THE UPSTART SPRING

James Nora

MLP

MID-LIST PRESS • DENVER

Copyright © 1989 by James Nora

All rights reserved. Published by Mid-List Press, P.O. Box 20292, Denver, CO 80220.

Library of Congress Cataloging-in-Publication Data

Nora, James J., 1928-
   The upstart spring

   I. Title
PS3564.054U67   1989   813'.54   89-3111
ISBN 0-922811-00-8

The author wishes to thank:

Kitty Hirs for her help and encouragement.

Oxford University Press for permission to use the selection by Christopher Fry, *A Sleep of Prisoners*, 1951, from which the title of this novel is taken.

Penguin Books for permission to use the poem by King Harald, from the translation by Magnus Magnusson and Hermann Palsson of *King Harald's Saga*, 1966.

The characters and incidents in this novel are products of the author's imagination. Although names of actual persons (e.g. President Lyndon Johnson) appear, no reader should try to identify the active participants in this story with people they know or think they know.

Printed in the United States of America

To my wife, Audrey.

And to my children,

Betsy and J.J.,

Marianne, Penny, and Wendy.

The human heart can go to the lengths of God.
Dark and cold we may be, but this
Is no winter now. The frozen misery
Of centuries breaks, cracks, begins to move,
The thunder is the thunder of the floes,
The thaw, the flood, the upstart spring.
Thank God our time is now when wrong
Comes up to face us everywhere,
Never to leave us till we take
The longest stride of soul men ever took.
Affairs are now soul size.

        Christopher Fry: *A Sleep of Prisoners*

PROLOGUE

The following narrative completes the agenda of remembering loved ones. Remembering the joy and the grief. The victories and . . . the losses.

Remembering a place and a time when we believed that anything was possible.

The transcriber of *The Elder Edda* wrote that he knew of one thing that never dies—the glory of the great deed.

But where are the heroes now? Where are the monsters worthy to test a hero's mettle? And where are the seas to batter with surly tongues the dragon-prows of longships?

Here are the heroes . . . and the monsters . . . and the seas.

ONE

This is how it began, two men talking about discovery—talking about doing what no one had achieved before. The two men, one uncommonly tall and the other of average height, wore green surgical scrub suits under flowing white clinic coats, from the pockets of which protruded stethoscopes, the sidearms of this particular frontier. They stood next to a long black-topped laboratory bench, which supported twenty cages. Each cage confined ten restless mice—but allowed their fetid odors to escape.

"We're getting close, Leif," Clay Ducharme, the smaller man, said. He opened a wire cage and snatched out a wriggling white mouse with a shaved ear in which a bulge pulsated rhythmically. "Three months ago, I transplanted C57 mouse hearts into A/Jax mouse ears and look at them. The damned things are still beating. Three months! How about that?"

"Outstanding," Leif Hanson boomed an appreciative response. "Looks like it's finally coming together."

"New combination of anti-rejection drugs."

"I've got the surgical techniques and . . ." Clay's pager interrupted Leif in mid-sentence.

"Dr. Ducharme. STAT! Emergency Room."

"I'll get back to you as soon as I can." Clay turned

and began to run along a corridor and down six flights of stairs while listening to his pager blare: "Dr. Ducharme. STAT! ER." He shoved open the swinging doors to the emergency room, which, as usual, reeked of antiseptics. Quickly he scanned this green-tiled barrack of gurneys, stainless steel carts, beeping machines, and harried attendants. To the left strapped on a stretcher was a man drenched in blood and the sour smell of whiskey. Not Clay's patient. A woman on the next stretcher vomited to intensify the olfactory assault.

The medical resident who had ER duty strutted to Clay's side and immediately began the detached presentation a trainee often makes to a staff physician: "Your patient, Dr. Michael Goldman, came in with severe chest pain. . . ."

"Dear God . . ." Clay murmured when he saw his patient, his friend—stretched out, pale and sweating and comatose, wired to a monitor—half-hidden by the hospital-green privacy-drapes. He took a deep breath and swallowed. "Dear God . . ."

"By the time we got the I.V. in, he arrested. But he's coming back. Lucky for him his office is just across the street. Damned lucky. Or we'd be wheeling him to the morgue."

Clay swallowed again. He glanced first at the monitor, which was now displaying a regular heart rhythm. Although his patient was unconscious, Clay still blew on his stethoscope to warm the diaphragm before placing it on the bony chest of Mike Goldman. "How's his pressure?" he mumbled.

"Coming back," the emergency room nursing supervisor said as she pumped the blood pressure cuff on his right arm. "Ninety over sixty, now." She deflated the cuff and loosened the Velcro fastener. "Very bad chest pain. He collapsed as soon as he reached the ER."

"Has his wife been notified?" Clay asked the nurse—and forced a smile to show her that he was grateful that she was taking personal charge of his patient.

"No one's had time yet," the resident answered for her. "We were lucky to keep him off the slab."

"I know. You've made that clear. I'll call his wife."

The woman who had been throwing up disgorged violently in the background. Clay first handed a fresh emesis basin from the supply cart to the vomiting woman and supported her head. Then he saw that Becky Goldman was already rushing into the emergency room with Mike's office nurse. He excused himself and walked over to embrace her—a petite dark-haired woman on the young side of forty. *Too young to become a widow.*

Becky rested her head on Clay's shoulder. Her face pressed against his chest. Muffled words: "Oh God." Tears dampened the lapel of his white coat. But then she stepped back, wiped her eyes, straightened herself to her full five feet two inches and asked, "Is he . . . how is he?"

Clay took her by the hand and led her to the stretcher. "He's not conscious right now." They both looked at Mike, tied precariously to life by an intravenous line.

Becky reached immediately for her husband—her fingertips brushed Mike's moist black hair from his forehead. "This is his fourth heart attack," she barely whispered. "His fourth."

"I know." Clay put an arm around her shoulder and thought of the crises they had experienced together with the previous three. "I know."

"Is he going to make it?" She clutched the side rail of the gurney tightly with one hand, while continuing to stroke Mike's forehead with the other.

Clay found it difficult to respond immediately. Instead, he watched the monitor.

But Becky searched Clay's face for an answer.

"Let's hope," he whispered.

"Am I breaking some hospital rules by being here?" Becky asked as she saw a nurse frowning at her. She kept squeezing the side rail.

"No matter," Clay said and placed his hand over hers on the gurney. "But we can talk outside."

"Will he be all right?" She reluctantly uncurled her fingers from the rail.

"We'll only be a few steps away if he needs us." He

took her arm and guided her to the waiting room, past the whiskey-smelling trauma victim, who was now thrashing against his leather restraints.

"It isn't good, is it?" Becky looked intently into Clay's eyes, which caused him to glance away. "You can be frank. We're old friends."

"We're running out of options." Clay waited for her to sit before he joined her on a cold Naugahyde settee with cigarette burns on the cushions. *Lousy damned place to comfort someone.*

"I know he can't go on this way."

"Coronary disease is a miserable disease." Clay immediately regretted making such an inept statement. "Mike's heart is essentially damaged beyond repair." Now he sounded more authoritative.

"There must be something. I mean, this is 1968. This is Houston. Not just the astronauts getting ready to walk on the moon. Houston's supposed to be the heart center of the world, too."

"One of the major centers, I guess," was what Clay said. What he was thinking about, however, was his conversation with Leif—and the story that was now capturing headlines. *If only we were ready today.*

"Anything? Any possibility at all?" Becky's question was a life rope floating only a few inches from her grasp

"If only we were ready." Clay was surprised that he had repeated the words aloud.

"Ready? Ready for what?" Her eyes locked on him like radar. "Ready for a heart transplant?" She lowered her gaze—and her voice to a whisper. "Are you considering that? I heard on TV they did one today at Stanford."

"I know." Clay frowned as he realized that his unguarded statement had now unlatched a door of hope.

"Isn't someone ready yet in Houston? How about at Baylor? DeBakey? Cooley?"

"I can't answer for them. All I can say is that at Southwest we've been doing a fair amount of research. Leif and I were just talking about it."

"When will you be geared up here?"

"Actually . . . I . . . let me talk with Leif Hanson."

"And? . . ."

"Maybe we can get started soon." Thinking: *The time has come. Damn it, the time has come.*

"Soon enough for Mike?"

Clay could not answer. But by facial expression he tried to convey some sense of optimism.

Within an hour Mike had regained consciousness and Clay transferred him up to the coronary care unit, making certain that Mike was stable before doing his other work.

The next step was to finish his talk with Leif. Clay walked down one flight of stairs from one green-tiled hall to another. The architect for University Hospital had probably heard that green was supposed to be the most psychologically restful color. So with the building only five years old, the patients and staff would have to live with monochromatic dreariness for many more years until redecorating would be justified.

Often it was difficult to catch up with Leif when he was outside of the operating room. But not today. The chairman of surgery was about to enter his departmental office. "Let's talk about heart transplants." Clay called out to him.

"Way t'go," Leif said. He was a Mack truck-sized man accustomed to towering over his medical and surgical colleagues, the little Volkswagens—blasting them aside with his horn. And with his smile. "Between us we've got the rejection and the surgery aced. We're ready, Clay."

"It's not quite that easy," Clay insisted, and did not smile. He wore the feistiness of a smaller man like scratchy homespun against his skin. This Volkswagen was not easily blasted aside. "A lot of preparing to do."

Leif pushed open the door to his limed oak paneled inner office and said, "Come on in, Clay, and we'll set our launch date now." He tossed the folder he had been carrying onto the antique oak dining table that served him and his surgical staff for small conferences. The round dining table, which had belonged to his grandfather, proudly displayed scars and nicks like battle ribbons—ribbons earned during the feeding of three generations of children in Bjorn

Hanson's farmhouse in Wisconsin.

"I want to start as soon as we can, but I want to do it right," Clay said and closed the door behind him. As he flopped down on the maroon leather couch he grazed his shin against the corner of the oak coffee table. "It's rejection. That's the problem I've been struggling with for over five years. . . . I think we may need something more than just drugs—despite what my mice show." He rubbed the injured spot on his leg. *Damned table.*

"Drugs are all the kidney transplanters use," Leif argued. "We were as ready last month as Barnard was. Then we let him get the jump on everybody. But we can catch up. This is Houston for godsake." Leif spoke in short bursts like a .30 caliber machine gun. His blue eyes were as fierce as they were intense, and were deeply set in a broad Scandinavian face topped by an oat field stubble of thick blond hair. After he finished pawing in the closet for a fresh scrub shirt, he said—now slowly, "From cardiology to the space program . . . this is where we touch the sky."

"You're getting fat." Clay did not allow himself to comment on Leif's extravagant statement. "A lot fatter than when we were in medical school." He glanced away from Leif's tree-trunk forearms and down at his own slender hands and wrists.

"The hell I am." Leif sucked in his gut and reflexly pumped his biceps. "It's all muscle." He threw his sweat-soaked green shirt onto the closet floor.

"Suit yourself. But the survival data on ex-football players who don't exercise enough isn't good." Clay removed his aviator-style glasses to wipe a spot off the left lens. "You're inviting a coronary."

"Let's cut the crap. We're not in here to talk about why I'm not as skinny as you are." Leif's bushy blond eyebrows pressed closer together revealing that there were scars in the right one, as if moths had been nibbling at an otherwise handsome tapestry. "Bottom line: why can't we start right now, Clay?"

"It's a damned conflict. For our patients, the sooner we start the better . . . *if* we've got the problems under control. But have we?" Clay again rubbed his aching shin. "It's been only a month since Barnard's first heart transplant. And that patient's already dead."

Leif tugged a dry shirt over his head and relaxed his belly muscles. "What bugs the hell out of me is that Barnard starts things off. Now every other damned heart surgeon will say if he can transplant a heart, so can I." He punched his arms into his white coat and patted his right hip for his stethoscope.

"Today Shumway did one," Clay said.

"Damn it, I know. That's the problem. Why the hell didn't Shumway do it first?"

"He should have been first. He's been doing the most research in this."

"But Barnard does the first one—human to human. Now you know damned well that DeBakey and Cooley and the rest are going to want to show their stuff, too." Leif was speaking more softly now, not blasting with his horn, smiling.

"And Hanson?"

"Hanson too. Damn it." Another smile. "Human heart transplantation's just starting, Clay. No one owns it yet. So we've got a good chance to really score with this."

"There'll be problems." Clay kicked off his loafers. His watchband was too big, allowing the face to slip around to the inner surface of his wrist. After twisting the watch into its proper place, he continued, "Barnard, all of them, are just using the old techniques of the kidney transplanters."

"So? . . . Something wrong with that?" Leif squared his shoulders and folded his arms across his chest. This pose made him appear even taller than his six feet six inches.

"Maybe a lot. And there's more show biz than science in what Barnard did. New immunology not just a new organ to transplant. That may be what we need."

"It doesn't have to be show biz, Clay," Leif slouched into a leather armchair. "We could make this first-class science. And I know you're damned excited about this or you wouldn't have brought it up. . . . With you and me and an experienced transplant immunologist, like Arthur, we could do it. We've got the people and the facilities. You think Arthur'd have the time?"

"I'm not sure. He's got his hands full with kidney transplants." Clay was thinking how readily Leif had dismissed his experience with small animal heart transplant research in favor of Arthur's established expertise in human kidney transplantation. *Probably justified, but not flattering.* "Arthur would sure be the man to help us, *if* he could find the time."

"Well for my part, I'm working in the dog lab tonight—improving my speed in transplanting the heart." Leif stretched, rubbed the flat of his hand across the late-afternoon sandpaper surface of his chin and said, "Why don't you talk with Arthur. You guys think about it. That's all I ask, Clay."

"Not *you guys*. You live in the South now. It's *you all* or *y'all*, if you want to get really down home. *You guys* is Chicago. Harsh. *Y'all* is soft, affectionate . . ."

"You're changing the damned subject."

"You noticed."

Arthur Johnson's immunology laboratories were on the seventh floor. Clay entered the stairwell on the second floor and began climbing—for the exercise. In addition to running at least three miles every other day, Clay almost always avoided elevators. So he ran the first three flights two steps at a time. The last two, one step at a time. At the end of the fifth flight, Clay stopped to catch his breath. After all, he told himself, he was over forty now. *But still in damned good shape. Five-ten and 140 pounds. The same as in college, running track.*

Interesting. Reminiscing about the Harvard track team.

Clay, from Mississippi, white. And who was his closest friend on the team? Arthur Johnson, from Alabama, black—a full scholarship student at Harvard College and later at Harvard Medical School.

Now both had achieved international stature in biomedical science.

Clay stopped at the entrance of Arthur's laboratory to wipe off droplets of sweat, which were clinging to his forehead and close-cropped brown hair. Even though it was January in a climate-controlled building, the Houston humidity could produce an incubator atmosphere, especially for people who run up five flights of stairs.

"Got a minute?" Clay called from the door.

Arthur rolled his chair back from the microscope he had been using and stood up. A thin brown man with a thick black mustache and gray eyes that shined like silver on mahogany. His unusually large well shaped head overpowered the rest of his body. "Come on in, my man. Pull up something and sit."

Equipment cluttered the laboratory. Too much equipment. Long black-topped lab benches with stainless steel sinks sprouted glassware, beakers, test tubes, retorts, balances, and centrifuges. Clay shoved a test tube rack and a book out of the way to make a space to sit on top of a bench.

"I've got a proposition. What do you think about our getting into heart transplants? I just discussed it with Leif."

"And he wants to start today. Or yesterday, preferably," Arthur said drily.

"R-i-i-ight. So I thought I'd check to see what you think. Kind of exciting stuff. We could get in on the ground floor. Might even become a leader in this."

"Fine with me. Happy to help." Arthur, unlike Clay, had lost all traces of his southern accent during his education and training in the North. "For as long as I'm here," he added.

"What d'you mean by that?"

"Varney was by."

"So what the hell's happened now?"

"He wanted to know how my search for a chairmanship is going." Arthur pulled a paper towel from a dispenser. "He wants me to leave the department. And he thinks I'm taking too long trying to find another job." He handed the towel to Clay. "There's something wet you're about to sit in."

Clay mopped the spot and sniffed the towel before

discarding it. "Acetic acid."

"Not good for your pants." Arthur began adjusting the dial on a photometer. "A new department chairman comes in and has a *vision* of how he'd like to see the department—his department—develop. So all the people who don't fit into that god-damned vision are expected to disrupt their lives and find jobs at other universities." Arthur kept turning the dial and grumbling, "It's one thing to try to get rid of the semi-competents, but to try to force out the good people in the department is unprecedented—isn't it?"

"But that's where tenure comes in. Jesus!" Clay slapped his hand on the lab bench. "To prevent this crap. And to guarantee academic freedom. You're tenured and the best man in the department. The only person in the whole damned medical school to win a Lasker—just one step from a Nobel Prize."

"And what the hell does that count when your chairman wants to get rid of you?"

"It counts for plenty. And maybe—just maybe—you've got Varney wrong."

"No. I'm afraid I haven't," Arthur said. "And he's doing the same thing to you, too, isn't he?"

Clay had not thought seriously in these terms before, but the memory of an earlier event returned. "Well as soon as he became chairman he did come by and say there are some people in the department who really are so accomplished that they require larger programs than the department can accommodate."

"Yeah, my man. And who were those people? Most of the tenured division chiefs, weren't they? He came with the very same story to me. Named you and me and the other division chiefs who have really accomplished something."

"It doesn't have to happen to anyone. I have no intention of leaving. Never would consider it."

A timer bell sounded and Arthur twisted around to flip a switch on an electrophoresis apparatus. "We need to sit down over a few beers sometime soon and talk about this problem with Varney in detail. In the meantime, I'll be happy to help on the heart transplants."

"We'll get together with Leif. He'll be glad to hear you're on board." Clay slid off the lab bench, and said slowly, thoughtfully, "We're really biting off something."

For the first time in the encounter Arthur smiled—but only with his mouth. "Not to worry. If we can keep Varney from screwing things up, and with you and Leif and me on the job, how can we fail?" Now the silver eyes smiled . . . just for a moment. "Speak of the devil," Arthur whispered.

Clay glanced quickly towards the door of Arthur's lab and saw Vincent Varney standing there, a porcupine of a man—short and squat and bristling. And just like that difficult-to-touch animal, he was skilled at stripping the bark off living things.

"I'm looking for Mawson," Varney announced.

"I think he's in the clinic," Arthur answered.

Varney pivoted away without saying thank you to Arthur or acknowledging Clay's presence.

Arthur stepped over to the door to make certain that Varney was not lingering to eavesdrop. "Be sure you understand," he turned back to Clay, "that if heart transplantation isn't a hell of a big success, Varney will use it against you as well as me. You're putting yourself at serious risk messing with it."

"I've never been much of a risk-taker, but this may be worth it."

Arthur offered encouragement: "Sure it's worth it. Hell, we're at the top of our game right now. We can handle Varney—especially since we're both so rich and famous."

"Maybe not so rich."

"At least, no more eating neck meat by the coal oil lamp."

"You mean you can afford backs and wings now?"

"Hell yes. Sometimes even drumsticks."

Clay thumped back down the stairs to Leif's office, avoiding the elevator, of course. Thinking: *Maybe once in your whole damned career along comes something like heart transplantation. New. Something to get your blood pumping in the morning. Oh Jesus, this could be great. . . . If . . . if I can keep Leif on a short leash and stay the hell away from Varney. And if we could only make it in time to help Mike.*

He now noticed, since he was not running up the steps, that the stairwell was actually chilly. Clay slapped his upper arms to warm himself. The overhead light was burned out on the fourth floor landing, and there were signs saying Wet Paint between the third and second floors. He sniffed the oil paint smell—was it really wet?—and touched the shiny beige cinder block wall with his right index finger.

It's wet. But at least the stairwells aren't green. He rubbed the paint-stained finger vigorously into the palm of his left hand before entering Leif's office. "Arthur's willing to help," Clay said.

"Outstanding." Leif came out from behind his desk and motioned to Clay to sit.

Clay waved off the invitation and said, "And by now you must suspect that I have a patient in mind for our first transplant."

"Mike Goldman?"

"He was my stat call to the ER. He arrested today."

"Heard about it. . . . Damned sorry."

"He's got a heart muscle like a soggy Kleenex. We've got nothing more to offer him."

"Then let's get cracking."

"I don't know if we can keep Mike alive for even a couple of weeks. And we've got so damned much to do to get ready. We need to construct reverse isolation areas in the recovery room and on the wards to keep the bugs away from the patients."

"Done in a week," Leif said confidently.

"We need to design the protocols and get them through the human research committee."

"A week—tops. This is January sixth," Leif fired short bursts of words. "Should have everything ready to go by the twentieth. Two weeks."

"You have no idea how much is involved." Clay shook his head vigorously. "Rejection of the heart and rejection of the kidney are different. The kidney can shut down for a couple of hours."

"And what's it matter if you can't pee for a while?"

"Ri-i-ight. But a heart can't stop for a couple of hours. Someone may have to fly out to Stanford or South Africa to see what they may be doing differently with the heart—if anything."

"See what Arthur says."

"And we've got to watch out for Varney . . . maybe we could let him participate."

"Hell no," Leif said. "I wouldn't piss on him if his guts were on fire. The guy's a Loki, if ever there was one. You've got to learn to stand up to that sonovabitch."

"I know. But Varney's my department chairman. I can argue, even fight, with normal people—and it's an exchange of views. But only a slight disagreement with Varney can lead to a vendetta."

"Forget Varney, Clay. We both want to start heart transplants. I'm willing to run with it. But I mean I'm *really* ready to run. So don't start dragging your ass."

"Barnard's first patient died," Clay muttered. "His second patient has only gone through four days. Shumway's patient is only a few hours post-op."

"So?"

"So we're going to do it right. No media crap. No loose cannons. I'm going to be all over you like a frog on a june bug to make sure this is good science without hype."

Leif smiled disarmingly before saying, "Take your best shot. But the bottom line is we're going to be the first to succeed. And I mean succeed."

"Damn," Clay said, "you're a real bottom line guy. With a risk-taking surgical personality."

"Yooo bet," Leif parodied a Norwegian accent. "Positive thinking." He grinned. "And a little Viking spirit of adventure."

"Or something." Clay started for the door, then stopped and looked back over his shoulder. "What was it the Vikings used to say when they entered a village? 'Not to worry . . . we only come to rape, pillage, and plunder.'"

"Yooo bet."

TWO

"It's a Mr. Eric Kristensen on the phone from *Life Magazine*," Leif's secretary stated the case cautiously. "He *says* he's your cousin." Mildred continued to stand at the door between her office and Leif's—uncertain as to whether she should have put the call through.

Leif picked up the phone. "Red?"

"Leif, good to hear your voice."

"It's been a hell of a long time." Leif nodded to Mildred that the call was acceptable and watched her turn to leave. He concluded she had spent the previous evening with Miss Clairol and had come away with a more attractive dark brown shade than her most recent too-brassy auburn.

"Much too long," Eric said, "I need to set up an appointment with you."

"Sorry, I don't do relatives unless they've got plenty of insurance and lots of money."

"Well, you know how rich most writers are. But I don't need surgery, I need information."

"Go ahead."

"I've been to Capetown and I've just finished out here at Stanford, looking at Shumway's case. As you can see I've picked up on this heart transplant story. I tried to reach you before I left for Capetown, but you were in the operating room."

"The OR's where I earn my living." Leif grumbled. As he talked, he sorted through letters, papers, and messages stacked in separate piles on his large oak desk.

"I was kind of surprised. I kind of thought that everything new in heart surgery comes out of Houston. But there's this guy in Capetown, South Africa—of all damned places—who pulls off a transplant."

"Yeah," Leif muttered.

"I thought you and DeBakey and Cooley were the tops in the world."

"We try to do good work." Leif felt a fingernail-on-blackboard scrape of annoyance with this cousin he had not seen or heard from in many years.

"Well, I'd appreciate some inside thoughts on Barnard and his operation. I'm flying from San Franciso to Houston tonight to begin work on a feature on NASA—preparations for the moon landing and all that. I'd sure like to get together with you when I get down there."

"Sure. Love to see you."

"I'll give you a ring. I'm going to be staying at the Shamrock."

"Right. Look forward to it." Leif replaced the phone in its cradle without slamming it—although that was what he felt like doing. Cousin Eric Kristensen had not handled the phone call too smoothly. *He wants to come to Houston to talk about Barnard. About* his *operation.* Leif knew Barnard all right. They had both been at the University of Minnesota at the same time. But Barnard had only been a surgical resident at the time Leif was already an assistant professor of surgery.

At shortly before 1:00 a.m. on January 23, Leif Hanson returned to his departmental office and dialed a call to Eric Kristensen to see if he had arrived at the Shamrock Hotel. He learned that Eric had checked in two hours earlier. "Get out of the sack, Red," Leif bellowed into the phone.

"What are you doing calling me at this hour?" was Eric's response.

"How'd you like to see a heart transplant?"

Eric didn't answer immediately.

Leif began tapping his fingers. "Listen I'm letting you and *Life* in on the ground floor. But you sure as hell don't have to come." He stiffened to his feet and stepped out from behind his desk.

"I'm just trying to find my damned glasses. I knocked them off the table when I answered the phone."

"Well, do you want to come or don't you?"

"Of course I do. Will you just let me wake up?"

"As fast as you can," Leif said. "Come right to my office."

Twenty minutes later, a slightly groggy Eric Kristensen joined the conclave in progress in Leif's office. Eric had obviously shaved and put on a fresh shirt, blue oxford cloth with a button-down collar. His English regimental tie and crisp gray three piece suit, while reflecting urbane taste and his high regard for the people with whom he was meeting, was out of place amidst the rumpled, middle-of-the-night attire of the other participants.

Leif exuberantly performed the introductions, announcing loudly: "This is my cousin Eric Kristensen." Then: "Red, meet Clay Ducharme. He's the head of cardiology here. Clay and I go back a long way together. All the way back to medical school. And this is Arthur Johnson. He's the head of our renal division. He's been running the kidney transplant program and he's going to look after the immunology on our heart transplants."

The two doctors shook Eric's hand. "I might have guessed you and Leif were related," Clay said as he surveyed the height of the new arrival.

"We're both about six-six," Leif said. "And no remarks about weight, please. Red's always been leaner and meaner."

"I doubt meaner," Clay said.

"I'll ignore that." Leif looked around for his last introduction. "And this is Joe Berry, the head of our photography department. You'll probably want to get together with him."

"You just let me know whatcha need." Berry took a step forward and gave a kind of salute, like a football official upon introduction at the beginning of a game. He was even wearing a striped shirt.

"I appreciate it." Eric nodded in return and asked, "How far along are things?"

"We've got a recipient and a donor."

"A *potential* recipient, but a mismatched donor," Clay said. "We don't just want to do a heart transplant, we want to be successful. We're all ready to move under the right conditions. These just aren't the right conditions—yet."

"But the recipient might not last the night," Leif said.

"And he won't last if he rejects a mismatched heart," Arthur countered.

The office door jarred open in front of Dr. Frank Sellery, in his green surgical scrub suit with short sleeves rolled up to display biceps that could only have come from pumping iron regularly. "Maybe more donors," he announced. "Three car pile-up on the Southwest Freeway. They're coming here." With his fingertips he cooly repositioned a lock of brown hair into its proper place on his suntanned forehead.

"This may solve the mismatch problem," Leif said. "Red, meet one of my surgical associates, Frank Sellery. 'Eric-the-Red' Kristensen is my cousin." Leif smiled. "When he used to have hair it was red."

That provoked a little laugh as the men emptied out of Leif's office and strode towards the emergency room—like a football team leaving the locker area.

As soon as the men arrived at the ER, the controlled chaos of stretchers, intravenous lines, and the harsh smell of iodoform and other antiseptics provided the background for the search for a potential donor. The doctors joined in the acute care of five accident victims. The reception door to the emergency room swung open and two more patients arrived on clattering stretchers.

"This one died on the way," an ambulance driver announced.

Leif moved quickly to the new patient. A young

woman with a grotesquely swollen and bloody face was not breathing. Leif felt for a pulse and listened to the heart. "She's dead," he agreed.

Clay Ducharme also placed a stethoscope on her chest. "Can we hook up an ECG monitor fast?" he called to a nurse. "No heart tones, but look, she still has good electrical activity of the heart." He pointed to the monitor.

Leif said, "Let's get an airway and an I.V. started on this one," and began closed chest cardiac massage, pushing rhythmically with both hands on the patient's sternum.

Clay inserted a needle into a vein in the patient's hand and started a bottle of intravenous fluid and medication.

Leif stopped the cardiac massage and listened with his stethoscope. "The heart tones are coming back. Damned glad you ordered the ECG, Clay. She may be our donor."

But first the dying woman's husband had to consent to the procedure, and the word around the ER was that he had been responsible for the three-car collision while driving intoxicated. The husband, Bobby Jack Bowen, a stubby young man with a cigarette stashed behind his right ear and a Confederate flag tattooed on his right upper arm, had other urgent concerns. "How much scar's this gonna leave on my chin?" he asked Leif while he gingerly fingered his bandage. "Y'all sure my wrist ain't broken?" Now he was whining softly and holding up the injured paw—like a frightened puppy. "Y'all sure that's what my x-ray shows?" Now glaring and speaking more like a knowledgeable and lawsuit-conscious medical consumer.

Copies of the consent form for donors and recipients arrived from the administrator's office. The legal firms representing the University of the Southwest and University Hospital had carefully developed the precise language of the documents to prevent the possibility of lawsuits. Leif had misgivings as he and Clay brought the consent forms to Bobby Jack Bowen. He expected a brush-off from this irresponsible twenty-one year old, and was surprised when Bowen promptly agreed. But Leif soon discovered that the donation of his wife's heart might influence the police to reassess favorably the circumstances surrounding Bowen's accident.

On the assumption that Mrs. Bowen might become a donor, Arthur Johnson had obtained blood for tissue-typing, returned to his laboratory, and had completed the tissue match by the time Bowen had signed the donor consent form. Leif was, of course, anxious to present the option of a transplant to Mike. He sent Sellery to get Clay and walked on ahead from the ER by himself. He needed a moment alone to prepare what to say.

"Leif's leaving to see the Goldmans," Sellery told Clay. "He asked me to get you."

"You put one cotton-pickin' hand on my patient until I ask . . ." Clay's speech reverted to Deep South. He took a few slow breaths and began again: "Dr. Sellery, I consider it a duty of the physician in modern medicine to protect his patients from the surgeon. I intend to discharge that duty. I will let you and Dr. Hanson know when I want you to see my patient." Clay stepped quickly to try to reach Leif before he could discuss the possible transplant with the Goldmans.

Eric Kristensen had been unobtrusively jotting down a few notes and following whichever doctor seemed to be doing the most interesting things at the moment. He fell into lockstep behind Clay.

"Been telling Mrs. Goldman what stage we're at," Leif said as Clay approached.

"So I see. Maybe a little premature," Clay said caustically.

"How do things look, Clay?" Becky asked.

"Well, we've done this special tissue-matching test," Clay explained, "even though we know so little about heart transplants. But a heart transplant is what you and I talked about a couple of weeks ago. And we're as ready as we can get in so little time. Do you want us to talk to Mike?"

"Of course." Becky was twisting her handkerchief into a knot. "Of course. What other hope has he?"

"I honestly can't think of any."

Mike Goldman, the skin of his face and chest moist and sticky like gray-tinted library paste, his hair in damp black coils, was sitting almost straight up in bed in his section of the coronary care unit. An oxygen mask covered his nose and mouth and a life-sustaining infusion of lidocaine dripped from a hanging bottle through a plastic tube into a vein on the back of his hand. His dark eyes darted from person to person as if trying to snap last photographs before the sun would set. But the electronic monitor of his vital signs was turned so he would be unable see it—and it was not beeping the way the other monitors were. The sound had been turned off so as not to worry a patient who was also a doctor and all too aware of the significance of the beeps and clicks and squiggles.

As Becky approached his bed he held his hand out to her. "Hi, honey," he managed to mumble inside the mask.

His wife leaned over and kissed him on the forehead.

"Mike, how you doing?" Clay asked. And: "You know Leif Hanson. And this is Dr. Eric Kristensen, his cousin."

Leif was about to correct Clay's introduction of Eric, but decided to let it ride.

Mike Goldman nodded to Leif.

"There's no point in kidding you, Mike," Clay said. "Medical management doesn't have anything more to offer."

"A Vineberg?" Mike Goldman pulled the oxygen mask away from his face so he could speak more easily.

"We're not thinking of a Vineberg," Leif said. "We're considering total replacement."

"A transplant?" Mike was gasping. He slid the oxygen mask back in place and gulped for air.

"Yes," Leif said.

"Me and Blaiberg?" Mike's face reflected the pain of trying to breathe, trying to stay alive.

"If you'd like us to give it a try," Clay said.

"I've nothing to lose," Mike Goldman said.

Leif maintained a glass-walled cubicle situated above and overlooking operating rooms 1 and 2. This permitted him to accomplish other tasks while supervising the preliminary and closing activities of surgical procedures. He could look through the windows and talk through the intercoms, write reports, dictate operative notes, return phone calls, and do the majority of his desk work without leaving the operating suite.

He seated himself in his cubicle above the two operating rooms and watched the preparations with a feeling of excitement that he had not known for years. Leif had been a pioneer in open-heart surgery. And there was no question in his mind as to the outcome of this procedure. Shumway's patient had died two days ago. Only Barnard's second patient, Blaiberg, was still alive. But after tonight, things would be different.

Leif flipped on the switch of the intercom to room 1. "How's it going in there?"

"Ready and waiting, chief," the surgical resident answered.

"Outstanding," Leif said. "So am I. Damn, so am I!"

But Clay broke the mood of unruffled expectation by pushing indignantly through the gallery and into Leif's OR cubicle. "Do you see what's happening in the waiting room and lobby?" he demanded.

"That's why I'm holing up in here. We didn't put in the protocol to tell the donor's family to keep their damned mouths shut," Leif said. "I've got the police guarding the OR."

"I'm not just talking about Bowen," Clay said. "There were reporters here before we even had a donor. Who leaked the damned story?"

"Can't keep a lid on something like this," Leif said.

"This is something we don't need. We'll look like Barnard."

"No we won't, Clay. I'm not going to let this turn into a three ring circus."

"It's a circus now," Clay argued. "Our reports should only be at scientific meetings and in medical journals. Not to the press. I warned you about this."

"Too late now, Clay."

"It's not too late. No one from the press knows a damn thing except what Bowen has told them."

"They know all sorts of things that they've been

piecing together all night. They can talk to any nurse or orderly and pick up all sorts of crap. Best to have one good accurate story rather than a lot of rumors and guesswork. That's why I invited Red to come along with us. Red's from *Life Magazine*."

Clay's jaw dropped. When he found words, he said, "Damn it, Leif, I thought your cousin was a doctor. I even introduced him as a doctor."

"Never said he was."

"I think this is highly unprofessional."

"Cool down," Leif said. "You'll feel different once we do the surgery, Clay. Come on, they're signaling for us to go on down."

Leif directed the orderlies wheeling Mike Goldman into operating room 1 and the donor into the adjoining room 2. The anesthesiology team, the surgical residents, and the OR nurses then took charge of the patient. Room 1, with its sparkling green-tiled walls, was the largest operating theater at University Hospital. It was used exclusively for cardiovascular surgery. This was Leif's domain. He glanced at the piece of equipment that identified the room as a cardiovascular theater, the heart-lung machine—a metal frame mounted on a stainless steel console suspending a large plastic bag through which the blood from the patient flowed to pick up oxygen. Leif mused that the mechanism of the pump itself, the rotating fingers compressing plastic tubes, differed very little from a device invented by Michael DeBakey while he was still a medical student at Tulane.

Surgical residents, in their respective operating rooms, draped both the donor and recipient with towels followed by layers of green sheets. Three residents assembled with Leif around the recipient, and three more residents were with Frank Sellery in operating room 2. Leif nodded to the circulating nurse to signal that he was ready. She spoke the message into the intercom. No response. Sellery and the rest of the team in room 2 were visible through the windows and across the hall that separated the two operating rooms. The circulating nurse tapped on the intercom. The electronic gadget refused to respond. She waved her hand to attract the attention of her counterpart in the other operating room.

"Never mind," Clay said, "I'll tell them." He stepped across the hall. "Frank, are you ready?"

"Just waiting," Sellery answered.

"OK, Leif's ready. Why don't you start?" Clay signaled to Leif, who was watching through his window.

Leif acknowledged the signal and bent over his patient.

"Stop the drip," Sellery ordered. "The drip's what's been keeping the patient's heart going," he explained to a medical student, who was assisting on the operation along with the surgical residents.

Clay went back to room 1 and stood on a low stool behind the anesthesiologist. He watched Leif's scalpel paint a red ribbon down the middle of the recipient's chest. Next came the power bone saw, humming as it ground through Goldman's breastbone, splitting the chest so that a large retractor could be introduced. The heart was beating feebly. And where the muscle should have been thick, there was a thin balloon of tissue, a ventricular aneurysm.

"The rate's slowing," the anesthesiologist said.

"I can see that," Leif snapped.

"And I'm not getting a pressure."

"Let's move." Leif squeezed the heart while one of the surgical residents worked on the incision in the right groin from which tubes connected the patient to the heart-lung machine.

"I'll see how Sellery's doing." Clay backed off the stool and bumped into a photographer and Eric Kristensen. Both wore proper attire—scrub suits and masks. High over the operating table on a platform was yet another photographer with a motion picture camera recording for posterity the opening of the chest. "How we coming?" Clay called from the door of room 2.

"We're ready," Sellery answered. Then he added to the photographer in room 2, "Get a few feet of this showing that the donor heart has stopped beating."

"OK, start removing the heart." Clay padded back to

room 1. "Sellery's taking the heart, Leif."

"Good, we're on bypass." Leif's fingers moved rapidly. He took pride in the reputation he shared with the other well known Houston heart surgeons of being one of the fastest in the world—doing as many as twelve to even fifteen cases in a single day. Quickly, almost unexpectedly, Leif pulled Mike's heart out of his chest and held it cupped in his huge hands. "That's a sight not many people have seen in a living patient." He nodded toward the empty chest. Then: "Where's Dr. Sellery?"

"I'll check." Clay stepped off his stool and walked briskly to room 2. "You ready?" he asked Sellery.

"Any time."

"Let's go then."

Frank Sellery made the final excision with scissors, lifted the heart from the donor's chest, and dropped it into a sterile stainless steel basin, which contained a saline solution. The heart, although removed from the body, responded to the stimulation of touching steel by contracting several times. It perversely began to beat—refusing to stop. Sellery stretched a wet gauze over the pulsating heart and called out, "Coming through. Hot stuff, coming through."

The surgical residents standing across from Leif at the operating table stepped aside to allow Frank Sellery, now re-gowned and re-gloved, to take over as first assistant.

The donor heart gave a final beat when Leif grasped it and rotated it in his hand, gauging its size and the size of the cavity into which it would be placed. After he trimmed the excess tissue from the donor heart to his satisfaction, the implantation began—sewing this new heart into the place where Mike's hopelessly damaged heart had struggled to survive. In a few minutes, Leif removed the last clamp from the aorta and the new heart began to twitch again. He applied the paddles of the defibrillator directly to the heart to use an electrical current to start it beating normally. A single countershock was followed by the heart beginning to contract forcefully. The electrocardiogram and blood pressure curves spiked on the monitor for everyone in the room to see.

"Looking good," Clay said.

A murmur traveled through the operating room, expanding into a spontaneous cheer. And applause. The newly transplanted heart was beating strongly inside of Mike Goldman's chest.

Frank Sellery was busy directing the cameraman overhead. "Get some of this," he ordered.

"Congratulations, big fella." Clay's eyes smiled over his mask at Leif.

"We did it." Leif was having difficulty trying to sound restrained. He looked at the clock. "Twenty-eight minutes of pump time."

The administrator and the public relations director of University Hospital were standing in the middle of Leif's office waiting for him. "Congratulations," John Ardrey, the administrator, said while shaking Leif's hand vigorously. His blue pinstripe suit accentuated his unusual thinness. His brown hair was also thin.

"You betcha," Charley Drones, the PR man, added and also grabbed for Leif's hand. "We'll be on page 1." Drones, who played Jeff to Ardrey's Mutt by being short and stocky, wore a flamboyant plaid jacket.

"Why?" Clay asked.

"Why? Because it's big news," Drones answered gleefully. "It'll be headlines all over the world."

"Not if we can help it," Clay countered.

"No circus," Leif warned. "We're willing to make some information available. We have one journalist with us now." Leif nodded towards Eric. "And we'd like to work with him exclusively."

"That won't fly," Ardrey said. "My office is already filled with reporters and broadcasters."

"Tell them to go home," Leif said.

"But we can't. Your friend, Dr. Barnard, has set the standard. The press will expect us to follow."

"I agree with John." Frank Sellery had now entered Leif's office, brushing his hair into place as he talked. He bent to sit in an armchair, but seeing that everyone else was standing, he straightened up and leaned against the chair.

"Who's with the patient?" Clay asked him abruptly.

"Your boy, Eck, and some of our boys."

"Well, I don't propose to waste time arguing press relations. We've got a patient to take care of." Clay walked out of the office in the direction of the recovery room.

When Clay was out of hearing distance, Sellery made his point. "Barnard started this thing with the media. The public will expect a full report."

"What the public expects and what the public gets are two different things," Leif said. "I want dignity in our program."

"You won't have to worry," Ardrey said, "*if* we provide a brief, informative report."

"You've gotta," Drones reentered the discussion. "There must be fifteen reporters and photographers downstairs. I've gotta give 'em something or they'll tear me to pieces."

"Really, Leif, you've got to release something," Ardrey said.

"All right. You may say that a heart transplantation was performed at the University of the Southwest. The recipient is in satisfactory postoperative condition. Further details are within the province of the doctor-patient relationship and will not be discussed at this time."

"That won't sell either," Drones argued.

"They know more than that already," Ardrey said. "The donor's husband hasn't stopped shooting off his mouth yet."

"That's all they're getting from me now." Leif started for the door. "If you'll excuse me, I've got to go to the recovery room to see my patient." He rumbled down the hall and into the postoperative area.

Recently constructed walls and doors separated a special section of the recovery room from the rest of the facility. A first door led into a vestibule where there were sterile gowns, masks, caps, paper boots, and antiseptic solutions. Anyone planning to go through the second door had to scrub, mask, and gown—just as if going into an operating room. This was the reverse isolation procedure to protect the patient from infection.

Clay, Wendell Eck, who was one of Clay's junior cardiology staff, a pulmonary physiologist, a surgical resident, and two special duty nurses were hovering around Mike when Leif entered the newly built isolation area. He was tugging on the second of his surgical gloves.

The transplant team worked for about two hours in the recovery room until everyone was satisfied that Mike was stable. Leif was the first to leave to start the morning surgical schedule. Clay followed to begin the heart catheterizations for the day.

Eric Kristensen was waiting outside the recovery room when Leif and Clay appeared. "I feel I owe you an explanation, Clay. You introduced me as Dr. Kristensen. I'm not a doctor. I'm a staff writer for *Life Magazine*."

"That's what I've learned."

"Leif invited me in the middle of the night. I'd just arrived in town to write a feature on the astronauts."

"The misunderstanding was on my part." Clay smiled. "I guess I just assumed that relatives of doctors automatically have to be doctors, too."

"One other thing. I don't think you have to worry about the publicity getting out of hand," Eric said.

"I made a strong statement about that after you left to go to the recovery room," Leif added.

"But you were the one who called *Life Magazine* in the middle of the night, weren't you, Leif?" Clay said as he turned and began to trudge in the direction of the cardiac catheterization laboratory.

Charley Drones and Frank Sellery had heard Clay's parting shot as they approached. "Clay's a bit reserved," Drones said. "But I know the value of this happening. What it means to the hospital. To the medical school. To Houston. In fact, to the whole damn world—for chrissake."

"But heart transplantation belongs to us surgeons," Sellery added. "The cardiologists are just along for the ride."

"Well, whoever gets the credit, it's still our baby here at Southwest." Charley Drones beamed. "We've left the

Baylor people eating our dust. I can't wait to hear what DeBakey and Cooley do when they see the morning papers."

As predicted, the heart transplantation did indeed make the headlines. Leif called home between his second and third operations of the new day. "Have you seen the paper yet, Slim?"

"I've seen it," Elaine Hanson said. "I was wondering what you were up to last night."

Leif paused, trying to decide if Elaine was inserting a zinger between the lines, but simply answered, "Now you know, Slim."

"It's on the morning network TV shows. Karen went off to school walking on a cloud. Very proud of her dad."

"I'm glad."

"For one day, it almost makes up for seeing so little of him."

Zing.

THREE

As he shuffled up from the driveway to his house, Clay saw Betty Sue opening the back door. After almost two decades of marriage, he still felt heart-skipping joy at the sight of his wife—seeing her now at the door, or glimpsing her in a hall at the medical school, where she was also on the faculty. Or detecting the scent of White Shoulders and knowing she was near. At this moment the setting sun was splashing red highlights on her chestnut hair. He paused to watch the shadows caress her face, the delicate features of a Saint-Gaudens cameo. And immediately he quickened his step.

"You're looking particularly proud of yourself. Come here and let me hug your neck." Her accent betrayed a trace of Mississippi as she greeted Clay with a hug . . . and a kiss. "How are you feeling?"

"Tired. And slightly euphoric," Clay said. "And I'll have to get back right after supper."

"How's Mike doing?"

"Incredibly well."

"You're on national TV, Dad." Andy, the oldest of the Ducharme children, made his presence known. He was mostly arms and legs poking out of jeans and a plaid shirt. "Walter Cronkite, Huntley-Brinkley. They're all talking about it. Walter Cronkite even mentioned you by name. But mostly he talked about Dr. Hanson."

"I guess I should feel honored."

"Hi, Daddy." A voice came from the kitchen. It was Melanie—ten years old, braces on her teeth and freckles on her nose. "We're having chicken jambalaya tonight. And I fixed most of it, didn't I, Mom?"

"She really did," Betty Sue agreed.

The bubbling sound and the spicy aroma of supper cooking drew Clay into the large open-beamed kitchen. The maple chopping block, the rows of spices, and the wide variety of copper and other utensils suspended from racks and walls announced in unison that this was a place for serious cooking. "Here's where I like to be better than anywhere in the world." Clay let out a groan. "But I've got to go back. I'll only have a few minutes to eat."

"It's ready," Melanie said.

"I guess it's an advantage living five minutes from the hospital," Betty Sue sighed. "At least we get to see you tonight. But being close, it's too easy to go back."

"This is a very special case. We can't let anything go wrong."

It was almost midnight when Clay returned home from the hospital. His throat was getting sore. Probably his usual January cold. But a cold was the last thing he needed when he had to take care of Mike, whose life now depended on being protected from germs.

"Your father called," Betty Sue reported as Clay entered the bedroom. She was propped up in bed under a fluffy floral comforter, a Dorothy Sayers mystery open in her lap. "He wants you to call him back tonight."

"Something wrong?"

"No. He just wants to talk to you about your famous case."

Clay pulled his tie loose and slipped out of his loafers. "It's too late to call back now."

"He said, no matter what time you got in, to call him."

Clay sniffed wood smoke and looked over at the white brick fireplace across from the bed. A faint glow and a crackling sound. "You had a fire tonight."

"It was a little chilly."

"Sorry I missed it. You sure there's nothing wrong with my dad?"

"I'm sure."

"Then I think I'll wait till morning."

"Suit yourself." Betty Sue looked down at her book, turned a page, and added: "But you know your dad. He'll probably stay awake until you call."

"I guess you're right. I'll call him in a few minutes. I haven't even had time to go to the john, for crying-out-loud."

"The price of fame."

"More like the price of notoriety," Clay said as he closed the bathroom door behind him, wondering if this phone call would involve some gratuitous lecture material.

Clay's father, Dr. Roger Ducharme, maintained a strong sense of self and family—a country doctor never at a loss for words or advice. Strong. A little too strong ever to accommodate an associate in his medical practice. Clay remembered filling in as a *locum tenens* in his father's office. If ever he had considered practicing with his father, the idea died during that week of vacation away from his medical residency, trying to care for his father's patients. Time and again he was confronted with: "Now, Clay, that's not the way your daddy would do that. . . . Now, Clay . . ."

Yet, Clay recognized that one reason he was a doctor was because his father was a doctor—and his father before him. He reflected on how five consecutive generations of Ducharmes had been physicians, starting with a certain André Ducharme who had traveled from New Orleans, his birthplace, to Paris to get his medical education. It was this same André Ducharme who had become somewhat of a celebrity under the Duelling Oaks in the 1830s. Young André, only nineteen years old, had inadvertently offended one of the greatest *maitre d'armes* in New Orleans, Marcel Dauphin. (Apparently it took very little to offend M.

Dauphin, who possessed unrivaled skill with the rapier.) But André Ducharme accepted the almost hopeless challenge, received the choice of weapons—and in a surprising, if not ungentlemanly, affirmation of personal survival, selected shotguns. It became a Ducharme family tradition for the fathers to take their sons before they reached their twentieth birthdays into New Orleans to City Park to the Duelling Oaks, where André Ducharme had been victorious over M. Dauphin in mortal combat. There paternal perceptions of honor and raw courage would pass to the the next generation. So Roger Ducharme had done with Clay. Soon it would be his turn to take Andy, but Clay was not sure about maintaining a ritual that both he and Andy might find uncomfortable. It was probably more than sufficient that Andy carried on the name of André.

Clay snapped off the bathroom light and returned to the bedroom. He swallowed saliva and felt the burning sensation in his throat. *Damn!*

"Everything still going all right at the hospital?"

"Better than I could have imagined." Clay began dialing and heard an answer halfway through the first ring. "Dad, sorry to call so late. Betty Sue said you wanted me to call no matter how late it was."

"That's fine, son. I was waitin'," his father said in a deep-voiced slow drawl. "Glad you were stayin' with your patient. That's the responsible thing to do. Lots of younger doctors don't do that now. As you well know . . . (Clay could sense that he was going to drag this out) . . . many's the night I've spent up with patients. In theyeh homes too. Home calls. I still make them."

"I know, Dad." Clay was trying to move the conversation along. "Is everything all right?"

"Except for the phone calls. The phone's been ringin' off the hook. They mentioned your name on the network news, you know."

"I heard about it. The kids told me."

"I'm worried."

"About what?"

"About what you're doin'. I want you to be verra

careful, son."

"I try to be," Clay said. *Especially with Varney waiting to ambush me.*

"Well, I'm just an old country doctor..."

There he goes again, Clay thought.

"... and I don't know much about this heart transplant business. But it could be trouble. I want you to be careful you don't jeopardize your career. We're all verra proud of you. Heah? But you be careful."

"I will."

"Don't go gettin' too big for your britches."

"Won't," Clay said, with a barely audible groan.

"It's a problem for lots of doctors." The elder Dr. Ducharme paused. "You know the story about the ol' niggeh who died and went to heaven and met St. Peter."

Damn, Clay thought, *I wish he wouldn't say nigger.* "I'm not sure I know the story," was all Clay said aloud.

"Well, the old niggeh got to heaven jes at lunchtime. And St. Peter said, 'Things are gonna be a lot better for you now. In heaven we're verra democratic. We eat cafeteria style and we all wait our turn in line.' So while they were waitin' in line, along comes this fella in a white coat with a stethoscope a danglin' from his neck and a head mirra on. And this fella rushes to the front of the line. So the old niggeh says to St. Peter, 'I thought you said evrabody waits his turn in line up here.' 'Well,' St. Peter says, 'don't you pay him no mind. That's jes God. He likes to play doctor.'"

Clay tried to force a laugh over the phone.

"You get the point?"

"I get the point, Dad. Please don't tell me the point."

"All right. But jes remember it."

"I will."

"When y'all comin' home? You reckon spring vacation?"

"Probably not. Maybe not till school's out."

"You tell Andy I found us a new fishin' hole back in that ol' swamp."

"I'll tell him, Dad. You get to sleep now. It's really late."

But it was not the older Dr. Ducharme who was in such desperate need of sleep. It was Clay. Yet the excitement of the day kept him wide awake. He tried to keep his arm around Betty Sue without moving.

But she readily detected the difficulty. "You think you're going to be able to sleep?"

"I hope so." Clay moved his arm, which was beginning to cramp.

"Your dad's very proud of you."

"I guess." Clay attempted to roll into a more comfortable position. "But it's funny. He can't just come out and say I'm proud of you, son. He always has to add a lecture. Tonight about caution. For crying-out-loud, caution is my middle name. I've been too cautious all my life. I didn't need a lecture."

"That's his nature. And he needs you a lot."

"I know. He's been so lonely for such a long time. What is it now . . . seventeen years since Mama died?"

"I was carrying Andy."

"I wish she'd gotten to see Andy—and Melanie."

"I do too."

"I became a doctor mainly because the Ducharmes lack the imagination to do anything else. But I guess I became a cardiologist because of Mama's heart problem. I wish she'd lived to know that."

"And to see you and Leif do a heart transplant."

"Funny, a heart transplant could have saved her. Except she might disapprove of heart transplants. Mama did a lot of disapproving in her day."

"It was just her way."

"I know. But I had to carry the burden of her Southern Baptist God off to college with me. Couldn't put six days of creation on a Harvard science exam. The first couple of years of college—I spent too much time agonizing about religion."

"I don't think our kids will suffer that way. We've raised them to think for themselves."

"I guess."

"Getting back to transplants, what about Mike?"

"I hope we did the right thing." Clay began to try to synchronize his breathing with Betty Sue's. That often helped him get to sleep. The problem was that Clay usually breathed at a slower rate. And tonight, because of his cold, he had to try to avoid breathing too directly towards Betty Sue. He began counting back from 1000 with each breath, 999, 998, 997. . . . *Dad will be disappointed if I don't take Andy to City Park . . . 996 . . . to the Duelling Oaks . . . 995 . . . where disputes were settled . . . by sword or shotgun . . . 994. . . .*

FOUR

The excitement of the previous night and day had stimulated Leif Hanson even more than Clay. While Clay was eventually able to sleep, Leif continued to prowl, wide-awake, around the recovery room and through the darkened corridors of University Hospital. Leif was fond of this time of night—when nocturnal housekeeping crews could scrub down the scuffed surfaces of the day.

But tonight, what of Leif's own scuffed surfaces? No sleep whatsoever the night before, and here it was almost two in the morning with his first open-heart case scheduled for 7:00 a.m. Almost no point in going home to bed. Yet he had to get some sleep. He returned to his office. Elaine would certainly be asleep by now. Should he go home?

There was so damned little for him at home.

Or try to catch some sleep on his couch? If he *could* sleep. He punched a sofa pillow under his head, stretched out on the cool leather couch, and stared at the ceiling. Not remotely sleepy. Too light. Leif turned off his desk lamp and settled back in the darkness. If he could fall asleep immediately, he would be all right. But if thoughts took over, there would be no sleep. He had to keep thoughts out. But what if he really fell asleep soundly?

Leif sat up and fumbled for the telephone, dialing O.

"Operator, this is Dr. Hanson. It's too late for me to go home now, so I'm going to try to sleep in my office. Could you be sure to call me at six? And if anyone needs me, they can reach me in my office. I'm going to turn my pager off."

"You have a good rest, Dr. Hanson," the operator said. "You deserve it."

Leif lay back and closed his eyes. What had been accomplished with this heart transplant was exciting. Not yet great science—but exciting. It was a beginning.

Stop thinking. Stop.

But within a minute, thoughts returned. Transplantation could be the new direction of his work. Maybe this was what he had been waiting for, preparing for, all of his life. This could possibly be a major contribution.

He *had to have* a major scientific contribution. Or a book. Or both. Something to dedicate. Something to make up for what had happened. Something so important that when he would stand up and say: this is for you—people would know the "you," would have to know the "you," and would find the dedication worthy.

Let transplants be a gimmick for some surgeons. For Leif it had the potential to be real science. Clay was too plodding. Now that it was started, they would all be forced to drive quickly ahead. It would be hard. There would be hairpin curves. But it was possible. All possible. Heart transplantation could be something worthy to dedicate.

Leif sat up and flicked the light on. He had to stop thinking. It would be morning soon. This would be two straight nights without sleep. Nine cases scheduled. He had to get to sleep. He turned the light off again. He would force his mind away from the events of the past day. No more thoughts. Perhaps memories. Memories. Try to remember back as far as he could. As a child he used to do that very thing. Escape into his mind. Into dreams. Chicago. The south side. He hated even to attend meetings in Chicago, because they brought back memories. . . .

RATS. A dark room illuminated by bright flashes of pain. Yellows and lightning blue sparks. Fur. Warm, thick, coin-tasting fluid trickling down his face and into his mouth.

Screams. A tall thin man in tears. What kind of a father am I? Living like this? In a slum. Allowing my family to live in a slum.

Next, the tall thin man was in bed. He inspected the recently healed scars on the little boy's face. The chewed eyebrow. A kiss. A grown-up handshake. Good-bye. No tears.

It was after four o'clock when Leif had last looked at his watch, and had confronted once more the memory of his father, Erik Bjorn Hanson, dying while still a young man. A young man who had just finished working his way through medical school. And had sustained a fatal complication of rheumatic heart disease during the first month of his internship. Then suddenly the shrill ring of the telephone pierced the darkness, summoning Leif Hanson from restless sleep to another day of surgery.

Only a week after surgery, Mike Goldman was sitting comfortably at the desk in his hospital room, trying to sort through what looked like many hundreds of pieces of correspondence.

"Have you ever seen such a change?" Leif asked Clay and Arthur. All were gowned as if for surgery. "Can you believe it? . . . Outstanding."

"It's very rewarding," Clay said cautiously. "Mike, you haven't looked so well in years."

"And never felt so well." Mike held up a letter. "From President Johnson." He reached for three more. "From both Texas senators and from my congressman."

"You've become quite a celebrity," Leif said.

"When can Becky spend some time in here with me?"

"What do you think?" Leif turned the question over to Clay and Arthur.

"I'd wait one more week," Arthur said. "While we cut your drugs back."

"Another week?"

"Don't sweat it," Leif said confidently. "You've got plenty of years ahead of you."

Clay and Arthur both appeared to be surprised at this statement and tried to show their lack of concurrence by frowning at Leif, without letting Mike see their expressions.

"How many years?" Mike asked in a way that did not really require a definite answer.

But Leif supplied one anyway. "Thirty years. Maybe more. Who can tell?"

During the first three weeks of his program, Leif Hanson's name dominated front pages and news broadcasts, as he performed a remarkable six heart transplantations. What was more impressive was that, of eleven heart transplants performed throughout the world, six were alive, and five of these were in Houston. Blaiberg in South Africa was the only other survivor. Through Christiaan Barnard and Leif Hanson, heart transplantation had become a media event.

In fact, it was already a ritual that after each heart transplant there would be a press conference. Although Leif had been up all night performing this, his sixth transplantation, he planned to complete his entire schedule of ten open heart operations. Leif was sitting in his OR cubicle between his third and fourth cases dictating an operative note when his phone rang.

"Dr. Hanson, this is Charley. We're waiting for ya in your hospital office. And the reporters are already down in the auditorium—chomping at the bit."

"I'm moving as fast as I can," Leif said. "I'll be right down." He hung up the phone, turned on the intercom, and peered down into operating room 2. "I'll be ready for room 2 in about twenty-five minutes." He glanced at the wall clock. That would be at ten-thirty.

The anesthesiologist waved up to Leif and answered, "We'll be all set by then. We'll aim for that."

Charley Drones, who looked like a pep rally bonfire, wearing burgundy polyester slacks and a burgundy and white houndstooth jacket, began to pace after he finished his call to Leif. "I'm sorry to getcha here so early, Dr. Ducharme. It's very hard to get everything to come out on schedule. I mean this is really a pressure business. It's tearing me up."

"Relax, Charley. I've got a few more minutes," Clay said.

Eric Kristensen had returned from New York and was also waiting in Leif's hospital office. He had already published his story in *Life* on heart transplants, including the first case in Houston, and he had told Leif he was considering writing another article based exclusively on the Houston experience.

"How are the patients this morning?" he asked Clay.

"Remarkably well," Clay said. "But it's almost impossible to take care of them all."

Eric pressed: "No rejection or infection?"

"Not as far as I can tell. But we shouldn't have lost Ahlstrom last week. The infection got away from us. While we were busy doing more transplants . . ." Clay stopped abruptly. "Scratch that. That's strictly off the record."

Leif took one step into the office and called out, "Let's go, team." He was with Sellery. They wore white coats over their green scrub suits—no one had stopped to change into street clothes.

"It's meet-the-press time in the old corral," Sellery added with feigned weariness.

Eric left the doctors at the door of the hospital auditorium and took his place with the journalists. Hanson, Ducharme, and Sellery sat behind the microphones at a table on the dais. "A heart transplantation was completed at University Hospital at 4:47 this morning," Leif opened. "The patient is in the recovery room and doing well. The names of the recipient and donor will be made available by the hospital administrator's office at the discretion of the respective families."

"You can't tell us the names yet?" asked the *Houston Chronicle*.

"Not at this moment."

"How about the other transplant patients?" UPI asked.

"They're doing as well as we could imagine," Leif

said. "But we don't know all the things to anticipate. We're exploring completely new territory." He paused to evaluate what he was about to say next, and continued. "If I may be permitted to compare this particular journey to the early Viking voyages, we've only found Iceland. Greenland and Vinland are a long way in the distance. Or maybe, since we're in Houston with the astronauts, I should say we're just beginning to reach for the stars."

"We understand that your first patient, Dr. Goldman, is out of isolation, and is walking around the halls in a business suit," said the *Houston Post.* "After three weeks that sounds most remarkable."

"We're very pleased with Dr. Goldman's recovery," Leif acknowledged.

"Any more information on the cause of Mr. Ahlstrom's death?" The *Houston Chronicle* again.

"I'll let Dr. Ducharme answer than," Leif said.

"Overwhelming infection. Sepsis," Clay said for the media. And to Leif he muttered, "Thanks a hell of a lot for punting that one to me."

"Did the autopsy show any sign of rejection?" The *Chronicle* wanted to know.

"We don't know yet. There are some suggestive findings. But, as Dr. Hanson said, this is all new territory."

"Is it true," asked the *Chronicle*, "that there are twenty patients in the hospital right now waiting for hearts and another thirty or more in motels and hotels around town?"

Leif looked at Clay and nodded to him to field the question.

"I can't vouch for those numbers. But I must emphasize that 'waiting for hearts' is not the way I'd put it. We're evaluating a number of patients who have been referred to Houston for heart transplantation. We've already determined that many of them are not appropriate candidates for transplanting. You must remember that this is an experimental procedure."

"I'm not sure I agree with that," Sellery interrupted. "We have five patients upstairs who'd be dead now if it weren't for heart transplants. I'd like to go on record as saying that this procedure is now well beyond the experimental stage and into the stage of clinical trial." His statement produced the desired reaction—a flurry of note-taking. At the last two press conferences, Sellery had emerged as a bit of a media star, fielding questions intended for Leif or Clay, holding forth with the reporters after Leif had terminated the conferences and had left.

"I think I'd modify that." Leif could see what Sellery was doing. It was time to take a stick to this wayward boy and make sure that everyone recognized who ran the show. "In fact I have an announcement. We have demonstrated the surgical feasibility of human heart transplantation. The next step is to carefully follow and study the patients we've already transplanted. To evaluate our procedures for controlling rejection and infection. Rather than do another dozen transplants, we want to take good care of the ones we have, and learn everything we can from them. To help *eventually* make this a standard form of therapy, rather than an experiment. Therefore, I'm declaring a moratorium on heart transplantation for the time being."

That shook up Sellery and the press corps.

"You wouldn't let someone die who desperately needs a transplant, would you?" the AP reporter asked.

"We would have to evaluate each case on its own merits," Leif said, watching the pain in Sellery's face. "But, until we've demonstrated the long-term effectiveness and safety of the operation, we must be cautious."

"You will be prepared to re-institute heart transplants in the future, then?" the *Houston Post* wanted to know.

"Of course. We're pioneering in this field. But we want to do it right," Leif said.

"This doesn't have anything to do with Mr. Bowen's charges that his wife did not receive proper care and was allowed to die so she could be a donor?" asked the *Houston News*. This paper had carried the allegation as a banner headline the day before.

Leif stiffened, then smiled. "You know better than that. And so does Mr. Bowen. Maybe this is the time to bring something out into the open. I've been reluctant to do it. But Bobby Jack Bowen has been harassing the Goldmans for the past three days. He went to the *News* with charges, because I told the Goldmans not to pay him. He wanted money for his wife's heart."

Another jolt through the room.

"I'll continue to be open with the press in the hope that there will be a dignified presentation of—let's face it—these very exciting times," Leif said.

That ended the press conference. Leif watched to see that Sellery did not remain behind as he had been doing recently. No need to worry. Sellery seemed anxious to get out of the auditorium.

So the team, with Eric in tow, quickly made rounds on the five transplant patients. The one who was still under the influence of the anesthetic didn't take long. A cardiology fellow and surgical resident were ministering to this most recent transplant recipient.

"Mr. Melton is from Mississippi. A high school English teacher from Davis Landing. Twenty miles from my home town," Clay began his presentation, but then quickly looked at Eric. "Scratch the name," he said, "it's not ready for publication yet."

"I won't use it till it's cleared," Eric said.

The other four patients were awake. And even though Leif spent only a few minutes with them, it gave each one enormous encouragement.

The real work of rounding would be conducted later by Clay. Leif started back for the OR. His next patient would be ready now. Eric followed, on the chance of getting a couple of minutes with his cousin before his next operation.

Leif opened: "You know I'm feeling more excited than anytime in my life. I feel like Leif Eiricksson searching for Vinland. Or King Harald Sigurdsson going into battle. It's great. I'm not forty-six. I'm twenty-one. I haven't averaged four hours sleep a night for three weeks and I feel twenty-one."

"Watch out for Stamford Bridge," Eric warned.

"What the hell's that supposed to mean?"

"Wasn't that where King Harald Sigurdsson was killed? Seems he went off into battle without his armor. The Vikings left their armor in their longboats. Isn't that what happened?"

"It was," Leif agreed.

"So hang on to your armor. And don't burn yourself out."

"Don't worry. I could go on like this for a hundred years. Honest-to-God, I feel invincible. I feel there's nothing in the world I can't do."

"Well, I feel very 'vincible.' All I'd like to do is get a little time to talk with you about the Houston transplanters. I'd like to consider doing a feature article now."

"That reminds me, some guy named Boyle or Broyles came by. He wants to write a book about me." Then Leif added mischievously, "So you may have to wait your turn."

Eric didn't answer.

Two medical students almost snapped to attention as Leif passed. They said simultaneously: "Good morning, Dr. Hanson." Even their voices snapped to attention.

Leif prodded Eric with, "I'm just joking. Do you know a writer with a name like that?"

"I know a Boylan."

"Should I tell this guy to get lost? He wants me to give him some sort of exclusive or something."

"I'd tell him to cool it, anyway."

"The whole idea sounds pretty fishy."

"It's not that far out. It's just premature. There may be a book here. The thought's even occurred to me. But first I'd like to try a feature article. So that's why I'd like to talk with you for a little while to fill in some very big gaps in what I know."

"Maybe we could get some time this weekend," Leif said, pushing open the doors to the OR.

"That'd be fine," Eric called after him.

"Ready for room 2," Leif announced as the operating room doors swung shut. God, he was high. Twenty-one?

Hell, he felt eighteen. He pulled his surgical mask over his face and began to lather his arms and hands, attacking each finger separately with the sharp bristles of the surgical scrub brush, thinking about Harald Sigurdsson, the last of the great Norwegian Viking kings. Tough, mean, treacherous. Called Harald Hardradi, Harald Hard Ruler, Harald the Ruthless. But a giant in many ways. Reported to have been seven feet tall. A warrior of unsurpassed courage and skill. A poet. . . . Yes. Yes, Leif would stand by his choice of Harald. After all, he was stuck with the middle name. His father's sense of history had burdened him with the names of two of the greatest Vikings. But today the burden felt light indeed.

After his final operation, Leif dialed Elaine from his cubicle office between operating rooms 1 and 2—to tell her he would be home early tonight. Early enough for supper. He had been wanting to share with her the excitement of the past three weeks, but their busy schedules never seemed to coincide. "Tonight we should have plenty of time," he opened. "I've got a lot to tell you."

"I'm sure you have," Elaine's speech was slurred, "and I'm really sorry, Leif. I have a steering committee meeting at the club."

"From when to when?"

"From six to whenever. Maybe ten or eleven."

"Ten or eleven? . . . You going to be sober enough to drive?"

"I haven't been drinking. And I resent the question."

"Whatever you say."

"It happens to be the truth. And if I have an occasional drink, it's none of your damned business."

"Whatever you say. Tell you what, Slim, why don't you look at your calender for the next two or three years. Maybe we could squeeze in one cup of coffee together during that time frame." Leif hung up before Elaine could answer. So much for his home life. He immediately began to dial another number.

"Hello," a woman's voice answered.

"You have any plans for tonight?"

"Whatever you'd like to do, hon."

It was after one in the morning when Leif finally arrived home. Elaine's Cadillac was not in the garage or driveway. And Elaine was certainly not in their bedroom. The meeting could not have lasted this long. Was she in bed with someone? Or could there have been an accident? He returned downstairs and poured himself a small chilled aquavit while trying to decide what to do.

No need. He could now hear the front door opening. Quietly. "Are you all right?" he called out.

"Fine," the words drifted back from an exceptionally tall slender woman disappearing up the winding staircase.

Damn her. He gulped down the ice and fire aquavit.

FIVE

Clay shivered as he drove his Volkswagen through the early morning darkness and February chill into the hospital parking lot. He turned off the ignition and sat slouching inside, teeth chattering, waiting for the drizzle to stop. But this had all the signs of being an all day misty-rain, so it was unlikely to improve. No point in delaying. Clay jumped from the car—and the drizzle promptly turned to a downpour. He limped the first few steps. *A recurrence of the heel spur from years of running? Or the beginning of arthritis?* He ran and splashed through a shoe-soaking puddle in front of the hospital door.

In his office he exchanged his soggy raincoat for a crisp white coat and went immediately to the transplant ward. There in competition with orderlies collecting and clattering empty breakfast trays, he conducted his work rounds, examining each patient, looking for clues to rejection or infection, studying the electrocardiograms and laboratory results. He wore two layers of surgical masks, because he still had a cold. The masks irritated his raw nose and made it difficult to breathe.

Mike Goldman was the next to last patient to be seen. Not only was Mike up and out of bed by 8:00 a.m., he was wearing a gray business suit. The most recent issue of *Life* with the article on heart transplants lay open on his bed. As Clay looked at him, he thought that if there was anyone who had ever fulfilled the description of "death-warmed-over," it had been Mike Goldman before his transplant. Now his color was good, but . . . he appeared a little less vigorous than on the previous day.

Mike counted the pills in his hand that Clay had just given him. "Hey, you've given me too many."

"I'm raising your steroid and Imuran doses again," Clay's words came muffled through the mask.

"But you just lowered them," Mike said warily, and looked down at the pills once more.

"I know."

"Come on, level with me."

"It's a hell of a strain having a doctor for a patient," Clay addressed his remark to an imaginary audience. "First of all, you can't charge them. Then they're always second-guessing you."

"Don't try to bug out of it." Mike was making no effort to begin swallowing the pills.

"Well, what can I say? This is as new to me as it is to you. And I'm flying by the seat of my pants. Your LDH-1 is higher today—that's the enzyme test I'm hoping will be our best early clue to rejection." He held up the latest electrocardiogram. "And you've lost a little voltage on your ECG. I just don't want to take any chances."

"Fair enough." Mike took four small steroid tablets in one swallow. "Keep being a mother hen."

"See you later, Mike." Clay started down the hall, pulling the surgical masks from his face—and bumped into Eric Kristensen, who was getting to be a little too much underfoot.

"You ready for a little coffee?" Eric asked cautiously.

"As a matter of fact, that's what I was on my way for. Wendell is doing the first two heart caths this morning."

"Coffee shop?"

"How about my office?"

"The price is right."

"I'm so damned tired." Clay rubbed both temples

with his finger tips as he walked. He had always been used to long hours and hard work, but the past three weeks had exhausted him more than he had ever been before. "I'm living on coffee, and I hate the stuff."

"Well, Leif's stopping the transplants for a while. That should give you some rest."

"None too soon." Clay covered his mouth and coughed from deep in his chest. "Maybe I can catch enough rest to get over my damned cold." He led the way into the outer office and asked his secretary for coffee—then into the inner office, which was much smaller than Leif's. No window. No paneling. No room for pictures, because teak bookcases occupied all the white plaster wall space to within eighteen inches of the ceiling. A row of diplomas from Harvard and Yale, specialty board certifications, and scholarly society memberships stretched across the top of one wall of bookshelves. The certificates were leaning against, rather than hanging from, the wall. A small L-shaped teak desk, with pictures of Betty Sue and the children on the small leg of the L, left room for only the desk chair and two brown tweed armchairs. "This transplant stuff is wearing me down. Coughing my guts out. My nose dripping. And that damned cousin of yours, working harder than I am and looking fresh as a daisy and strong as an ox . . . to mix clichés. Makes me feel damned puny. Worrying and coughing and worrying."

"You worrying about Mike?" Eric took one of the armchairs.

"Worrying about all of them." Clay flopped across from him in the other.

"There are only six heart transplants alive in the world, and you've got five. You and Leif must be doing something right." Eric hid the probing nature of his discourse behind a disarming smile.

"Maybe."

"Maybe?" Eric asked. "What does it take to turn you on?"

"Twelve straight hours of sleep for openers."

Clay's secretary, a tall, fortyish, Rosalind-Russelltype brunette, handed each of the men the requested mugs of coffee.

Eric nodded his thanks before slipping in his first question: "You think something's wrong?"

"There's reason to believe something could go wrong." Clay was rubbing his temples again.

"Why?"

"Because the name of the heart transplant game is man against nature."

"Isn't fighting any disease working against nature?"

"Not at all," Clay said. "Let me tell you what a French surgeon said a few centuries ago: 'I dressed the wound. God healed it.' And I think that pretty well summarizes what doctors used to do. We dressed the wounds and allowed nature or God to heal them. Hippocrates said, 'First, do no harm.' Because it's so easy to do more harm than good, we've got to be damned careful."

"But do you think you're doing harm right now?"

"No. Of course not. If I did, I wouldn't be involved in this. But it's certainly time to stop our transplants and study our work carefully to see if we could be doing harm. I'm sure as hell glad Leif made that decision."

"What could you do differently?"

"We've just got to come up with something new in immunology." Clay had still failed to recognize the agenda of Eric's questioning. He enjoyed teaching, so he continued his easygoing "bedside teaching" of third-year internal medicine to a knowledgeable layman. "I know it. Arthur and his people know it. Leif knows it. We need to know how to work *with* the body to accept 'non-self,' the foreign heart, as 'self.'"

"How's that?" Eric asked in an offhand friendly manner.

"You see, when a germ or a cancer cell or a heart transplant appears in the body, the body can tell that these things don't belong there." Clay studied the coffee mug he was holding in both hands. "They're non-self, so they've got to be destroyed. It's destroy *or* be destroyed. But not for the heart transplant. In this case it's destroy *and* be destroyed."

"Yet all the body can see is that the germ, the cancer cell, and the heart transplant are non-self," Eric suggested tentatively.

"That's absolutely right. The body can't tell which non-self is good and essential to tolerate. And which is bad and truly must be rejected." Clay stopped to take a long drink of coffee. He breathed into his cup. Steam came back and clouded his glasses for a moment.

"Well then, is the medicine you're using for rejection working with nature?"

"Just the opposite. We're bludgeoning the body's defenses so that it can't reject the germs of infection or cancer *or* the heart transplant. That's why we lost Ahlstrom." Clay took another swallow of the strong black coffee. "We didn't leave him sufficiently able to fight infection. And that's what killed him."

Eric started jotting down a few notes. "But what can you do differently?"

"Well, for three years, my wife and I have been working on something called induction of tolerance. Putting human hearts into humans has very limited clinical value. There'll never be enough human donors to go around. Through induction of tolerance, we might could—might be able to—" he corrected his Mississippi vernacular, "take the next step and use animal hearts. Possibly pig hearts." Clay at last noticed that Eric was writing. His voice darkened. "What are you doing? This isn't for publication. I thought we were just having a friendly chat."

"Sorry." Eric put the notebook away. "You didn't say off the record. But I'll regard it as that."

"I've got to do the next three heart caths." Clay swallowed the remainder of his coffee and pushed up out of the chair. He decided he was not about to say anything more concerning his research.

When Clay returned to the transplant suite in the early afternoon, he saw, of all people, his department chairman, Vincent Varney, writing in the chart of one of the heart transplant patients. At his side, at the two-tiered white Formica desk of the nurses' station, was Clay's junior associate, Wendell Eck, engaged with him in what appeared to be earnest discussion. Varney was no more than five feet five inches tall, and greatly overweight (sometimes charitably referred to as Dr. Five-By-Five, when he was not being more irreverently called something else). But his obesity had a solid look about it. By comparison, Eck was over six feet tall, balding prematurely, and although the initial impression was one of slimness, thin arms and legs, he had a soft, almost eunuchoid appearance, with a protruding lower belly. Their conversation stopped abruptly as Clay approached.

"I've been reviewing the charts and making some notes I'd like you to pay close attention to," Varney opened, removing his wire-rimmed glasses and pointing them at Clay. His demeanor went beyond aggressive all the way to hostile. "And as soon as these patients are transferred from the surgical service to medicine, I will hold you responsible for seeing that no reporters, especially that reporter from *Life*, are allowed access to them."

"Dr. Varney was expressing interest in the management of the gastrointestinal risks to our patients on steroids." Eck smiled stiffly and achieved an unnatural jovial tone of voice.

"That's right, Clay, I don't think proper attention is being paid to the protection of the GI tracts of these patients in the presence of the high doses of steroids they're getting."

"I imagine you wrote specific recommendations in each chart," Clay spoke quietly, cautiously.

"I did. And since the charts are legal documents, and since there are medicolegal considerations, it would be unwise to ignore the recommendations of an authoritative consultant in gastroenterology, who also just happens to be your department chairman."

"I look forward to reading your notes with great interest." Clay struggled to dampen a flare of Ducharme temper by speaking slowly—trying to avoid provoking his department chairman.

"Also," Varney said, "I understand you're already writing articles on the heart transplants."

"That's correct."

"I would like to see the papers before they're submitted for publication. As your department chairman, I feel it is highly appropriate that I evaluate their content before they are released under the imprimatur of this department of medicine."

"I'm only senior author of one of the articles," Clay said.

"It goes without saying that I will have to *approve* that article."

Clay felt his face and ears getting hot and his mouth tighten. "The other articles have the chairman of the Department of Surgery as the senior author. I'm afraid you'll have to debate that issue with Dr. Hanson, your fellow chairman." *Keep cool, Ducharme. Cool.*

"I'll expect you to send me the other articles as well," Varney said. "And I want to see them soon." He turned to leave. "By the way, I've made it clear to Dr. Johnson that he's been spending too much time with your heart transplants. I'm pulling him back." Varney bared his teeth in a lockjaw smile. "You and Leif may have to work without much help from him."

Clay sat down next to the chart rack. He was swearing inaudibly, while watching Varney walk—no, waddle—down the hall.

"Don't sweat him." Eck offered to provide a release for Clay. "He's just behaving like his usual nutty self."

"That sonovabitch," Clay sputtered. "That dirty . . . pressuring Arthur and threatening us with his area of expertise." He stood up and began to pace. "Except that son . . ." Clay again choked back an expletive, "thinks every area is his area of expertise. He considers himself the world expert on everything. But Leif summarized his knowledge pretty well."

"How's that?"

"Well since he's an expert on ulcerative colitis and

other diseases characterized by diarrhea, he's been said to know more about shit than anyone else in the world."

Eck laughed ingratiatingly. "That sounds like something Dr. Hanson would say."

"And Varney's detractors say that shit is all he knows anything about," Clay continued. "But he really seems to believe that he's an expert on everything in medicine."

"Could he actually have something to offer the program?"

"No. Nothing." Clay opened a chart without actually reading it—thinking about the confrontation. "This is typical Varney. *Expertise*." Clay slammed the chart shut. "As department chairman, he's been sending out into practice a bunch of cold carbon copies of himself. Students and residents who've acquired a lot of expertise—who have knowledge without wisdom. And no heart. And that's the sort of internist this medical center is turning loose on the public."

"But what's Varney after in this transplant stuff?"

Clay took a deep breath. "He wants *in*. This is big. It's exciting. And he wants in. He wants to see his name on the papers. And if he can't get in, he'll try to screw us." Another deep breath. "I'd let him in to keep him off our backs, but Leif won't. So Varney may get all over me like ugly on a bulldog."

"But he just can't come out and ask if there's a way he could be involved?"

"No. That's too normal. Too civilized." Clay began speaking softly now. "For years I've tried to understand that man. I've bottled my temper rather than have a confrontation with him. I know he's come up the hard way. The first in his family ever to go to college." He returned the chart to the rack. "But Leif and Arthur have come a lot further. Without becoming bitter, vengeful, inflexible bastards."

"Varney's just schizy." Eck leaned forward in a confidential manner, his elbows resting on the chart rack.

"I wouldn't go that far," Clay said. "As cardiologists I don't think we're qualified to make that diagnosis."

"The man's in psychotherapy."

"Come on. How do you know that?"

"There are lots of things I know that people don't give me credit for knowing," Eck said petulantly, almost effeminately. "Varney is in psychotherapy."

"Well, so . . . psychotherapy's great. I've sometimes thought if I could afford it, I'd enjoy treating myself to psychoanalysis. Might help me control my temper better. That doesn't make me schizy—or Varney schizy. Maybe it'll calm Varney down." Clay's tone made it clear that he did not care to pursue the topic further. He had rounds to complete. He walked away from Wendell Eck to finish his rounds alone. Otto Schneider was the final transplant patient for Clay to see.

"Good morning, Doctor." Otto, small and thin and gray, raised his hand in a perfunctory wave and smiled.

Of course it was afternoon, but Clay was anxious to skip over this apparent disorientation by saying, "Did you have a good lunch?"

"Lunch?" Otto asked. He was unwilling to abandon his frame of reference. "I ain't had breakfast yet. You seen my comb?" He began to run his thin gray fingers through his thick gray hair.

"I haven't seen it, Mr. Schneider. You're certainly looking well," Clay changed the subject. Indeed, Otto Schneider's recovery had been the most dramatically rapid of any of the patients—except for this persistent disorientation. His heart transplant had been far and away the best tissue match. Clay backed unobtrusively from the room and returned to the nurse's station to write a progress note on Schneider.

Clay returned home from the abrasive ambience of the hospital unable to talk about work—or to say much of anything. He felt the confrontation with Varney still twisting his gut. And his chest hurt from coughing so much. When something was bothering him he would eventually pour out every detail to Betty Sue. Sometimes it took a day or so. And it usually took Betty Sue to find just the right time, place, and occasion to encourage the catharsis.

The time was later in the evening. The place was the kitchen, warmed by stove and oven and family. The occasion was placing a pewter pot of freshly brewed Earl Grey tea between them on the round maple table after the dishes were cleared.

"Is it a patient or a colleague?" Betty Sue began as she reached out for Clay's hand.

She knew the problems. Clay recognized that. In many ways, she knew them better than he did. Still an assistant professor herself, while men with half her accomplishments held tenured positions in her department. Her academic work was important to her, but what was most important to both her and Clay was their family and life together. With this sense of priority, problems at work were usually well controlled. "It's a colleague who should be a patient," Clay finally answered.

"Varney?" Betty Sue supplied the name without having to think about it. "It figures. . . . By the way, Arthur Johnson called earlier. He said he needed to talk to you."

"Arthur predicted that Varney would try to use heart transplantation to get at us. And he's starting his attack on both of us." Clay poured an ounce of tea into his cup. *Not strong enough yet.*

"I'll never understand the search committee picking Varney for chairman. And the dean accepting him. Everyone around here knew how abominably he behaves."

"He's done some passable basic research."

"But he's always behaved in such a hateful, spiteful way towards almost everyone in the school. Yet knowing how disagreeable he was, the dean accepted the search committee's recommendation."

"Well, the dean didn't want him. He kept sending the recommendation back to the committee and the committee kept giving Varney back to the dean." Clay poured for Betty Sue and then filled his own cup, inhaling the soothing aroma of the bergamot.

"People used to say Varney can't get along with anyone. With Hanson or Ducharme or Johnson or

Knoblauch." Betty Sue dropped a tablet of saccharin into her cup. "Now what they say is that it's too bad Johnson and Ducharme and Knoblauch and the others can't get along with Varney. Amazing! Only Leif seems to have escaped."

"Well, Leif's a chairman." Clay swallowed some tea. Just right. He took another sip and let the flavor linger.

"But I think Varney is also fixing to cause Leif as much damage as he can. So if there's any way he can get at you or Leif or the others through this transplantation project, I agree with you that he will."

"Except heart transplantation is currently a success."

"Let's hope it stays that way," Betty Sue said.

"We've got more experience than anyone in the world," Clay paused and allowed his voice to capture the despair he felt, "but I'm not sure we know what we're doing."

Betty Sue reached across the table and took Clay's hand again. "I think that your patients are very lucky to have you so involved. If anyone is going to learn the answers and do the right thing, you are."

Clay let out a nervous laugh. "You want to put that in writing and send it to Varney?"

The jangling of the phone broke into the conversation. Clay wearily got up and limped the first two steps on a painful foot to take the call. It was Arthur Johnson. He was still in his laboratory at the hospital and wondering if Clay could see him.

"Be there in five minutes," Clay said.

"You're not going back?" Betty Sue stepped to block the door—only half-playfully. She wrapped her arms around Clay's neck. "We need some time together."

Clay reached out to hold the soft warmth of Betty Sue, drawing her to him, not wanting to let go. "And of course, you just happen to be wearing an extra dollop of White Shoulders," he whispered. Not wanting to let go. "I'll be back as soon as I can." He reluctantly escaped from her gentle grip—from the warm sweet-scented Betty Sue out into the cold drizzle, polluted by the acrid smell of not-too-distant power plants and oil refineries . . . which brought on a spasm of coughing.

As usual Clay took the stairs up to Arthur's lab. And as usual he arrived there trying to catch his breath. "What's happening?" Clay asked when he entered the lab, which appeared even more cluttered than usual. A new phase microscope and a new incubator vied for the limited counter space.

Arthur was standing studying computer printouts, which were spread over a lab bench. "Greetings, my man. Something damned interesting." Uncharacteristically, Arthur did not look up at Clay. "I've been comparing the tissue antigens of the people we've been typing for heart transplants and those we've been typing as potential donors."

"And what've you found?"

"Well, we've typed thirty-six people with early-onset coronary heart disease for possible transplant. And I think there may be a difference in their tissue type when we compare it with the controls." Arthur kept his gaze fixed on the printouts.

"Something there you could look at to identify the patient at risk?" Clay moved closer to see.

"Maybe even more than that. Maybe there's an immunologic insult involved in coronary disease." Arthur reached for a pack of Chesterfields.

"Is the difference significant?" Clay asked. His mind raced ahead to the possibilities of this observation.

"We need more patients." Arthur was avoiding looking at Clay. "But with only thirty-six, the chi-square is just a shade below significance."

"That's still great. The potential's there." Clay watched Arthur extract a cigarette. "I thought you gave up that damned smoking a year ago."

"Just started up again. And no lectures," Arthur said, still not looking at Clay.

"Well, I can't understand . . ." Clay began.

"How an intelligent human being . . ." Arthur picked up the usual sequence of the sermon. "I don't really want to smoke. And my ulcer's acting up right now."

"And smoking riles your ulcer."

Arthur went ahead and lit his cigarette. "Clay, talking about tissue-typing—it was just an excuse." Finally Arthur looked directly at Clay. "It could have waited till Monday. The data aren't even significant yet."

"But it's close. And it could be damned important. It may open a whole new area into the cause of coronary disease," Clay countered, not hearing what Arthur was trying to say. "You should be happier than a deacon counting the collection," he added.

"I've been fired," Arthur whispered. "That's why I needed to talk to you. I've been fired," he repeated firmly.

"Wha-a-at?" Clay shook his head in disbelief. "Varney said he was pulling you back from heart transplants, that's all."

"Late this afternoon, Varney called me in for a little chat."

"You can't be fired. You've got tenure." Clay threw his arms up and began to pace within the cramped space of the lab. "You work a hundred hours a week. You're the best man in the department."

"He told me I was spending so much time with transplantation problems that I was not doing all I should for the rest of the renal division. He thought maybe someone like Mawson should head the renal division."

"That ass? He just finished his fellowship. A young assistant professor heading an important division? He can't pull that."

"Sure he can. Tenure has to do with my professorship. It has nothing to do with my administrative responsibility as chief of a division." Arthur absently flicked the cigarette in the direction of an old petri dish he was using as an ashtray. "So now . . . I can work for Mawson, one of the least capable people I've trained in many years."

"Why the hell did you give him a job in your division?"

"I didn't. Varney did. I see it clearly now. He was grooming Mawson to help get rid of me. Just like he's grooming Eck to get rid of you."

"Come on. We can't be replaced by such inconsequential people."

"There's a lot that goes with the title. Just being called the chief gives you control over things. That's all I had when I came here. There was no renal division. I was given a title. I started from scratch—and built the whole damned thing with my grants and my blood. A title is important." Arthur turned away and began folding the printouts.

"Well, even Mawson has enough integrity not to accept such a thing. And I know Eck wouldn't. I trust Eck and I think you should trust Mawson."

"Mawson has already accepted the job. He's known about it for a week. He's just conveniently away in Washington right now at the time Varney actually springs this on me. But his secretary told me. He'd already been discussing what her new duties will be when he takes over my office."

"I can't believe it."

"You'd better start believing. And you'd better keep an eye on your boy, Eck. He's the same as Mawson."

"You're going to bring this up to the dean, Monday, aren't you?"

"No." Arthur dragged deeply from his cigarette. His hands trembled slightly.

"Well, then I will."

"Don't increase your own problem. All I needed was to talk with someone. I just need to try to figure things out. . . . The hell of it is, I just knew Varney would use transplants to get at us."

"What happened is that a destructive sonovabitch became chairman of our department."

Arthur snapped open and shut his Zippo lighter. "He attacks and we're supposed to take it. We just try to go along to get along. A hell of a way to live in academia . . . and then it doesn't even work."

"Well, we're going to make something work at the dean's office."

"Not possible. For chrissake, you've been in the service. The dean has to support the chain of command. Varney's a zealot. And you'd better learn what I've finally learned: you can't appease a zealot. His game is 'I'm OK—You're Not OK,' and he's incapable of accepting any other point of view. And since we're not OK, there's nothing we can do to appease him that's OK."

"I've got to talk to the dean."

"Please don't. It'll damage both of us. I've got a job offer out east. I've visited twice. I love Houston. And I'd love to stay here, but it looks like I've got the job if I want it. One of the items on the agenda for this visit is to meet with a real estate agent to look at houses." Arthur inhaled his cigarette deeply and held the smoke in his lungs for two or three seconds before he exhaled. "So, my man, it's just a matter of nailing down details. Let me just get out of this school quietly. And get another job and try to be productive at some other place."

"I want to help."

"It was a help to be able to talk. A real help. I needed it. Now I just need to get away as quietly as possible. I leave Sunday afternoon. The final negotiations for my new job begin Monday."

"I don't want you to leave. You're my friend . . . one of my closest friends."

"We won't stop being friends just because I've moved."

"What will our heart transplants do? Mike may be rejecting."

"I won't be moving for a while. But you're the real expert on heart transplants now. I just got you started."

"I wish that were true. I wish that the knowledge were there. Whatever—I need you to come see Mike with me tonight."

And when they arrived at his room, Clay saw Mike had greatly improved since morning. The pallor had disappeared and his dark eyes were shining like obsidian.

"All we need is Leif and we can play a rubber of

bridge," Mike greeted them.

"I guess the extra dose of steroids and Imuran was what we needed."

"I feel great," was Mike's answer.

"Your electrocardiogram is back to normal." Clay scanned the tracing. "We've got sick people to look after, and not waste our time on malingerers."

"What, no bridge?" Mike laughed.

"See you tomorrow," Clay called back as he and Arthur left the room.

In the hall Arthur said, "It looks to me like you've not only learned how to diagnose, but how to treat, rejection of the heart."

"Maybe. . . . So why do I feel I'm walking through a Viet Cong mine field? Or now a Varney mine field—with Varney waiting behind a rock to blow me away?"

SIX

Adjacent to the surgical recovery room was the newly remodeled ward for the heart transplant patients. More luxurious rooms. More life support equipment. There the team made rounds on Thursday.

"Schneider's still out in left field waiting for fly balls when there's no game going on," Feinstein, the psychiatrist, was saying, his back against a green-tiled wall, standing straight. He wore a boutonniere in the lapel of his Italian silk suit and lifts in his tassled loafers to help him attain a height still less than five and a half feet.

Clay was looking down the corridor for Arthur, who should have been back from his job interview and now be on team rounds. He finally said, "I know Schneider's confused as hell. I could understand it before surgery. The cardiac output for his whole body was less than the brain alone is supposed to get."

"What's his output now?" Webb asked. Webb was the psychologist, tall, black, with a florid Afro hairstyle.

"Almost six liters. Normal," Eck said confidently without deferring to Clay.

"He's just got a long-standing organic brain syndrome," Feinstein said. "He may never recover. And he was probably a nut even with good circulation to his head. This heart thing just made it worse."

"Can't you do something for him?" Clay asked.

"I can't even talk to him anymore," Feinstein said.

"I can't either," Webb added. "The little Nazi won't have anything to do with his Jew-boy and nigger shrinks."

"Actually he relates pretty well to Leif. Except Leif almost never gets to see him. And he still relates reasonably well to me." Clay avoided comment on Otto's racism, opened Schneider's door, and waved to him—wondering if he knew which meal he had eaten today.

"Come in," Otto said. "Come in."

"Can't right now, Otto. I'll drop in later during rounds."

"Good, good," Otto said to the wall. "Good," he said to the wall again. "But somebody better look at this sore in my mouth."

That caught Clay's attention. He pulled a penlight and tongue blade from his pocket. "Open."

Otto opened.

"You've got a cold sore."

"I know that."

"Do you get them very often?" Clay discarded the tongue blade into the waste basket.

"No. Probably got it from that Jew next door."

"If you're speaking about Mr. Berkowitz, he doesn't have any cold sores. Herpes cold sores are not good things to have when you have a transplant. But you're taking such low doses of medicine, we should weather this with no trouble."

"I know that. I still got it from that damned Jew."

"Talk to you later," Clay backed out of the room, thinking it was fortunate that the anti-Semitic Schneider did not know that the heart transplanted into his body was not Aryan, but Jewish. The donor, who had been an eighteen year old physics major at Rice, was related to a prominent Houston rabbi.

The next patient they rounded on was Martin Ford, who, curiously enough, had also been an auto worker, like Schneider, but from across the border in Canada. Almost ten years older than the thin and gray Otto Schneider, but he had looked a robust ten years younger when he entered the hospital. The muscular, jovial Martin Ford of three weeks earlier was not the man the team saw today. His arms and legs were losing some of their muscle mass. And he just lay there. Not smiling. Not even talking.

Clay listened to Ford's chest with his stethoscope and looked at his electrocardiogram and other laboratory studies. "How are you feeling, Mr. Ford?"

"Fine," Ford mumbled.

When they left Ford's room, Clay was shaking his head. "I'm having a hell of a time keeping his rejection under control without poisoning him with steroids and Imuran. Today he's taking four times as much as Schneider. And he still smolders. It's just damned lucky he isn't getting herpes—or it would really eat him up."

"What's making his muscles deteriorate so fast?" Webb asked.

"The steroids. The damned corticosteroids. And inactivity."

"I thought steroids built up muscle."

"There are different kinds of steroids. The kind to combat rejection tears muscle down."

They walked to the next room to see Fred Berkowitz, who was a prominent real estate developer from Miami. His surgery had made the front page of the *Miami Herald*. The clippings were on his wall.

Clay repeated the examination ritual and concluded with: "You're looking very well today."

"Feeling just great, Doc." Berkowitz held out a box of chocolates. "Have some."

"Just one." Clay selected a dark chocolate cream.

The final patient was Mr. Yancey Melton, a fifty-two-year-old, high school English teacher with a modest goal. He had told Clay that he wanted to live long enough to see his first grandchild and to see his son graduate from medical school. Clay watched the technician wheel the portable X-ray machine next to the bed of the cherub-faced, rotund Mr. Melton and thought about the special bond he shared with this patient. It was more than their being from neighboring small towns in Mississippi. And it was more than their both being Faulkner scholars, not superficially acquainted with Faulkner's works, but in-depth scholars. It was a love they shared for the South and its people. Clay looked forward to some more good conversations after Mr. Melton had recovered from the acute effects of his recent surgery. But for the moment there would be no conversation. The technician was taking too long.

"Be back to see you later," Clay said as he waved from the door to Melton's room.

Melton waved back and smiled.

As this Thursday morning's rounds drew to a close, there still had been no appearance of Arthur Johnson, who routinely rounded with the heart transplant team. Arthur had been scheduled to return to Houston Wednesday from his interview for the department chairmanship in New York. Perhaps he had needed to stay over an additional day.

Clay made his usual climb up the stairwell to Arthur's laboratory. "What's the good news?" he began.

"No good news." Arthur dug in the ashtray for his lighted cigarette. "Can we go into the lab office?" A couple of lab technicians were within earshot, so he led Clay into the small office adjoining the laboratory.

"What's wrong?" Clay asked as he pulled the door closed behind them.

"First thing Monday morning, my first appointment for a three day visit with the search committee was with the dean." Arthur sat on top of his desk and offered the only chair to Clay.

"Sounds like the man to start with." Clay dropped heavily into the black vinyl and chrome swivel chair.

"He greeted me with: 'I understand you're no longer chief of the renal division at Southwest.'"

"What?"

"Varney gives me the word Friday night, Houston time, after everything is closed up in New York. And Monday morning, before things have opened up in Houston, they know in New York that I've been canned."

"How the hell could that happen? . . . God damn it!" Clay slammed his foot on the floor.

"Not very easily. Someone had to go far out of his way to spread the word on a weekend. He'd have to call people at home."

"Varney? But that's crazy. If you want someone to leave, you don't undermine his chances for another job," Clay said. "That is if you're competent." He kicked at the floor again.

"Competence is not Varney's strong suit. But maybe Mawson did it. Maybe both." Arthur made a fist with his right hand . . . then slowly opened it and rubbed his fingertips across his mustache.

"I wouldn't put it past either of them." Clay swiveled the chair forward and back thirty degrees. It responded with a grating squeal.

Arthur lit his next cigarette from the stub of the last one. "Oh Jesus, I'm really in a bind now."

"I know. God, I know."

"I made a list on the plane back from New York." Arthur dragged deeply on his cigarette and coughed. He cleared his throat. "In the past two years, I've been contacted by seventeen different medical schools to consider the job of chairman of medicine. But now what school wants to hire a chairman who can't even hang on to his job as a division chief?"

"I understand why you're feeling so down, but I don't think what's happened is as serious as you believe."

"It's serious. Take my word for it. One right after another, my interviewers raised the question of my problem with interpersonal relations. Hell, no one wants a guy at any level who's a potential troublemaker."

"But anyone who knows you . . ."

"That's another problem. Who knows me? Except for my research, who knows me? I've been so damned involved in my work I haven't spent enough time cultivating the right people. I don't have that many friends. Hell, I've never even been married. So when it comes to pushing, who's going to say, I know Johnson. He's all right."

"I am, for one."

Arthur gazed down his cigarette and studied the smoke curling from the end. "Thanks, Clay." He glanced back at the cigarette. "But do you know me?" Almost a whisper.

"I know you, Arthur. I've known you for over twenty years. I know you." Clay revolved the chair a few degrees and looked squarely at Arthur. "And I've had to admit to myself many times that you're twice the man I am."

"I appreciate the sentiment. Unjustified as it may be."

"No. You're the same productive man you were last week. Varney can take away your title, but he can't take away your accomplishments. The people in New York are going to find out what happened here."

"You still underestimate the value of the title and what all this means," Arthur insisted. "I've been thinking about it since Monday. Walking through the interviews with the members of the search committee like a zombie—knowing what had happened. Trying to explain my problem with interpersonal relations. I probably can't even get a job at a junior staff level now, even if I try to impose on my friends. I'm too senior. People aren't looking for full professors as second or third or fourth men in divisions. They're looking for young assistant professors. I'm overqualified."

"You're not going to have any trouble at all," Clay said with all the confidence of an outside observer. "Which medical school is it in New York? And who's on the search committee? You've got friends here, Arthur. And we're going to help."

"Thanks. But you've only had a couple minutes to think about this situation. I've been sweating it since Monday. Now stop and put yourself in my place. Because—God forbid—you may soon be in my shoes. Varney replaces you with his stooge, Eck . . ."

"Don't say that. Varney and Mawson may be bastards, but I think Wendell is a loyal friend."

"Sure. Like Mawson, he's made a point of telling everyone how loyal he is." Arthur started fumbling for another cigarette. "My God, Clay, haven't you ever heard of protesting too much?" He located a new pack and tore the top off. His hands betrayed him by shaking as he was pulling on the cellophane and foil. "Let's just say you're looking at a chairmanship and you're fired from your present job and are replaced by a junior ass—call him Smith rather than Eck. Or whatever name you want. What would people think?"

"They'd think it was pretty strange. And I'd hope my friends would make an effort to learn the facts."

"You'd hope?" Arthur was now lighting a fresh cigarette off of the previous one. "That's the problem. Hope isn't enough. We're all so damned busy doing our own thing. We haven't got time for anything else. No time to learn facts, for godsake. No time for friends. We're all stretched thin. And it's every man for himself. And if someone goes down, we can say: 'Damn, that's too bad. Really too bad.' But inside we're saying: 'Damn, I'm sure glad it wasn't me.'"

"That's too cynical," Clay said.

"No. It's just the way it is. And this hypothetical problem that I'm suggesting isn't hypothetical at all. I'm now down the tubes. Maybe you've still got a chance." Arthur waved at a pile of boxes in the corner. "You know what those are?"

"Not off hand."

"The contents of my office in the department of medicine. While I was away Varney and Mawson had my stuff removed from my office and carted up here to the lab." Arthur slid off the desk and stepped over to the boxes.

"What kind of crap is that? You might expect it in a disreputable used car dealership. But in a supposedly dignified medical school?"

"You've got the right word. Disreputable." Arthur's hand trembled more noticeably as he tapped the ashes off his cigarette into the ashtray he was carrying with him. He set the ashtray down on the floor and yanked open the flaps of the top box. "But Varney's clever."

"Not that clever."

"Yes. Clever. Cunning. He can create a very plausible story to justify his making changes in the department. He doesn't want the strong independent people around who won't kiss his ass. He wants the ass-kissers like Mawson and . . . I won't say Eck, because you don't want to believe that." Arthur inhaled his cigarette deeply. "Now, for you, it's pay attention to the warning. Don't wait until they dump your books and diplomas out into the hall." Arthur carefully removed a diploma from the opened box, examined it, and turned it around so Clay could see it.

The glass was cracked.

Arthur muttered, "How about that? Universitas Harvardiana. Summa and all that stuff. And they broke the god-damned glass."

Clay looked at the diploma and said, "Jesus, I sure am sorry."

"The glass can be replaced." Arthur returned to the desk and leaned against it. "Varney started slowly three years ago, and we haven't moved. Now he's got to escalate till we get the message." Arthur flicked the ash off the stub of his cigarette. "Clay, while you've still got a chance, get out of here. For godsake, get out of here."

"The hell I will. I love Houston. And I like being part of a city and medical community where the sky's the limit."

"That's what I thought. And look what it's got me."

"We've got to talk to the dean."

"No. Let me keep looking for jobs for a while." Smoke from Arthur's cigarette wafted into his eyes. He squinted and jabbed the cigarette into the ashtray. "And let's bust our butts on this transplantation research. If we could really prevent rejection, we could write our own tickets anywhere."

"That's a more positive attitude." Clay forced his lips into a smile and his voice into a tone of enthusiasm. "All we have to do is immediately come up with a breakthrough in research that should normally take many years to achieve. Keep our patients alive. And hang on to our jobs while under constant attack. Hell, we've got 'em right where we want 'em."

"Piece of cake, my man," Arthur upped the ante of counterfeit ardor. "We'll lick this problem. Stockholm, here we come!"

But Clay's pager began to beep a stat call to the transplant ward. "Damn," he muttered.

"If there's anything I can do to help, I'll be right here."

"Thanks," Clay was saying as he ran from the lab. "Damn! Damn! DAMN!"

In the heart transplant ward, the head nurse motioned to Clay from the door of Ford's room. "He doesn't look good," she whispered. "Feeling faint. We took his blood pressure—seventy over fifty-five."

Clay rushed into the room. "Let's get an I.V. with some Isuprel to bring that pressure up."

"We've got everything you need at his bedside."

He entered Ford's room hiding behind a persona of professional self-assurance. "Mr. Ford, I heard you were feeling a little faint."

"A little," Ford mumbled.

"We have some medicine here that's best given in the vein. So I'm going to have to start an I.V." Clay examined the back of Ford's left hand after putting a rubber tourniquet around his arm. Nothing. The veins remained collapsed. Nothing in the wrist. He would have to go fishing in the antecubital fossa—and fast. "Arm board!"

Ford's arm was extended and a padded board was shoved under his elbow and taped in place. Clay began palpating the fossa in the bend of the arm for anything that felt like a vein. He could just barely detect the brachial pulse. There would be a vein next to it. He introduced the needle, pulling back very dark blood. The tubing was connected and the I.V. fluid began flowing.

The nurse handed Clay the Isuprel, which he began pushing slowly into the tubing, while watching Ford's monitor. The heart rate began to increase, but the blood pressure was not changing appreciably. More Isuprel.

"How's the pressure now?"

"It's coming back."

Clay discontinued the Isuprel and slowed the I.V. rate. "Feeling better?" he asked Ford.

"Yes," Ford answered tentatively.

During the next hour Clay inserted an arterial line and stayed at Ford's bedside, watching the monitor, which was now revealing a very gradual lower drift of blood pressure. "Could you call Dr. Johnson's lab and ask him if he could come down here," he whispered to the nurse.

Within two minutes, Arthur was standing at the door of Ford's room.

Clay met him there and reviewed the recent events.

They both took positions at Ford's bedside to watch his pressure. Very gradually it diminished: 108 . . . 106 . . . 103 . . . 100. This, over a period of one-half hour.

Arthur nodded his head at Clay, indicating that they should step away from the bed.

"I'd jolt him with an amp of Solu-Cortef if he weren't already so full of steroids," Clay whispered.

"I'd do it, anyway," Arthur said.

"But he's got a ton on board right now."

"All I can say is, in kidney transplants, we use enormous doses in rejection episodes."

"OK." Clay beckoned to the nurse. "Let's get another amp of Solu-Cortef ready."

After the medication, Ford's pressure began to rise again. This time it remained steady for three hours before starting to drop once more. Another dose of Solu-Cortef. More Isuprel.

"We're in for a long siege," Arthur said.

"We may need some relief. The surgeons ought to know what's happened to their patient." Clay asked the nurse, "Could you get a hold of Dr. Hanson?"

The word came back that Dr. Hanson had left at two for Atlanta and would not return until Friday evening. He was giving a talk there. Sellery was taking his calls.

"Sellery is someone we can do without," Clay whispered to Arthur. "How about Eck? He could alternate with us if this goes on for a long time."

"I'd prefer to get by without Eck," Arthur said. "Why don't you go to supper? We can manage between the two of us—unless this drags on for several days."

So throughout the night, Clay and Arthur remained with Ford. Falling blood pressure. Medication with Isuprel and Solu-Cortef.

Again falling blood pressure.

More Isuprel and Solu-Cortef.

By sunrise Ford had been stable for almost two hours. Clay, seated at the bedside, struggled to stay awake. He studied a thin slab of light as it projected from under the shade and peered dustily across the room to focus on the top drawers of the dresser. The light was gray with a tint of orange and it reflected varying shades of color off the particles caught in its gaze. Specks of silver, specks of gold, and a spirochetal filament floating lazily through the beam. And . . . and Clay's head nodded and jerked back up. He rubbed his face with both hands and straightened to a stand. Perhaps a short break outside the room would help. He signed to Arthur where he was going before he walked, no paced, up and down the hall.

Mr. Melton was standing at the door of his room. He said, "And then, life wasn't made to be easy on folks: they wouldn't ever have any reason to be good and die."

This was obviously from Faulkner, but Clay couldn't place it. "Good morning, Mr. Melton," was all he said.

"Good morning, Dr. Ducharme."

"You're up early."

"And you've been up all night."

"I thought we were being very quiet. Very discreet. Do you think the other patients know?"

"I don't think so. How's Mr. Ford?"

"Better."

"That's good. He's a very nice man. He's been very sick"

"Yes."

"It's been a difficult night."

"It has."

"But do you know, in the midst of all this difficulty, what has been beautiful?"

"I can't imagine what."

"Seeing the white Dr. Ducharme and the black Dr. Johnson working together. With love. And mutual respect. It's been beautiful."

"Dr. Ducharme," a nurse called.

"Excuse me, Mr. Melton." Clay turned quickly towards the nurse. "Got to get back to Mr. Ford. Looks like we've still got a far piece to go."

SEVEN

Leif arrived home Friday evening, unaware of the crisis with Ford, which the team had just successfully overcome. On the drive in from the airport, he remembered that he had half-promised Eric some time to talk. The prospects of a pleasant weekend ahead were heralded by blooms of azaleas, which had begun to compete with the camelias in bringing the warmth of pinks and reds to the chilled gray yards of late February in Houston. This could be an ideal weekend to spend at the ranch. The talking with Eric could be done out there. And Leif could show his cousin this retreat so essential to his well-being, almost as essential as it was to the land-hungry Scandinavian and German immigrants two and three generations earlier. His was a working ranch of 2200 acres of prime land two hours from Houston. Leif would have liked his grandfather, Bjorn Hanson, to have seen this ranch. At least Eric could see it. Leif reached his cousin by phone at the Shamrock to offer the invitation.

However, as often happened to Leif's plans for family or social events, emergency surgery took precedence. So he had to call Eric back to cancel the trip to the ranch, but promised to meet with him in the office after the unavoidable Saturday surgery.

Eric was waiting in Leif's office, relaxing on the leather couch. He moved his legs as Leif plopped into the adjacent armchair. "You all done with surgery for the day?" Eric asked.

"I hope so."

"I hate to bug you, but I need more information if I'm going to do a feature on the Houston transplanters. And Hanson in particular."

"Fire away."

"All right," Eric began unpacking his briefcase, "how about stuff from early childhood? All I really know is about one summer together on our grandfather's farm, almost thirty years ago. That was it until I came to Houston to do the NASA story."

"Nothing much there. Born and raised in Chicago. That's all I'd say about that."

"Come on, I really need to know more about your early years. I could get the 'born and raised in Chicago' out of *Who's Who*."

"Well, let's play it by ear," Leif said without enthusiasm.

"We can start with that summer, if you want. And work in both directions." Eric placed a tape recorder on the coffee table and punched the "on" button. "You don't mind this, do you? After a few minutes you won't even notice it's here."

"It's all right," Leif said stiffly and sat up straighter in his chair.

"You remember that summer in Wisconsin pretty well?"

"Yes."

"It was the summer between high school and college for you?"

"Yes."

"If I remember correctly you spent a lot of time learning about Norwegian and Viking traditions from our grandfather. Becoming acquainted with *Growth of the Soil* and Knut Hamsun. Sitting around the dining room table with him reading the Sagas. Every night after chores were done.

Sitting around the table reading with him."

"Yes."

"You're really not making this interview very easy. Can you try for two syllables? Or three?"

"I'll try."

"Your mother died of a heart attack the day before your high school graduation ceremony. That's how you happened to come up to Wisconsin for the summer."

"Yes . . ." Leif said softly and at last amplified a response, "she'd bought a new dress for my graduation and for church that Sunday. I'd been promising to go to church with her for weeks." He looked over at the tape recorder and said, "Can you turn that damned thing off for a while?"

"Sure." Eric hit the stop button. "All this is off the record?"

"Yes. While I sort some things out. I don't plan to spill my guts to you. I don't know why my childhood should enter into this at all."

"Come on, Leif, you're not a shrink, but you are a doctor. Childhood is damned important."

"Not for the record."

"All right. Not until you say so. For now it's just for me to try to understand you and to add to what I know from thirty years ago."

"What do you think you know?"

"I know your father died when you were two and your mother died when you were sixteen and that you're still upset that you didn't go to church with her when she asked you to."

"That's what I was worried about from this interview. Superficial. Simplistic."

"Then help me not be simplistic. Help me get to the guts."

"Why do you need to get to the guts? Why can't we just talk about heart transplants today? Not about my childhood for godsake!"

Eric took some deep breaths. He looked around the room at the volume-crammed limed oak bookcases, which matched the wood paneling, and glanced at the paintings on

77

the wall. Good quality museum prints. There was a tight cluster of nine relevant diplomas and certificates. The top row, Leif's bachelor and MD degrees from Yale and his DPhil from Oxford. The next row, his surgical residencies. The bottom row, his surgical specialty certifications. Eric took another deep breath and asked, "So how does losing your parents at such an early age make you feel about yourself?"

Leif rubbed his hand over his chin and answered, "You really stink, you know that, Eric?" Leif continued to rub his chin. "But . . . as Willy Loman put it, '. . . kind of temporary.' Is that the sort of an answer you want in the guts of an interview? Kind of temporary."

"I also know you were poor in Chicago. After your father died."

"Poor? How does frequently sleeping in bus stations and railway stations and Jackson Park sound? And begging for food during the peak of the depression? Example—one of many—I remember once my mother took me into a restaurant on Sixty-third Street. I was about six. And she told the owner, 'He hasn't eaten since yesterday. Could you just give him a little glass of milk?' I'd been in school all day with my stomach growling. So what did the owner do? He gave me a T-bone steak dinner. And my mother, too. T-bone steak dinners only cost twenty-five cents then. But he gave us his top of the line. And insisted that I have a second glass of milk."

"Nice guy."

"Yes. Damned nice. So after the war, with my pockets bulging with my discharge money, I went back to repay him "

"And what happened?"

"The restaurant was closed. Just a hole-in-the-wall restaurant. I asked around. The guy in the liquor store next door said the owner of the restaurant had been gunned down in a hold-up the month before."

"*Uff da.*" Eric slipped into Norwegian vernacular and added a low whistle.

"Getting killed. Just the price of doing business on

Sixty-third Street. Maybe even the reward for being nice."

"This is all off the record, huh?"

"That's right."

"When do we get back on the record?" Eric tapped his fingers on the tape recorder.

"It depends on what you want to talk about."

"Maybe get back to when you came up to Wisconsin. You know we all felt very sorry." Then Eric added: "At least for a while."

"Oh?"

"Well, I never thought I'd come right out and say it." Eric concentrated on stroking the back of the couch, avoiding Leif's gaze. "But I've got to admit that I resented you in Edin. You know, after a couple of weeks."

"I was getting too much attention? Poor little orphan?"

"Something like that," Eric said. "Of course I can look back on it now and see the reasons." Eric took his glasses off and placed them on the coffee table. "What did you feel about me that summer?"

Leif remained silent for a moment. Then he began slowly, "Envy. Some resentment. But mostly envy. You were damned lucky. Living with both parents and our grandfather." Now more rapidly, "A big farmhouse and a big farm. Your own room. And I'd grown up without a father in what we called a slum in those days. I guess they call it a ghetto now. Sixty-third Street. South Chicago."

"Wisconsin gave you some roots?"

"Yes. But only for a few months."

"And then our grandfather died."

"Less than two months after I'd gotten out to Yale."

"But he remembered you in his will."

"He gave me *Growth of the Soil* in English and Norwegian. And the Sagas in English and Norwegian. I guess he hoped I could teach myself Norwegian."

"And he left you the dining table you used to sit around and read together."

"That was a nice touch, wasn't it? And there it is." Leif nodded towards his conference table.

"I recognize it. My mother wrote me when you had it moved up to Minnesota. When you joined the faculty there."

"When I finally finished my training and had a place to put it." Leif continued to look nostalgically at the table. "And he left me more than enough to supplement my scholarship at Yale."

"I know he felt bad that there was so little money when your father was growing up. He blamed himself for your father and one other child getting rheumatic fever."

"The other child was my father's sister. She died when she was eight. And my father died when he was twenty-five. All either of them ever needed was penicillin. But no one had developed penicillin yet."

"Medicine's come a long way."

"Not fast enough for my father. But I'm going to make medicine move fast now. You can damned well count on it. . . . No more standing still. '. . . yet we will make him run.'"

Eric squinted his eyes as if trying to place the fragment of the quotation, but quickly moved on with the interview. "I often wondered why you and your mother never came up to Wisconsin during the Depression. There was plenty of room. And, God knows, there was plenty to eat."

"Most of the time I had enough to eat. It didn't stunt my growth. My mother was a nurse. She felt she could support us. Pride. Stubborn pride. But a few times she had to ask our grandfather for money. When we had no place to sleep. And he'd always wire twice what she'd ask for and invite her to move up to the farm."

Eric began to tap his recorder again. "When are you going to let me go back on the record?" He moved the machine a few inches closer to Leif. "The origin of your conference table is on the record, because I already knew about it."

"All right start the damned machine."

Eric proved to be skillful at his job. He got Leif to open up about many things from the early years, things that Leif had not planned to share. But many times Leif would preface a remark with: "This is off the record." A full one hour cassette carried the story up to that summer when Leif left Edin, Wisconsin to begin college at Yale.

Another cassette took Leif through college, the war, into medical school, and beyond. Even a simple recitation of the highlights of these years could not fail to impress the readers of *Life*. Phi Beta Kappa. 1941 All America football team. Postponed medical school to enlist in the Army Air Corps.

"And you were a god-damned hero, too, weren't you? What'd you win? The Medal of Honor?"

"Distinguished Service Cross."

"But you wanted the Congressional Medal of Honor?"

Leif grunted—then said wistfully, "Just like Harry Truman, I would have preferred it to being president."

"Where'd the Rhodes Scholar come in?"

"Between my second and third years of medical school. Then I returned to Yale. Finished my M.D. and went into my surgical . . ."

The second cassette clicked off in mid-sentence.

"We're on a roll," Eric said. "You game for one more cassette? It's pretty rare to have this much time without your pager going off, isn't it?"

"I guess."

"Looks like I only brought two cassettes. You don't happen to have one, do you?"

"We don't use that size."

"There's a store right across the street. Could you just sit tight till I get back?"

"Unless something comes up."

"I'll be right back."

Leif picked up and handled the cassettes, wondering how Eric had been able to extract so much information from him. From here on, he would have to be more discriminating in what he discussed with Eric.

But it had been enjoyable, remembering the early days at Yale. He rested his head against the back of the chair and allowed the memories that he had just shared with Eric to wash over him.

Remembering Davey running from the Quonset hut slamming the front door and yelping when he sighted his father. The big man scooped up the three-year-old child and held him overhead with one arm. Davey put his arms out like an airplane. "Brrrr." He made his airplane engine roar.

Out of the olive drab metal Quonset came Elaine, strikingly tall and slender with short, curled, brown hair. She gave Leif a light kiss on the lips. Davey was still being an airplane overhead. "Hi," Elaine said.

"I've got a war surplus P-51 up here, for sale, cheap."

"I'm sorry we only buy jets now," Elaine said. "Prop models are passé."

"I'm a jet," Davey said.

"You are?" Leif gave the boy a push higher into the air, letting him fall to chest height before catching him and carrying him into the Quonset. "What kind?"

"A jet wrocket," Davey squealed. "Pick me up again, Daddy, so I can touch the ceiling."

Leif stiff-armed Davey into the air.

"You fly jets," Davey said.

"Well, I hate to lose esteem." Leif dropped the boy again and caught him waist high. "But I have to admit I didn't fly jets."

"Yes," Davey insisted.

"I used to fly airplanes with propellers," Leif said.

"Yes, that was in the old war," Elaine said. "In the olden days."

"It wasn't that long ago. As a matter of fact I was checked out on the P-80, but I did my shooting from 'stangs and P-38s."

"Did you shoot anybody?" Now Davey was impressed.

"Well," Leif searched for a way out, "I did shooting, because that's what you do in wars. But I shot at other planes mostly." He hung his raincoat up. "Why don't you get your football. I'll bet we'll have time to play before *supper."*

"OK." *Davey ran to his room.*

"Get your jacket, too. It's chilly out," *Leif called back to him.*

"Do I have to?" *came the expected answer.*

"Yes," *Leif and Elaine answered simultaneously.*

"Honey, I've got a cake in Betty Sue's oven. I've got to run get it."

"Why, always, Betty Sue's oven?"

"Because the Ducharme Quonset has the best oven in the village." *Elaine waved at her small gas range.* "This darned oven doesn't bake worth a darn." *Elaine closed the thin plywood door behind her.*

"Let's go, big team," *Leif called.*

"I'm coming," *Davey entered the front room with one arm in the sleeve of his upside-down jacket.* "This dahn jacket."

"Let me give you a hand, champ." *Leif turned the jacket around and zipped it.*

Father and son went to the field behind the Quonset.

"All right, remember what I showed you," *Leif said.*

"Ahms, togetheh." *Davey brushed his white-blond hair off his forehead, put his elbows against his middle, and held his hands outstretched together.*

Leif lofted the miniature football through an arc of six feet. Davey caught it. "OK, bring the ball back by your ear and let her fly."

The ball spiraled to Leif. "OK?" *Davey asked.*

"Fine." *Leif backed up one step and threw again.*

Davey caught it and passed it back a little short, but Leif reached out for the ball.

"You hurried your throw too much. Now concentrate." *Leif stepped back another step.*

Davey let his arms fall and lowered his head.

"Now, nobody's being mean to you. When the coach tells you something, you don't pout. Put your arms up."

The little boy didn't move.

"Davey, put your arms up." *Leif's voice was quiet.*

"That's a good boy."

They exchanged several more throws. Davey missed only one. Then Leif centered the ball once to Davey, who dropped it, picked it up, and ran wide around left end.

Leif chased the boy noisily, but slowly, and tackled him just after Davey called, "Touchdown."

After the game, father and son decided to see if there were enough dandelions in the field to make up a spring bouquet for Mommy. About twenty feet from the doors of the back row of Quonsets ran a dirt road that had always been closed to traffic before construction on the new physics building had begun. Now, many Quonset-dwellers used the road and kept their cars parked in back.

A student drove by at excessive speed, as Leif and his son waited to cross the dirt road. Dust billowed its choking wake behind the car. The road was unusually dry. Leif shouted: "Slow down." But the car had gone too far for the driver to hear.

"We don't park in back," Davey said.

"No, we have a little more consideration."

Davey had to search before he found three scraggly dandelions, which he proudly presented as a bouquet to his mother. . . .

The balloon of reverie burst at the pinprick of Eric's voice. "I'm back."

"One more cassette and that's it for today," Leif warned.

"You're the doctor," Eric said. "By the way, while I was buying the cassettes, I was thinking about your picture of yourself. . . . Temporary."

"So?"

"I think I've got a better one for you. How about a redwood?"

"In what sense? Physical size?"

"Think about it."

The beeping of Leif's pager intruded.

"I knew it was too good to be true," Leif said as he picked up the phone and dialed the page operator. "This is

Dr. Hanson. . . . Five minutes. . . . OK."

"No more cassettes today?"

"I'm afraid not. And I have a request. When you're through transcribing the cassettes, I'd really like to have them."

"No problem."

"When do you have to turn this article in?"

"As soon as possible," Eric said. "Is there one more time we can get together again?"

"I've got a hell of a tight surgery schedule next week."

"How about next weekend?"

"I hate to delay things for you, Red."

"A couple more hours is all I need."

"You might want to talk with Clay Ducharme. We go back almost twenty years to when we were medical students and residents. I was a couple of years ahead of him in school."

"Sounds good. Maybe he's got a little dirt on you." Eric picked up his tape recorder and slipped it into his briefcase. "Call you later in the week."

"Fine. . . . And about redwoods. . . . Oddly enough, I have some feelings about them. Maybe I'll tell you sometime."

Like to hear it." Eric snapped his briefcase shut. "One last thing. You know when we were together that summer in Edin, we talked about becoming doctors and writers. I think in the sense that we were both going to do both."

"And I became the doctor. And you became the writer."

"Yes. Except I wonder, are you still a *skald*? Do you still write poems? I was thinking maybe we could use one in the article."

Leif opened a lower desk drawer, withdrew a manuscript about two inches thick, and dropped it in front of Eric. "Didn't our grandfather always tell us that being a poet was part of being a Viking?"

"So you still write?"

Silence. Leif was momentarily disturbed by the question. "I guess we should say: I try to write. I've always wanted to write. So I've written these poems. And even part of a novel. The hell of it is, it seems to take as much time and effort to become a good writer as it does to become a good surgeon."

"And you don't have the time?"

Another long pause. "I've got to find the time. Somehow. It's a damned frustrating conflict."

Eric waited.

"The feeling . . . somewhere I may be losing the feeling. But . . . I'll get going on it." Leif allowed an abrupt laugh to escape. "I mean how can you maintain your membership in the Vikings without writing poems?"

"How can a Viking surgeon have wound-dew covered hawkfells without the kennings?"

"We try to spill as little 'wound-dew' as possible."

"And collect much 'Rhine gravel'?"

That elicited a more natural laugh. "The Houston heart surgeons do earn much Rhine gravel. But we're worth it."

The pager call was to the emergency room. Although there was a moratorium on heart transplants, all patients with terminal head injuries were kept alive until the heart and kidney transplant teams could be consulted.

"She's only a little kid," a young woman intern with curly black hair told Leif. "Riding her trike. She got out of the driveway and into the street. A delivery truck hit her."

Leif looked at the child in her blood-soaked T-shirt and blue jeans. "What were the parents doing when this was allowed to happen?" he asked with a surprisingly accusatory tone.

"They were all in the driveway," the intern whispered, nodding towards a young couple standing only a few feet away. "She kind of lost control of her trike. They just couldn't get to her in time."

Leif glanced at the grieving couple and said nothing.

"They're trying to salvage something from this.

They'd like to donate her heart."

"I see."

"I told them we weren't doing heart transplants for a while. I said maybe they'd like to consider donating her kidneys."

"And? . . ."

"They want to donate her heart. They seem to think that's more important than donating kidneys."

"Why don't you get in touch with Dr. Johnson, or anyone, from the kidney transplant team? I'll go talk with the parents and explain things." As he walked slowly towards the devastated couple, he began to wish there were, at this very moment, a recipient—a child. The time was rapidly approaching to end the moratorium. If they could start doing babies and children . . . now that would really be worthwhile.

EIGHT

Clay had come to the conclusion that Eric was not just a reporter. Eric was a Roto-Rooter in a Brooks Bothers suit, dedicated to scraping the insides out of the transplanters. As vigorously as Clay had resisted the media intrusion into heart transplantation, he recognized that he had now lost that battle. So maybe to compensate his family for recent neglect and the stress he had been bringing home from work, he could provide them with some reason for pride: an article about Clay in *Life*. Thus today he would make a concession to the reality of the insatiable appetite of the media and to the faintly gnawing hunger pangs of his own ego and allow Eric to write about him in *Life Magazine*.

"I know you're busy as hell, so I promise to hold this to one hour tops," Eric said apologetically as he sat down in Clay's office. He placed his tape recorder on the corner of Clay's desk. "I won't use this if you object—but it's in the interest of greater accuracy."

Clay gave a noncommittal grunt.

"I'm trying to find out what Leif is really like. What makes him tick. And I thought that you could best help me."

For a moment Clay remained silent before allowing a thin self-deprecating smile to show. "The reason for *this* interview is to find out what *Leif* is really like?" His smile widened.

"Yes." Eric opened a notebook on which he had some questions. "Of course, you're also a key player on the transplant team, but I don't know much about your background except that you're an Ivy League liberal, who strangely enough comes from Mississippi, and that you and Leif were medical students together at Yale."

"We were also residents at Yale."

"I'd like you to think of some specific time or event at Yale that may have foreshadowed what Leif, what both of you were eventually to become. What led Leif and you from Yale to the Houston of today? I'd like to get something of the flavor of those days. Leif whetted my appetite when I last talked with him."

Clay removed his glasses and rubbed his eyes. "That's hard. I don't know of any single event."

"Well, how about something that captures some flavor or influenced your thinking?"

"Let me see. Our families socialized quite a bit even though Leif was a resident in surgery and I was in medicine."

"You lived in Quonset huts."

"Yes. When we were residents. Sachemville was the name of the place. It was down below the physics lab."

"Any particularly flavorful episode."

"You're big on flavor, aren't you?"

"I'm big on beating that word into the ground, I guess."

"OK. Something's coming to me. Leif's thirty-fifth birthday party. Just a couple of months before I finished my medical residency. And a year and a couple of months before Leif finished his surgical residency—which was longer than the medical residency. As I recall, it was an unusually warm spring evening. . . ."

The sound of Brahms' First Symphony on the phonograph in the Hanson Quonset greeted Clay and Betty Sue as they approached. The Hanson residence differed from its look-alike hemi-cylindrical neighbors by virtue of a rose trellis, which partially obscured the plywood front wall.

Clay pulled a flat package from under his arm and handed it to Leif, who was already at the door to greet them. "The Cleveland?" He nodded towards the phonograph.

"Szell. And what's this for?" Leif asked.

"For kicks, and for your birthday," Clay said. "From the Ducharmes."

"The Messiah." Leif held up the white Westminster album. "You guys shouldn't have."

"But you're glad we did," Clay said.

"You've been telling me about Clay's Westminster Messiah for six months," Elaine said.

"Believe me, it's beautiful." Leif opened the table model Zenith phonograph that rested on a room divider of bookshelves made of twelve inch wide boards spaced on cinder blocks. On one side of the divider was the miniscule kitchen: apartment-sized refrigerator and stove, small sink, and a narrow table that could accommodate only two adults and a small child.

"Well, let's hear it," Betty Sue said.

"I wonder if my needle's all right." Leif wiped each record carefully.

"Sure it is," Elaine said. "I can't wait."

Clay watched Leif delaying removing the Brahms. "You may have to wait a couple of minutes," he said and smiled at Leif.

"Why?" Elaine looked puzzled.

"Leif can't stop the Brahms on a dominant seventh. It demands a resolution."

"You guys have got me all choked up." Leif smiled sheepishly, and did indeed wait for the response to the dominant seventh before putting the new records on the spindle.

"Please sit down everyone." Elaine motioned towards two black canvas sling chairs and the couch, covered in slightly frayed green and brown plaid.

The two couples sat quietly for a few minutes, listening until the end of the first recitative, at which point Elaine disturbed the silence with some statement to Betty

Sue. *A few more comments passed between the women as the men continued to listen to the music.*

"I suppose we can't demand complete silence." Leif got up. "The girls have usually got a lot to hash over."

"We're sorry, Leif," Elaine said.

"It's OK, dear. I'll get us something to drink."

"We're having coffee soon," Elaine warned.

"I had in mind some 'adequate little red wine.'"

"I'm on second call," Clay said. "I'll have to skip the wine."

"The coffee is just about ready," Elaine added.

After pouring the coffee, Elaine began showing Betty Sue some photographs.

"This is the new house Elaine's sister is moving into." Betty Sue handed Clay a picture.

Clay whistled. "Where is this?"

"Grosse Pointe Farms," Elaine said, "right on Lake St. Clair, just past the Yacht Club."

"Isn't that something." Betty Sue continued to admire the house in the photo.

"What does the husband do for a living?" Clay asked.

"Works for Chrysler."

"Are you sure he isn't Chrysler?"

"This is your older sister," Betty Sue said. "Margaret's her name, isn't it?"

"This is my younger sister, Dorothy." Elaine sipped her coffee. "Can you imagine moving into a place like that at twenty-five?" She drank more coffee and said absently, "Can you imagine just living in a place with a bathtub instead of a tin shower stall?"

"Or a furnace with a thermostat, instead of these little coal stoves that you burn yourselves on when you walk by," Betty Sue added.

"They roast you in the front room, while you freeze in the back." Elaine contributed to the litany.

"But you can't beat the Quonsets for economy," Clay offered.

"Oh, they're drafty substandard barns and you know

it," Betty Sue said. "The only thing that makes them livable is that all your friends are in the same boat."

"But when the relatives live in mansions, it puts the screws in the old man." Leif stood up. "You should see her sister Margaret's house. You could put two of Dorothy's in it. And her folks' home, where she grew up. A castle practically. And I provide a tin and plywood shanty."

"Leif, I didn't mean anything." Elaine took his arm. "I told you I married you for your money, and I'm just going to wait you out." She laughed. "Now let's talk about Handel."

"No. It's not right," Leif said.

"I don't care where we live, just so it's with you." Elaine pulled Leif beside her on the couch.

"For goodness sake," Betty Sue joined in. "We all like to gripe a little. Don't take it to heart."

Leif stood up and walked to the phonograph to turn the records. "Maybe it's me then," he said. "I want something better. When I was a student, a junior resident, it was all service to humanity. All science and service. My work was what counted. What did it matter whether I got paid or not? Now, I think maybe I'd like to make some money."

"It's not an immoral ambition," Clay said.

"I'm almost frightened that it is." Leif eased himself into a canvas sling chair and tried to find a comfortable position for his long legs over the curves of the metal frame. "If money or personal ambition ever become important to a doctor, really important, I'm afraid they can influence his judgment, or take up too much of his thought and time."

"Doctors are only human, Leif," Clay said. "I think about my work a lot, but I think about my family and some good things I'd like to provide for them and myself. I have no guilt feeling about this."

"Maybe doctors should be more than human beings," Leif continued. "I think they have to be slightly obsessed with a vision. I always thought I had the vision, but now I'm worried about what my vision is."

"I see nothing wrong with highly trained individuals,

like doctors, receiving good income for their services," Clay argued. "It's right out of Adam Smith."

"I'm not really worried about doctors in general, I'm just worried about myself. And I can't seem to express the conflict." Leif drained his coffee cup. "Let me put it this way. Ralph Houseman has sort of been my ego-ideal. I always thought, if I could be a sharp academic surgeon like Houseman, what more could I want? But today I look at Houseman with his frayed collar and his old Nash, and I think I've got to do better. I've got to go out and make a buck—and the great crusade be damned." Leif shrugged. "This upsets me."

A brief period of silence. No one chose to continue to address Leif's concern. Finally Elaine said, "I think it's time we get the dessert."

"I'll join you." Betty Sue stood up.

"Are you ready?" Elaine called from the kitchen. She came back carrying a birthday cake with lighted candles. Betty Sue turned off the lights and an inharmonious rendition of "Happy Birthday" began.

"Seven candles, one for every five years," Elaine said.

"I'm touched." Leif blew out the candles.

"We won't ask for a speech," Clay said. "All we want is cake."

"I'll take care of that." Elaine brought in plates and began to cut large chunks of chocolate cake with thick chocolate icing.

Betty Sue followed and began to refill the coffee cups.

"This is really very pleasant," Leif said.

"It's the company," Clay added.

"Funny . . ." Clay said more to himself than to Eric, "as hard as the living conditions were, we really loved those Quonset days. When doctors are in training, you worry each day that you won't survive to the next. Then the next day, you're afraid that you *will* survive—and will have to endure yet another day of agony. But when you look back, you remember the happy times. And there were happy times. Leif and I loved our time at Yale." Clay smiled. "Is that the sort of flavor you want?"

"Exactly." Eric turned the cassette over. "As you said, you socialized a lot at Yale."

"Yes."

"Do you still?"

Clay hesitated. "Not too much," he mumbled.

"Why?"

"I guess we're both too busy."

"Does Leif have any home life at all?"

"What makes you ask that?"

"For one thing, I've never been to his house. *Almost* got to go to his ranch—but I've never been to his house. Not that I regard myself as a high priority item. But I find it kind of strange. Since I am his cousin. And I've never laid eyes on his wife or children."

"I'm afraid I can't help you on that. Those are questions for Leif."

"Well, I don't want to go into a really deep analysis of either of you guys, but I may still be missing the handles on both of you. This article may take longer than I thought."

"Maybe we don't have handles that are easy to grasp."

"It's kind of funny. Leif's my cousin and, granted, I haven't seen him for almost thirty years, until now—but I'm getting closer to understanding you than I am to Leif. There's still something missing."

Clay didn't offer an answer for an uncomfortably long period. "There may be something missing. But you'll have to get it directly from Leif."

"I hope you're not referring to his playing around? Although that's common knowledge."

"What do you mean playing around? Not on your life! That's just vicious jealous gossip. You must know that."

"Oh, boy," Eric said, "I've stepped in the cow chips now."

"One missing piece is . . . I'm not going to tell you.

It's up to Leif. But you damned well better believe that Leif does *not*—repeat—does *not* play around. Lord! Where the hell could he find the time?"

"Whatever you say, Clay."

"It's not whatever I say. It's a fact. And I don't want you to be spreading rumors."

"I have no intention of spreading rumors."

"All right. Sorry to get steamed."

"I admire your loyalty."

"My loyalty is to the truth."

"Right."

"Leif is as close as you'll ever get to a real hero. In every way he's a hero."

"Right. . . ." Eric waited for Clay's storm to calm. "Right. . . . Could I ask you just one more thing?"

"Maybe."

"Since you know him so well, could you give me a one word image? Or a few words of analysis?"

"I don't analyze my friends." Clay said. But he thought again of a dominant seventh. Leif as a dominant seventh—seeking, demanding resolution.

"Well let me give you a word. I see Leif as a redwood. Does that bother you?"

"It depends."

"Imposing—like a redwood."

"I agree. I admit to being in great awe of Leif, but I wouldn't want him to know. I'd deny I ever said it. "

"Grew up without a father. In desperate poverty. Learning to do whatever had to be done to survive. So I see him as having the shallow roots of a redwood. Always looking for permanence. For roots. And always willing to take a risk—maybe even cut some corners."

"Well I see him as being able *to endure* with the roots he has. Just like a redwood." Clay rose abruptly from his chair and stepped to the door. "So if you're looking for an exposé, fella, you've come to the wrong place."

During the next four weeks, as spring luxuriantly unfolded in south Texas, Clay found himself essentially confined indoors caring for the five living transplant patients, making sure that they were being protected from infection and rejection, while he was learning as much as ethically and scientifically possible about the transplanted heart in the human subject. He had missed the peak of the azaleas, and now lacked the time to walk in his backyard to witness the blossoms of his beloved magnolia tree reaching out to the roses, whispering, exchanging fragrances. He had even had to abandon his aerobic running program.

With experiments confined to mice and rats, how could he achieve an immediate major advance in immunology that could be safely used in heart transplant patients? More than just contributing to progress in science and the program at Southwest, the well-being of the patients was the critical issue. Not to mention that his own career as well as Arthur's depended on it.

Before going home to supper, Clay climbed the six flights of stairs from the ground floor to visit Arthur in his laboratory to learn the latest about his job prospects. "How did the trip to California work out?"

"I haven't been invited back. The word is out that there's something drastically wrong with me."

"Damn. Damn! What can we do? Who can we call?"

"Nothing to do. I just have to work harder."

"You're already working too hard."

"I can't sleep. So I work."

"You're sometimes here in the middle of the night."

"I'm always here in the middle of the night. I've finally struck a balance."

"What kind of balance?"

"I wake up around two in the morning. Leave for work at two-thirty. Get home around ten at night. . . ."

"What are you trying to do? For godsake, what are you trying to do?"

"Numb the pain—just trying to numb the pain."

"You've got to get the hell out of Houston. Get out of academic medicine."

"And do what?"

"General practice. Anything."

"I wish I could."

"Then do it."

"I'd be a menace. I'm so narrowly specialized, I'd be a menace in general practice. Besides that, I'm going to come up with an answer to this god-damned rejection, and then I'll write my own ticket."

"You haven't been going to rounds or conferences anymore."

"No time."

"You mean it hurts too much?"

"That too."

"Why didn't you go to the ACP meeting in Chicago? You could have told your story there to the right people."

Arthur finally lit the cigarette he'd been tapping on the back of his hand. "I'm too embarrassed to talk to anyone."

"You can't keep this up. You know that, don't you?"

"I know."

It was already one-thirty in the afternoon on the first Sunday in April. Clay had rushed off before breakfast and was now admitting another new patient to the coronary care unit. He heard himself being paged and picked up a phone at the nurses' station.

"Sorry to bother you at the hospital, but are you coming home for dinner?" Andy opened.

"I wish I could, son. I won't be able to. Go ahead without me."

"Mom's special. Chicken Ducharme."

"I've got a new patient who's very sick." Clay felt he was being a little too abrupt, so he asked, "How was church?"

"I may never return to that church, Dad," was Andy's entirely unexpected answer.

"What happened?" Clay asked guardedly.

"The sermon was on violence."

"Seems appropriate considering what's occurred this week."

"That's the point. This week a Baptist minister, who

has been awarded the Nobel Peace Prize, was violently murdered. And in our Baptist church in Houston, our Baptist minister preaches on violence, obviously alluding to what happened in Memphis."

"And? . . ."

"And he never once mentioned the name of his fellow Baptist minister, Martin Luther King," Andy said. "Never once in our lily white church did our gutless minister have the courage to utter the name of this black man."

"That distresses me too," Clay said. "I'd like to talk to you about it when I get home." Again he was trying not to sound short with his son, but a nurse was waving anxiously at him.

When Clay finally arrived home he asked immediately where Andy was.

"In bed for the past hour," Betty Sue said.

"Maybe he's still awake." Clay looked into his son's room and whispered, "Andy."

No answer. Andy was lying on his back, straight as a soldier at attention. His feet now reached all the way to the foot of the bed.

"Sound asleep." Clay continued to watch his son.

"I'm sorry you couldn't get home sooner." Betty Sue led the way out of Andy's room.

"He's pretty upset about Martin Luther King."

"We all are."

"I'll talk with him in the morning. Andy's sense of justice is very well developed. He's a truly compassionate young man." Clay walked into the kitchen. "I have to have a little something to eat."

"He needed to talk with you, Clay. We *all* need a little more of your time. And your dad called. He needs to talk to you, too."

"I feel like I'm being torn six different ways."

"I know that."

Clay removed a carton of skim milk from the refrigerator and poured a large glassful. "I suppose he won't go to bed till I call."

"You know he won't."

"I'd better get it over with." Clay dialed.

The phone was picked up immediately after the first ring. "This is Dr. Ducharme," the familiar deep voice answered.

"Dad, how are you?"

"I'm fine, son. Haven't heard from you for a while."

"I know. I'm sorry. I've been awfully busy with this transplant stuff."

"Haven't heard much about it lately, either. Your patients all doin' well?"

"Pretty well."

"You fixin' to come home for spring vacation?"

"I don't see how we can."

"I've got somethin' for Andy."

Clay waited for his father to continue.

"That sweet sixteen you used when you first started huntin'."

"Your sixteen-gauge shotgun?"

"Yes."

"You do take Andy huntin', don't you?"

"No."

"It's a real good thing for a father and son to do together."

"Andy really isn't into hunting."

"How do you know if you don't give it a try? Isn't there good huntin' in Texas?"

"I've heard there's lots of good hunting."

"A young man shouldn't grow up without knowin' how to hunt."

"I think that's more if you live in a small town or on a farm. We're big city folks now, you know."

"I think big city folks hunt, too."

"I guess some may. But I'm no longer into shotguns. Andy and I are trying to be more gentle."

"Spring vacation would be a good time to come home. You might could go into New Orleans. To City Park with Andy."

That's what he's leading up to, Clay thought. "The shotguns under the Duelling Oaks?"

"You're here today, because André Ducharme..."

"I know, Dad," Clay interrupted. "But maybe Americans are too much into guns. Some nut has killed Martin Luther King. And frankly, our family is deeply disturbed about it." Clay had not intended to blurt that out. And now he waited for what he expected to be a stereotype of a Mississippi racist response. Or even something akin to the cheering that took place in some Dallas clubs at the news of the assassination of President Kennedy.

"I am too, son," was the surprising response. "It was despicable. The man was doin' good."

NINE

Although many were expecting that it would eventually happen, it still came as a surprise when at one a.m. on the third of May, Denton Cooley performed a heart transplantation at Baylor's St. Luke's Episcopal and Texas Children's Hospitals. Exactly five months to the day since Barnard's first unsuccessful attempt at a heart transplant. Only fifteen weeks after Leif had begun his own series with Mike Goldman.

It was clear to Leif that now the race was on. How long could Mike DeBakey stay out of the competition? How soon before Chris Barnard and Norm Shumway would start up again? How many other heart surgeons would feel obligated to become involved?

While Leif and the majority of cardiovascular chiefs in the country were in Washington discussing heart transplants at the National Academy of Sciences, Denton Cooley remained in Houston and performed a second transplant. Before the week was out, Cooley had transplanted three hearts. Leif's reaction to Cooley's entry into the field of heart transplantation was predictable.

"Damn him." Leif rumbled into Clay's office waving the *Houston Post*. "Three cases in five days." Leif had just returned from the meeting. "You know, I wondered why

Denton wasn't in Washington. Mike was there. Now I understand. He was staying home doing more transplants."

"You've got to hand it to him," Clay said, rolling his chair back from his desk. "He's started off with a bang."

"You know what it means for us, don't you, Clay?" Leif did not wait for an answer. "It means we've got to get back into transplantation. If we hold back any longer, not only will the recipients start going over to Baylor, but they'll be getting all the donors."

"That's the wrong way to look at it."

"Well, let's look at it this way then. Arthur has purified some antilymphocyte globulin. So we're ready to go with an important new advance. Our program has more to offer than anyone else's. Why should we sit on our asses and let Denton take our patients—when we can do more for them?"

"Sounds reasonable," Clay said. "Except..."

"Except what?" Leif stood towering over Clay with his arms folded across his chest like a jinni rising from a lamp.

"Except I'm not sure we have more to offer. And it's still damned hard taking care of these patients and doing everything else. I've got a site visit coming up on my cardiology grant—three million bucks. Just preparing for that could take all my time." Clay came out from behind his desk, took an armchair and encouraged Leif to sit with a motion of his hand.

"Then why the hell don't you let Sellery and your boy, Eck, do more work, Clay? Just look over their shoulders. See that they're doing it to your satisfaction. You've got to learn to delegate responsibility. I sure as hell have." Leif seated himself carefully in the matching armchair. It looked too flimsy to hold someone his size if he didn't use care. Over the years he had learned to be cautious with furniture that was not sturdy.

"I hate to tell you this—since he's *your* boy—but I don't have confidence in Sellery. I don't like to trust him with more than an ingrown toenail."

"He's all right in some things, Clay." Leif finessed

the remark. "You know we've really got the program here. And we're going to be the ones to make a major contribution. Look at our patients, Clay. Bottom line: five men, the picture of health. They'd have been dead if it weren't for this operation."

"Leif, they look the picture of health to you because you don't see them enough to realize how sick they still are. Mike Goldman's face is beginning to look like a pumpkin from the steroids. And his ECG voltage keeps dropping. Ford had a hell of a first-set rejection. Arthur and I spent thirty straight hours with him, keeping him alive—while you were out of town."

"But the antilymphocyte globulin may add a lot."

"It may. . . ." Clay was obviously resisting, speaking slowly. "But it's not really new. Starzl has been using that stuff for years in his kidney transplants. And I think Cooley already started using it on his first case."

"How the hell do you know that?"

"I know."

"Well, what about the thing you've been working on? Induction of tolerance. For using animal hearts? That's *really* new."

"Believe me I'd love to use it. But it's not remotely ready for humans. Too many problems yet."

"Well, Eck tells me that you can already transplant across different species. Mouse to rat. Rat to mouse."

"Sometimes it works. But it has to work all the time before we take the next step."

"We've got to stay ahead of the game. Maybe it's time to transplant between large animals. Sheep, pigs, baboons. And I'd like to do that part—with induction."

"As soon as we possibly can. As soon as we get consistent results."

"Why not now?" Leif rested his fists on his knees and leaned forward. "We haven't done a transplant in over three months. What do you want to do, putter along for years with mice and rats? You've had three months."

"Look, my research has to be impeccable. For the sake of the patients and for my own sake. My reputation is on the line. And so is my ass with Varney. So I don't want anyone rushing off half-cocked."

"But we don't have time anymore. For godsake, Clay, don't you see that?" Leif stood up, once more looming over Clay, and paced a few steps in the cramped office, before he eased himself back into his chair. "Heart transplantation is here. Patients and their physicians are demanding it. Now. And if you've got a technique that's better than anything else going, you're obligated to bring it out promptly."

"Not until it's ready," Clay said. "We're pushing too hard. I know you can't believe it, but there's a limit. You've got the idea that if you throw enough money and energy at a problem, you can solve anything." He paused a moment and added: "And I think there may be a limit to how far we can go doing these experiments on human beings."

"Damn it, Clay, you can be infuriating." Leif bounced out of the chair once more.

"I'm sorry," Clay said softly. "But I'll share another insight with you. All of us, Southwest included, may have started heart transplants about two years before anyone was really ready."

"Ass-dragging," Leif shot back as he stamped from the office . . . thinking: *transplantation research is too important to be left in the hands of people like Clay. Damn Clay and his caution anyway! At least we can go ahead with the antilymphocyte globulin. Whether Clay likes it or not.*

Frank Sellery once more proved to have a talent for finding donors. He rooted through emergency rooms (sometimes called ghoul rounds) and found two donors in Houston in two days. Two other donors arrived on charter airplanes from Chicago and Tucson.

Within the week, Leif Hanson had performed four more cardiac transplants, using the antilymphocyte globulin. His total was now ten. And nine were alive. When they were all out of isolation, Leif arranged a group portrait, in color. Nine "healthy" looking men, well-groomed, in business suits, artfully posed. The wire services flashed the picture around the globe. And the portrait came out just in time to make the cover of *Life* for Eric's article. In fact it provided just the impetus needed to push the article into publication. Leif's results seemed to support his most recent contention at a national medical meeting: heart transplantation was becoming a valid clinical option for some forms of advanced heart disease. On the very day in May that Leif made that statement in New York, his most recent patient began to reject. Just eighteen days after surgery. And Mike Goldman was completing a two-day stay in the hospital for what was being recorded as yet another episode of rejection.

But whatever the unpublished problems may have been with some of the patients, Leif was able to point to one indisputable fact. Nine men were alive and doing reasonably well. All of them probably would have been dead by now were it not for heart transplantation.

Heart transplants— a miracle of modern medicine. Leif's pictures in *Life* proved it.

"If you're planning on another transplant, fella, forget it," Clay said as Leif entered his office, unannounced, one afternoon in late May.

"No transplantation, today." Leif sat in a chair without pausing for an invitation and wasted no time. "You know you haven't given a talk out of town since we started doing transplants."

"Your boy Sellery has been handling most of those chores for you. I see his picture in the paper all the time. Very photogenic—must get his hair styled every week, at least. Besides you've been giving enough of the talks so people know you're in the business."

"I'm trying to stay close—closer to home, Clay."

"So am I."

"But there are a couple of talks coming up that should be given."

"Send Sellery."

"I will on one. Chicago. American Society of something-or-other. But the second talk is too important for Sellery—and the institution making the invitation wouldn't accept him anyway. But they would be pleased to have you or me. The annual Cushing Lecture at Yale, very soon—in June."

"That's a surgery department lecture. It's always been given by a surgeon. It's a great honor."

"I know. And I've struggled with it, Clay. The title they suggested is 'Heart Transplants: Present and Future Prospects.' You're in an ideal position to give it."

"And you, as a surgeon and our fearless leader, are in even a better position. It's an honor. Don't let my riding you about being out of town too much get to you. For this trip, you have my blessing to go back to Yale."

"It's not that." Leif rose slowly to his feet and repeated, "It's not that." He began to pace—slowly. Distracted.

"I know," Clay said. "I understand."

"Damn it. It's still too painful." Leif rubbed his hand along the back of the brown tweed chair and noticed that the fabric was getting thin.

"It doesn't go away. I understand."

"May I tell them if I absolutely can't come, you'll take it, Clay?"

"Sure. But they want you."

Clay's secretary opened the door halfway and said apologetically, "Sorry for interrupting, but your next patient is ready in the cath lab. It's Mr. Kramer."

Clay stood up immediately. "Please excuse me, this heart cath is on a member of the hospital board." He took a step towards the door, turned and said: "You think about that talk at Yale. This is one you've absolutely got to give."

"June in New Haven is kind of tough to take." Leif watched Clay leave and tried to block out the memory. He seated himself once more in the worn tweed chair—in Clay's small office without a window. The memory would not be denied.

June. Late spring. The senior residents would soon be leaving and the new interns starting out as doctors. As Leif returned home, Davey, clutching his football, ran half a block down the back row of Quonsets to meet his father.

"You're quite a way from home, champ." Leif rubbed the boy's head and took hold of his hand.

"Mommy said I could."

"Just so you don't leave the block or get near the street."

"I won't," Davey said. "Guess what we got at nursery school today."

"A rocket ship?"

"No."

"A herd of elephants?"

"No."

"I give up."

"Guinea pigs," Davey said. "They're so cute." He laughed delightfully. "They're just tiny." Cupping his hands to indicate their size.

"When you study to be a doctor, you'll see a lot of guinea pigs."

"Will they let me play with them?"

"If you want."

"Do you play with them?"

"No. Well, maybe sometimes."

"Could we buy a guinea pig fohr me?"

"Not right now, son. There's no room in the Quonset." Leif nodded to a medical student as they walked along.

"We could keep him in my room."

"Your room would smell like a barn in no time."

"Please, Daddy?"

"No. Now that's it." Leif looked down at his son. Why was he playing the heavy with this little kid? Would it hurt to indulge him? Maybe it was just that his head had been aching all afternoon. It now throbbed with each step. "We'll see about it," Leif relented.

"Mommy, Daddy's home," Davey ran into the Quonset, slamming the screen door.

"Hi, dear," Elaine called. "Easy on the door, Davey."

"Hi, Slim."

"Hard day?" Elaine began a cautious interrogation.
"So-so." Leif sat on the couch. Elaine joined him.
"Mommy, Daddy's going to get me a guinea pig."
"That sounds like fun," Elaine said to Davey. Then to Leif: "That's all he's been talking about—the guinea pig at nursery school. He's been so excited about them he hasn't given much thought to the t-e-l-e-v . . ."
"The television's bwroken," Davey said.
Leif smiled. "Anything else you'd care to spell?"
"Get a new one," Davey said. "Hank says so."
"I'd like to get a new one, Davey, but I don't think we have enough money."
"Why don't you go out and play for a few minutes?" Elaine suggested. "So Mommy and Daddy can talk."
"But I want to tell you," Davey pleaded
"Out," Leif pointed to the door.
Davey tugged gently at his father's sleeve. "Lift me up, Daddy, so I can touch the ceiling," he pleaded.
"Out," Leif said.
"All wright." Davey frowned the fierce frown of a three-year-old before running from the house.
"I've got the granddaddy of all headaches." Leif got up from the couch.
"Let me get some aspirin," Elaine said.
"Thanks," he followed her into the kitchen. "And I have to go back to the hospital for a while tonight."
"Why? . . ." Elaine began. But there was a sound of tires skidding on the dirt road. Not loud. A barely perceptible skid.
Leif went to the screen door to look for Davey.
Davey was nowhere in sight.
Marilyn Borcher, who lived next door, got out of her car . . . and screamed.
Leif and Elaine ran from the Quonset. "Davey." Up the incline to the dirt road a few yards away. "Davey."
And there, at the right front wheel of Marilyn's car, covered with dirt, lay Davey.
Bloody foam oozed from his mouth and nose. Blood ran from an ear.

His skull was crunchy to the touch like a broken shell over a boiled egg. Evidently the wheel had run over, or partially run over Davey's head.

Leif rapidly palpated his son's neck, back, chest, and extremities before gently lifting him.

"Drive us to the hospital," Leif shouted to Marilyn.

"I can't." Marilyn was trembling. She fell against the car and slid to the ground. She lost consciousness, her face twitched a little, she wet herself, and then she began to awaken.

"Throw her in the car. You drive. We have no time."

Elaine opened the car door. Leif slid into the front seat carrying Davey. Elaine yanked and shoved Marilyn into the back seat of the Borcher car. The car lurched down the bumpy back road to Whitney Avenue and squealed out into traffic. Elaine accelerated to fifty miles per hour and leaned on the horn, weaving, running stop signals.

Leif stared at his son, cold and wet, blood foaming down his face, tugging hard for each irregular breath. He lifted the eyelids and saw the sightless dilated pupils through which no recognition passed. The eyes that used to blaze sparks of mischief were now ashes. The child began to jerk his shoulders convulsively. Leif pulled up the boy's shirt. The ribs were retracting, "My God, he's obstructed," Leif yelled. "Hurry! For godsake, hurry."

Not even a pocket knife to get him an airway. Leif bent the boy's head back and pressed on Davey's tongue with his fingers, trying to suck out the obstructing material. He spit out mouthful after mouthful of blood and saliva. You're not going to die. Your old man's not going to let you die. "Do you hear?" he said aloud. "You're not going to die," he shouted. Oh God, no brain stem. No contusion. Please. No brain stem or contusion.

Elaine jolted the car to a stop in front of the emergency room. Leif carried his son into the hospital, and yelled, "Tracheotomy set."

He put Davey on an examining table. A resident, a nurse, an intern, and a student crowded around the small patient. The tracheotomy set was there.

Leif tore it open, seized a knife, and incised into the midline of the neck. Blood welled up in the wound, very dark blood. He had tried to go down to the trachea in one stroke, but he had not pressed hard enough.

He fumbled with a sponge to get the blood out of the surgical field. Clay Ducharme, who had been in the emergency room seeing a coronary patient, was now listening to Davey's chest with a stethoscope.

"There's no heartbeat," Clay said.

"Get some adrenaline and needle the heart," Leif's hands trembled as he bluntly dissected around the little trachea. A hissing sound told him his scalpel had penetrated the trachea. "Suction," Leif called.

The intern obliged.

The small tracheotomy tube was pushed into the incision. More suction. Oxygen was directed into the tracheotomy.

Clay injected adrenaline into the heart. Blood and more viscid secretions were suctioned. More oxygen into the tracheotomy.

"No heartbeat," Clay said. "No respirations either."

How long since the heart stopped? How long? More than four minutes? Yes. . . . Yes!

The brain would be irreversibly damaged. Leif felt dizzy.

A Band-Aid, which had covered an old and inconsequential scratch on Davey's head, hung limply. Leif lifted the child's eyelids. Closed them. Dropped his scalpel on the Mayo stand. And walked slowly away.

Through the blur he could see the men's room door. He locked it behind him, turned on the water in the sink full force, and sat on the toilet seat. He stood up for a moment, wanting to rush back to hold Davey. But he sank back on the seat and leaned his head against the wall. The water was splashing out of the sink. Leif turned it off. He had to go help Elaine.

Elaine was sitting on a table in one of the examining rooms. Clay Ducharme was with her. Clay awkwardly put his hand on Leif's shoulder. "What can I say?" He had tears in his eyes. *Elaine was not crying. She was just staring across the room.*

"There's nothing left to do here." *Leif helped Elaine off the table. She leaned her head against his chest.* "There's nothing anyone can do," *Leif said.*

An emergency room nurse brought a booklet of forms. "Have you decided what funeral director you want called?" *she asked.*

"We'll pick one for you, if you want," *Clay said.*

"That would be fine," *Leif whispered.*

Elaine said nothing.

When they returned from the funeral, Leif had little memory of who had attended the service or what had been said. He stood by the door and leaned on the bookcase while watching Elaine slump into the couch and kick off her shoes. Her parents stood uneasily in the middle of the room. The copy of John Donne protruded in its row on the bookshelf. Leif pushed the book in, then withdrew it. "I've got to go back again," *he said.* "Just for a few minutes." *He slid the copy of Donne into his jacket pocket and went out into the cold drizzle.*

Leif found the grave filled in when he reached the cemetery. Only a few minutes to fill such a small grave. Flowers. How Davey would have enjoyed these flowers. To think that they all belonged to him.

Leif dropped to his knees by the grave and dug his fingers into the soft mounded earth. Then he stood. Pulled the book from his pocket and looked around. Nobody to hear. The selection: "XVII. Meditation."

He read aloud: "The church is catholic, universal, so are all her actions: all that she does belongs to all. When she baptizes a child that action concerns me, for that child is thereby connected to that head which is my head too, and engraffed into that body whereof I am a member. And when she buries a man that action concerns me; all mankind is of one author, and is one volume; when one man dies one chapter is not torn out of the book but translated into a better language. . . ."

Leif's eyes skipped a few sentences and he continued reading: "Who bends not his ear to any bell which upon any occasion rings? But who can remove it from that bell, which is passing a piece of himself out of this world?"

The drizzle was condensing into larger drops. The soft dirt of the grave was becoming mud. Leif crouched beside the mound and whispered, "Good-bye, Davey. I'm sorry I let you down, son. I really let you down." He squeezed a handful of dirt, released it, wiped his hand on the wet grass and walked rapidly to the car. No more to build on there.

The memory spurted from his grasp.

It was now time for supper. Except Elaine would not be home. For several months now, she had rarely been at home at mealtimes. On the infrequent nights when he would be able to get home to dine with the family, he would usually eat alone, because the housekeeper had already fed Karen and Mark. This was deliberate on Elaine's part.

But to hell with it!

He dialed a number where he could find supper . . . and . . . what passed for affection.

TEN

The feature in *Life* on the Southwest heart transplant team became a cover story and carried the title: "The New Vikings." Eric even incorporated a poem by Leif into the puffed presentation.

But Clay recognized that Eric had failed to find all the handles he had sought. Eric had learned very little about Davey—or how after the death of their son, Elaine and Leif had begun to erect separate walls of private grief. Nor had Eric appreciated the sense of desperation in Elaine's social activities. Of course, he learned that their younger son Mark was mongoloid, but he had not discovered the tragic circumstances surrounding his birth. How Elaine had almost hemorrhaged to death and required a hysterectomy—all while Leif was tied up in surgery in another operating room. These were handles Clay could have provided. Maybe he should have told Eric more. Certainly Leif would never tell him. But how could this material possibly fit into a splashy article on the "New Vikings"?

And unfortunately, the cover story that brought such celebrity to the team also made it difficult for them to accomplish the very research needed to take heart transplantation up the next rung of the investigative ladder. Medical and quasi-medical organizations from all over the country (and many out of the country) were requesting their presence at a variety of functions. Clay and Arthur adamantly refused to go. And Leif tried to be selective, declining most invitations, while reluctantly agreeing to attend only those that best served the purpose of maintaining the momentum of their heart transplantation program. Sellery continued to do the bulk of the traveling.

Prior to heart transplantation, Clay had been almost a model father in attending the school activities of his children. But this spring, for the high school track meet at which Andy won first in state in the mile, Clay was not in attendance. Betty Sue was.

"I feel terrible missing your hour of triumph," Clay told his son, who was still awake at midnight when Clay returned home from the hospital. "Nothing less than a life and death situation could have kept me away."

"I understand," Andy said without bitterness. "These things happen." He pulled down the sheet to his bed and crawled under it. He had taken to wearing only Jockey shorts to bed.

"It's the serious drawback to a career in medicine."

"Fair exchange for what you can accomplish."

"I guess." Clay sat on the edge of the bed. "You did a 4:08 mile?"

"Just barely beat out the guy from Lubbock who won last year."

"Do you know that's ten seconds better in high school than my best in college?"

"Performances are getting better in all events. New records all the time."

"But a first in state is a real accomplishment in Texas. I only took a second in Mississippi—when the competition wasn't as tough."

"Training's the secret. Your dad probably didn't start running you around the track when you were five, the way mine did."

"Well, with Rice being so close, it seems a pity not to take advantage of its athletic facilities."

"Anyway, all that running finally paid off this year."

"I'm very proud of you, Andy." Clay reached over and mussed Andy's chestnut colored hair—the same color as Betty Sue's when she was his age.

Andy patted his hair back into place. "I appreciate it," he mumbled self-consciously.

"You're going to surpass your old man in everything. And that makes me very happy. Track. Academics. I know you're a lot smarter than I am . . . you got so many smart genes from your mother."

Clay eventually persuaded Leif to come to grips with his unwillingness to return to New Haven and give the Cushing Lecture in June—which he did. What Clay heard from friends in New Haven was that Leif received something as close to the welcome for a returning hero as a staid institution is capable of mounting. Before returning to Houston, Leif also attended a Heart Association dinner in Los Angeles to receive an award. That the official award-giver was the movie actress, Roxanne Molnar, in no way detracted from the event.

But even staying in Houston provided no guarantee that productive research could be done. Present and future heart transplanters from all over the world made pilgrimages to Houston during the hot summer months. Visitors from Barnard's group dropped in from South Africa to observe the management of a relatively large volume of transplant patients. Argentina, Chile, Brazil, England, France (a priest was the recipient), Canada, Poland, and Czechoslovakia, joined the list of countries establishing programs in this exciting frontier of medicine. Heart transplantation had become a source of national prestige. Cooley's group in Houston, and a team in Poland performed animal heart transplants, both of which proved to be unsuccessful. It was already becoming apparent to many investigators that if heart transplantation were going to become a useful clinical procedure, animal hearts or artificial hearts would eventually have to be employed.

By the very magnitude and intensity of their work, the heart transplanters did not share fully in the growing national anguish over the escalating war in Vietnam and the most recent assassination—that of Bobby Kennedy. Even for Clay, time simply did not permit despair over occurrences that were deeply troubling many sensitive people in the United States during this period.

The transplanters had enough problems of their own at Southwest. Patients who had looked so robust after their surgery were now showing toxic effects of the drugs used to keep them alive. Clay was having to spend inordinate quantities of time with their management. The mood at Southwest had changed—so gradually that it was imperceptible at first. However, a knowledgeable observer from the outside could recognize the change. Such an observer returned to Houston after months of absence: Eric Kristensen.

"What the hell's happening here?" Eric confronted Clay. The meeting was in the brightly fluorescent-lit hall outside of Clay's office, in the early evening.

"What do you mean?"

"I mean the place is down. Everyone's just dragging."

"The swamp's been drained . . . and I guess we're up to our asses in alligators."

"And it's not much fun, anymore?"

"Not much," Clay said. "What brings you back to Houston? You decide you'd like to check out the heat and humidity in August?"

"No. What I decided to do was write that book. So I thought I'd come back and concentrate on the transplanters and the first five patients," Eric said. "Last time I was here I kind of got hooked on the excitement."

"There's still excitement. But the wrong kind." Clay stood in front of the door, not inviting Eric inside the office.

"You haven't got the answer yet?"

"I'm not sure we even know what the hell the question is."

"I've got a proposition for you." Eric's confidential tone competed with the underlying buzz of his reportorial Roto-Rooter. "How about letting me spend a whole day with you. To see what's happening?"

"Why would you want to do that?"

"Well, it might turn up in my book—if you don't object. But since that's not likely to impress you, maybe there's something I can do to help."

"*Life* just gives you time off to do a book?" Clay was incredulous.

"It's a good job—writing for *Life*."

"Damned good job, I'd say."

"So how about it?"

"A full day? Dawn to whenever we have to stop?"

"That's what I want."

"I think I'll work your tail off."

"I'll take the chance."

"One thing," Clay lowered his voice, "this is my own hidden agenda. Leif is talking about doing still more transplants. He's accepting referrals and he's anxious to do some more with antilymphocyte globulin. If you have a chance after you see how busy we are, maybe you could add your voice."

"You've already got most of the living heart transplants in the world."

"I know. But he's worried about Cooley getting ahead of him."

"Hard to believe. Worrying about Cooley getting ahead?" Eric shook his head in disbelief. "But he really seems to have taken hold of heart transplantation as the one great thing he was put on this earth to do."

"Seems that way."

"Well, to get to my five patients, how are they? Mike's out of the hospital practicing medicine, isn't he? And is old Otto as nutty as ever?"

"Nutty is not quite the word I'd prefer to use," Clay said.

"How about Ford and Berkowitz and Melton?"

Clay paused before saying, "I'm assuming you're asking these questions out of genuine interest in old friends. Anything for your book would have to come from them. This is off the record."

"I understand."

"Well, Ford isn't looking too chipper, which you'll see tomorrow. Be prepared. And except for tomorrow when you'll be accompanying me for just the one day, you won't have access to the heart transplantation patients except during visiting hours and with their permission."

"Wow! Getting tough." Eric kept looking over Clay's head into the office, shifting his weight restlessly from one leg to the other.

"Our department chairman, Varney, has made that policy clear. You see the first five patients aren't on the surgical service anymore. They're on the medical service. I won't go into it, but no more heart transplants have been or will be transferred to the medical service."

"Too bad. Being Leif's cousin doesn't cut the mustard anymore."

"You've got the big picture."

Eric looked through the open door into Clay's office and asked, "Can't we sit down someplace?"

"I know this looks rude as hell, but I can only give you a couple more minutes. We're that busy."

"OK, what about Berkowitz?"

"Doing reasonably well. But not terribly happy. He's learned that having a heart transplant was a hell of a tough way to get his picture in the paper."

"Or in *Life*?"

"He's still pretty proud of his picture being in *Life*. In fact, he's got a copy of it framed and on the wall of his hospital room. But what's been eating him lately is what he hears from one of the men who was admitted for a possible transplant at the same time he was."

"So what does he hear?"

"Well, Berkowitz thought he was the lucky one when he got a heart and this other man waited around for several weeks and finally went home. In fact he might have been said to have lorded it over his competitor for a transplant. Except the guy who lost in the transplant sweepstakes is one of several of our transplant rejects playing eighteen holes of golf a day. And Berkowitz has

only been out of the hospital once."
"Is this still off the record?"
"Off the record."
Eric let out a sigh and asked, "So how's Melton?"
"Mr. Melton is unfortunately still in the hospital. He wanted so damned little. He wasn't looking for immortality. Seventeen months is what he wanted. Just long enough to see his first grandchild and to see his son graduate from medical school. That wasn't asking much. Just seventeen months."
"Isn't he going to make it?"
"I hope he is. But what's eating my gut right now is: wouldn't he have had a better chance if we'd left him alone? I mean there are all these guys out playing golf who weren't *lucky* enough to get transplanted. And we've got just one patient effectively out of the hospital. The rest are usually in pajamas." Clay rubbed the back of his neck where his collar was irritating him. "So that picture you ran in *Life* was really pretty phony. Only Mike left the hospital that day. The rest got back into their pajamas." Clay started to enter his office. "Well enough of that. I've really got to split now. See you tomorrow at my house for breakfast."
"At what time?"
"Five."
"You've got to be kidding."
"You asked for it. A typical day."

After more hospital work and before going home for supper, Clay returned to his office. He sat behind his chair and flipped open his pocket notebook. Underlined was: *visit Arthur*. Arthur had just returned home from a second visit for a chairmanship at one of the more prestigious medical schools in the country. Only one other medical school had interviewed Arthur since the fiasco in New York. But now, with this second visit to a really top school, he seemed to have a fighting chance to escape from Varney's sick sphere of authority.
But it was getting late so Clay decided to phone rather than trek up five flights to the immunology lab. He

was frankly too tired. He sat behind his desk, with the only source of light for the windowless room being the desk lamp, and began twirling the rotary dial, clicking off the four numbers of Arthur's extension. "Well, tell me the good news," Clay said as soon as Arthur answered the phone.

"No good news, I'm afraid," was Arthur's answer.

"What happened?"

"It's kind of a long story—with a new twist."

"Well, at least tell me a little now. We can get together tomorrow and thrash it out."

"I don't know why they had me out for a second visit. I really don't."

"Because you're one of the best candidates for any chairmanship in the country. That's why."

"According to some, perhaps," Arthur said. "That's what one of my interviewers said. An associate dean. He opened with: 'We've got a strangely mixed report on you. Some say you're absolutely the best there is. And some say you're absolutely the worst . . .'"

"What a lousy thing to say," Clay interrupted. "What a lousy god-damned thing to say!"

"From then on it was downhill. A couple of people wanted to know what my problems were with my chairman. A couple more expanded to the subject of what my problems were with interpersonal relations in general. And then the chairman of surgery really outdid the rest."

"What did he say?" Clay waited. The room was too dark. But the switch to the overhead light was not within reach. He clutched the phone tightly and continued to wait through the long pause.

"He said their reports were that I had bad interpersonal relations—and worse. Damn it, Clay, I hate to sound like a complainer all the time. It seems every time we talk, all I do is bitch about my personal problems. I just hate myself for doing it."

"What the hell do you think friends are for? Now get on with it. What did this surgery chairman mean by *worse*?"

"It's hard for me to even tell you about this. It was like spending three full days in the principal's office for being a bad boy, instead of being a respected candidate for an important position."

"Why the hell did they ask you to visit?"

"I don't know."

"And what's the thing that's hard to talk about?"

There was a long pause. "Damn, it's hard to even get the words out."

"Well, get 'em out anyway."

"You know my work and reputation are my whole life."

Clay answered quietly. "I know that, Arthur. Of course, I know that."

"My work is my life. Everything."

"What happened?" Clay persisted.

"The chairman of surgery said he heard that the honesty of my research was in question."

"Oh damn! Damn!"

"I could take the interpersonal relations bit. But this thing is out of control now. It's been suggested. People will never be sure again."

"I'm going to have Leif call that damned surgery chairman and set him straight."

"It won't do any good. Just make it worse." Arthur was silent for a moment. "I think they've got me by the soul," he finally said.

"The hell they have," Clay shouted into the phone.

"I used to think if you were very good at what you did. And worked twice as hard as anyone else. And were creative on top of all that—you couldn't lose," Arthur said. "But when creativity comes up against power, it's no contest. No contest."

Clay had to think of a new argument to combat this entirely understandable despondency. All he could finally offer was a weak: "I want us to talk about this tomorrow."

"I'm willing," Arthur said wearily. "And thanks for calling. I'm sorry. Really sorry to be such a bother. I mean—really sorry . . ."

After ending the conversation with Arthur, Clay internally debated seeking out Varney for a confrontation.

But Varney would already be home by now. And what good would it do? Varney would be ready with justifications—he always covered himself.

How could this go on in a respectable university? And why? Every time Clay thought he had Varney figured out, the man slipped away. Yet he knew there were lots of Varneys in academia getting away with these things over and over again. Jealous, spiteful, envious people who resented excellence in others—who considered excellence a threat. And who felt the need to destroy. When the creative juices start to dry up and you still want to see things happen, the next best thing is to destroy. Clay stayed with that thought for a moment. He finally decided he had read it someplace. Was it in Camus?

Of course, the gentlemanly thing for the victim is to leave quietly. In a "dignified" way. But Clay also recognized that Arthur could not just go out into country practice. He was most certainly overspecialized. His whole life was research. What could he possibly do? Varney was reducing Arthur's options to almost none. Why? Could it be that Varney just didn't understand what he was doing? No. He knew. Of course, he could still plead that he had no idea all this was happening. An alternative possibility occurred to Clay—could it be that the Varneys like the Claggarts of the world were just plain evil? Clay suddenly felt exhausted. *The darkness of the room.* So tired of all this crap. Tired of thinking about Varney. *Dark.* Tired of analyzing. Tired from lack of sleep. Even tired of Arthur's problem. *Tired. Damn it. Tired!*

Now if he could only force himself out of his chair, he could go home for forty-five minutes for a quick supper. Then back to the hospital for a few more hours.

He rested his head in his arms on the desk. *Only for a moment. Don't fall asleep.* He groaned and closed his eyes. *Frontiers of science. Excitement. Personal satisfaction solving a problem.* Trying to become man working with nature.... *No. No way, Ducharme. Heart transplantation will* always *be man against nature.... Sure as hell better look for another way.* Look where? Where? *Maybe the new research grant. Rewrite some sections.* Get out of the crisis care loop? *Something different.* Prevention? *Whatever.* But heart transplantation was not the answer. Not at this time, anyway. In the excitement of the quest it was still hard to accept such a punishing conclusion. Clay wanted to run from it.

But like a Zen slap, it was there—stinging his face.

ELEVEN

"Five a.m. and the coffee's on?" Eric inhaled the aroma of percolating coffee the moment Clay opened the front door. "God, that smells good." He shook hands and began sniffing and looking over Clay's head for the source of the fragrance. "So this is when your day starts?"

"Been doing this for many years." Clay led Eric into the brightly lit kitchen, with its colorful wallpaper, cherry cabinets, and copper cooking utensils. "Sir William Osler observed that medical students are divided into two categories, the larks and the owls. So I learned to take advantage of my lark-nature as a medical student and've been getting up at four-thirty or five ever since. It's when I do my best work."

"Except that before this transplant business started, you used to write your papers and books and grants in the morning," Betty Sue, apron-clad, looking more like a typical housewife than a professor, commented from the stove. And added: "Good morning, Mr. Kristensen. You like your coffee black?"

"Good morning. Yes, please. Black and thick."

"Now Clay's most creative hours are consumed by the transplant program." She handed Eric a steaming mug and continued, "So if you can influence your cousin to slow down, we'd sure appreciate it in the Ducharme household. Leif's got the hospital packed with patients just waiting for hearts."

Clay stepped over to the built-in range top to help. "Betty Sue is basically not a lark. She gets up early in self defense." He gave the grits a final stir and ladled the cereal into a bowl.

"Is breakfast ready?" called a boy's voice.

"That's our son, Andy," Betty Sue explained.

"A lark?"

"A four-plus lark. He always does his homework in the morning. His sister, on the other hand, is impossible at this hour, so we're not going to insist that she join us right now." Betty Sue carried a bowl of scrambled eggs to the table. "That tall skinny drink of water coming around the corner is Andy. And this is Mr. Kristensen, Andy." She patted Andy's hair into place.

"Hi." Andy seated himself by swinging his leg over the back of the chair. "Bless this food to our health and us to thy service," he started and finished the grace before the guest knew what was happening.

Betty Sue passed the eggs and grits. "I should explain that the reason the eggs are lighter in color than you may be used to is that we throw most of the yolks away. The cardiologist in our family worries about our cholesterol."

"I don't think you'll notice any difference in taste," Clay added. "We do have a little problem with high cholesterol in the family. And I try to keep it under control. I think that prevention will prove to be an infinitely saner approach to coronary heart disease than heart transplants. And that's on the record."

"The eggs are delicious," Eric said. "Really good. Fluffier than the usual scrambled eggs. And the grits and hot biscuits. This is the way to start the day." The biscuit Eric was holding exuded its warm aroma and dripped margarine. He attacked it with too large a bite, but managed to ask, "How does everyone stay so slim with meals like this?"

"We watch our diets pretty carefully," Betty Sue said. Then she noticed that Eric was looking at Andy, who was already reaching for seconds. "Except for our son, who's a bottomless pit."

"I read your stuff on the astronauts," Andy said. He was slapping gobs of margarine on a biscuit. "Pretty good." A forkful of eggs and a bite of biscuit. "But that thing with Grissom and those guys burning up in Apollo 1. That was a bad scene. Very bad."

"It was." Eric saw that Clay had already finished breakfast so he took a last swallow of coffee.

"You know anything more about that than what's been written up?"

"Probably not," Eric joined Clay in pushing away from the table. "Seemed that they were just trying to do things too fast. Too much worry about being first." He untangled his legs to stand.

"They sound like heart surgeons." Betty Sue kissed Clay good-bye and stepped to the door.

On leaving the house, Eric said, "I like your son."

"Andy's an amazing boy, even if I do say so myself. So smart that he keeps his parents on their intellectual toes every minute. But the really great part is that he's just plain nice. And what I hate about transplantation right now is the time away from Andy and Melanie and Betty Sue. This is a particularly critical time in Andy's growing up for his father to spend time with him. Time that can never be replaced. Just a simple thing like watching 'Star Trek' together. I don't think we've seen more than one episode as a family since heart transplants started. And helping Andy with his physics and chemistry. And American and French literature. Things I know fairly well. A lot of togetherness is being sacrificed—and I resent it."

The men reached University Hospital at 5:30 a.m. and began rounds on the heart transplants first. "These are work rounds," Clay explained. "We review the charts, order tests, and do a lot of work before the patients wake up."

The next stop was the coronary care unit. Then to the patients awaiting heart surgery that day. After that came the first patients on the morning schedule for cardiac catheterization. "Did Dr. Eck explain this test to you so that you feel you understand it?" Clay asked the woman with frosted hair. Mid-thirties. A stack of books and papers on her bed and bedside table in her deluxe private room.

"I think he made it very clear." Her answer was no-nonsense precise. Her facial features were no-nonsense precise, too. Like polished marble.

"I'd like to review with you this procedure and why it's being done . . ." Clay did not get to finish.

The patient talked over Clay's last couple of words. "I'm having a heart catheterization today because my cardiogram and symptoms say I'm working on having a heart attack. You're going to freeze a spot on my leg and put tubes in my arteries and veins and measure pressures and oxygen and inject dye into my coronary arteries to see if they're plugged." She paused before asking, "Do I pass?"

"You seem to have the picture," Clay said. "But now the big question. Do you understand the risk?"

"There's a small chance that a blood vessel will be damaged and even a smaller chance that I could die."

"That's putting it pretty bluntly."

"I know," the woman said. "It's just that it's damned important that we find out what's going on. So we take a little risk. There's a risk every time you get in your car." For the first time she slowed her rapid staccato patter and added, "Especially on the Southwest Freeway. A bunch of damned maniacs out there."

"Are there any questions I can answer for you?"

"No, Dr. Ducharme. I've just heard that you're the best. That's why I'm here." She turned away to direct her attention to a sheaf of papers, as if she were dialing her telephone in the middle of a conversation she wished to terminate. Then, off-handedly, she asked, "Oh, there is just one thing. How long is this going to take?"

"We'll start at eight and we should be through before nine. And you'll be wide awake during the whole procedure, so you'll be free to ask questions as we go along."

Once outside her room, Clay said to Eric, "This woman represents what may be the start of an epidemic."

"How's that?"

"Well, young women aren't supposed to have coronary heart disease. But I've had two women this year, both in their thirties, who had fatal heart attacks. And this woman is right when she says she's working on having a heart attack."

"What do you think's happening?"

"I'm not sure. But there seems to be a pattern taking shape. They're now out in the dog-eat-dog world. Young executives. This gal owns one of the biggest and most successful real estate businesses in Houston. They're all hard-driving and heavy smoking. Their cholesterols are high and they're on the Pill."

"*Uff da.*"

"*Uff da?*"

"Sorry. That's Norwegian for *oi vay.*"

"You old wordsmith, you." Clay smiled and lead the way into the cardiac catheterization laboratory, a darkened room, eerily lit by video screens, in which X-ray machines and cameras occupied the center, and electronic recording devices lined the walls. The X-ray table was more like an operating room table. Sterile surgical drapes, surgical instruments, and a high intensity surgical spotlight completed the OR ambience. "Are you sure you want to see all of the heart caths today? I have five to do. They're pretty mundane next to heart transplants."

"I want to see. You bet."

After completing the fifth catheterization, Clay looked at his watch and said, "Sorry to tell you this, but we have a meeting starting five minutes ago. So that last cath took care of our lunch break."

"What's the meeting about?" was Eric's question as they half-walked, half-ran along the corridor to the conference room of the department of medicine. They were both still wearing sweaty, green scrub suits covered by white coats. Eric's coat was at least two sizes too small.

"It's the weekly research conference of investigators involved in the heart transplant program. A few of us used to meet at twelve, in what we jokingly called 'Darkness at

Noon.' Now we meet at one in what could better be termed 'Mayhem after Midday.' I chair the mayhem."

They entered a small paneled conference room which contained bookshelves filled with bound medical journals along three walls, a long rectangular table, and not enough chairs for the twenty people who had gathered. Varney was there, standing at the head of the table.

Clay said, "Damn," when he saw him. "First meeting he's ever been to."

"Should be fun," Eric whispered.

"Don't count on it."

"I'll just try to scrunch down and blend into the woodwork. Maybe he won't remember who I am."

"I'm here today . . ." Varney began.

"Dr. Varney, could we just wait another minute or two?" Clay said, carefully avoiding a tone of confrontation, and slid into a chair at the middle of the table. "I'll certainly be pleased to recognize you when we start. I'd just like to wait a couple of minutes more for our surgical colleagues."

Varney began to respond, but ended up just glaring at Clay and dropping into his chair.

Within a minute Sellery strolled in and smiled to the assembly. "Sorry I'm late. Tied up in the damned OR." He fingered his hair carefully into place and slipped into the chair next to Clay.

"Will Leif be here?" Clay asked him.

"Are you kidding?"

"I didn't think I was."

"He's out of town. Didn't you see this morning's paper?"

"Afraid I missed it."

"He was out with Roxanne Molnar. In Los Angeles. Three times in two months with the beautiful Roxanne. I believe our chairman of surgery is going Hollywood."

"Let's can the god-damned small talk about Hanson's social life and get on with the meeting," Varney snapped. "Some of us have better things to do."

"I agree." Clay stood up. "A number of problems have been coming up the past few weeks that indicate our attempt at coordinating our research program is becoming seriously fragmented."

"That's why I'm here. Are you planning on recognizing me?" Varney demanded.

"I'm very pleased to recognize the distinguished chairman of the Department of Medicine." Clay's words skidded close to sarcasm, but avoided a head-on collision with Varney.

"A few months ago," Varney jerked to his feet, "before all this heart transplantation crap started we had a very congenial department, a lot of good camaraderie."

"Bullshit," one of the doctors sitting near Clay said—but not loud enough for Varney to hear.

"Now we have everyone at each other's throat. And I hold you, Ducharme, responsible for this state of affairs."

Clay took a couple of breaths before answering. "How did you reach that assignment of responsibility?" He forced the words out evenly.

"This whole ridiculous heart transplantation program was your idea."

"I've advanced the idea that our institution is qualified to investigate heart transplantation," Clay continued to speak slowly, enunciating each word too precisely. "I grant you that the research has suffered because of the damned publicity and emphasis on the clinical aspects. And if I'd had any idea that things could deteriorate like this, I never would have become involved." Clay was beginning to cool down a little. "But this is not a time for recrimination. It's a time for us to do some serious science and get answers as quickly as possible."

"Not so fast," Varney said. "I think this is an excellent time for recrimination. I get my ear bent every day by members of my department who are madder than hell. And you'd better hear what they have to say." He motioned to a young doctor to take over.

The young doctor, short and blond and solidly built, grabbed the baton without missing a stride. "Clay, it's real nice of y'all to talk about hepin' each other. But it appears to me that all we're doin' is hepin' Hanson and Ducharme. I mean, you're a full professor with tenure. And I'm an assistant professor. This transplant business is my chance to do some work that will earn me an associate professorship with tenure here or at some other good school. This is my chance. But who are the first authors of all these papehs that are comin' out? Hanson or Ducharme or Johnson. Even poor ol' Sellery doesn't have a first-author papeh of his own."

"Every report that has mentioned any contribution you've made has carried you as one of the authors."

"Sure. In a twelve author papeh I'm number nine. That doesn't cut it."

"But there's never been more than a couple of sentences in our papers that had to do with your work."

"Whose fault is that?"

"Certainly not mine. If you can develop a paper out of what you're doing, please do it. But if you think for your one sentence contribution to a fourteen page paper based almost entirely on my own work, I'm going to write the whole damned paper—and then put your name first as senior author, you're crazier than hell." Clay was raising his voice, letting too much of the Ducharme temper escape.

"Well what have I got that's new to say after you spill it in one of youh papehs? Or Hanson has put it in his?"

"If all that you have to say can be said in one or two sentences, then you obviously don't have a paper. But I think you've got enough material for a couple of papers. If you buckle down and work on it. But I'm not going to write your papers for you."

The young doctor began to back off. "Well, look, can't my name be one of the top three on some of these papehs? Then I'll be listed in the *Index Medicus*."

"Not unless you earn it."

There was a short pause before an older doctor, with hair parted not far above his left ear and plastered over too much shiny scalp, said, "My gripe is similar. You and Arthur have been using one of my technicians to share night call on tissue typing."

"You volunteered her services. And Arthur trained

her. She's a good hematology technician."

"Well, Arthur's been reviewing the data on the tissue matches and so have I. Some of the work is being done in my lab by my technician. And, to be blunt, I want to write a report."

"I think it's a little too early to draw conclusions," Clay said.

"Well, I don't. And I want to be the one to report it as first author."

Varney nodded approval for the hematologist.

"I don't see Arthur here," Clay said. "Why don't you work it out with him?"

"Let's get on with the business of the urine." This came from a distinguished looking doctor with gray hair and a gray mustache twisted at the ends.

Clay always visualized him as the type of doctor he would expect to come out of the operating room and solemnly announce, "Yes, Mrs. Smith, your son will play the violin again."

Instead, he announced that he wanted to get on with the business of the urine.

Another equally distinguished looking physician with horn-rim glasses joined in with: "Yes, let's get this urine business cleared up once and for all. The protocol clearly states that the twenty-four hour urine samples are to be sent to my laboratory."

"That was the preliminary protocol."

"The preliminary protocol was not abrogated."

"The hell it wasn't."

Clay was trying to intercede between the two internationally recognized professors who were almost coming to blows over the ownership of the urine. "Gentlemen, gentlemen," Clay was shouting. "There's enough urine to go around."

"How about shit?" someone called from the back.

"We've had more than enough," Clay said. "If we can't restore some semblance of decorum and undertake constructive discussion, this meeting will stand adjourned."

"I'll give you something constructive," Sellery got

into it. "The way you've been talking about our having enough transplant patients to study makes it sound like you're calling for another moratorium on heart transplants."

"I guess that's about right."

"Well, it won't fly. I won't stand still for it. And I know Leif won't. This is an operation—just like tying a ductus. We're surgeons. And whether patients come to us to get a ductus tied or a heart transplant, we're going to do it."

"And who's going to take care of the patients after the transplant?"

"We can. Or whoever wants to help. You can't dictate what kind of patients we're going to accept for surgery."

Clay just shook his head slowly. "Unbelievable. You're in Capetown or Paris or London. You have no idea what's happening to our patients."

"The hell I don't. I see them as much as you do. And these trips aren't just joy rides. I helped set up the heart transplantation program in Paris. And in London I had some good talks with Sir Peter Medawar. You will admit that he might be an expert in this field, won't you?"

"Since he won a Nobel Prize for transplantation research, he should qualify as an expert," Clay said with undisguised sarcasm.

"Well, Pete says we're on the right track. And to keep going."

"Pete?"

"Yeah."

"If there's nothing else, let's adjourn."

Betty Sue Ducharme raised her hand. "I had a research report on a technique for solubilizing transplantation antigen. It might have an application to human heart transplantation if the concept of induction of tolerance ever becomes a reality."

"Do you have some slides?" Clay asked.

"I do. But I think this is a bad day to present the data." Betty Sue was going to let it go and started to sit down. "No. No, I've got to say something." She jolted up again. "This meeting is unreal. Where are the compassionate physicians? Heart transplantation is getting a lot of publicity. Mostly the wrong kind. And if we fail, people will say science failed. But this isn't science or art or medicine that we're dealing with here. This is . . . heart transplantation has become a bunch of egos turned loose with a dangerous toy."

Someone muttered, "Pushy damned broad."

"I guess this isn't a good day to present the data," Clay said and glared at the doctor whose remark he had overheard.

"Sorry to have made a speech," Betty Sue mumbled while she gathered up her slides and papers.

"Meeting adjourned."

Eric and Clay walked silently and slowly back to the locker room to change out of their scrub suits. Clay finally spoke, "If I'd known the meeting was going to deteriorate like that, I wouldn't have invited you."

"I know."

"You can tell Leif not to believe every glowing report he reads about himself in the newspapers and magazines. Things are going to hell in Houston." Clay pulled on his white coat. "And what the hell is this Roxanne Molnar business?"

"Beats me. You haven't given me time to read a newspaper today."

"Well, the day has hardly begun, fella."

To illustrate the point, Clay saw four patients in his office before giving a lecture at three. Then they rounded on the patients who had received their heart catheterizations and heart surgery that day. Since Leif wasn't in town, there were only three heart surgery patients in the recovery room rather than a dozen.

"Can't Sellery do more cases in a day?" Eric asked.

"He'd love to, but there isn't that much willingness to send him many cases. Certainly no difficult cases. Anyway, three open hearts is a very busy day for most cardiovascular surgeons." Clay looked at his watch. "It's half past six. I reckon we have about four hours of rounds left, but I need and want to spend some time with my wife and kids first. So come on home with me for supper. We'll be back here at eight."

"You need a break from me tagging along. And I need a break, too."

"Betty Sue's planning on it. We're having Chinese food and I do the stir-frying."

"It's tempting, but I'll see you at eight."

It was five after eight when they started to round on the other hospitalized heart patients, and nine when they got back to the transplants.

At midnight, standing out in the parking lot, Eric said, "If this is how it is when there's very little surgery and no new or sick transplant, how do you handle things when you've got problems?"

"For one thing, someone else has to help with the caths and lectures and seeing the other patients."

"Do you enjoy these hours?"

"I hate them. As I told you, I'm a lark. After about seven at night, I function on half a brain. I really need eight hours of sleep a night to perform well. Mike DeBakey, as I'm sure you've heard, thrives on four hours sleep. They say he's never slept more than four hours a night during his entire adult life. So this would be a relatively light day for Mike."

"And this is why you'd like Leif not to do any more transplants for a while."

"This has been no put on," Clay said. "This is the real world of Houston transplants. Today we got all our work done. Anything more that's added to our schedule means something's got to be subtracted. And the quality of our work is going to hell. It's bad enough when you give a poorly prepared lecture like I did today. But it's criminal when the well-being and even the lives of our patients are on the line."

Showing Eric around all day and through the evening had blocked from Clay's consciousness his plans to meet with Arthur. On arriving home after midnight, he suddenly remembered the missed appointment. But it was too late now. Even Arthur would have finished work by this time of night. Clay crawled into bed without bothering to change into pajamas—and fell asleep immediately.

At 4:30 a.m., Clay quietly arose without waking Betty Sue. Andy would be up soon enough. If only he could ease out of the house and let everyone get an extra half-hour of sleep. Lord, he needed some sleep too. His eyes burned so painfully, it was hard to keep them open. And he felt like he was getting another cold. His nose was plugging. "Damn," he grumbled as the back door squeaked shut.

The hospital cafeteria opened at five, and Clay was first in line for orange juice, bran muffins, and coffee. He bolted his breakfast and reached the transplant suite fifteen minutes later, where he wearily began to make rounds by reviewing charts. Melton was running a low-grade fever, which would demand prompt attention. And Otto had been wandering around the wards most of the night causing more than a little disorder. Clay would have to do something about that, too.

The night nurse in the transplant unit approached Clay with: "Did you hear about Dr. Johnson?"

Clay felt a sick feeling in his gut as he asked, "What about Dr. Johnson?"

"It's very sad."

"What about Dr. Johnson?" he almost yelled and then clenched his teeth.

"A security guard found him in his lab around midnight. Comatose. Probably an OD."

"Is he? . . ." *Oh God, I promised to see Arthur. Too damned busy.* "Is he? . . ."

"He's alive. In intensive care."

Clay rushed from the transplant suite heading for the intensive care unit, saying to himself: *god-damn you Ducharme. You let him down. . . . Just like you let your mother down. Just like . . .*

There was Arthur, unconscious, with an endotracheal tube in his throat hooked up to a respirator, which was clicking and hissing as it breathed rhythmically for him. The troubled gray eyes were closed, but worry creases remained on his face, pulled and distorted grotesquely by adhesive tape. Clay looked down at the lifeless face—feeling sick. Thinking. Thinking . . . *so god-damned busy yesterday. So god-damned busy you couldn't hear what Arthur was trying to tell you. Always too busy. Always too tired.*

A young but balding medical resident was at Arthur's side. "Barbiturates," he explained. "But he has no family around here. We didn't know who to call."

"He has friends," Clay said. "Didn't you call anyone?"

"We called Dr. Varney. I mean he's the department chairman."

"Terrific," Clay snapped.

The resident adjusted a dial on the respirator. "It was lucky the security guard came by when he did." Another adjustment of the dial. "I think he should be all right."

"If he didn't sustain brain damage," Clay said.

During the remainder of the morning, Arthur's suicide attempt was a prime topic of conversation when the paths of faculty members crossed on the wards and in the halls.

"You can't attack the jobs and pride of men in their forties," Henry Knoblauch, the neurologist who consulted on the heart transplant team, was saying as he stood with Clay at the foot of Arthur's bed in intensive care. Henry frequently had to wear, as he did now, a back and neck brace, because of a war injury. "Even the most secure people are skirting around mid-life crises. But when some bastard undermines their security, you can't help but have a disaster. Any moderately sensitive human being—let alone someone with medical training—can appreciate this."

"But Varney is not even a moderately sensitive human being. He's either so profoundly disturbed himself or so incompetent an administrator that he can't act appropriately," Clay said bitterly, looking at Arthur, who was still hooked up to the hissing respirator.

"I think both explanations fit. Incompetent. And disturbed."

"So what have we been doing about it? Talking about it now and then. Commiserating—but not too deeply. Then we go back to doing our own thing."

"And we're busy as hell just doing that."

"So then we let this happen to a good friend."

"What the hell could Arthur have done to Varney? It's gotta be more than working too much on transplants—or a little disagreement at a conference." Henry tugged at the collar of his neck brace. "I mean, everyone acknowledges that Varney hates almost everybody. I guess we really shouldn't ask what Arthur's done. Or what we've done."

"All right. Then what the hell's going on inside of Varney?"

"I'm a neurologist, not a shrink. Maybe there's really nothing personal. Maybe he just wants to develop his own department."

"Bullshit." Clay kept watching Arthur for movement—for any signs of consciousness.

"He *did* inherit a powerful department from Leister. But the senior people were all Leister's appointees—carrying on Leister's vision for the department. Varney now wants to develop the department according to his own vision."

"You don't really believe that?"

"Hell no! . . . Just trying to be charitable." Henry inserted a finger between his neck and brace to relieve some pressure. "Varney is a seriously disturbed human being."

"But there are competent ways to do things."

"I didn't say he was competent." Henry adjusted the brace on the opposite side.

"And Varney got the chairmanship because he did some research once. Because a guy stumbled on something in a test tube or came up with something in mice doesn't qualify him to deal with people."

"But that's how they pick chairmen." Henry moved his head slowly to the side and winced in pain. "I wonder which of us is next on his list."

Clay let the last remark go. "Your back is really bothering you a lot today, isn't it?"

"Lately it's been worse than usual," Henry said.

"You learn to live with pain. But it's a hell of a way to live." He turned slowly, stiffly, in the direction of the hall. "Gotta see some other patients. Let's look in on Arthur in an hour." He walked gingerly to the elevator and pressed the button.

"What are you doing for the pain?"

"I'm trying everything. Even a psychiatrist. That's the reason I run a pain clinic. Hell, that's the reason I became a neurologist in the first place. To try to figure out something to do with my own pain."

The elevator arrived and Clay, who always avoided elevators, joined Henry. "Does biofeedback work for you?"

"I think it helps me quite a bit." The door squeaked shut. "And it sure seems to do a lot for some of the terminal cancer patients. But my problem is minor. It's Arthur we've gotta worry about."

On his fourth trip of the day to intensive care, Clay found the respirator disconnected and Arthur breathing without assistance—although he was still unconscious.

Wendell Eck was also in the intensive care unit seeing another patient. He was wearing a green surgical scrub shirt without a white coat, which revealed how thin his arms were. He stepped over to Clay's side and looked disapprovingly at the unconscious Arthur Johnson. "It's really too bad," he said. "A bright guy, but so unstable."

"He was severely stressed," Clay shot back. And then, without realizing it, he began to share a confidence with Eck. "I ah . . . I didn't realize. I didn't realize how stressed he was. I was too damned busy. We were supposed to talk yesterday, but I didn't make it."

"Not your fault," Eck said. "He's done this before. At least a couple of times."

"Wha-a-at?" Clay asked angrily.

"I understand that when he was in college he tried it. And during his internship, too."

"Where did you get that crap?"

"From Mawson. It's too bad. But Johnson's just an unstable guy. And that's one of the reasons Vinny had to keep an eye on him and finally replace him. You can't have a guy this unstable running an important service."

"Mawson told you this?"

"He knows Johnson better than anyone."

"Mawson is a slimy, god-damned liar trying to cover his ass. I went to college with Arthur and we were interns together. I've known Arthur for many years, and you'd better believe that Arthur never had a previous suicide attempt. He's overcome a lot in his time. And I don't want you telling lies about him. And I don't want Mawson starting lies. Varney's been doing everything to Arthur he can to destroy him."

Eck changed his tack. "Well, Varney sure is a snake. We all know that."

"And Mawson needs to be set straight."

"I'll sure tell him he was mistaken."

"*I'll* tell him," Clay said. "But right now I've got to find out why Mr. Melton is spiking a temp."

When Clay returned to the transplant suite he was able to appreciate that his protocol for managing the patients was fully in force. A medical resident had already taken blood and urine cultures on Mr. Melton. However, two physical examinations during the day had failed to disclose a source of infection. Thank God for house staff and hospital routines, he thought. Somehow, someone minds the store in the midst of crises. But Mr. Melton's temp was still up. He tied on two surgical masks before entering Melton's room.

"How are you feeling now, Mr. Melton?" Clay's muffled voice filtered through the masks.

"Not bad." Yancey Melton greeted Clay and by gesture invited him "to sit a spell." His gray flecked brown hair was neatly combed, and his normally round face was becoming even more round from his steroid medication. He was wearing Ben Franklin reading glasses and holding a volume of Eudora Welty in his lap. "Got another cold, have you, Dr. Ducharme?"

"Yes. And you're running a little temp."

"I know."

"We're trying to figure out why." Clay sat in a

bedside chair. "Have you got any ideas?"

"I believe so."

That took Clay by surprise. "What's your idea?"

Yancey smiled. "It's just my sinuses." He pressed under his left eye. "This one has been hurting a little. I usually run a temperature when it plugs up."

"Did you tell this to the medical resident?"

"I honestly wasn't sure what he was looking for. He really didn't ask me anything—or say much to me. That's no criticism. He was truly very busy. And I just plain didn't know what he was trying to find."

Clay shook his head slowly from side to side. "You think it might be useful for doctors to talk with their patients now and then?"

"It might."

"I'm going to have an ENT doctor visit you and then see you later."

"That will be fine. By the way, I think Mr. Berkowitz would like to talk with you this evening."

"He's next on my list." Clay left Yancey to call an ENT consultant and then went to the room of Fred Berkowitz.

"Why have I got diabetes?" was the angry greeting of the bald, and now, moon-faced Berkowitz as he pointed to his supper tray.

"I beg your pardon?"

"I came here with a bad heart. I get a transplant. Now I can't even go home. And to top it off I get diabetes. Why? And why can't I get a decent meal instead of this stupid diabetes diet?"

Clay was not prepared for this discussion. "Well," he began, "I hope the strict diet won't last long. We're just trying to stabilize your insulin and food intake."

"But I didn't have diabetes when I got here. Why do I have it now?"

"Part of it is the steroids you take to prevent rejection. They make your face round and sort of bring out diabetes. Four of our nine patients have diabetes now—although no one started out with it."

"That's terrible."

"I agree. And there may be more to it than that. It's something we're puzzling over. I'm going to have our endocrinologist come by and see you."

"Will he get me better meals?"

"I'll ask him what he can do."

Berkowitz was beginning to dampen his hostility. "Whatever you can do, Doc," he mumbled.

"Talk to you later," Clay said as he left Fred's room.

"So how's the hairless Jew?" Otto Schneider was waiting for Clay in the corridor.

"If you're referring to Mr. Berkowitz, he's fine. And you and I are going to have to have a little talk."

"No we ain't."

"Yes we are."

"I don't like him."

"I'm afraid that's your problem. My problem is that you keep my patients awake at night, wandering around into their rooms. The nurses were very unhappy with you last night."

"I don't give a shit."

"But I do."

A nurse signaled to Clay that his ENT consultant had arrived.

"I have to talk with this doctor. But then we'll have to talk some more."

"No we won't," Otto said. "By the way, I heard your little nigger doc is dead."

Clay whirled around, clenching his fists. He waited for the surge of anger to subside sufficiently to allow him to speak. "Mr. Schneider, you're our patient and we try to be understanding about all the facets of your illness and your personality, but there's a limit to our forbearance. If you're referring to Dr. Johnson, you will please recognize that he *is* one of the most distinguished doctors in the entire country. He is *not* dead. He's doing quite well, thank you."

"Shows how little you know, Doc. Ain't no one doin' well. Not the patients. Not the doctors."

TWELVE

The early morning air was heavy with moisture, but still cool and clean, as Leif drove his Mercedes into the parking space reserved for the chairman of surgery. Clay often occupied the unreserved space next to Leif's with his little Volkswagen, and so he did this morning. The best time of day during summer in Houston, Leif was thinking as he strolled towards the hospital.

Soon the exhaust fumes from the crush of traffic would swirl through the wet haze and veil the sun with a net of gray—until that orange fist could angrily burst from its Lilliputian bounds and burn away the cool. And leave behind the torn fabric of fumes and heat in Houston. But for now the fabric was intact and the walk through the palm tree-landscaped parking lot to the hospital employees' entrance was pleasant.

Although it was a full ten minutes before the hour, a queue of orderlies and cleaning people had already formed in the vestibule, holding time cards, waiting to punch out as soon as the clock permitted. Ten minutes to wait until they could get credit and pay for working until seven.

Not part of the queue was a stocky young man, whom Leif had noticed several times in the past. Short, blond, slanted eyes. Mongoloid. Diligently pushing a stiff-bristled broom. He was undertaking the responsibility of his duties with obvious dedication as he moved quickly back and forth across the entry way, cleaning the same area more than once, pausing too often to brush a few specks of debris into a plastic dust pan. Rather than going immediately to his office, Leif stood by the elevator and continued to watch.

The queue at last began to move keeping time with the clicking of punch against card. The stocky young man smiled at his fellow workers as they stuffed time cards back into their pigeon holes and hurried from the vestibule—without returning his smile. Now he could sweep where they had been standing. Next he rolled his cleaning cart down the hall, past Leif, to the utility closet, unbuttoned and removed his gray hospital jacket, and hung it on a hook in the closet. Rather than blue jeans, he was wearing bib overalls. OshKosh B'Gosh. His blue work shirt was buttoned at the collar.

The young man returned to the vestibule and confidently reached for his time card, distinguished from all the others by a red dot in the corner, pausing only a moment to orient the card, dot-side up, dot into the punch. Then he replaced the card into his own slot—marked by a red dot. Now he could go home. He stepped out the door and into the parking lot. Ah, there was the sun-fist poking up from behind the row of palm trees. The young man held his hands toward the sun, but it was too early to feel its warmth.

A gray-haired woman, in her sixties, rattled to the entrance in an ancient Chevy.

Some day she would have to try to let him walk home alone. But would he be able to find his way?

Leif hurried on to the operating room and phoned Eric as soon as he reached his office cubicle. "Hope I'm not waking you, Red. Remember in February, we were going to visit my ranch? What the hell, it's only August now. Only a few months late."

"I'd almost forgotten. I guess I wouldn't mind getting out of this damned Houston humidity."

"You just have to learn how to live with it. You rush from your air-conditioned home to your air-conditioned car to your air-conditioned office. And in the summer you don't do anything outdoors until 10:00 p.m."

"When do we leave?"

"How about Saturday? My associate, Frank Sellery, will cover for me the whole weekend."

"Sounds fine."

"We can talk this weekend till we both get tired of it."

"I do need a lot more material," Eric said. "I wasn't satisfied with the article."

"I thought it was good. You write very well."

"The article was too superficial."

"You can't go into great depth in a magazine piece."

"I know. But I'd like to have known something about Davey."

Leif pulled the phone away from his ear for a moment and took a breath before he answered distantly, "That's not relevant to heart transplantation."

"But I think it's very relevant to you. Do you have a photograph of him?"

Another breath with an audible sigh. "Of course."

"Could I see it?"

"Certainly."

"Maybe we could talk about him a little more."

"If you want."

"Tomorrow I'm going to visit the first five patients you transplanted. I don't think I can handle any more than that in my book. Anyway I only really got to know the first five."

"You know they're on the medical service now?"

"Yes."

"Varney may try to give you trouble. Let me know if he does. I'm not allowing any more of our heart transplants to be transferred to medicine because of that nut. . . . That's off the record."

"Clay's already warned me."

"Mike won't be a problem, of course, because he's out of the hospital. Practicing medicine full time. The world's second longest surviving heart transplant."

"And quite a testimonial to the Hanson team."

"I guess," Leif acknowledged with becoming modesty.

Now came the long postponed trip to the ranch. Only Leif, Eric, Karen, and Mark went. Elaine declined to go. As they drove Leif could sense the excited anticipation that the children were experiencing.

In the heat of the day, they swam in a large rectangular swimming pool, which was surrounded by redbud, mimosa, and palm trees in a professionally landscaped array. The ranch was a working ranch, but the living area provided a resort ambience. After swimming came horseback riding. Leif looked at his son, Mark, and thought of the young man with the broom. Although Mark sat a horse well, he would never be an All-American or a Phi Beta Kappa. In fact it was doubtful that he could ever be taught to read or support himself—except, perhaps, by sweeping. And there was slender, blond Karen, always shy and withdrawn. Of course her shyness was easy to understand. She was just ten years old, but she stood two inches under six feet tall—so painful for her among her fifth grade classmates. She slouched to try to disguise her height. Considering the heights of the parents, Leif had often thought, they should only have had sons.

Coming in from a ride across the ranch they left their horses at the stable and Leif inadvertently said, "How Davey would have loved this place."

Eric looked at Leif and waited for him to continue.

Leif said, "I don't know what made me say that." They walked in uncomfortable silence.

"You don't easily forget the death of a child." Eric eventually pushed words into the empty space.

"No," Leif said. "I live with death every damned day of my life. I fight it every way I can. I've grown a hide on me like an elephant. So I don't hurt so much every time it wins one from me. I've tried to forget my lost battles. But Davey . . . I can see him so clearly . . . that's one loss I can't forget. . . . And that's one I can't forgive myself for."

Mark, a short, chubby six year-old, was trying to attract his father's attention. His slanted eyes crinkled and his tongue protruded slightly as he smiled up at this giant beside him.

Leif rubbed the boy's head. Gave him a pat on the shoulder . . . and looked past the child into the distance. "I've got to do something for Davey. Something important. Something that'll last. A volume of poems and dedicating it to him." He kicked at the sod as they walked to the house. "Except I'd want it to be a good volume. And I'm afraid my poems aren't very good."

"The ones I've seen are quite respectable," Eric said. "I mean you've already had one published in *Life*."

"I'm afraid I know better. But I'm going to endow a memorial scholarship at Yale."

"That sounds like a good idea."

"You know what else I've thought of?" Leif didn't wait for an answer. "I've heard they've got these memorial groves of redwoods in California. I thought I'd look into endowing some redwoods in Davey's memory."

"Redwoods? . . . Interesting." Eric smiled. "And you've got the money to do what you want."

"I guess. But it's strange, isn't it?"

Eric waited for him to continue. They paused by the swimming pool while the children went ahead to the house. Eric prodded: "What's strange?"

"This need to do something that'll last. Something that goes beyond death. . . . Maybe some of it's for me. But a lot of it's for Davey. Whatever the reason—it drives me." He looked absently into the pool. "It's what made King Harald write poems and fight battles." Leif glanced over at Eric. "You mentioned Stamford Bridge once. Do you know the poem Harald composed before that battle?"

"The battle he never should have become involved in," Eric added. "I don't think I could recite it. Wasn't it something about doomed warriors?"

"The important line is, 'my head always high in battle,'" Leif said. "The rest of it goes:
    'We never kneel in battle

Before the storm of weapons
And crouch behind our shields;
So the noble lady told me.
She told me once to carry
My head always high in battle
Where swords seek to shatter
The skulls of doomed warriors.'"

Leif sensed that Eric was not appropriately awed by the poem of King Harald, the hard ruler. "That poem is over nine hundred years old," he prodded. "Do you think you or I will ever write or do anything that will live nine hundred years?"

The surgical schedule for Monday following the trip to the ranch was unusually light for Leif. Only five cases. And Leif finished these by early afternoon. He even had time to make rounds with Clay on the transplant patients.

During rounds a short doctor with gray hair and a scraggly gray mustache approached the team. The shoulder of his brown tweed suit coat looked like something had been spilled on it. He observed Leif looking at his coat and opened in his prominent Scottish burr with: "My introductory lecture to students, interns, and residents in pediatrics is that the fir-rst prer-requisite for a pediatrician is the pur-rchase of a vomit colored suit."

This evoked the desired response of laughter from both Leif and Clay.

The doctor in the "vomit-colored" suit was Maxwell MacGregor, the chairman of pediatrics at Southwest, and widely regarded as one of the world's most distinguished pediatric cardiologists. "When you've got a moment I need to talk to both of you." He looked first at Leif and then at Clay.

"Now is fine. We've finished rounds," Leif said.

"What brings you to the heart transplant suite, Max?" Clay then added jokingly, "You're not thinking of getting into the heart transplant business, too, are you?"

"That's just exactly what I wanted to talk to you about. I need a verr-ry frank and honest opinion. I've got a patient," MacGregor began. "Just a dar-rlin' child. You know the astronaut, Jim Kelly?"

Clay said he didn't.

"I know about him," Leif said. "I read about him in *Life*. His daughter has some unspecified heart problem. I remember that."

"Well, I was about to send poor dar-rlin' home to die. Fibroelastosis. Then I thought with my good colleague, Clay, and our excellent surgeon, Leif Hanson, doing so well, maybe we don't have to send her home to die after all. I asked the Kellys if they would like to have me talk with you. They would."

"Transplant a child?" Leif was thinking out loud. "I've been considering it."

"There'll be new pr-roblems," MacGregor said. "But she's already had one cardiac arrest. I wasn't sure we could resuscitate her." He paused. "In fact I wasn't sure we *should* resuscitate her. But maybe this could be the reason for bringing her back to life. Maybe there is something to offer the child. What do you think, Clay?"

"Honestly, Max, we're sitting on a volcano. We shouldn't think of this as a clinical option. It's still an experiment. And to be honest, we're pushing ourselves to the limit just to keep our present transplants alive."

"Nine out of ten, alive," MacGregor said.

"Some of the living are a lot sicker than the newspapers would have you believe," Clay said.

"Oh, I know that," MacGregor said.

"Bottom line: let's give it serious thought," Leif said. "And while we're thinking, why not do her tissue typing and skin tests?"

Clay weighed the suggestion before turning to Wendell Eck, who was on rounds with the team. "Could you go with Dr. MacGregor and get some of those things started? Just on a remote possibility?"

"Right."

"I appr-reciate it," MacGregor said.

As MacGregor and Eck were walking down the hall, Clay muttered to Leif, "I don't want us to get mousetrapped into another transplant."

"Maybe children will accept heart transplants better than adults."

"There's no good reason to believe that."

"But we don't know."

"Do we have to try out everything in human subjects?"

"No. But don't you use newborn hearts in your mouse-to-rat experiments?"

"That's just because we need a small size. We transplant the rat hearts into the mouse ears and vice versa."

"But could some of your success be due to the fact that you're using immature tissues?"

"I seriously doubt it."

"But you don't know, do you?"

"No, I don't know."

"Well, just stop and think about it. Wouldn't it be marvelous if kids turned out to be the best recipients of all? I mean wouldn't that be something? To take a dying inoperable kid. Give him a new heart. And give him many, many years of life?"

"It would, Leif. But it's not very likely at this stage of our knowledge."

"But isn't it worth a chance? My God, the kid's already died once. Why can't we give the little kid a chance?"

So, Leif and the Hanson team prepared to perform their most appealing heart transplantation to date. The recipient: Kathy Kelly, a beautiful, five-year-old girl, red hair, freckles, always tenderly holding her Raggedy Ann doll. Shortly after the decision to transplant, she survived her second cardiac arrest. Leif was picking up his phone to dial a local TV station to broadcast a plea for a donor child who would have a heart small enough to fit into Kathy's chest when Sellery stormed into the office.

"Nine-year-old drowning victim in intensive care at Texas Children's Hospital," Sellery announced. "Already been tissue-typed. But Cooley's got no kid-sized recipients right now."

"Outstanding." Leif replaced the phone in its cradle. "Cooperation. Good press for both of us. Outstanding."

Kathy's recovery after surgery was spectacular. The day after receiving a new heart, she was actually sitting up in bed coloring in a Mickey Mouse cartoon book.

Three days later, photographers displayed her in the arms of her astronaut father, clutching her well-worn and sterilized Raggedy Ann. Another picture was of Leif and Jim Kelly and carried the caption: "Two explorers of new frontiers." The photos traveled all over the world via wire service. Heart transplantation had climbed the battlements through a rain of rocks and hot oil to reach a media pinnacle. Even the back-biters and jealous non-involved faculty physicians and surgeons at the Houston medical schools (except Varney) appeared to be impressed. A third widely distributed picture showed Leif in his scrub suit holding Kathy in his arms. The accompanying story quoted a surgical resident as saying that the only differences between a heart transplant by Dr. Hanson and an appendectomy by the average surgeon was that heart transplantation took less time and had lower mortality. Leif recognized that this was a catchy thing to say, but he tried to give the impression that he found the statement to be highly embarrassing hyperbole.

Hyperbole notwithstanding, Leif sensed it was all coming together now. This could be the major direction of his work with transplants. Saving children.

"Black Jack" Bottomeley, the Houston billionaire, had somehow anticipated this striking interface between the space program and heart transplantation. Two weeks before the Kathy Kelly transplant, he had sent out invitations to the astronauts and the transplanters to come to his River Oaks estate for a little party. Apparently the two groups of people—the astronauts and the transplanters—were now becoming Houston's new famous sons. The new pioneers. Or to borrow from Eric Kristensen's cover story, the new Vikings.

Elaine had rarely been attending social events with Leif for a year or more, and when the invitation from Bottomeley first arrived, she informed Leif that she would not be going. But when the Saturday of the event arrived, she changed her mind.

A uniformed guard admitted the Hanson Mercedes through the gate to drive up the floral-lined road to an imposing structure that initially looked like Tara. But as they got closer, the residence assumed the style, if not the full dimensions, of the US Supreme Court building, with Corinthian columns three stories high. The heat and humidity wrapped itself around the Hansons as they walked up the steps and presented their invitation to an elegant black butler in full livery. They were a fashionable thirty-five minutes late. And they seemed to be the first to arrive.

The butler escorted them into an immense rosewood paneled library, which displayed a larger-than-life portrait of the lord of the manor above the mantel. Near the fireplace sat the smaller-than-life, gnarled figure of "Black Jack" Bottomeley. He did not leave his chair, but leaned forward on his cane and extended an arthritic hand. "So you're the famous Dr. Hanson?" The South was still in his mouth. Years of living in London and Zurich had not changed his speech. Pure west Texas. "I like the way you work. Hard. Decisive. Not afraid to take a risk. I sure do like that."

Two middle-aged women, his nieces, stood *American-Gothic*-like at each side. Behind his chair hovered a male attendant. No one else was in the room.

"I hope we're here on the right night," Elaine said.

"Don't fret yourself, my dear. People are just starting to arrive." Bottomeley nodded towards the library door.

A contingent of several astronaut couples was strolling in, as if unawed by the surroundings. The Kellys came over to meet their host and join the Hansons. Jim Kelly had red hair as did his wife. Both were slim and vigorous and well rested. The days of tension surrounding the event of their daughter's heart surgery were in the past. They had waited until Kathy was asleep. Max and Clay had reassured them that it was all right to go out for a few hours, because

Kathy was doing so well. Jim Kelly handled the introductions of the astronaut couples. There was a Gemini astronaut who had already had a space shot. And some rookies who had not been up yet. The men headed for a bar that was set up in the library. Liveried bartenders and bars adorned several of the rooms.

Leif, with Elaine at his side, eventually wandered off looking at books and catching bits of conversations. The library appointments were the best that money could buy. Rich woods and leathers. He wondered if someone had turned a very good decorator loose in here with *carte blanche*. Thousands of books. Matched leather bound sets. As it they had been purchased by the yard. For this corner, two yards of dark green morocco—perhaps in a Dickens or a Thackeray. And for this area, four yards of a deep rich, burgundy, full calf, imperial binding. Any authors will do.

The library was filling up, so the Hansons went to the music room. Other transplanters were arriving: Denton Cooley, Sellery, Clay, and several more from Baylor and Southwest. The astronauts congregated mostly with the astronauts, the transplanters with the transplanters—and the wives with the wives. Leif mused that it looked like it was going to be a really swinging night.

Hunting and auto racing were the big topics of conversation that Leif overheard among the astronauts. "For bear," one was saying, "Alaska's the only place."

An immediate response was, "Bear is all right, but while it lasts, Africa's for the real game."

"Africa's closing down," was an insider's rejoinder.

"There's nothing wrong with hunting right here in Texas. More deer taken each year in Texas than in any other state." A rookie got into the act.

Eric Kristensen appeared. Apparently his involvement with both groups of people and his being in town was sufficient to warrant an invitation.

"You look like a lost waif," Elaine Hanson said as she glided away from Leif to welcome Eric. She could have stepped out of *Vogue* in her beige silk tunic pants outfit, complemented by a single strand of pearls and a tumbler of vodka with a splash of tonic. "You must know more of these people than I do. But I'll introduce you to those I know that you don't. And maybe you can introduce me to some more astronauts."

"I'll be happy to do what I can." Eric returned a nodded greeting towards Leif.

"Except they're so short." She squeezed Eric's arm. "I always need to stand next to a tall man."

"They're average height," Eric said.

"I don't think I like average people."

"Average height. Not average people."

"Average anything," Elaine said. "River Oaks finally got a tall tennis pro on their staff. I really hate towering over men. And to be a head taller than someone who's trying to teach me tennis is too much. Do you play tennis?"

"A little. When I have the time."

"That sounds like Leif." Elaine tugged at Eric's arm. "I hear some music." She downed a large swallow of vodka and parked her drink on a coffee table before they followed the sound of "Deep Purple" to a ballroom that matched the size and grandeur of the mansion. Crystal chandeliers, polished parquet floor. And nothing more ostentatious for an orchestra than thirty pieces. "Leif dances like a fullback," Elaine said. "How do you dance?"

"Like a tight end." He led Elaine onto the floor.

"Good hands," she said.

"What?"

She squeezed his hand. "Ends have to have good hands."

"I guess."

"That's what you played in college?"

"Yes," Eric said.

"Among other things?"

"You mean like basketball?"

"That's not exactly what I meant." She laughed.

"Actually, basketball may have been my better sport."

"But not tennis?"

"I've got a pretty good serve."

"And how are your strokes?"
"Out of practice."
"That can be remedied."
"No time. Still working on my book."
"Too bad." Elaine laughed musically and slipped away after the dance.

As the liquor flowed, the party became more lively. Scotch, bourbon, gin, vodka, and aquavit. There must have been a strong Scandinavian influence among the early Texas oil men, because aquavit was very popular at gatherings like this. Clay and Betty Sue appeared on the dance floor. And Elaine changed partners twice more before finding Leif—and actually dancing with him.

"You seem happy tonight," Leif said. The music was slow. Something from the forties.

"I am."

"Why?"

"I'm not sure. Do I have to know why?"

"No." Leif felt how tense Elaine's arm and hand muscles were as she kept him at a distance.

"It might be the little Kelly girl."

"You mean because she's doing so well?"

"I suppose," Elaine said. "When you do something for kids, I feel your work is really worthwhile. Saving the lives of kids. Now that's . . . that's something beautiful."

"A big part of my work is with kids."

"That part of your work is good. Up to now I've thought this heart transplantation was just another ego trip. But if you could save kids. That would be beautiful."

"I'm working on it."

"Why don't you just do kids? Do ten cases a week instead of thirty or forty. Cooley does mainly kids, doesn't he?"

"He does a lot of kids, but he doesn't do many more kids than I do. And we both do a lot of adults. But you're on the right track. I'd like to do even more with kids."

"Could you ever consider cutting back?"

"It's possible."

"Spending some time with your family?"

"I spend time." He felt her tight arm muscles continuing to hold him away.

"Do you know what grade your daughter is in?"

"Come on, Elaine."

"She's so shy. She needs her dad. She loves you so."

"I'll do better for her."

"For starters, what can you do about her height? She's getting so damned tall."

"Tall parents."

"She feels like a freak. That's what makes her so shy. Only when she's with you can she feel like she's the little girl she really is."

"Let me talk to a pediatric endocrinologist."

The music changed to a fast tempo and the Hansons and Ducharmes left the floor. "Clay and Betty Sue," Elaine called. "How good to see you. It's been a long time."

"It has," Betty Sue said.

The men stepped over to the bar for drinks. They exchanged a few words with Eric who had been explaining to the bartender that aquavit should be served chilled—not on the rocks.

"You must be so busy with your work and your home. I don't know how you do it," Elaine began with the conventional remark of the non-working wife to the working wife.

"She has a live-in servant," Clay joined in, "me."

"Not for the past few months, I haven't," Betty Sue corrected. "When they were students and residents, I thought it couldn't be worse. But it can. And it is."

"It's been a while since I've thought of those old Quonset days," Leif said.

Clay looked around the room. "This is far removed from a Quonset hut."

"Yes," Elaine said softly, "far removed."

There was an uncomfortably long pause. "Why don't we get together at our house next week?" Betty Sue asked. "To allow old friends to enjoy each other's company again."

"I think I'd like that," Elaine said.

"How about Monday night? Too soon?"

"I'm in San Francisco Monday." Leif checked his pocket agenda. "But I'll be home Tuesday."

"Tuesday's fine for me," Clay agreed.

"Eight o'clock," Betty Sue said.

"It's been years, hasn't it?"

The slow music started and the couples returned to the dance floor.

"It's been a long time since we've gone out together that way," Leif remarked. "Visiting friends."

"We can do it for appearances."

"We might enjoy it." Leif looked over at Clay and Betty Sue, dancing, holding each other close. "We were happy like that."

"That was a lifetime ago."

Leif tried to draw her closer. "Just for appearances," he explained.

But Elaine pulled back. "I don't think your blond scrub nurse would like this."

"Damn it, Elaine. Can't you loosen up a little?"

"I don't know how I can." She watched his face. "You don't understand, do you?"

"Try me."

"I thought you were an expert on people in pain."

"We've shared a lot of it together."

"But don't you know that when you reach out again and again and again, and your hands get burned every time, you just can't keep reaching out? Don't you know that?" She was whispering, but the words came out more like a hiss. Drops of water on a hot iron. "God, I've tried. I really have. I've tried to reach you. But I've had to give up. Just to keep my own equilibrium, I've had to give up."

"Is it worth one more try?"

"I doubt it."

"Can you at least think about it?"

"That much, I can do. I'll think about it."

THIRTEEN

Sunday morning following the Bottomeley party Clay arrived later than usual for hospital rounds. This was the day Arthur was to be discharged, so Clay first went to his room in the psychiatric wing. Clay had been visiting Arthur daily, bringing him his mail and things he needed from his home and office. For many days Arthur had been on a locked ward, but over the past week he was easing out of restriction preparing for discharge.

"Home today?" Clay asked as he entered the pastel green room, without bars on the windows, and handed Arthur several pieces of mail

"That's what they tell me." Arthur was already dressed in street clothes. He dropped the letters into his open suitcase.

"Can I drive you home?"

"Thanks, anyway, but my car's still in the parking lot. I may have to call on you to give me a jump start. It's been sitting there quite a while."

"Well . . . you're looking good. Really good." Clay tried to hit an enthusiastic note, but he was coming across flat, one tone away from awkward.

"Thanks."

"I ah . . . I suppose you heard, Leif did another

transplant."

"I heard."

"Little girl."

"Saw her on TV." Arthur nodded towards the the television set mounted on the wall.

"I hope you'll be getting back to work soon. We really need your ideas and help."

"I think you'll be stuck with me around here for good." Arthur turned his attention to packing. "As bad as it may be, the job here is the best I'll ever be able to get from now on. I really blew it with my attempt."

"Why?" Clay finally blurted out the question. "Why did you do it?"

"I was wondering when you'd get around to asking that." Arthur folded his pajamas and stuffed them into the suitcase. "As you must know, suicide is usually not a rational act. And I don't think it's subject to a reasoned analysis. In fact, if I've learned anything, I've learned this: you can't reason with someone who's depressed. You can't use logic."

"But if we could have talked."

"We did talk."

"But we'd planned to meet the next day." Clay was standing at the foot of the bed. "I didn't finish till midnight. Then I assumed it was much too late to call."

"You don't think our failure to meet contributed to what I did, do you?"

"I don't know."

"Forget it." Arthur picked up his cigarette pack from the bedside table. His tremor was worse than ever. "Believe me I wasn't sitting around waiting to meet with you. I told you suicide is an irrational act. There's nothing new we could have discussed that would have altered my plans." Arthur stuck the wrong end of the Winston into his mouth, but caught the error before lighting the filter tip. "You did the most anyone could. You listened. You cared. That's what was important. You couldn't have reasoned with me. The most rational thing I did the days before I OD'd was calculate my barbiturate dosage. What I didn't calculate was the night watchman coming in so early."

"How'd you like to . . ." Clay was about to ask if Arthur would agree to spending a few days in the Ducharme guest room, but decided that such an offer smacked of lack of confidence in his friend's ability to cope at home, "have Sunday dinner with us?"

"I appreciate it, Clay. But I've got a mess facing me at home. Been away too long."

"Anything we can do?"

"Nothing. I'll be fine. I promise you."

"Will you be coming to the lab tomorrow?"

"Maybe for a couple of hours. To check my mail. And then I have to spend an hour with my 'parole-officer' psychiatrist."

"We all need all the support we can get."

"I know. Sometimes I think what I need is a little primal scream therapy." Arthur finally lit his cigarette. He handled it for a moment. Studied the lit end as it encroached on the white paper. Finally he said, "Except some things are just so bad you can't scream." Now he inhaled his cigarette deeply. "There I go again. The god-damned self-pity. I'm sorry."

"I'm listening," Clay said. "And there's nothing to be sorry about."

"It's not like I was getting my ass shot off in Vietnam. Or starving to death in the streets of Calcutta or on the edge of the Sahara. I'm just having a little trouble with my job."

"There's enough trouble to go around."

"Yeah." Arthur took another long drag on his cigarette.

Clay wanted to ask him to call Monday morning, but rejected the idea. He would call Arthur instead. That would appear less meddlesome.

And on Monday morning, Clay did call the lab. Arthur answered and sounded to be in reasonably good spirits.

But it was on Monday afternoon when a disaster

occurred that caught everyone by surprise. Kathy Kelly, who had been actively playing in her room for the last two days, became lethargic and wanted to take a nap after lunch. Clay had spent only a few minutes with her on rounds in the morning, joking with her about her Raggedy Ann. At 10:00 a.m. she had looked as vigorous as imaginable.

At 1:00 p.m. Max MacGregor sought out Clay. "She's got a friction rub and she's lost QRS voltage on her ECG. Just since this morning."

"Only six days since her transplant."

"Really acute."

"We've got our work cut out for us," Clay said.

Kathy held tightly to Raggedy Ann through the afternoon and evening and on into the night. Her eyes were open wide, watching everything happening around her. Clay and Max worked through the night. The parents were also with her as much as possible. However, in modern-day intensive care in the medical centers, there is little room for family among the machines, tubes, and highly specialized personnel, each doing his, her, or its job. In fact, it was sometimes hard to find the patient in the midst of the people and paraphernalia. A few tufts of scraggly Raggedy Ann hair were visible.

By about four in the morning, the rejection crisis seemed to be under control. The Kellys were told they could get some sleep. They went to a hospital guest room down the hall. Shortly after four-thirty, Kathy's blood pressure began to show an unmistakable fall.

"How you feeling, dar-rlin'?" MacGregor asked as he increased the speed of the Isuprel drip.

"I want Mama." She began to cry.

"In a little bit," Clay said. The pressure dropped further.

"Mama, Daddy," Kathy sobbed.

"It'll be all right," MacGregor opened the drip fully. "Get me more Isuprel," he told the nurse.

Kathy's heart rate was slowing. Her electrocardiogram showed widening QRS complexes. "Mama," she whimpered.

"Let's move on that Isuprel," Clay shouted. "Bag-breathe her." The electrocardiogram was now a straight line. He hollered at a lanky surgical resident, who was just standing there, "How long does it take for a cardiac arrest to get through to you, fella?" Clay spread electrode paste on her chest, positioned the paddles, and jolted the child with 40 watt-seconds of electric current. Her back arched. Her arms and legs stiffened. But her heart beat didn't return. He increased the current to 80 watt-seconds and shocked her again. And again at 120 watt-seconds.

"Let's intubate," MacGregor said. The resident began pushing on Kathy's chest while Max struggled with the laryngoscope and placed a tube in her trachea.

Clay hooked oxygen and the respirator bag to the tube before taking over the cardiac massage. Max controlled the respiratory functions. Kathy's eyes were still wide open, but unseeing now.

"Get the Kellys and have them wait outside," MacGregor told a nurse who had just entered the room.

Clay was undergoing an experience of *deja vu*. As an internist-cardiologist he didn't have children as patients. But here he was trying to resuscitate a dying child. This had happened before. When? "Let's have an ampule of bicarbonate. Push! Into the tubing! Into the tubing! Be ready to shock her again." Nothing. No response. Where had this happened before? Where? When? Of course. *Davey Hanson. New Haven. Leif's son.* "Is Dr. Hanson around?" Clay asked as he continued the cardiac massage.

"I believe he's out of town," the resident said.

"Are you the one who said this procedure is easier than an appendectomy?"

"I'm afraid so," the resident mumbled and looked away.

"Well, it's your turn to massage her heart," Clay stepped back and told the nurse, "Give me some glucagon and more bicarbonate." The electrocardiogram was still a flat line. "How's she aerating?"

"Getting plenty of air in both sides," a bearded intern said. He had just entered the room in response to a "cor-zero" call. "Well, wait, correct that. Now she's beginning to sound stiffer."

"Keep bagging."

"She's bubbling."

Brown fluid oozed from her nose and mouth. The endotracheal tube suddenly detached from the oxygen line, and the brown ooze changed to a gush pouring out over Raggedy Ann.

"It's all over," MacGregor said. "Clean her up as fast as you can. I've got to talk to her folks." MacGregor waited by the door, trying to get himself under control. "But how can I tell them?"

The Kellys read his face when he came out. "She's dead, isn't she?" Jim Kelly asked.

"We thought we could save her," Max said.

"We didn't get to say good-bye." Mrs. Kelly's tearless eyes burned into Clay. "Couldn't we have had a chance to say good-bye?"

"Everything happened so fast," was the best Clay could answer.

"She was all alone. We didn't get to say good-bye."

"It happened so fast."

"Loved ones should have a chance to say good-bye."

"We all loved her."

"Not the way we loved her."

"I know."

"We didn't even get to say good-bye."

Clay eventually wandered through the early morning solitude of half-lit corridors back to his office. He stumbled into an armchair and reached over to slam the office door shut with enough force to make a crashing sound. Then he just sat in the dark. He would let Leif sleep an hour or two before calling him.

You've screwed up again, Ducharme. Like you did with your mother. With so many patients. With Arthur. Could anyone believe how much damage you've done as a doctor? Never should have gone into medicine. Never. You damned fool!

Clay had known in May that heart transplantation was not succeeding. But he had to keep pushing it. And let Leif keep pushing it. And now a little girl was dead. . . . But she would have died anyway. Poor excuse. They should have waited a couple of years. Been better prepared. Done it right. But where was the glory in that?

Now how the hell was he going to get Leif to stop transplants? . . .

Is Varney going to love this! . . . God damn it!

He rested his head on his desk like a first-grader being disciplined by his teacher and promptly fell asleep—only to awake within a half hour. Dreaming . . . thinking of his mother and the calls she had kept making to him in New Haven that summer, complaining of her heart. Of course he checked with his father who assured him, with that great Roger Ducharme self-assurance, that nothing was wrong—just female crockiness. Then came the day when she called him at the hospital. He angrily dismissed her symptoms, told her to consult with doctors in Mississippi (as if she could bypass a Ducharme doctor for another opinion), and warned her not to call him at the hospital.

She died that night.

And so father and son learned their most painful lesson about humility in the practice of medicine. Clay shook his head and muttered to himself, "What a lousy human being you are. And what a lousy doctor."

He groped in the darkness for the desk lamp, twisted the switch, and lurched to his feet. Then staggered behind his desk and slid open the bottom desk drawer looking for his shaving kit. No time to go home now. He would just have to call Betty Sue and get back to work.

And fight with Leif to stop transplants.

FOURTEEN

From his French Provincial-furnished suite at the Fairmont Hotel, Leif looked out over San Francisco towards Coit Tower, remembering the first time he had seen this city and nearby Muir Woods. He had just earned his wings and gold bars and had flown to Hamilton Field to await his assignment to the Pacific Theater. Each morning his squadron remained at Hamilton until noon. If there were no orders by that time, the men could take the bus into San Francisco for twelve hours of recreation before returning to the base. So for three days Leif devoured the city and the redwoods, not as a condemned man gorges himself on his last meal, but as a lover learns and delights in the discovery of each new perfumed secret of his loved one. Thus whenever anyone needed a talk delivered in San Francisco, for Leif it was almost always, "Have slides, will travel."

Leif gazed into the blue distance of sky and water. The peacefulness of water. And the Viking challenge of an unconquered ocean. But he was close to conquest. And he was close to peace with himself over the direction of his work.

He stepped over to the white and gold desk where he had been organizing his presentation. He already had slides of Kathy Kelly—something to impress his audience. There were still a few minutes to spend before going to breakfast and on to the lecture hall. He snapped a rubber band around his plastic slide box and turned on the television for the morning news.

And there was a picture of Kathy. After a week she still rated national coverage.

He twisted the volume control to hear what NBC had to say about his success.

But that was not what the news anchor had to say. What he announced was that Kathy Kelly was dead.

Leif slumped into the desk chair, listening until the report of the death of a child gave way to a commercial for underarm deodorant. With his shoulders bent, his arms resting limply on his thighs, he listened to how Ban fought wetness better. When a dog food commercial took over the next advertising spot, he straightened to his feet and punched off the switch. Once more he stepped to the window to look out on the city. A sudden fog was seeping in from the bay, darkly filling recesses in North Beach and roiling up Telegraph Hill to obscure—in wetness—all but the top of Coit Tower.

The jangling phone stabbed wildly into the fog. It was Clay telling him what had happened to Kathy.

"NBC beat you to it."

"Sorry. Just wanted to let you sleep a little extra."

Leif gave his talk as the first speaker on the program and caught the earliest possible flight back to Houston. During the entire trip home his throat was so tight he had discomfort swallowing. The tension and pain traveled into his chest and down to his belly, puddling there like cold gravy. Then back to his chest. . . . *Saving kids*. The ultimate direction for his work. *So damned close*. To make the taste of failure more bitter.

Elaine's eyes were swollen from crying when Leif arrived home. She was sitting on the edge of their king-sized bed staring into the fireplace.

"What's happening?" he asked and awkwardly tried to put his arm around her.

She jerked away. "Didn't you know? Your little child died."

"The little Kelly girl? Of course, I knew. That's why I'm back early." Leif tried to reach for her again.

Elaine jumped to her feet and spun away. "Where were you when she needed you? Where are you always when people really need you?"

"I thought everything was all right," Leif tried to explain. "I didn't know anything would go wrong."

"Of course you didn't. You never know about things going wrong," she spit the words out. "The child is dead. Just another kid."

"What do you mean: *just* another kid? There's no such thing to me as *just* another kid. And you don't even know that. You usually don't give a damn about any of my patients. I lose patients all the time. Kids. Adults. But more important, I save patients all the time. And this one child you know about. I lose her and . . ."

"This one was different," Elaine interrupted.

"I don't understand."

"You never do."

Leif loosened his tie. "Ahh . . . maybe I do. Of course I do."

"No you don't."

"Whatever you say, Slim."

"Don't patronize me."

Leif just stood there—trying to figure out what to say next. "We've got to get ready to go to the Ducharmes," he offered.

"No, we don't. I sent regrets. While you were screwing around in San Francisco, Clay was up all night with your child. And we can't revive that relationship. They're happy. They've grown together. I'm not enough of a masochist to expose myself to such comparisons."

Since he was not going to the Ducharmes, Leif intended to round at the hospital after he slammed out of the house. He was not on call yet. And he was churning inside. He kept driving on past University Hospital, past the

Warwick to a high-rise overlooking Herman Park. He had the fleeting impression that a cream-colored VW van was following. Rather than stopping in front of the apartment house, he drove around the block, parked, and walked back. The van was parked across the street from the entrance. Leif looked at it for a moment. No one in it. He decided it was his imagination. He unlocked the outer door and took the elevator to the twentieth floor and knocked two shorts and a long on the apartment door.

"Who is it?" asked a woman's voice.

"Joe for the dry cleaning," Leif said.

The chain released and the door opened. A blonde stood on her toes, wrapped her arms around Leif's neck, and said, "Welcome home, Joe." The door closed behind them. "I'm a mess. I didn't expect you."

"I came back early," Leif said. "Kathy Kelly died."

"I know, hon. I felt so bad. But you did your best."

"Did I?"

"Sure you did, hon. Sure you did."

"You always try to make things right, don't you?"

"I try," she said. "Now sit down and I'll fix you a nice tall gin and tonic."

"Three shots," Leif said and eased himself onto the blue brocade sofa.

"Then I'll fix myself up a little." She was wearing a snug tee shirt and shorts, leaving no guesswork about the remarkable contours of her body.

"No point in putting something on now that will be coming right off," Leif said.

"I like to look nice for you." She handed him the drink and disappeared into the bedroom. The apartment was clearly luxurious beyond the range of a nurse's salary, even the personal scrub nurse of the chairman of the Department of Surgery. Very large rooms. Early American furnishings. Some antiques. A terrace that overlooked the park. "Do you have your pager?" she called out.

"Sellery's taking call until midnight. So I'm turning it off until then."

"We can have a wonderful evening. I've got some

good steaks and some good wine. And you pick out the music."

"How about *The Rite of Spring?*"

"Not before supper," she entered the living room. A beautiful mature woman. A little taller than average. Deep blue eyes. Her professionally lightened hair flowed softly over her shoulders. She was wearing a navy blue silk lounging outfit with a neckline that opened to the waist. "You brought me this from Paris," she said.

"I have good taste. He stood up and went to her. "You know that shoots it, don't you?"

"Before supper?"

"Before, during, after."

"You must have missed me." She curved her body into him as he drew her close.

"There's just one tie on this." He pulled and the garment fell from her shoulders to the floor.

Leif appeared at the the funeral with Jim and Helen Kelly. Then Leif Hanson and Jim Kelly issued what might best be called a joint communiqué. To the effect that there are always risks at the frontier. And we must keep trying. Keep reaching for the stars. They said that NASA and the astronaut program had to recover from the deaths of Grissom, White, and Chaffee. An AP reporter grumbled that it included everything but, "Let's win this one for the Gipper."

Kathy Kelly's death devastated the other transplant patients and required intensive efforts to reassure them. Schneider demanded three electrocardiograms in one day. The back-biters got in their bites. Clay Ducharme's response was now almost stereotyped. He called for another moratorium to try to find out what went wrong. Leif's response away from the media was just the opposite of what he had displayed at the press conference. Moody. Almost withdrawn. Obviously deeply worried.

This worry was accentuated when DeBakey's long-awaited entrance into heart transplantation took place on

August 31, with a typical DeBakey flourish—shortly after Leif's well publicized failure. For DeBakey's performance, not only was the donor's heart used, but both kidneys as well. So that three simultaneous transplants took place. This really captured the headlines. Furthermore, it was rumored that their heart recipient was an immunologic freak. Poor cellular immunity. He could not reject the heart even if he wanted to—so went the rumor.

As president of Baylor College of Medicine, DeBakey commanded the resources of an entire medical school. And also at Baylor was Cooley, an equally aggressive and talented competitor. Leif had made the commitment to heart transplantation as his ultimate career goal. But right here in the same city were two of the most gifted surgeons in the world, who could attract the patients and the donors and prevent Leif from achieving what he was so urgently seeking.

Ensconced at the top of the list for the next heart transplant was a Chicago industrialist and real estate developer, named Seymour Cohen. Not unrelated to this pecking order was the fact that Mr. Cohen through his lawyers had been in serious negotiations with Leif and administrative officials of the University of the Southwest regarding the endowment of a Cohen Institute for Cardiovascular Research. Cohen's people, it was rumored, had proposed an initial gift of $25 million. The major impasse was administrative. Cohen and Hanson wanted this to be an autonomous institution, under Leif's control, affiliated with, but not totally under the jurisdiction of, the University of the Southwest.

Mr. Cohen, who was a widower and childless, maintained a suite at the Warwick Hotel, which he was too sick to occupy. He had been in Houston for almost two weeks "waiting for his heart" at University Hospital. Clay vigorously resisted the idea of Cohen or anyone else having a heart transplant. And during this period, the law of supply and demand prevailed where Clay's arguments failed. The only donors in several weeks had been the child released by

Cooley to Hanson and the adult under DeBakey's control. The problem of finding donors to satisfy the need of recipients had been predictable, and was now acute. So Cohen waited for his heart, a shell of what must have once been a most dynamic man. Shell is not entirely correct. Heart failure bloated his belly and legs with fluid. He was also another example of what happens when the heart cannot get enough blood to the brain. Frequently he had trouble completing a sentence. Sometimes from shortness of breath. More often because his mind wandered.

One evening Cohen said to Leif, who visited his hospital room regularly, "A hundred and eighty-seven."

Leif didn't know the significance of the statement. He said, "I beg your pardon."

Cohen had to catch his breath. "That's a hundred and eighty-seven ambulance sirens since I've been here." Several more labored breaths. "Each time I wonder . . . is it bringing a heart for me?"

On a night in early September, Seymour Cohen's heart arrived at the emergency room inside a young man with a gunshot wound to the head. Ambulance siren number 241. A vigorous battle with the coroner over the ownership of the young man's heart ensued. If his brain was dead from a gunshot wound, he was a homicide victim and belonged to the coroner. But Leif Hanson was not going to let a young and vigorous heart go to waste because of the legal technicality that the victim was a coroner's case.

Leif also faced another front of opposition: Clay Ducharme. "First, we shouldn't be doing another transplant." Clay accosted Leif by the elevator outside the ER. "But if you persist, we've got five people who are better matches than Cohen for that heart. Five desperate patients. And one appears to be our best match ever."

"I've promised Mr. Cohen," Leif said.

"Just tell him the truth. This isn't a good match."

"Same as Ford." Leif pushed the elevator call button.

"It's a lousy match, just like Ford."

"Ford's heart's been doing fine for eight months."

"He's doing miserably."

"Bullshit." Leif punched the button again.

"You don't know," Clay argued. "You don't even see him once a week."

"Not true."

"The hell it's not."

"The heart goes to Cohen." The elevator door snapped open and Leif stamped inside.

"Cohen can live for weeks." Clay joined him. "Our good match is like Mike Goldman was. He's on an I.V. drip of lidocaine. He could die tonight."

"Bottom line: my mind is made up, Clay."

"Who the hell do you think you are?" Clay shouted. "The great God Hanson? Walking through the halls of this hospital and placing your healing hands on whoever strikes your fancy? I choose you to live, Seymour Cohen. And I condemn you to die, John Doe. What sort of crap is this?" The door opened with a clap and Clay thundered out of the elevator and turned left towards the transplant suite.

"If you want to do something good for Seymour Cohen, why don't you let us use your god-damned induction of tolerance for animal transplants?" Leif walked briskly beside Clay.

"Because it's years from being perfected."

"We don't have years. Time's running out on our program—and you tell me years," Leif said. "I can't wait any longer. Don't you understand? I'm giving you fair warning right now. I'm going to do animal transplants or something equally dramatic, and I'm going to do it soon. With or without your help or blessing."

"You'll just have to," Clay shot back.

Two weeks after Seymour Cohen's transplant surgery, the Cohen Institute for Cardiovascular Research came into being under the directorship of Leif Harald Hanson (as an affiliate of the University of the Southwest) with an initial contribution of $22 million and an eventual endowment estimated at almost $100 million.

FIFTEEN

The death of Kathy Kelly continued to torment Clay. Now in late September, he would still think of her two or three times a day, while trying to concentrate his energies on the research grant application he had recently rewritten to emphasize prevention of heart disease. He had also had three lengthy, but unsatisfactory, meetings with Leif on the future course of heart transplantation at Southwest. In the past Clay and Leif had often had heated but ultimately friendly exchanges, usually ending in compromise. And usually resolved through Clay giving in much more than Leif. Not so at the last three meetings.

On the twenty-fourth of September, the National Heart Institute sent sixteen people, professors from other medical schools, on a site visit to spend two days reviewing Clay's application for over $3 million of research funds. Researchers from many departments and divisions at Southwest were coinvestigators on the grant, including the chairmen of biochemistry, pharmacology, and statistics. Leif Hanson and Arthur Johnson were also on the grant. There was even a cell biologist from Baylor—just to give the application a multi-institutional flavor.

The meeting took place in the fruitwood paneled board room of the medical school under the watchful eyes of oil paintings of previous deans. On the first morning of the site visit for a large grant proposal, it was usual for the dean to begin the series of presentations. And the dean spoke forcefully, making it clear that there was no question that this project would be an asset to the medical center. Clay followed with his initial outline of the proposal. The chairman of the department from which the grant originates would be the next presenter.

But Varney did not appear.

Clay announced an early coffee break and immediately phoned the departmental secretary.

"Dr. Varney asked me to tell you, if you called, that he won't be available this morning," she said coolly.

"Thanks a bunch for letting me know in advance."

"He gave specific instructions to wait for your call."

Clay returned to the conference room and arranged for the other department chairmen who were coinvestigators on the grant to talk next. Leif Hanson's presentation was highly effective. Then senior investigators, like Arthur Johnson, spoke. Arthur was at his impressive best. No hint of his recent problems. He did not even smoke during the session. One visitor went on record as saying that Arthur's contribution to the grant as it related to hypertension was clearly one of the strongest points in the proposal. Other investigators followed during the afternoon and next morning.

The site visitors reserved the final hour of the second day for a closed meeting between the entire committee and Clay, the principal investigator. Clay was nervously aware that this was the most sensitive part of the session. He looked at the chairman of the committee. *Really overweight. Not what you'd expect of someone evaluating a grant in preventive cardiology.*

The chairman smiled encouragingly at Clay and nodded for him to begin.

Clay took a deep breath and launched into his summation. He had not spoken more than a few sentences when Varney barged into the meeting and proclaimed, "I am Professor Vincent Varney, chairman of the Department of

Medicine. I was unable to be here yesterday."

"That's quite all right, we know you support this excellent grant proposal," the committee chairman said.

"I need to make this committee aware of some things," Varney persisted. His bristles were combat ready.

"It really won't be necessary, Dr. Varney. We really are getting down to a delicate stage of negotiation." The committee chairman was trying hard to be courteous. "This is supposed to be a closed session between our committee and the principal investigator."

"Well, Mr. Chairman . . ." Varney would not be deterred, "you must be made aware that as department chairman I have no intention of allowing cardiology to take over my department of medicine. We simply don't have the space for a grant of this size."

It took the chairman of the site visit a moment to try to assimilate what Varney was saying. Having apparently decided he understood, he began: "We realize, the entire committee realizes, Dr. Varney, that space is a problem everywhere." The site visit chairman, who is supposed to be the critical evaluator of the application, found himself in the surprising position of having to defend a grant application before the chairman of the department from which it originated. "The committee is really satisfied with the amount of space already available to conduct this research."

"I'm not sure that I can continue to guarantee the amount of space the grant requires." Then Varney returned to a pitch he had used earlier to selected department members. "There are some members of my department who are really so accomplished that they must have programs larger than our department can accommodate."

The site visit chairman was speechless. He fingered the metal frame of his glasses and looked around at the faces of his fellow committee members, seeing shock and disbelief. Finally he offered an irresolute compromise. "The committee understands space problems, and would certainly support a proposal of the principal investigator to rent space near the campus in lieu of overhead."

But the battle was over. A grant that lacks the

support of the department from which it originates cannot be funded. Varney had just shot down the entire financial support for cardiology—and for Clay.

Several close friends of Clay called the next day to ask what was going on at Southwest.

A cardiologist from Pennsylvania called. "How could he let you spend a year on the damned application, put all your grants together in one program of projects, and then destroy them all at the last minute? And how could he waste our time?" At the end of the call, and without even recognizing what he was doing, Clay tore the phone from the wall and hurled it across the room, cracking a panel of the door.

Leif Hanson received similar calls from friends who had been on the site visit committee. Leif asked for a meeting with the dean, where he and Clay found that the dean was less indignant than they had assumed he would be. And he was apparently disinclined to pursue the problem further.

Now it was Arthur's turn to try some consoling when he visited Clay's office. "I'm really sorry, Clay. There are lots of things I'm happy to share with you. But being on Varney's shit-list isn't one of them." Arthur dropped heavily into a chair in front of the desk. "He's out to destroy you as well as me."

"The dean isn't prepared to do anything to the dirty sonavabitch," Clay said.

"What can he do? The grant's already lost."

"He can fire Varney for being an incompetent chairman and a destructive bastard. The guy is tearing up the medical school." Clay came out from behind his desk and sat in the chair opposite Arthur.

"I think the dean's a little afraid of him," Arthur said. "You heard what Varney did this morning?"

"I can't face hearing it."

"You'd better know," Arthur said. "He fired Henry Knoblauch as chief of neurology."

"Oh damn!" Clay twisted out of his chair and began to pace within the confines of the small office.

"Said he hasn't been productive enough in research to provide proper leadership of such an important division as neurology. And, just to put icing on the cake, he charged him with insubordination."

"Insubordination? This isn't the god-damned army!" Clay shouted. "And Henry's doing enough research and writing on his textbook for a hundred papers. . . . I can't believe what's happening . . ."

Arthur kept touching his cigarette pack and looking at Clay's No Smoking sign on the desk.

"Go ahead and smoke," Clay finally said. "I may have to take it up myself."

"No, I can hold out," Arthur took the pack from one pocket, fondled it a moment, and placed it in another pocket. "I guess we've all been wondering why we came here now. I know I have."

"We came because the previous department chairman made fantastic offers. He was trying to build a great department."

"And I think he did."

"Then he resigns. And we get a new chairman." Clay interrupted his pacing to sit on the edge of his desk.

"Who can prepare for these things?" Arthur said. "There was a chance that the new chairman could have been a good one. There was even a chance that Varney could have matured into the job." He now got as far as pulling a cigarette from the pack—but replaced it. "You know what wakes me up at night?"

"What?"

"I keep thinking: what if I'd stayed in Boston? I was director of an immunology program. And associate director of the renal service. I had a nice lab and enough time for research. Now I'm a director of nothing. I came here because I wanted the chance to run a major clinical service. But now I don't run anything."

"Varney can't last," Clay said.

"A new chairman isn't going to bring my reputation back." Arthur again pulled a cigarette from the pack, but crushed this one in his hand and threw it into the waste basket. "You know I've even thought of killing . . ."

"Varney?"

"Yes, except I couldn't figure out how to do it and get away with it." Arthur let out a sound somewhere between a sigh and a grunt. "Then I considered the possibility of a hit man."

Clay watched Arthur shake another cigarette from the pack and said, "Smoke the damned thing."

Instead, Arthur shoved the cigarette back into its package. "But I've decided that Varney isn't worth killing. Percy Foreman allows as how some people in Texas may need killing. Varney needs killing. It's just that he's not worth killing. And I'm not going to allow that man to diminish me further by dwelling on my hatred of him."

A telephone call from his daughter brought the news to Mr. Yancey Melton that he was a grandfather. Clay ordered a bottle of champagne, and an impromptu celebration took place in the green-painted doctors' lounge of the transplant unit—a room furnished in vinyl and Formica with all the style of a bus station.

"Goal number one," Mr. Melton said. "In six hours I'll be seeing my grandson."

"And you'll be seeing other grandchildren . . ." Clay caught himself too late. He was being uncharacteristically expansive—almost sounding like Leif.

"I'm not going to be greedy," Mr. Melton said.

"And your son is in his last year of medical school now. Your second goal is approaching."

"Yes. My son is talking about being a cardiologist."

"I admire his good taste." Clay held his plastic champagne glass up to toast.

"He's a fine young man."

"I know. I've enjoyed meeting with him."

"He's also made a bit of a study of Mr. Faulkner."

"Do you both share the same perceptions about Mr. Faulkner's work?"

"Some." Yancey glanced at the airline tickets in his hand, looked up, and smiled. "Of course, my boy belongs to the decade of the sixties. He perceives Faulkner as being very old guard. He responds to Faulkner's humanity, but feels it didn't go far enough. Not nearly far enough. He considers him a flaming racist, actually."

Clay smiled. "I've got a son of the sixties, too." He he took a sip from the plastic glass. "My son regards me as establishment. And here I thought I was a flaming liberal."

"Our young people are feeling issues of injustice deeply."

"I guess."

"Does your son want to follow your footsteps into medicine?"

"He's hoping to go to Harvard for pre-med."

"You must be very proud of him."

"I am. Very proud."

"Your taxi's here," a nurse interrupted.

Yancey Melton, courtly and reserved in his Old South manners, stood up, hesitated for a moment, and then embraced Clay as he said good-bye.

As he rode in the required wheelchair from the hospital, Mr. Melton carried with him Clay's deep but unexpressed concern for his safety. His rejection had been so difficult to control. And infection was such a constant threat. *But if he can't go home to see his grandson, what's been the point in having a heart transplant?*

Only two hours after Yancey Melton left the hospital, Mike Goldman was readmitted to his old room near the nurses' station, short of breath, his belly getting big from retaining fluid because of his heart failure.

"My pants don't fit anymore," Mike announced as soon as Clay entered the room.

"How long's this been going on?" Clay asked while feeling for Mike's pulse.

"I've had to let my belt out a couple notches today."

"And you didn't keep your appointment yesterday."

"I've been feeling great."

"Or trying to deny. Look, we've got to have an ECG twice a week on schedule. And an LDH."

"It's just that I've been feeling . . ."

"I know you've been feeling great," Clay interrupted. "Now be quiet a second while I listen." Clay placed his stethoscope on Mike's chest.

"Sound OK?"

"A little friction rub. We'll get your ECG now."

Almost two days were required to get this rejection episode under control. *What was it? His third—or fourth?*

It was a subdued Mike Goldman on whom Clay rounded the morning after the worst of the episode had passed. Some of the amenities had been returned to his hospital room—an acknowledgement that this was not to be a short stay. Pictures of his wife and children. Books. TV.

"How you feeling?" Clay opened.

"I'm not going to have to worry about living thirty more years, am I, Clay?" Mike countered.

"What makes you say that?"

"The way I feel. And we both know that now they're rejecting hearts all over the world. You can't pick up the paper without reading about it." Mike smiled pensively. "I could have died this time, couldn't I?"

"I . . . guess so," Clay groped for words.

"It's all right. We've got to be honest. I've got to make plans. Level with me, Clay. As a friend."

"Heart transplantation is a long way from becoming a standard treatment."

"I'm not asking for medical philosophy," Mike said. "I'm asking about me."

"How can I answer that? That's in the movies that the all-wise doctor says, 'You've got six months to live.'"

"I know that."

"Then what do you want?"

"I need a ballpark figure to make plans. If I've got a year or less I'm not going to spend all day in the office. I'm going to stay home till after the kids go to school. And I'm going to be back home when they return. I'm going to be with Becky. And we're going to do some things we've always wanted to."

"Like what?"

"Crazy as it may sound, I've always wanted to learn to play the harmonica. And Becky and I have always wanted to learn to sail a boat. There's something so peaceful about water."

"I see." Clay was not looking directly at Mike. He was trying to appear to be engrossed in reading the latest cardiogram. Finally he said: "Once you get through this episode I don't see why you shouldn't go sailing and learn the harmonica."

"Do you see why I should be in my office from eight in the morning to six at night? Mike tested Clay.

"No," Clay said and began furiously unwinding the roll of ECG.

Mike nodded his head in recognition of the answer. "There. That wasn't hard to say after all. Was it?" Mike didn't wait for a response. "In some ways it seems unfair. But I've been lucky in many ways. There's not a better wife in the world than Becky. Four great kids. And I've just seen my youngest daughter going off to her first day of school, holding her big brother's hand. I never would have seen that if it weren't for the heart transplantation. You know I never would have lived to see that."

"I know."

"And my oldest daughter, Esther. She's got a dance recital coming up in a few weeks. I'm definitely going to be around to see it. She's going to be another Margot Fonteyn. She's a beautiful girl. She and her little sister are going to do a routine to 'Me and My Shadow' that'll knock 'em out."

"Sounds like fun."

"You think you and Betty Sue could come and see them?"

"I'd like that."

"I'm just carrying on like a proud father." Mike smiled. "And I am. I'm so proud of my kids."

"You have every reason to be." Clay waited for Mike to continue.

"I suppose the unfair part is that I'm just beginning to get the hang of life. Just learning how to be a reasonably competent doctor. In fact, I'm just learning how to fix the plumbing in the house. And grow decent roses. More important, I'm just learning to be an acceptable human being." He looked intently at Clay. "It takes so damned long to learn these things. Then by the time you begin to get it together, life is over."

"Most people never get it together no matter how long they live." Clay began rewinding the roll of ECG.

"Maybe. But Becky got it together before she was thirty. My folks got it together. I know you and Betty Sue have got it together." Mike paused to catch his breath, then mumbled, "I'm not sure that Leif Hanson has got it together—or ever will."

"Why do you say that?"

"Something about him. He's never satisfied. Always trying to get one up on DeBakey and Cooley."

"Well, that's the way surgeons are." Clay placed the roll of ECG on the nightstand. "Strange breed of cat. Competitive as hell. Maybe that's why Houston is the heart center that it is. Good healthy competition."

"The people, like me, practicing in town don't think the competition is all that healthy. And some people I know at Baylor and Southwest think the competition is downright sick."

"It's a matter of opinion."

"You know I haven't seen Leif Hanson in months. The most I've seen is his picture in the papers or magazines. Or on TV. Usually with that movie actress, Roxanne Molnar. Seems they're trying to keep up with Barnard dating Gina Lollabrigida. But Leif still averages thirty or forty operations a week. He's quite a man."

"He is," Clay agreed.

"But I don't think he's got it together. I don't think he'll ever be satisfied."

Otto Schneider found out about Yancey Melton going home. Berkowitz had also had a trip home. Mike Goldman was at work most of the time. Even two of the more recent transplantees had left the hospital. Every week Schneider came up with a new demand for discharge. And a new reason. The previous week his reason had been to help start a heart transplantation program for the state of Michigan. Following Mr. Melton's discharge he upped the ante. He had volunteered his services to President Johnson. It was imperative that he leave for Washington immediately.

Clay talked him out of it. The man was hopelessly disoriented. But he was also becoming a nuisance, roaming the wards at night, walking into the rooms of the other patients. He had taken a particular dislike to Fred Berkowitz and was making frequent anti-Semitic statements in his presence.

In fact the nights were becoming progressively more difficult at the hospital for all of the heart transplant patients. Schneider never seemed to sleep at night. Berkowitz and Ford were up a great deal of the night, too. One night when Schneider would not stay in his room, Clay had asked him why he refused to sleep.

His answer was childlike in its simplicity: "I'm afraid I won't wake up. Night is death."

But the next night Schneider's misbehavior escalated to an intolerable level.

"What happened now?" Clay asked the nurse on duty when he arrived on the ward at two in the morning, still groggy after having been awakened from a sound sleep.

"Otto has spray-painted swastikas on the doors of Goldman, Cohen, and Berkowitz. He's also sprayed 'DEATH TO JEWS AND NIGGERS' on the wall around the corner from the nurses' station. And four letter words all over the place." This young blond nurse, a recent graduate of the program at Southwest, looked like someone who should still be going to proms and malt shops, not facing a guerrilla attack on a hospital ward. She was trembling as she talked. "To top it off, he cut eye-holes in a pillow case, wrapped himself in a sheet, and went from room to room like a Ku Klux Klansman. He's completely flipped."

Clay reached for her hand and said, "It's OK, Miss Swanson. I'll take care of things."

Her hand was still trembling.

"It's OK," Clay repeated as he escorted her back to

the nurses' station and patted her shoulder.

"You've got to do something about that nut, Clay," Mike Goldman called from his door.

"You're supposed to be in bed."

"How can you sleep in this madhouse?"

Berkowitz came from his room. "Can you believe it? That man's got to be locked up. What are you going to do?"

"We'll take care of it." Clay took Berkowitz by the arm and walked him into his room.

Now to Schneider. Clay's jaw muscles tightened in the effort to control his anger as he confronted the culprit, who was sitting on his bed. "Mr. Schneider, you can't be allowed to behave this way."

"Why're the Jews getting all the hearts?" Schneider shot back. "Don't worry, I know. And I've wrote President Johnson about this." He jerked his legs up onto the bed without removing his slippers.

"Why do you think . . ." Clay paused. He was going to try to reason with him. Try to enter Schneider's mad *Gestalt* and reason with him. But he abandoned the undertaking and said, "What are you bucking for? A section eight?"

Otto exploded into a laugh. "Section eight," he repeated.

"Why are you acting this way? The other patients can't sleep."

"The hell witha other patients." Schneider jiggled his legs on the bed.

"Well, then I can't sleep."

"The hell with you, too," Otto said and looked directly at Clay.

"Is it that you're trying to get home?" Clay had all he could do to ignore the aggression.

"I gotta go to Washington first."

"Then home?"

"Maybe." Schneider crossed and uncrossed his legs.

"You've never told me about your home. You live right in Detroit?"

"Right in Detroit."

"A house?" Clay sat heavily in the bedside chair.
"My own house. And it's all paid for."
"That's great, Otto." Clay's tone was more relaxed now, but he was still seething inside.
"All paid for."
"That's always a great accomplishment."
"I worked for it."
"I'm sure you did."
"Nobody ever gave me nothing. No nigger welfare."
"I'm sure you worked hard."
"You know I once worked eleven straight years without a day off."
"That's something."
"I mean I never even had a Saturday or a Sunday or a vacation off."
"That's really a long spell." Clay was willing to accept the statement, as hard as it was to believe.
"Then I had my first heart attack. But I had my house paid for."
"Nice neighborhood?" Clay asked absently.
"Used to be."
Clay waited.
"I gotta see what's happening to it."
Clay waited.
"A nigger moved next door."
Clay tried to play it down. "That's good for balanced schools. Honest open housing."
"That's good for shit," Otto said. "What d'you know? Where d'you live?"
"Right near here."
"Niggers next door?"
"No."
"Then what do *you* know? I worked my ass off. Gotta beautiful house. Beautiful yard. Nice lawn. Good neighbors. Thirty thousand dollar house. Got it paid for. And then my neighbor—s'posed to be my friend—moves to Arizona. House just like mine. But not half paid for. He sells for fifty and moves to Arizona."
"Anyone else sell?"

"A guy across the street. House like mine. He didn't keep his yard up, though. Sold it for thirty-five to a nigger dentist and he moves out to Farmington Hills."

"But look, blacks who can pay that kind of money for a house are going to be a cut above whites who could pay the same. They'll be professional people, educated, interesting. They'll help the neighborhood, not hurt it." Clay stopped abruptly. What the hell was he doing, he asked himself, acting as if he did not know about block-busting?

Otto looked at him with a look that said it all. Pity, if he were that stupid. Contempt. "The week before I came down here . . ." he started talking in a tone one would reserve for transmitting simple information to a small child, "I got a offer on my house. I wasn't trying to sell. The same Jew-boy real estate crook offered me twenty-two." Otto sat there on his bed, looking at Clay. "I gotta go back and see if we should sell. My wife's worried."

Clay could have argued, thrown a few more standard liberal pitches at him. But what was the point? There would have to be another meeting with the psychiatrists to see what could be done for Otto Schneider. Could they put him through the ordeal of a heart transplant and then lock him up in a rubber room? Now that would be some accomplishment for this new miracle of modern medicine!

Clay retreated from the ward and shuffled through semi-dark corridors to his hospital office. Three in the morning. Too late to go back to bed. No way to get to sleep now. In fact, even in the absence of calls from the hospital, he had found himself waking up in the middle of the night more and more lately. Worrying. The worrying had begun gradually, about three weeks after the first heart transplant, and had kept building until it was now a central reality of his life. Just like Arthur Johnson. Waking and worrying. Even exhausting work could not guarantee sleep. He pulled a stack of electrocardiograms from a basket and began to read them and dictate the findings.

Between tracings his mind escaped from the discipline of the task at hand. Worrying about the patients. Of course. But now worrying about his job. Trying to figure a way to get some smaller grants to keep his program together. What a mistake it had been to put the large program project grant together. So many jobs in his division had depended on it. And he never even considered the possibility that Varney would sabotage the grant. But if Varney could destroy a big grant, he could do the same to any other grant that Clay would submit in the future.

Clay tried to concentrate on the next electrocardiogram. But he kept thinking: why did he ever take this job at Southwest? Would he have to pick up and move? Just to satisfy that bastard Varney? No! Houston was his home! Clay dictated the report on the electrocardiogram in hand: a recent inferior infarct. But the screws were tightening. Maybe he could look into a position at Baylor. They had their political problems there, too. Yet things were more in the open. Cooley and DeBakey could be at each other's throats. But they were just going for the throat. Arthur had it figured out, all right. At Southwest, they preferred to go for the soul.

Here they were at the most exciting period in the history of science, a period when people like Leif and the people at NASA felt that anything was possible, that the sky was the limit. And where were their energies invested? In senseless battles. Power plays. Struggles for dominance. Hanson and Varney and maybe DeBakey and Cooley might get turned on by these intellectual equivalents of warfare, but Clay was poorly suited for such struggles. And so was Arthur Johnson. *If we could just be left alone to do our work.* Clay slammed the next electrocardiogram on the desk. *Hell! They won't leave you alone. How naive can a forty-two year old man still be? They won't ever leave you alone.*

The only potential source of light in the cave of despair in which Clay seemed to be hopelessly wandering was glowing faintly from some recent experiments. After five years of trying to develop the methods for inducing tolerance across species barriers, he was at last getting long-term survivals of mouse hearts in the ears of rats.

The thoughts began to spin as in a centrifuge: *Work like hell . . . maybe in two more years—a breakthrough.*

Spinning: *Except now that Varney's screwed us, almost no time for research. Got to write new grants.* Spinning: *See Leif again. Stop transplants. Then restart with something worthy of a Nobel.*
Really start fighting. No more appeasing Varney. But keep the damned Ducharme temper in check. No more broken phones.

SIXTEEN

Shortly before midnight, Leif locked up his laboratory and went out to the parking lot where his new Porsche now occupied the hospital's premier parking place. He had been trying all day to reach Clay to talk. Of course he had seen the housekeeping staff scouring away the graffiti Schneider had painted in the transplant suite the previous night. Schneider's escapade had then prompted Sellery to discharge Otto in the morning, without consultation, and before he or Clay could object or countermand the order. Leif was certain that Clay would still be infuriated over the discharge, and would need a little soothing. He also recognized that Sellery was really doing what Leif most wanted—even though he would have opposed the move if he had been asked. Otto would be all right at home for a few days. After all he was in the best physical shape of all the patients. Maybe he would calm down away from the hospital.

And there were more important matters to discuss with Clay. He wanted to tell Clay that he was working on a mechanism to provide temporary funding of Clay's program through the Cohen Institute. He would be willing to help with no strings attached—as a friend. And, as a friend, Clay might also be willing to bend a little on opening up his research on the induction of tolerance for animal transplants. Not a cold marketplace trade-off. Just friend helping friend.

So after missing connections all day long, who was standing in the faculty lot inspecting the new red Porsche parked next to Clay's dusty tan VW? Clay Ducharme.

Leif came up behind Clay and said, "Want a ride?"

"Is this yours? A little Porsche? How do you fit?"

"Plenty of room in the cockpit."

What happened to your Mercedes?"

"Still got it," Leif said.

"This is a beauty. Kind of makes my Volkswagen look tacky."

"You don't have to drive a VW." Leif unlocked the door.

Clay slid into the front seat. Soft glove leather. "Now that's a new car smell," he said.

Leif got behind the wheel. "Remember when we were residents, joking about ending up as frayed-collar, Nash-driving academicians? Well, our collars aren't frayed. And at least I've been willing to buy the kinds of cars I want." He shut his door—a solid sound. "Why don't we go to my house for a drink?" Leif turned on the ignition.

"Hell, Leif, it's midnight. Maybe you and DeBakey can thrive on four hours of sleep, but I can't. With the Schneider crap, I got almost no sleep last night. And then that nut who works for you sends him home."

"Calm down. Let me talk to Sellery about it."

"You'd better. He wouldn't listen to me anyway. But he's a loose cannon. You've got to get him under control."

"I will, Clay. He means well. Good intentions."

"He's still a menace." Clay stroked the dashboard and surveyed the interior. "It's a beautiful car. But can you tell me what the hell we're doing out here at midnight?"

"Working. That's what we were put on this earth for, wasn't it?"

"Leif, we're all screwed up with this clinical transplant business. We've got to cut our losses and get back to basic research before it's too late. And I've got to spend my time working on new grants. Let's have a two year moratorium—and then we can restart the program with induction of tolerance."

Leif began backing the Porsche out of the parking lot. "Remind me to talk about grants with you."

"Why?"

"Just remind me."

"Where do you think you're going?"

"First, let's talk about transplant antigen and transplanting pig hearts to humans."

"Not tonight!"

"Just an hour, Clay," Leif aimed the Porsche towards River Oaks, ten minutes away. "It's an exciting scientific challenge." He turned on Kirby. There was almost no traffic at this time of night.

"God knows I want heart transplantation to succeed. I've got a big emotional and professional investment in it. But my thinking is changing. I realize that there are far more important things in medicine than trying to salvage a few hopelessly damaged hearts."

"Like?"

"How about getting adequate nutrition and minimal hygiene for a billion people? Or for heart disease, how about preventing the damage in the first place? Over a million cardiovascular deaths a year in America. And we're screwing around with something that can help only a few hundred a year, at most."

"Not if we go into xenografts. We could raise pigs for medical as well as nutritional needs—an unlimited supply of donor hearts."

"Two years, if we work like hell on it. Maybe a year to trying pig hearts in dogs or baboons."

"Too long, Clay. Not nearly soon enough. . . . Then how about the artificial heart? DeBakey's got those calves over at Baylor with plastic hearts in them. And they look good."

"The calves only survive a few months. And would you like to spend your life with a hose coming out of your chest hooked up to a refrigerator-sized air compressor?"

"It doesn't always have to be a big hose and a big air

compressor. For godsake, the space program is miniaturizing everything."

"Well, when that technology is all refined so that there are hundreds of cows peacefully grazing on the hillsides with miniature atomic hearts beating inside them, let me know."

Leif slowed down as he entered the exclusive residential neighborhood called River Oaks. The oaks were mostly live oaks with small dark leaves that survived the year round. Many trees sported luxuriant beards of moss. A chauffeur-driven limousine was the only other car within sight. It turned abruptly into a long palm-lined driveway.

"Remember a guy named Haupt?" Leif asked. "Took a year of training with me a few years back. Developed a heart model all on his own. Like the one in DeBakey's calves. Had it before he worked for DeBakey. Also had it while he was working for me. And now he's working in Chicago."

"I remember now. His heart model never got off the ground."

"Off the ground now. Haupt's calves are living with the hearts working in them." Leif turned left into a curving lane in which only trees and gate houses were visible from the street. "The big problems in these damned plastic hearts have been the valves and the clotting. Well, maybe you'll grant me that the Hanson valve has turned out to be one of the better designs around." He slowed down for a cat wandering across the traffic-free street.

"I'll grant you that."

"Better record as far as clotting problems. So we redesign the Haupt artificial heart and put modified Hanson valves in it and we have a new artificial heart that's strictly our own ."

"Why not wait until DeBakey's people perfect it?"

"Because, damn it, this is where I've made my commitment. I'm going to make animal transplants work. Or I'm going to make artificial hearts work. Can't you understand?"

"These things take time if you want to do them right. And there are more important medical problems. Can't *you* understand? And there are people problems right here that also need attention."

"Like?"

"Varney."

"He's a lightweight." Leif smiled. "A *fat* little lightweight."

"Don't count on it. For the first time he's got me really worried. I'm having serious trouble sleeping now. A god-damned sleep disorder like Arthur's."

"Varney will hang himself."

"He may hang us first," Clay insisted. "How the hell am I going to fund my division?" Clay was rubbing his temples. "Did you have any more talks with the dean about my grant problem?"

Leif smiled, knowing he had an answer to the first question. But he responded to the second. "I talked to the dean."

"Well, what did he tell you?"

"Varney made good sense as far as the dean was concerned. For the good of a balanced medical school, you can't let one area become so big that it squeezes out everything else. Cardiology is too big. It needs to be cut back."

"And you accepted that crap?"

"Hell no. But I accept that Varney always covers his ass. And as far as the dean was concerned, his ass was covered in this."

"Is the dean just going to let this go on until Varney brings the whole damned school down?"

"He's a little afraid of Varney." Leif now turned at his street in River Oaks.

"Hey, let's get back. We've had our talk. I've got to get home."

"Just a quick one." Leif pressed the radio control button to open the tall iron gate and the Porsche rolled past the gatehouse onto the imposing grounds of Gray Rocks. The house itself rose like a Gothic cathedral at the end of the winding driveway.

Clay said, "Your house always reminds me of

Sterling Library. You been in all the rooms yet?"

"Every one."

"The American dream," Clay injected a full syringe of sarcasm.

"What any other poor boy can achieve if he makes two million . . ." Leif stopped in mid-sentence. "Scratch that last remark."

Of course, rumors abounded that Leif and Cooley and DeBakey each collected somewhere around two or three million a year. But those were just educated guesses.

Leif unlocked the heavy oak door. A dry air-conditioned blast met them at the interface with the humid air from the outside. They closed the humidity out. "The bar's open," Leif said, as he led Clay down an oak paneled hall to what in lesser houses might have been called a family room, also oak-paneled, and with a floor-to-ceiling stone fireplace.

Elaine's voice called to Leif, "Did my vagrant Viking decide to come home tonight?" She etched the words in acid. "What happened? Did your blonde throw you out early?"

"I've got Clay with me." Leif sounded a warning. "Besides I was home for supper. Didn't anyone tell you?"

They entered the baronial recreation room to find Elaine sitting at the bar, on a maroon leather stool, which clashed a shade off from her bright magenta hostess pants outfit. She was slim and tan and more than a little drunk. "What, you needed to bring protection home tonight?" She slurred her words only slightly.

"Not at all," Leif said guardedly. "We've been working on some problems. You know how busy we've been since we started the transplantation program."

"*You've* sure been busy." Elaine etched another line.

"Gin and tonic?" Leif asked Clay.

"That would be fine."

"You know how many nights your good friend from Yale has spent in this house since the first of January?" Elaine asked.

"Clay knows how many nights heart transplantation has taken up. He's spent enough of them with me."

"I was speaking to Clay," she said. "Do you know

how many nights?"

"I certainly agree. Leif has to spend a lot of nights in the hospital," Clay said the words awkwardly.

"Bullshit," Elaine slurred. "Bullshit," she repeated. "I'm giving him credit for tonight. It's before one o'clock. This is his eighty-fifth night at home." She pointed her martini glass at Leif. "I guess eighty-five out of 280-some *ain't* bad."

Leif handed Clay a drink, which he swallowed half of immediately.

Elaine stood up. She towered about six-four in the heels she was wearing. "I'll now leave you two to hatch up whatever plots you might have in mind to hatch up. Maybe you can form a cartel and corner the *lutefisk* market." Elaine swayed a little on her first step and then did the fashion model slink across the room. She did not bother to look back.

Leif swirled the ice cubes of his gin and tonic.

"She's counting the nights," Clay said.

"I see she is."

"I'm afraid you're in trouble."

"The American dream," Leif said.

SEVENTEEN

It was almost nine months since the first heart transplant had been performed in Houston. During this entire period Clay had not had a night or weekend off. Clay remembered how his father had often made the point that when starting out in family practice he had not had a night or weekend off in the first five years. Never mind that back then his father was only seeing five to ten patients a day— the majority of whom he could help only a little. Things were different now. There were ever-present pagers to seek you out wherever you might wish to find solitude. And Clay desperately needed solitude. Away from the pager. Away from the phone. Away from the patients. And mostly away from contentious colleagues.

As devoted as he had been to his aerobic running and to all other aspects of personal health, Clay had even been unable to participate in minimal exercise for several months. He decided that now with Mike Goldman stabilized, with Yancey Melton home for a few days, and with his own resources almost totally depleted, he would take Saturday and Sunday off for self-renewal and family-renewal. There were bridges to his children and even to Betty Sue that had fallen into disrepair. He had to stop thinking about what had happened to his grant. And what might be happening to his career.

For Saturday they would drive down to Galveston. Catch some crabs. Picnic on the beach. And Clay would run along the beach with Andy. Reactivate his exercise program. Then home to bed early. On Sunday, yard work, more bridge-building with the family, and lots of sleep.

Of course Clay was concerned about who would be able to take care of the patients, but Leif assured him that he and Frank Sellery and Wendell Eck, who had just been promoted to associate director of cardiology under Clay, could manage fine. Leif further assured Clay that he would keep a short leash on Sellery. And if they had any problems they would call on Arthur Johnson.

The time spent at the beach with Andy proved to be a high point for Clay. They talked of happy memories and of making new memories. They discussed justice and injustice, science and history and literature and trying to get into Harvard.

"There'll be no problem there," Clay said. "As I've told you before, you're a lot smarter than I am, and I got in." Clay picked up a flat rock and winged it for three bounces off the water. "What do you want your major to be?"

"Probably biology. It's a good major for pre-med. But I'd like to take a lot of English courses."

"You sure you want pre-med?"

"It's a family tradition." Andy flipped a rock and got four bounces.

"You could always break with the tradition." Clay stopped at an inlet where they had caught crabs on their last visit to Galveston.

"No. It's a good tradition. I really want to help people."

"Medical school interviewers tend to shy away from candidates who say they want to help people."

"Why?"

Clay stuck his hand into the plastic bucket feeling for two pieces of bait. "Helping people can burn you out. Better to emphasize your love of science. Loving and caring for people could eventually break your heart."

"Is your heart broken?"

"Not yet. But sometimes it comes close."

"I guess I'll have to take that chance then." Andy finished tying some salt pork onto his line and cast the bait out as far as the thick cord would reach.

When Clay arrived back at work on Monday, he found that Sellery had been at it again. His discharging Schneider without seeking a word of consultation should have forewarned Clay as to what could happen over the weekend. First thing Saturday morning, Sellery had drastically altered the carefully regulated regimens of anti-rejection drugs on the inpatients. At the nurses' station, Clay leafed through the order book, swearing under his breath. *Damn it! So this is an example of Leif keeping a short leash on Sellery. Damn it.* And for some reason, Yancey Melton had returned early from Mississippi and was unwilling to talk with anyone but Clay about the reason for it. This much was known, while at home he had developed a cold sore on his lip. And now he had several cold sores. Clay left a message with the operating room supervisor to ask Sellery to call him or drop by his office.

Sellery did not return Clay's call or attempt to see him at his office. So Clay sought and found the elusive Sellery in the surgical outpatient department. "I've been trying to get hold of you all day," Clay began while standing in the door to Frank's office—a painful disharmony of wood and metal furnishings. The walls appeared to be covered with every certificate Sellery had ever received from pre-school to post-doctoral training.

"I know, I tried several times to callya back," Sellery said unconvincingly.

"If you've been looking at any of the order sheets, you'll see that I've returned to the original dosage schedules," Clay said just above a whisper because of the proximity of Sellery's secretary outside the open door. "It was kind of hard to figure out what you were trying to accomplish. You cut the immunosuppressants abruptly on everyone except Melton."

"Well, I think that they should be on practically no immune suppressants if they're gonna return to a normal life."

"Damn, this is really scary," Clay said in a normal tone as the secretary moved away to her desk and Clay stepped entirely inside the office. "Look, I've been trying my damnedest to reduce dosages systematically. And I've been using every clinical and laboratory clue we possess to make a decision on each patient." Clay was trying unsuccessfully to speak with restraint. He closed the door behind him. "You've just screwed everything up without considering the clinical evidence or the general protocol."

"All right. I did what I thought was best," Sellery snapped. "What I'd really like to see is stopping all the immune suppressants on half the patients and keeping the other half on their drugs. I mean, what the hell d'we know for sure about rejection of the heart in the human?"

"Heart transplant patients are now dying all over the world from rejection," Clay was almost shouting.

"I don't know that rejection has been documented," Sellery countered.

Clay had been through so many of these fruitless discussions with Frank Sellery. "I can't believe this. You're talking about repeating animal experiments in humans, just to see if half the humans will die the same way half the animals died?"

"We don't know that the humans will die."

"You're a menace, Sellery. You know that? Something's got to be done about you."

"Just look out for yourself." Sellery slammed a folder onto his desk, stiffened to his feet, and strode aggressively past Clay to the door. "I've gotta go to the recovery room."

Clay stood there alone for a moment, wanting to explain to Sellery about Melton. Because of his herpes cold sore, if there was any one of the patients who *had* needed a rapid reduction in immunosuppressants, it was Yancey Melton. But Sellery had apparently overlooked him after his return from Mississippi. Clay had to see Mr. Melton again.

Clay and Yancey were used to talking at night on the frequent occasions when Clay would have to return to the transplant suite to reassure some of the patients. The bright light of day could hold back the terror of death. But as the night-shadows would appear, the size of the terror would expand until the darkness would become one great shadow of terror. Yancey Melton, however, was not one of those who experienced night terrors. He would usually be awakened by the commotion and would call to Clay as he was leaving. Then they would talk, sometimes of Mississippi, often of Faulkner.

"I've just had a weekend off, too," Clay opened. "Was it hot in Davis Landing?"

"Davis Landing gets some good Gulf breezes." Yancey Melton was not his usual outgoing self. And rather than remaining in street clothes, he had returned to bed. His face was round and flushed.

"Could I see your mouth again?" Clay asked.

"Two more new ones since this morning." Melton pointed to the new cold sores as Clay gently directed the tongue blade and light to study the lesions.

"Tomorrow we're going to get some new antiviral medicine from M.D. Anderson Hospital," Clay said. "It'll fix you right up."

"I know you'll do your best." Yancey extended his hand towards the bedside chair, inviting Clay to sit.

Clay was happy to get off his feet. "You know, I'm sorry," he said, "we've been worrying so about those crazy cold sores, I haven't even asked about your grandson."

Mr. Melton waited a moment before answering softly, "He died before I got home."

Dear Jesus, Clay thought, *so that's why*. He should have known something like that had changed Melton's mood. "I'm so sorry," he said.

"His lungs. Hyaline membrane disease, they called it," he said the words so quietly Clay could hardly hear.

Clay bent forward to ask: "They couldn't get him to New Orleans or Jackson in time?"

"I guess not."

"Your daughter's young," Clay offered a little glibly. "There's plenty of time to have as many more kids as she wants."

"I hope so."

"You're not to worry." Clay perceived how ineffectual he was being. He sat in awkward silence for a moment before squeezing Yancey's arm and quietly withdrawing.

The likelihood that Yancey Melton would survive to see a grandchild was now seriously in doubt in Clay's mind. By trying to suppress rejection they were walking a tightrope across the chasm of a biological law. On either side was disaster. And the tightrope was getting slack.

The next morning while Leif was in the operating room, Clay took a long distance phone call for him from Detroit. Schneider was dead. He had stuck a shotgun against his chest, pushed the trigger with his toe, and blown a fist-sized hole into his heart. Clay rushed from the corridor phone, where he had taken the message, to reach Leif from the privacy of his office.

Within five minutes Leif had finished his case and returned Clay's call from his OR cubicle. "He was our best chance for a long-term survivor," Leif said. "A good match. Our best chance."

"His wife said he was despondent about his house and his neighborhood. Also Berkowitz let him know who his donor was. Otto told his wife he found out he had a Jew-heart in him."

"This really shoots our program," Leif said.

"And Mr. Melton has about twenty sores in his mouth this morning. I've never seen herpes invade so fast."

"I'm really sorry to hear that," Leif said. "But . . . we're still the most successful. Nine of twelve alive."

"DeBakey just lost one, but he also did two more last week. He's got four out of five alive."

"And the whole medical school under his thumb to make his program a success," Leif added. "What's the score on Cooley?"

"He lost a couple of kids last month. One he tried to

do both a heart and lung transplant on."

"But what's the total?"

"He's got six out of ten still alive," Clay said. "Denton screwed himself on those last two cases. He would have had six of eight alive. Then he tried two kids."

"Well, we've got to have someone to replace Melton when he dies."

Clay started to add something. Then he stopped and shook his head. "My God, what are we saying? Do you hear what we're saying over this damned phone? Listen to us. What the hell are we talking about?"

"I'm talking about trying to keep this program going. I'm talking about working my ass off. We can't lose our momentum now."

"No. We're not just talking momentum. Numbers. Escalation. Body counts." He banged his fist on the desk, which caused the phone bell to resonate. "This has become a blood sport. Nothing to do with healing or science. What the hell has happened to us? And what's happened to human dignity?"

"Don't pull human dignity on me. What's so dignified about coming in here, clutching for life, and have it slip away while we putter around in our laboratories? This is a battle to be won. And I'm going to win it."

"No matter how many people have to be sacrificed?" Clay asked softly.

"That's right," Leif said. "No matter *who* is sacrificed."

"I'm getting the picture." As he replaced the phone in its cradle, he muttered: "Damn, am I getting the picture."

Clay returned home tense and despairing—but at least he was at home for supper to spend some quality time with his family Despite all the crises at work, here, with his family, was where the meaning to his life resided.

Then came a problem. It began innocently enough. Melanie burped, excused herself, and laughed, saying that she and some of her girlfriends had been having burping contests during the lunch hour at school. And that she was getting pretty good at it.

Andy said, "Gross. Disgusting."

It occurred to Clay that he had not been interacting as much with Melanie as he had with Andy, so he announced: "When I was in the army, I was a champion burper. And I can easily out-burp anyone in this family any day of the week."

A perfectly innocent—and perfectly stupid—beginning for a family crisis.

The challenge was immediately accepted. And the burping began in earnest.

"This is really crude," Andy protested.

But the gulping of iced tea and the swallowing of air—and the burping—continued until the phone rang. Betty Sue answered. It was their minister's wife.

Suddenly Andy let out a howl of rage.

Apparently Melanie had made a face at Andy—an expression of self-satisfaction at having enlisted the support of Clay in this generally unacceptable activity.

Andy began to scream at his sister while Betty Sue and Clay tried to quiet him to be able to carry on the phone conversation.

Clay knew that the screaming was coming through clearly to the minister's wife. "Please leave the kitchen," he said softly.

Andy refused.

Clay demanded: "Leave the kitchen."

Andy continued to refuse.

"This is my house and you'd damned well better behave before I knock you across the room."

Andy lunged out of the kitchen. And within a minute a shattering noise came from upstairs.

Melanie called out: "Andy just kicked in the door to the hall closet."

After the phone call was over, Clay and Betty Sue surveyed the damaged door before going to Andy's room.

"You've got to learn better control," Betty Sue began.

"You have one of these rage reactions every couple

of years. I'd thought you'd grown out of them," Clay added.

"This is serious." Betty Sue went to put an arm around Andy, but he pulled abruptly away. "These out-of-control rages could get you into serious trouble some day."

"I've learned rage from my father. Maybe even inherited it," Andy said.

"Wha-a-at?" Clay yelled.

Andy turned to Clay. "I'm never going to let you manhandle me again. I can't wait to get out of YOUR house and get to college."

How could Clay sleep that night? When had he manhandled Andy? Certainly Clay had a temper he was always struggling to control. Yet he felt he had never been more physical towards Andy than any of the best of fathers who cherish their children.

But that's not what matters. What matters is what Andy feels. And Andy feels differently about it. Andy is . . . a Billy Budd. Such perfection that the "Arch Interferer" can't allow it. So he's been burdened with the flaw of rage reactions. Damn it, a potentially fatal flaw. Could get himself killed. Says he gets the flaw from me. And he may be right. The damned Ducharme temper. That got the first André into a fatal duel. . . . Dear God, I'm not only failing at work, I'm failing at home. I'm failing my son.

To hell with work. To hell with heart transplants. To hell with Leif. To hell with grants. And to hell with that goddamned Varney. What counts is my family. To hell with all the rest.

Oh Andy, don't you know I love you more than my own life?

Seymour Cohen died. Only a few weeks after surgery. Poor tissue match. His death required an immediate strategy meeting around the oak table in Leif's office. Clay wearily took a chair next to Leif and ran a finger across a now familiar nick in the beveled edge.

"Bottom line: our transplant program is about to die

with our patients," Leif began to address this *Nightwatch* assembly of grim faces. "Frankly, gentlemen, I'm getting desperate. We've got to do something fast. So I want us to think of two new possibilities. One or the other of these will be put into play by *this* team in the very near future. *Repeat*, very near future."

"We sure need something new." Sellery came in on cue as if he had been rehearsing.

"One is animal hearts to man through the induction of tolerance or some other new immunologic technique. And two is . . ." Leif nodded towards Haupt, "two is the artificial heart. Most of you remember Gerhardt Haupt when he was on our service. He's now a new member of our team."

"Sure, good to havya back in Houston, Gerry," was Sellery's greeting.

Haupt was short and muscular with tightly curled blond hair and of an age that was difficult to assess. Perhaps forty. "Good to be back," he spoke with a slight accent.

"Dr. Haupt is going to head our new artificial heart program. Dr. Johnson is developing some new antisera from thymus, which may be our new immunologic technique. And Dr. Sellery and I are going to start working with large animals to get the surgical bugs out of cross-species heart transplants. And I guess we'll just hope that Dr. Ducharme and his group will progress sufficiently in induction of tolerance to make that a viable option as well."

Arthur said nothing.

Clay nodded his head slowly and negatively, but also said nothing. And no one acknowledged his lack of agreement.

After the meeting Clay was joined by Wendell Eck, walking down the hall and up one flight to Clay's office. They had no sooner seated themselves when Varney walked in unannounced. Since there was no chair for him except the one behind Clay's desk, he remained standing by the door. "I have solved the problem of rejection," he proclaimed matter-of-factly.

"Oh, my God," was Clay's initial response.

He knew how he and Leif had just been struggling with the problem. *And in waltzes this stupid ass, announcing he's solved it.* Clay used all the self-restraint he could muster to say, "I didn't realize you were working on it."

"It's about time someone started working on it," Varney jabbed.

Clay prepared to counterpunch, but Wendell Eck jumped in with: "We'd certainly like to hear about it, sir." Eck's tone was most conciliatory. "Here, why don't you take my chair."

"I'd first like to have a commitment that you will use my protocol on your next heart transplant." Varney seated himself grandly in the worn tweed chair. "In fact it may not be too late to use it on some of your present patients. Today, even. I'm sure Cohen would have benefited from it."

"Obviously I can't give a commitment until I know what the protocol is."

Varney was hedging. "I got the new chief of my renal division and his kidney transplant people to use it, and they're sold on it. Varney looked at Eck and then at Clay. "I guess I have a witness here to document where the protocol came from." He handed a sheet of paper to Clay.

Clay glanced at it and said, "Cytoxan? That's your breakthrough?"

"I've been studying the literature extensively and talking with pharmacologists and immunologists," Varney said. "It has properties far superior to Imuran, and I'm surprised that it isn't used in heart transplantation."

"But it is used," Clay said. "Arthur suggested it when Mike Goldman was having his second rejection episode. Mike's been on it for several months. Cohen *was* on Cytoxan. Cooley's group uses Cytoxan in some of their patients. It seems to have *slight* advantages in *some* of the patients, but no consistent advantage over Imuran." Clay tried, unsuccessfully, not to have his words assume the tone of a lecture. "And it really doesn't come close to solving the problem of rejection."

"You've been using Cytoxan?" Varney asked Eck directly.

"Yes. Yes, we have, sir."

Varney reached over and took the page of protocol back from Clay. He offered a thin bristly smile and pushed out of the chair. "That's one for you."

"Small consolation," Clay said. "Christians, one. Lions, how-the-hell many?"

That produced a broader smile from Varney as he waddled from the office.

Clay didn't speak immediately after the encounter. But when he put his thoughts together he said, "I think that little scene captures what goes on in ninety percent of medical research. A new gimmick, a new drug, a new machine, a new operation comes along and what do we do? Try it out on some poor unsuspecting patients."

"But the drugs and operations and gimmicks were developed to be used in patients. That's the whole purpose."

"And when the gimmick doesn't work, or does great harm, who pays?"

"I guess we all do." Eck shrugged his shoulders.

"No. The patient is the one who really pays. Can we go back and replace Mr. Melton's old heart to see if it won't work better than the transplant?"

"Not when it's pickled in a jar," Eck said. "But then how do you get any progress? Chances have to be taken. Some sacrifices have to be made."

"I'm familiar with that argument. And I don't have the answer, except to say that there's a difference between knowledgeable research—and most of the crap that goes on in medicine today. Crap that's no more profound than let's try Cytoxan out on a bunch of patients and see if it works. Or let's do heart transplants on humans and see if it works. Or, almost criminally, let's stick an animal heart or an artificial heart into a human and see if that works. Right out of the horror films. And if it doesn't work—what the hell! It's all for the sake of progress. Science."

"What can I say?"

"I'm beginning to feel like hell about heart transplantation."

"We're just not moving ahead right now."

"That's not it." Clay looked down at the floor and at his hands clutched together in his lap. "I hate to feel like a Third Reich experimenter. Just trying to find out if something works in humans."

"Our patients aren't in concentration camps. They come to us for help. And by God, we're giving it to them. We're doing good."

"We're killing them and charging them for it. And the poor misguided fools don't know it." Clay pounded on the arm of his chair. "They think we care about them. Do they know that most doctors are interested in what's good for their medical careers, first? And what's good for the patients, second?"

"My God, Clay, you really are down. I think you're overworked."

"I know I'm overworked."

Eck uncrossed his thin legs and rose to his feet. "I guess I'd better get back to work."

"We've really got a couple more problems to discuss, if you've got a few minutes."

"Sure." Eck slouched back down into his chair.

"You know that next July all of my grants, except one small one, expire?"

"Vinny-the-snake really stuck it to us, didn't he?"

"No question about it. The problem is I had almost all of the funding for our division tied up together in that one grant. Including most of the salaries. I don't know if you realize that our division runs almost exclusively on my grants, not on hard money."

"That's the way it is most places, isn't it?" Eck's face failed to mirror the concern that Clay was expressing.

"Unfortunately. Everyone lives on soft money. From grants—mainly from the federal government through the NIH. The medical schools have abdicated their responsibilities for funding. And if our grants aren't funded, we've had it."

"But you've got tenure and a full university salary, haven't you?"

"That's right. But I'm the only person in our

division, tenured or otherwise, with a full hard money salary. Everyone else gets part or all of their salaries from my grants. That's more than twenty people, including you."

"Well, he's got funds, as a chairman, to pick up some of these salaries. Mine and a few others."

"Did he tell you your salary was safe?"

"Well, yes. As a matter of fact he did." Eck shifted his weight in the chair.

"Who else has a safe salary?"

"Oh, I don't recall. To be honest I mainly wanted to check on my own salary."

"But he didn't share with you any other plans?" Clay now got to his feet and moved behind his desk, where he seated himself slowly, deliberately—sitting as tall as he could.

"What do you mean?"

"Simple. Ever since Varney became chairman, I've sort of heard his plans secondhand through you."

"Well, we just happen to meet in the hall or something." Eck shifted his weight again.

"You know, I'm really struggling with a problem. I don't know how to handle it. When two people who should both be telling me the truth about the same thing tell me just the opposite—I mean there are allowances to be made for misinterpretations and misunderstandings and shades of meaning—but answers should *not* be directly opposite."

"What are you driving at?"

"Something that happened a couple of years ago. Something that Varney told me. But when I mentioned it to you, you denied it."

"I don't know what you're talking about." Eck changed from his usual subservient tone to a more forceful response. "You're really fighting with everyone today, aren't you?"

"No, I'm confronted with having to come up with large sums of grant money by July. Which means I may have to retreat temporarily from part of my responsibilities—including most of my involvement in transplantation. And that's patient care as well as research."

"So what's this got to do with what we're discussing?"

"I can't put it delicately. So here goes." Clay leaned forward on his desk. "If I'm going to turn over some responsibility to you, I need to know that I can rely on you."

"You can."

"And trust you."

"I don't like the sound of that." Eck started to push out of his chair. "In fact I think I resent it."

"Why don't you sit down and listen to the dilemma," Clay said. "A couple of years ago, when Varney was named chairman—before he even took over the job—he said you came to him and applied for my job."

"That's a lie." Eck sat stiffly at the edge of his chair and glared at Clay.

"So you told me when I brought it up before. And I apologize for reviewing it again. But Varney had this discussion with me in what seemed to be a very sincere manner. Sincere for Varney, anyway. He said: 'Poor old Wendell Eck is trying to find himself and his niche, and he came to me and asked if he couldn't be put in charge of the clinical cardiology service. And leave Ducharme running the research and training.' Apparently because Ducharme could get the grants."

"That's not true. I never went to Varney with such a proposal."

"Well, I told Varney that the clinical and training and other programs couldn't be divided. Varney pushed only a little bit more, saying you felt you weren't cut out for research and wanted to devote all your energies to clinical service and teaching."

"That never happened."

"Well, since Varney wasn't entrenched yet as chairman he backed off."

"Of course." Eck stood up and started for the door. "I don't really like this discussion. I don't like being cross-examined or called a liar. I've told you that such a conversation with Varney *never* took place."

"Even playing golf?"

"What the hell does that mean?"

"You're the only one in the department who plays golf with Varney. Maybe you share confidences then."

"I'm not going to listen to this shit anymore." Eck opened the door. "And unless I get an apology, you've lost a friend." He closed the door hard.

Clay sank back in his chair, trying to understand. He asked himself if he was wronging Eck.

Who was lying? Varney or Eck?

His belly began to reflect the tension—as if a sharp finger were repeatedly punching him. The problem at home with Andy. The problems here at work. *Damn it, the politics of academic medicine almost guarantee failure for serious science.* An almost impossible biologic problem was demanding a prompt solution. So what were they doing? Ignoring the problem and concentrating on disabling the problem-solvers. *And you can't even tell from which direction the attacks are coming.*

Is it Varney? Is it Eck? Is it both?

One thing was sure. Under these working conditions and with the obvious failure of their methods to stop rejection, a moratorium on heart transplantation should be an institutional policy—not something left to the discretion of the chairman of the Department of Surgery. Trying to reason or argue with Leif had proved useless. They had to get out of heart transplants before disaster forced them out.

Clay pulled a yellow legal pad from a drawer and began to compose a letter to the dean with carbon copies to all department chairmen, including Leif Hanson and Vincent Varney, calling for a medical center policy requiring an enforced moratorium on heart transplantation. He even included a summary of the data on rejection and infection among the recipients.

It was a drastic step. But he had to take it.

Before closing the memo, another thought occurred to him. What about the artificial heart? Should he also ask for an institutional policy to prohibit its use in humans? The artificial heart by its very design could not help but lead to bleeding and clotting problems—and strokes.

Clay decided against diluting the impact of his letter on the moratorium by adding anything about the artificial heart. Anyway, it should take Haupt years to get his pieces of plastic to work.

To hell with the artificial heart! And to hell with everything else at the medical school.

What was really important was what was happening with Andy.

EIGHTEEN

At midnight Clay was roaming along the darkened corridor of the transplant suite, trying to make his quick bed check rounds prior to leaving for home. Only half of the overhead lights were on and the ward staff was less than half the number of the daytime crew. No interns or residents were in sight, which usually signified the absence of an immediate crisis. He peered into Mr. Melton's room

"Can we talk just a minute, Dr. Ducharme?" Mr. Melton called out. His words were slurred and muffled, because his mouth was actually partially eaten away by the herpes virus.

"I'm sorry. I thought you were asleep." The room was muddy dark, illuminated only by the light from the hall. Clay fumbled for the light switch.

"Please don't put the light on," Mr. Melton said.

As Clay's eyes accommodated to the diminished light, he could see the grotesque mask that Yancey Melton now possessed as a face, as if someone had plastered raw hamburger over his features, destroying tissue around his left eye and making his nose and mouth hard to distinguish. Clay had been a coward. He knew that. Why else had he reviewed Mr. Melton's chart during the day, but had only now stopped to look into his room late at night? Why indeed? Too cowardly to be confronted by the spectacle of the destruction of this once proud and compassionate man. Disgraceful cowardice!

"I've tried to prevail, as Mr. Faulkner would have it," Yancey said. "But I've failed. Now I'm only trying to endure. And failing at that, too."

"No. That's wrong, Mr. Melton. You have prevailed," Clay said.

"I wish it were true, Dr. Ducharme," Yancey attempted to enunciate clearly through a damaged mouth that refused to respond normally. "I know it's not your fault. You and the other doctors are all doing your best. But I'm no longer a man. I've been turned into a non-person. A thing."

"Please don't say that."

"What I say is correct. I've become a thing to shoot medicine into. A thing to look at with pity—if looked at at all. Or sometimes looked at with revulsion. . . . People don't talk to me anymore as if I were a human being. I'm not looked upon as being involved in my own life . . . only the recipient of treatments . . . a laboratory specimen."

"Oh God," Clay said, "this is what we've been doing to you?"

"Heart transplantation is a dehumanizing experience. You doctors should know this. You must be made to know this."

"We've been trying so hard to find answers. To save you and the others," Clay said. "But . . ." he searched for the right words, "but it looks like we've lost sight of the 'you' we were trying to save."

"And I've lost sight of my own humanity. I've allowed myself to become a thing. . . ." Yancey was too short of breath to speak for a moment.

"No," Clay said. "Don't you see. You've gotten up on your hind legs and said, 'Damn it, look at me. I'm a man.'" Clay reached for Yancey's hand and held it hard and hoped that the dark would not reveal the tears on his face.

"Thank you," Yancey said.

"I'll see you in the morning," Clay said. "Try to

sleep."

"The pain prevents sleep."

"I'll be sure that the nurse brings something for the pain."

"Thank you," Yancey said. "See you in the morning."

But Yancey Melton died that night. Alone. Clay had wanted to be certain his family would be with him at the end, but had misjudged when the end would be.

One disaster followed another in disorderly sequence. The day of Yancey Melton's memorial service in the hospital chapel, Mike Goldman came to Clay's office. Clay had already seen three of the heart transplant survivors. All distraught. There was sadness at the death of one with whom they had shared so much. But in truth, the death of Yancey Melton had put each of the survivors abrasively in touch with his own imminent death. Clay was prepared for Mike Goldman to ask for an electrocardiogram and enzyme studies to allay the anxiety.

But Mike said: "Esther has cancer of the bone. Osteogenic sarcoma. They want to remove her leg at the hip tomorrow."

"Oh . . . no. No!" was all Clay could say. He came out from behind his desk and put his hand on Mike's arm—easing him into a chair.

"My little dancer. They want to do a hind quarter resection on her." There were silver tear-salt streaks under his eyes.

"I'm sorry—so sorry." Clay pushed his chair closer to Mike's and reached for his arm again as he seated himself beside him. "We were going to her dance recital tonight."

"The dance recital is still on." Mike's eyes were beginning to glisten. "She won't come into the hospital until after the recital. Even though her leg hurts like hell. She won't disappoint her little sister." He used the heels of his hands to wipe his eyes. "They've spent so much time on their routine."

"When did you find out?" Clay dug into a desk drawer for tissues and handed the box to Mike.

"Yesterday. My other kids don't know yet," Mike said. "Her leg's been hurting for weeks. She just thought she'd sprained it dancing." Mike pulled out several tissues and handed the box back to Clay. "You and Betty Sue will come tonight, won't you?"

"Of course we will."

"She just wants to go on as if there was nothing wrong."

That evening, the Ducharmes and the Goldmans sat together in the community hall of St. Andrew's Church. The room, which had a stage of satisfactory size for small recitals, obviously doubled for other functions, as indicated by the folded tables against two walls and the folding chairs for the audience.

The ballet and modern dance efforts by the younger children produced more than a little discomfort in the audience. Clay squirmed in his seat, looking around the auditorium through many tormented faces to seek out the smiling ones that identified the immediate families of the current performers. As the dancers got older, the performances got better. Some were not bad. Esther Goldman and her sister appeared on the program as the finale.

The house lights dimmed and a single spotlight focused on stage left. The music began—introducing the inevitable routine of children's dance recitals: "Me and My Shadow." The spotlight enlarged to an avenue-beam of white . A truly beautiful young woman appeared in top hat and tails. Cane, black silk shorts. Long, beautifully formed legs. Promenading—without apparent effort—along the avenue. Her little sister, identically dressed followed her, stepping into Esther's leg-shadows with almost equal grace. Clay looked around. No squirming in the audience. No torment.

And onstage, no clue that each graceful movement was being paid for in the hard coin of pain.

Then the reality broke through the dream and Clay wondered which leg would be the one removed tomorrow. Another turn. Some high kicks. The music ended. The audience applauded with genuine enthusiasm. Some even stood.

The family and friends could be identified by the tears.

Mike Goldman closed his practice. Whatever time he had left would be spent with his family. They would have to live off accounts receivable. Clay visited Esther Goldman in the hospital several times. Mike and Becky were always there. Esther was talking about the new artificial leg they would build for her. She was most appropriately named Esther—a regal young woman of courage and beauty.

November brought relief from the almost intolerable heat and humidity of the season extending from May to October. And as the northern part of the country began to shiver, this part of the South became not only livable, but enjoyable. Those who owned convertibles put the tops down. People played tennis and sat on their patios during the daylight hours rather than confining such activities to the night. At Southwest, however, work was the activity—work engulfed by an ever enlarging tide of desperation.

Although the dean had not made a moratorium compulsory, Leif had been complying voluntarily. This allowed Cooley to push ahead with five heart transplants in November alone. Between DeBakey and Cooley, twelve heart transplants had been performed, during Leif's last period of moratorium. After Cooley performed his fifth transplant of the month, Leif asked Clay to meet him in his hospital office.

As soon as Clay entered, Leif confronted him with: "I just can't wait around and watch those two clowns doing all the work. Don't you understand? We're almost out of the transplant business right now." He pushed himself away from the oak conference table and sat in a leather armchair.

"They have nothing new to offer and neither do we yet." Clay slid onto the couch. "We've got to do the basic research first—on lower mammals not on humans. And I won't have time to help with a new transplant. I'm trying to put in some grants to keep our cardiology division alive."

"Don't get uptight about the damned grants," Leif said. "Things will work out. And I've got a recipient. And a donor."

"I'm not aware of them," Clay said.

"Patient of Max MacGregor."

"Max? I find that hard to believe."

"Max is going to meet us here."

"What kind of a patient?"

"A young child. Single ventricle and pulmonary hypertension."

A secretary tapped at the door and ushered Max into Leif's office. "Leif, Clay," Max said, "high-level meeting?"

"A patient of yours, Max. A child named Grosset," Leif said.

"Sad story," Max said. "Lee Grosset. The poor lad's inoper-able."

"How about a transplant?"

"You don't understand. This is one of these cases—we see two or three a year. The parents essentially say cur-re him or kill him. They're at their wits' end. The child is taking so much out of their-r family. They're on the ver-rge of divorce." Max joined Clay on the couch. "They say they can't take the child home again. Not as sick as he is. They can't stand it. So they want an operation. Cure him or kill him." Max pulled a pipe out of his pocket and began to pack the bowl. "Verr-ry sad. I think maybe a foster home could help solve it. Except they can't come to grips with their-r own feelings."

"Why not a transplant?" Leif insisted.

"We're not executioners, Leif," Max said.

"Thanks for your vote of confidence."

"There's no lack of confidence involved. The child has pulmonary hypertension. You'd have to do both a heart and lung transplant."

"I'm prepared to do it."

"But the patient is not prepar-red to survive," Max

said. He put his pipe back in his pocket.

"Lung transplants don't make it," Clay added.

"We've got a good respiratory care team."

"Look, Leif, Clay and I both saw the baby that Cooley tried the heart and lung transplant on in September. She just wore her-rself out trying to breathe. . . . It's been tried. We don't have to do it again."

"Because Cooley didn't succeed, we shouldn't try ?"

"Because none of us knows enough yet to do a heart and lung transplant," Clay argued. "Do a few dozen in dogs, pigs, and baboons. When you've got some long-term survivors, we can talk about it."

"Listen, the Grossets came to me for help and we have a donor."

"You'd be doing yourself a great disser-rvice." Max leaned forward towards Leif. "You'd be an executioner, which is just what these par-rents want. But eventually the guilt will catch up with them. They'll know what they've done. And they'll lash out. They won't be able to toler-rate their own guilt. So they'll need to blame someone. *You.* And they'll set you up for a lawsuit big enough to warm the heart of Melvin Belli." Max dug his hand into the pocket of his brown tweed jacket and pulled out an envelope. "In fact, I think I have a letter from the Grossets with me. It's marked 'per-rsonal' so my secretary didn't open it. I stuffed it in my pocket to read sometime today."

"Letters marked personal are usually unpleasant," Clay said.

"I've had a few that threatened my life and my family's safety," Leif added.

"Then you know why I didn't rush to open it," Max said. "Let's hope it's not unpleasant after all, but just an explanation that they've consulted with Dr. Hanson." Max tore open the envelope and began to read. The expression on his face revealed the letter's contents. He handed it to Leif and said to Clay: "They say I'm a ter-rible doctor. That I've never shown any feeling for their baby. That I regard the baby as some sort of freak. And that they've now gone to a doctor who knows what he's doing. Our friend, Leif."

"We all get those letters, Max," Clay said.

"I know," Max said. "I've been a doctor for well over thir-rty years and every time I get one of these, it still tears me up."

"Well," Leif said, handing the letter back to Max, "it took me much less time to learn to handle this sort of crap. I may get more publicity, but I also get more attacks. In fact, did you know that only last week the police intercepted a nut in the emergency room of this hospital, who had a gun and was looking for me?"

"I heard about it," Max said. "I guess surgeons are tougher than cardiologists."

"They have to be. . . . The Grosset case looks like a no-win situation," he said abruptly and stood up. "Anyway, Cooley's already got credit for the first total heart and lung transplant." Leif walked towards the door, much more obvious than he used to be about signaling the end of a meeting. "But I'm going on record right now. We've got to maintain the viability of our clinical transplant program. By the time we're ready to try something new we won't have the patients or the mechanisms in place to perform a heart transplant."

"Leif . . ." Clay began to protest.

"I'm sorry," Leif said. "Cooley is getting way ahead of us. He's done eighteen transplants to our twelve. DeBakey's already done nine. We pioneered in this field. We've set the pace for everyone else, and now we're falling behind. At your insistence, Clay, I stopped doing transplants in September. But if we're going to make the major breakthrough in heart transplantation, we're going to have to keep our program alive somehow."

"You're talking mindless escalation. Our leadership has to be in research. Not repeating the same stupid mistakes on every case," Clay said.

"Our leadership has to be in the operating room, too. We're going back to doing transplants."

"Till we get it right?"

"Yes. And to keep our program alive, damn it!"

"What the hell's the use," Clay stalked out of the

office shaking his head. "We argue the same god-damned points over and over and over again."

Maxwell MacGregor accompanied Clay down the hospital corridor. He huffed out a breath and muttered, "I'm finding progr-ressively more madness in heart transplantation. Did Leif really say Cooley *has the credit* for the first heart and lung transplant?"

"He did. And that's the main reason for not doing it—not because we're not ready for it scientifically."

"Incr-redible. And he counts the number of transplants like there's a scoreboard, and his team is now behind in points?"

"Points. Body counts. It's not just Leif. It's a great many of the cardiovascular surgeons. Ambition. Competitiveness. *Hubris*," Clay said. "It's reaching a dangerous level."

"They're getting verr-ry close to crossing over ethical and mor-ral lines."

"It's worrying the hell out of me. But I think Leif is basically too honest to cross a line."

"You don't think that fr-riendship, like love, can be just a tr-rifle blind? Leif is a verr-ry large man. I think he's capable of having a verr-ry large flaw," Max shoved the letter from the Grossets back into his jacket pocket.

"I hope you're wrong."

"I hope so, too. But there are those who regard his womanizing as more than a minor character defect. He carries a terr-rible burden that you and I have been spared. Big and handsome and wealthy and—and verr-ry powerful. No wonder nurses and socialites and movie stars are anxious to hop into his bed."

Clay was no longer confident in making his customary defense of Leif against rumors of any sexual improprieties. Too much information was accumulating from too many sources. The best he could do was tentatively question one possible indiscretion. "You don't think he's actually shacking up with Roxanne Molnar?"

"And you can't think that he flies all the way to Hollywood to have a cheeseburger and fries with a well known sex goddess." Max brushed his fingertips across his scraggly mustache. "Twice he's been in Hollywood when I desper-rately needed him to do emergency sur-rgery on babies. Twice I had to rely on that bungling Sellery. Both babies died. . . . So next time there's an emergency congenital heart, as much as I hate to refer a patient away from our own center, I'm going to send the baby over to Cooley."

"I'm sorry to hear that."

"And I'm sorry that your friendship with Leif makes it hard to hear such things."

"I'll try to be objective," Clay said pensively. "I'm afraid . . . that our friendship is in jeopardy. Since transplantation began all Leif and I seem to do is fight. About cases like this baby. About what's appropriate. About experimental procedures." Clay stopped at the stairs. "I've got to find an olive branch to restore some peace between us."

The olive branch that Clay offered Leif was a Saturday visit to his laboratory with a complete status report of the current experiments in induction of tolerance. Compared to Leif's laboratory, Clay's was small. Smaller even than Arthur's—and more crowded, because the lab office and one-fourth of the bench space held tiers of mouse and rat cages. The majority of Clay's experimental rodents were in the animal quarters, but even the few that currently resided in the lab for special observations gave off a disagreeable odor. Microscopes, centrifuges, photometers, sonicators, and other pieces of equipment marched stiffly up and down the black laboratory benches.

"Even though my thinking has been changing on the importance of heart transplantation, I want you to know how much I still want it to succeed. And how hard I'm still working at it." Clay opened a cage and pulled out a black C57 mouse with a swollen ear. He held the ear close enough to a lamp to allow Leif to see that the swelling was pulsating. "We're closer than we've ever been before."

"A rat heart in there?"

"Yup. For six months. And the critter got nothing

but transplant antigen."

"Outstanding."

"Here's its electrocardiogram." Clay handed Leif a Polaroid picture photographed from an oscilloscope. "The tall spikes are the denervated rat heart and the fast complexes are the mouse's own heart." Clay waved in the direction of four rows of cages. "Every mouse in this section is just like this one—six months on transplant antigen alone."

"Absolutely outstanding."

"Unfortunately these cages . . ." Clay stepped over to three different rows, "all contain mice like this one." He captured a squirming black mouse and pointed to a scab-encrusted hole in the mouse's ear. "As near as I can figure the mice with the living hearts and the mice with the rejected hearts were treated exactly the same."

"But you've got more successes than failures by far."

"Not good enough. Why so many failures? What's the difference between the groups? That's what I've got to find out." Clay slipped the mouse back into its cage. "But with a lot of work and a little luck we might have things in shape for you to start large animals within a year. I just want you to see how hard we're working on this. But you've also got to see how far removed it is from growing rat hearts in mouse ears to putting large animal hearts into the chests of humans."

"Maybe the difference is in how you make the antigen."

"Or in how we schedule the doses. Unfortunately, these experiments all take time."

"You going to show me how you make the antigen?" Leif asked in an offhand manner.

Clay studied Leif for a moment, smiled, and said: "Sure."

NINETEEN

As soon as Leif had left Clay's lab, he almost ran back to his office, convinced that he was not only on the right track, but was nearer his research goal than he had realized. Leif began writing notes on the research that Clay had just shown him. *We're close. Damned close. Why can't Clay see that? Clay's unwilling to contribute to the solution, so he'll just have to get out of the god-damned way.*

With Frank Sellery, Leif had been doing a number of experiments, but they had been having to rely mostly on massive drug suppression of rejection. Each time they transplanted a pig heart into a sheep or a baboon, it contracted into a tight ball that would not beat. But Clay's experiments were working. He had shown Leif one success after another—all the while emphasizing the experiments that were failing.

Unfortunately for Leif's program, Cooley and DeBakey continued to monopolize the Houston headlines. Some of Leif's former patients, who had become discouraged waiting for transplantation to start again at University Hospital were now turning up at Baylor. One evening a donor appeared at the emergency room, but the Southwest team reluctantly transferred the patient to Baylor, because they had no suitable recipient. An immediate transplant took place at Baylor—and apparently the tissue match was poor. What was not appreciated at first was that both the recipient and the donor had originated at Southwest under Leif's jurisdiction. And both ended up at Baylor.

Frank Sellery uncovered this intelligence and confronted Leif with it. Leif took the information to Clay Ducharme and Arthur Johnson, and said if Southwest was going to stay in the cardiac transplantation business, they would have to start doing the procedures again. Even poor matches. If Leif Hanson's patients were going to have cardiac transplants, Leif Hanson was going to do them, not Denton Cooley or Mike DeBakey.

There were no more donors for three weeks, but when one became available a heart transplant was started on the basis of blood type only—before notifying Clay. Not until two hours after surgery did the lab report the results of the tissue match. But it was the good fortune of the recipient that the match turned out to be Southwest's second best. Leif now had the opportunity to see if thoracic duct drainage would work as a new method to fight rejection.

What attracted the news media was that the same donor who provided the heart had also donated kidneys for two patients, a liver for another, and a lung for a fifth patient. This lung transplant was in a private patient under Frank Sellery, and the indications for the operation were obscure to Leif, who had been too busy to evaluate the case himself. Anyway, the banner headlines belonged to Leif again. Leif had learned how to play the media game.

FIVE TRANSPLANTS FROM ONE DONOR
HANSON TEAM
SCORES SURGICAL
SPECTACULAR

Leif's moratorium had been entirely voluntary. The dean and the department chairmen had failed to support Clay's call for a policy of enforcement. This latest success seemed to attest to their sound judgment.

Leif usually took time off with his family at Christmas, going either to Acapulco or Hawaii for a week.

This year, as soon as school let out for vacation, Elaine took the children and flew to Detroit to be with her parents in Grosse Pointe. Actually, Elaine had told Leif that she wanted to go home alone with the children and suggested that he not accompany them. Leif was not too deeply enmeshed in his research to analyze this request to spend Christmas apart. *What's she up to? Thinking of a divorce?*

But there was nothing he could do about that today. Better to concentrate on something more productive. He was still trying unsuccessfully to duplicate the transplant antigen techniques that Clay had been using. He kept telling himself that he had seen the process. He had seen the results.

"What I find totally frustrating is how something that appears to be so straight forward can continue to elude us," Leif told Sellery as he cleared off the black lab counter and put away the last of the reagents for the day's experiment.

Sellery placed some glassware in the stainless steel lab sink, wiped his hands on a paper towel, and said, "Why not get Wendell Eck to prepare some transplant antigen so we can move ahead? Or maybe Arthur Johnson can do it for us?"

"I shouldn't ask Eck to help," was Leif's less than forceful response. "He works for Clay."

"Clay's tied up with other things. Besides, he showed you how to do it, himself," Sellery contended. "Clay can't dictate who his associates collaborate with."

"Maybe I can ask Clay to make some," Leif said without conviction.

"He won't do it. And he wouldn't help you even if he could. He doesn't want to share. He's jealous. And he's pissed at us for starting the last transplants without him."

Leif was about to challenge this perception of Clay when Sellery came up with a compromise. "Let me ask Eck. You won't have anything to do with it."

"I ah . . . that's ah. . . ." Leif struggled with the options. Was it ethical? Was it wrong? In a legalistic sense, it was not wrong at all. *Clay is contributing to the problem. Not to the solution. And he isn't getting out of the way.* Leif undercutting Clay through Eck. *Not what good friends do to each other*. But Clay obstructing Leif. *Not what good friends do*. "Maybe you can bend ethics just a tad. For the greater good. . . . But I won't participate in this. This is between you and Eck. If you want to do it—it's between you and Eck. I don't know anything about it."

"Understood."

So Sellery asked Wendell Eck on Christmas Eve day to make a batch of transplantation antigen using liver and spleen from a pig whose heart would be transplanted into a baboon.

In the barn-smelling, large animal quarters, Leif pretreated the baboon with massive doses of steroids, then the solubilized transplantation antigen. They moved the baboon and the pig to a sterile animal operating room, which contained two operating tables, a heart-lung machine, anesthesia machines, and monitoring equipment—very similar to the heart surgery rooms in the hospital. With Leif and Eck operating on the baboon at one table and Sellery operating on the pig at an adjoining table, they quickly transplanted the pig's heart into the baboon and watched for a reaction. The heart began to twitch.

"No instant rejection," Leif shouted. "First time this has happened. How 'bout that?" Instead of the heart contracting into a hard ball that would not beat, the heart continued to twitch—ventricular fibrillation. Through one application of electrical shock they were able to convert the rhythm to normal sinus and keep the transplanted pig heart beating in the baboon for two hours before it contracted and stopped.

As Eck was leaving the animal surgery laboratory, Leif asked him not to mention this particular experiment to Clay Ducharme. Not just yet. He said he wanted to *surprise* Clay. It looked as if they were making progress. A long way to go—but progress at last.

On this December 24, Apollo 8 was about to circle the moon. Television sets all over the hospital tuned into the media event. The space program people were working at the Manned Spacecraft Center in Houston and the transplanters were working in their laboratories during the supper hour. No time off for Christmas Eve. Clay was walking through the basement corridor past the hospital cafeteria on his way to the parking lot and home. He stopped and took a couple of backward steps. The cafeteria was almost empty, but standing in line were two nurses, an orderly, an intern, and Leif in his green scrub suit. Clay went into the cafeteria. "I didn't know we had any emergency surgery tonight," he said.

"We don't. I'm just finishing up some animal studies." Leif was surprised to see Clay and feeling more than vaguely guilty about the work he had been doing with Eck.

"You're not eating here on Christmas Eve." Clay took the tray from Leif.

"Elaine and the kids are in Grosse Pointe for Christmas. There's no one at home except the housekeeper." He spoke softly so the people in line wouldn't hear. *Why did Clay have to see me?*

"There's family at my house." Clay took Leif by the arm, and Leif, to avoid any further embarrassing discussion, left the line with Clay.

When they got outside the cafeteria, Leif said, "I'd really rather not. I've got a lot of work to do."

"Look, Scrooge, everybody takes off on Christmas Eve. Even you. So since you've nothing better to do, you're coming to our house for supper."

Leif said: "I just can't. Believe me, I appreciate the invitation, but I just can't accept." He turned and walked quickly down the hall. *Why did Clay have to see me?*

Leif kept walking through the tunnel and back into the Basic Sciences Building, where researchers kept their animals. He was about to go past the domestic animal lab when he saw that Gerhardt Haupt was still in there. "Another workaholic?" he called through the door, and decided to go on into the barn-like room, complete with stalls and bales of hay, which was home for three calves with artificial hearts, walking on treadmills, while hooked up to their life support air compressors. "Doesn't anyone go home Christmas Eve?"

"Too much vork. Too little time," was Haupt's answer.

"How's the calf work going?"

"Very well, I think."

"My animal transplants have just begun to look a little better."

"That is very good."

"When do you think the Haupt-Hanson heart will be ready for humans?"

"Ooh . . . that is hard to say."

"How about the spring?"

"Ooh . . . I think . . . well, if these calves last until spring they will have lived longer than any other calves with artificial hearts—ever."

"You think the modified Hanson valve will prevent clotting and bleeding better than anything else?"

"I think maybe yes."

"Because you sure as hell don't want to replace someone's heart and give him a stroke."

"No."

"Is that what's been holding DeBakey back with his calves?"

"I don't know. The strokes are serious problems everywhere."

"You know if anyone else is about ready to do humans with the artificial heart?"

"I don't think so."

Leif gently handled a thick plastic tube that connected the chest of the calf to the air compressor. "You know, our heart transplant program is getting in jeopardy. Plenty of potential recipients in the world—but very few donors."

"This is true."

"Everyone is recognizing that human donors aren't the answer. It's got to be animal donors or artificial hearts."

"Of course."

"But, as you say, too little time."

"Yes."

"Unfortunately we're running out of time." Leif

stepped to the next calf and patted it on the flank. "I'd like to set a deadline for us of this spring to have our breakthrough. Otherwise we might be out of business. We've got to be able to go with either the artificial heart or an animal heart by spring."

"When in the spring?"

"How about April 15? This is Christmas Eve. We can celebrate on income tax day."

"The spring . . ." Haupt said in a tone of resignation that bordered on despair. "The spring. . . ."

"Let's shoot for it. Be ready to go with either the animal hearts or the artificial heart in the spring."

So Leif began his drive home through the dark streets towards his empty house. He turned out of his way to cruise slowly down Rice Boulevard and past the Ducharme house. There it was—comfortable looking. Tudor. He geared down to first. Not a very large yard, but a good pecan tree and a live oak in front. A magnolia and a tall palm at the side. Bright yellow squares of windows, winking as shadows of occupants moved across the living room.

Why had he rejected Clay's invitation? What else did he have to do tonight? Elaine had deliberately separated him from his kids at Christmas. His nurse friend was visiting her family in Lubbock. What else did he have to do? The invitation probably still held. Leif cut the Porsche into a U turn and parked in front of Clay's house. He flipped off the ignition key and sat quietly in the car. This could be a chance to tell Clay that he was close to having temporary research funds for him through the Cohen Institute. The problem was that the newly appointed administrator of the institute had not yet worked out the logistics. There was very little chance of a slip-up, but he had better wait.

Sitting alone in his car on Christmas Eve.

Afraid to go into a house and visit with old friends?

Just sitting. Afraid to go in?

Finally he snapped on the ignition, slammed the accelerator to the floor, and peeled rubber away from the curb—heading back to the hospital.

TWENTY

Just as the Ducharme family was sitting down to supper—in the dining room because it was a special occasion—the phone rang. Clay let out a groan and stepped to the kitchen to answer the call.

It was Arthur Johnson. "I hate like hell to bother you tonight, but I'm finishing up some work."

"Well, come on over here and share Christmas Eve with us," Clay said. "You need some time off. Come on over. We'll wait for you. We're just about to eat."

"I won't hold you up long," Arthur said. "A couple of things have happened this week. I've been moved out of my lab. And something else."

"Oh damn. Damn!"

"Varney's assigned my lab to Mawson, as chief of the renal division."

"How can he do that? You've got grants and contracts. You've got to have space to do the work."

"He's given me an old storeroom to use as a lab. Except there's barely enough room to pile my equipment to the ceiling, much less work with it."

"Well, after Christmas we're going to see the dean. This crap has got to stop." Clay punched at the cabinet next to the phone. "And what else has happened?"

"I saw the Dean yesterday." Arthur did not respond to the question. "He says space is very tight. Suggests I might be able to rent something somewhere."

"But Mawson doesn't even do bench research."

"He's now the chief of the division."

Clay tried to think of something encouraging, but he ended up saying, "Arthur, I'm so damned sorry. Just get out of here. Take any kind of job. Just get out."

"I reached that conclusion some time ago. I've contacted over a dozen friends to ask for a job," Arthur said. "I just seem to embarrass them. They have no jobs for me."

"Wait a second," Clay said. "How about Leif. Who says you have to be in a department of medicine? I'll bet he could create a transplantation research division in surgery just for you."

"I don't think so."

"It's a natural," Clay insisted.

"I hinted to Leif about a job a couple of months ago. He didn't pick up on it," Arthur said. "Anyway things are going to work out. You get on with your supper."

"Come on over and share it."

"I wish I could, but I've got a . . . another engagement. By the way, I left a stack of things on your secretary's desk. Maybe you could go over them?"

"Sure you can't have supper with us?"

"Sorry."

The second declined invitation in an hour was what Clay was thinking as he hung up the telephone. But during supper he kept picturing Arthur alone on Christmas Eve. Arthur had said he had another engagement. Was that just bravado? No one should be alone on Christmas Eve. And certainly no one who had been going through the stresses that Arthur had been experiencing. Clay was beginning to worry. Yes, about another suicide attempt.

After supper, Andy began building a fire in the living room fireplace, while Melanie got out the recording of Dickens' *A Christmas Carol*, the old Lionel Barrymore rendition. Clay glanced around this comfortable living room. Over the fireplace hung an excellent museum reproduction of a still life by Renoir. The original resided at the Fogg Museum at Harvard. Several other reproductions of Impressionists and paintings from other periods tightly filled available space on three walls. Two original abstracts by Texas artists. One was in the style of Jackson Pollock. A comfortable room for Clay. A comfortable evening. But what about Arthur? Clay stared at the fourth wall of the living room. Floor-to-ceiling bookcases, about a thousand volumes, the classics from the Greeks to the twentieth century. Plays, novels, poetry, history, philosophy, and theology. Comfortable. *But what about Arthur?* Betty Sue poured chestnuts into the basket of the fireplace corn popper. For the Ducharme Christmas Eve tradition, the family would light the Advent candles, gather around the piano and sing a few Christmas carols, and then listen to Lionel Barrymore do Scrooge while they roasted chestnuts. This was a routine from which Melanie would permit no deviation. (Although Andy, as he got older, was less committed to the ritual—particularly listening to the Dickens-Barrymore recording.)

DAMN IT! WHAT ABOUT ARTHUR?

Clay could not enjoy any of this. He left the family group during the carol sing and went to the kitchen to dial Arthur's home.

No answer.

Where could he reach Arthur at the hospital? No office. No lab. He called the hospital operator to see if she had a new number for him. She didn't.

"Come back and join us on 'Silent Night.'" Betty Sue called into the kitchen.

"I can't. I just can't. I don't know where Arthur is."

"He said he had another engagement, didn't he?"

"That's what he said."

"Does he carry a pager?"

"I don't think he does anymore." Clay began dialing the hospital operator again. Arthur still had a pager, but he didn't respond. "Now I'm really getting worried."

"He wouldn't necessarily have his pager turned on tonight on Christmas Eve, if he's not on call."

"He has no clinical responsibility anymore. So I

guess he's not on call."

"Then he's probably out at a Christmas Eve party or service." Betty Sue took Clay's arm. "Just come back and sing 'Silent Night' with us and we'll turn you loose."

"I'm worried."

"I am too. Would it do any good to look for him in the hospital?'

"Where would I look?" Clay joined the family at the piano.

"Start at the old lab. Look in all the labs that are assigned to the department of medicine," Betty Sue suggested.

"Sorry to spoil Christmas Eve."

"We understand," Andy said. "Maybe just one verse of 'Silent Night' will have to do."

Arthur was nowhere to be found in the hospital. Clay had him paged on the overhead and checked the materials Arthur had left for him. Tissue typing data correlated with predisposition to coronary disease. From the office Clay went to Arthur's home. The house was dark. Not even a porch light. He contemplated calling the police to look inside, but seeing that Arthur's car was gone, Clay uneasily concluded that he was indeed away on another engagement.

And so he was.

On a deserted beach in Galveston, Arthur parked his Buick Riviera and stepped out on the hard packed sand. At that very moment astronauts were circling the moon. Their families in Houston were hearing their voices coming from this great distance.

The moon's cold, silver light reflected off the gently corrugated gulf waves, whispering derisively along the sand—colder still as clouds began to cover its face. In the darkness, how could one distinguish where the land ended and the water began? Where Earth ended and what began?

Cold. . . . Cold and dark.

Arthur opened the trunk of the Buick. It was now too dark to see inside. He felt around until his hand touched what he sought—and slowly withdrew a length of flexible rubber hose.

The responsibility for all the necessary and unhappy details from the discovery of the body to the memorial service fell on Clay.

He wanted to offer some words at the service, but decided to defer to protocol, which called only for Arthur's minister to speak. He also feared what he might say—feared for his own self-control with respect to some of his colleagues at the medical center.

The weather, damp, drizzly, and cold, was not unlike that accompanying another funeral, a few years earlier in New Haven. More than a hundred people from the medical center attended—including Varney, Mawson, and the dean. All three insisted on getting up without invitation to give brief eulogies and to cite Arthur's remarkable accomplishments and contributions to medicine. Several times, as first Varney and then Mawson eulogized Arthur Johnson, Clay wanted to leap from his seat and scream, "Murderers." He wanted to rush at these men and choke the hypocritical words back into their throats. Each time his muscles tensed, he felt Betty Sue's grip on his arm tighten. And Clay's own good judgment prevailed. It would have been a final dishonor to Arthur's memory to disrupt his service by calling attention to the contribution these bastards had made to his death.

At the end of the service a variety of comments could also be heard. *Such a waste of a fine mind.* But there were others. *He finally succeeded. Tried it several times before. In college. Internship. A few months ago. Always an outsider.* The dean subscribed to both points of view. The death was regrettable. A waste. But Arthur was a troubled man—however bright. A man who had made many previous attempts. Besides that, he was despondent over his ulcer.

After Betty Sue had driven off in her car, Clay met briefly with Leif and Henry Knoblauch, standing out in the drizzle in a Baptist cemetery on the outskirts of Houston.

Henry repeated what he had said before: "You can't

attack the jobs of men of our age."

"He could have had his pick of the best jobs," Leif said.

"That was last year. This year he couldn't find anything. He tried. If Varney could have just left him alone for a while," Clay muttered. "Allowed him to have a decent lab till he could produce some more good work. And the rumors had time to die down."

"If anyone would let the rumors die," Henry said.

"He was absolutely essential to our transplant program," Leif continued, "absolutely essential."

"Would you have offered him a job in the department of surgery?" Clay asked.

"He should have been a chairman. A chairman of medicine," Leif said.

"The question was," Clay pressed, "would you have offered him a job?"

"I, ah . . . actually, I thought of it. But I was worried about embarrassing him. He should have been a chairman."

"That's the problem. People couldn't think of him as someone whose situation had been so quickly and drastically changed. He just needed a decent place to work, a place where he would be respected."

"He would have been great in our department." Leif brushed the accumulating moisture off his hair and began unlocking the door of his Mercedes. "But I was worried that a job in our department was beneath him."

"I guess a lot of people thought that," Henry said softly as they walked away from Leif and proceeded on to Clay's VW. "But you know there's an almost subtle element in what Varney did to Arthur. And what he's doing to me. Isolation. Segregation. Taking away the relationships that give life meaning. It's the loneliness, Clay. It's the loss of meaning. The alienation. For people like us, *who we are* is defined by *what we do*."

"And if what we do is taken away? . . ."

"Then who the hell are we?"

"But, damn it, Henry, we're more than our jobs."

"Are we?"

"If we're not, we damned well better learn to be."

"Easier said than done. Much easier said than done. I'll be candid with you, Clay, Varney's now got *me* on an emotional ragged edge."

"Do you think Varney is smart enough to be doing these things deliberately?"

"Deliberately attacking what gives meaning to our lives? Imposing on a fellow human being an anguished sense of alienation?"

"Or is taking away the titles and the labs and the offices just legitimate means to an administrative end?"

"It doesn't matter, Clay. Don't you see? It doesn't matter what the reason. Arthur was reduced to a lonely, alienated, non-person, whether it was for a grotesque administrative goal or out of totally evil intent. Whatever the reason, a man who was of great stature in American medicine has just been dropped into a muddy hole. And taking away his lab and his salary last week was the final shovel of dirt in his face."

"His salary? His salary! Arthur never told me."

"There are things just too humiliating to talk about."

"Then how did you find out?" Clay began fumbling for his car keys.

"Varney's secretary is my patient. She was terribly upset. Varney was discussing it with Mawson right in front of her. What he did to Arthur. What he was gonna do to me. She's looking for a new job. She can't stand the crap anymore."

"They can't take away the salary of a tenured professor."

"Of course they *can't*. They just say the salary goes with the job of chief of the renal division. And we simply don't have another salary. Sorry."

"They can't take away the salary of a tenured professor. That's part of tenure."

"Tenure is also supposed to protect us from all the other shit Varney dumps on us."

"All Arthur had to do was go to the committee on privilege and tenure." Clay found the keys in the pocket of his raincoat.

"Which is chaired by Mawson, as of the first of November."

"Damn!"

"With the help of a lawyer and the American Association of University Professors, maybe Arthur could have started getting a salary again in six months or a year. Of course Varney would have then argued that Arthur shouldn't even have had tenure, because of his emotional instability and because he was making absolutely no contribution to the department."

"They take away his office, his lab, and all of his functions in the department—and then they can say he's not doing anything in the department."

"That's what Varney can say."

"And we helped dig the hole that Arthur has been dropped into, today," Clay said, just above a whisper. "Dear God, we helped dig the hole."

"No, I won't take that much of a guilt trip. But maybe we could have done more to prevent his hole being dug, if we weren't so damned busy struggling to avoid the pitfalls that were being dug for us."

"Doctors by and large are a dangerous lot." Clay jabbed the key into the lock of the VW. "A little bit smarter than the average. A little more cunning. And that's where the danger lies."

"Because people expect a bit more from them than they do from a used car salesman? Because they've been endowed with the gifts to do more good?"

"Or greater evil." Clay gave a shudder from the cold. He studied the troubled expression on Henry Knoblauch's face. "What's happening in your life, Henry? Things getting any better at all?"

"You got a minute more?"

"That doesn't sound good. Let's sit in the car, out of this damp."

The men crammed themselves into the confines of the VW. Henry sat with difficulty because of his neck and back brace. He finally said: "Varney's got me, too. I'm being retired."

"I don't understand," Clay said.

"At forty-five years of age, I'm being retired. Varney has made what he feels is a very generous offer. Half-salary as long as I don't do anything more in medicine. As soon as I start to practice again—see one patient—my retirement benefits are completely canceled for life."

"I've never heard of such a thing," Clay said. "You don't want to retire, do you?"

"Of course not."

"Well, don't retire."

"I'm being forced to." Henry stared ahead through the windshield, which was now clouding with condensed moisture from within the car. "I thought I figured out what he had against Arthur. But I can't figure why he's after me."

"Why are you being forced to retire?"

Henry still didn't answer the direct question. "I pronounced some of the heart donors brain-dead. That's all I've had to do with the transplant program. But he was out to get me even before the transplants started."

"Henry, answer me! Why do you think you have to accept retirement at forty-five?"

"Total disability—that's what he's calling it."

"You've had trouble with your back for twenty-five years. Before you even went to medical school."

"It's not my back. It's what I took for my back."

"What happened?"

"I couldn't sleep. Biofeedback and aspirin weren't controlling the pain. So just at night, I took morphine. Prescribed for me by another neurologist. And not every night. I had two prescriptions for ten tablets each. Over a period of almost three months. When I asked my neurologist for a third prescription, he said I should go easy on the stuff. And I accepted the suggestion without protest."

"How did Varney get in on it?"

"I'm afraid my colleague must have told him." Henry wiped a little condensation off his part of the windshield. "Does twenty tablets in almost three months sound like an addiction?"

"Doesn't sound like addiction to me."

"I know it violates the accepted approach to handling chronic pain. And I know there was an emotional element related to Varney's taking away my title and my lab. So I've been back on aspirin and biofeedback for over a month. I don't sleep except when I'm so exhausted I'm practically in a coma."

"Don't let him push you into retirement."

"He's got me Clay. He says he'll bring this up to the state board and they'll lift my license."

"I'm sure they wouldn't do such a thing."

"They might. And then I may never have a chance to practice again. And worse, what's left of my identity, my personhood, as a licensed physician will be taken away. He's got me. I take a *generous* half-salary retirement or he sees that they lift my license." Henry twisted in his seat trying to find a comfortable position. "Varney's clever. And so he's able to add Knoblauch to his list of non-persons."

On January 2, Blaiberg—Barnard's second patient—celebrated his first anniversary with a transplanted heart. And Mike Goldman, the world's second longest living heart transplant patient reentered University Hospital. His anniversary was only three weeks away. Mike's belly was full of fluid again, and he was so short of breath he could hardly speak: "I guess I've been trying to deny it. Figured if I denied it long enough and hard enough, it'd go away."

"You're going to have to spend time in the hospital," Clay said.

"I know."

Sellery was the first member of the surgery staff to see Goldman. "My God," he told Clay in the hall outside of Mike's room, "you've gotta keep him alive. He's almost made it to a year. If he dies now, think what it'll do to the program."

"What about what it will do to *him?* And to his wife and kids?" Clay shot back. "I don't know about you, Sellery. What the hell keeps going through your mind? Why are you in this damned transplantation business?"

"For the same reasons you are, Ducharme. And for the same reasons Hanson is. It's the glory road. Except I don't waltz around talking holier-than-thou shit. I'm honest enough to admit it."

"I see," Clay said. "Well, are you getting enough glory, Dr. Sellery?"

"Not quite. But I will." Sellery looked at Clay through narrowed eyelids. "You really don't like me, do you?"

"Does it matter?"

"No."

"Then why ask?" Clay started to push open the door to Mike's room.

"You always get your digs in. Let me give *you* one, Ducharme. You're not even honest enough to admit why you won't help Leif and me with your god-damned transplantation antigen. Jealousy. Spite. You want it all for yourself. You and some of the other guys keep bitching about Varney. How jealous he is. How he can't stand to see people succeed. But I don't see any difference between you and Varney. No difference."

"That shows how perceptive you are."

"You're damned right it does," Sellery said smugly. "Varney's run out of ideas and techniques to do anything exciting in research. So he stakes out his territory and raises hell. And you . . . you can't do heart transplants. You're not a surgeon. And that eats your guts out, doesn't it? Heart transplantation is a surgical procedure. And the surgeons get the credit. And that eats you."

"The hell it does," Clay scoffed.

"The hell it doesn't! You older guys are all alike. You, Varney, all of you. You can't stand to see anyone else get ahead. You resent younger doctors. You resent each other. You do anything you can to screw each other." Then Sellery smiled. "Well, Dr. Ducharme, your turn is coming. We're gonna do what you said we couldn't do. And then you can take your god-damned antigen and stick it." Sellery's smile broadened with self-satisfaction as he turned and walked away, brushing a hand over his carefully groomed hair.

Clay watched Sellery turn the corner and took several deep breaths before continuing into Mike's room.

"Having a few words with Sellery?" Mike asked.

"I'm sorry, I didn't know you could hear," Clay said. "You're looking so much better, already."

"Sure. My blood pressure's back up."

"Thanks to Isuprel and Solu-Cortef." Clay stood at the foot of the bed.

"How long do you think I'm going to need this I.V. drip?"

"I don't know, Mike. I'm just glad to see your pressure coming back."

"I can breathe a lot better," Mike said.

"Has it been worth it, Mike?"

"The transplant?"

"Yes." Clay eased himself into the bedside chair.

"I think so. I've had some good months. Time with my family." He nodded towards the harmonica on his bedside table. "And I did learn to play that thing—you've heard me play it."

"I admit you sure learned it fast. A regular virtuoso."

In three days Clay discontinued Mike's Isuprel infusion. But within twelve hours he had to restart it. Mike's blood pressure dropped. Over the next several days, Clay used progressively larger amounts of Isuprel just to maintain a blood pressure and cardiac output that would keep Mike conscious. Large doses of immunosuppressants and relative immobilization in bed eventually produced pneumonia. Fortunately, the pneumonia responded to a new antibiotic and cleared within a week, but Mike could not be disconnected from his intravenous lifeline of Isuprel.

Three times during this hospitalization, Clay drew blood for matching with potential donors.

Mike was unaware of what the blood was being tested for until Leif and Clay came into his hospital room together and told him the results of the third match.

"Mike, we have another donor for you, if you'd

like," Leif began. He stood stiffly at the side of the bed and kept his eyes focused on the lab reports.

Clay took his position at the other side of the bed and placed his hand on Mike's arm. "It's another C match, but the donor doesn't have any antigens that you've been sensitized to by your previous donor. At least as far as we can tell."

"You want to give me another transplant?" Mike tried to smile.

"We want to give you the opportunity for another transplant. The decision is all yours," Leif said.

"What do you think? I owe you a lot. I want to cooperate."

"You owe us nothing," Clay corrected.

"Start the whole thing all over again?"

"If you'd like," Clay said. "But I've got to be honest with you. This new donor may have some antigens that we still can't detect."

"Start the thing all over again?" Mike said softly to himself. "Start all over?" he whispered.

"If you want." Leif said.

"Could I have a little time to think?"

"Sure." Leif now rested his hand on Mike's shoulder.

"How much time have we with the donor?"

"A few hours." Clay said.

"How much time have we with me?"

"Maybe a little longer."

"Could I see my wife and children?"

"Of course."

"I know kids aren't supposed to come into the hospital."

"So we'll break the damned rules," Clay said.

Becky Goldman and the children came to see Mike. Esther was on crutches. They talked and basked in the warmth of each other's love for over an hour. Mike tried to make the good-bye kisses appear to be just routine. Routine kisses. Routine hugs. Perhaps he clung to Becky's hand a second too long. Squeezed a little too hard.

Was that what made her say she wanted to stay longer?

But Mike insisted that everything was fine—he just needed a little rest now.

Then he asked to talk with Clay. "I've decided." Mike looked almost serene. "If it's all the same to you, I'd rather decline your offer. You reach a point when grasping too hard for life becomes undignified. I'd rather go with whatever dignity I have left."

"I . . . understand," Clay said.

"Thanks for everything."

"I wish we could have done more." Clay pressed Mike's hand.

"You've done a lot. And it's all been worth it."

"Are you sure?"

"I'm sure."

"I'll be looking in on you every little bit." Clay waved awkwardly as he backed out of the room. He wanted to say something more. Something about . . . friendship. Perhaps he could say it on his next visit.

Mike asked his nurse if she could get him morphine for pain. It would take several minutes for her to check out a narcotic. Time enough to pull the I.V. needle from his hand, terminating the life-sustaining Isuprel drip.

Still dreaming of learning to sail. Swimming out to the sailboat where Becky was waiting. Swimming with Esther at his side. Her beautiful, long, tan legs kicking rhythmically.

Mike reached out. A cold wave splashed over him. He lifted his arm and dug a stroke into the icy, grinning face of the water. He smashed yet another stroke into the unyielding water and lifted his head to gasp for air.

Then the icy grin began to disappear. The chilling waves became warm and smooth. And yielding. Enfolding with compassionate arms of welcome this one so long lost in the cold of life.

He felt the warmth.

The embrace.

The welcome.

Clay had just finished consoling Becky Goldman when he heard a stat emergency call directing him to Ford's room.

He ran down the hall, trying to pull a cloak of composure over his shivering despair and fear.

"The Isuprel drip is wide open but his pressure keeps dropping," the nurse said.

Oh God, Clay said to himself. "Put two more ampules in it." He listened to Ford's chest. "Mr. Ford, how're you feeling?"

Ford mumbled, "Fine" through his plastic oxygen mask.

"And let's have ten milligrams of glucagon and a gram of Solu-Cortef." Clay watched the monitor. The rate continued to slow. He felt for the carotid pulse—which was barely palpable. "Let's have a full one milligram ampule of Isuprel. I'll put it directly into the tubing."

A slight increase in rate resulted from the combination of drugs. Ford lay on his bed, pale and apprehensive, watching a black and white re-run of "The Beverly Hillbillies" on the 23-inch color television set mounted in the corner of his room.

"Is his wife around?" Leif asked when he entered, coming up from the recovery room in response to the stat call.

"She's back at the motel, Doctor. She usually comes in around eleven."

"Why don't you give her a call and ask her to come in now," Leif said, "and turn the defibrillator on, please."

The nurse pushed the on-off button of the defibrillator, which was part of an emergency cart next to the bed. She then spread electrode paste over the paddles that would be used, if needed, to apply the electrical current to the chest. "The Beverly Hillbillies" continued to cavort on the television screen. Something about Mrs. Drysdale, the next door neighbor, resenting the presence of a menagerie of animals on Jed's estate.

Leif watched the electrocardiogram becoming irregular and disorganized. He grabbed for the defibrillator paddles and applied one high up in the midline and the other at the left side of the chest. He pressed the discharge button. The patient stiffened, but the electrocardiogram did not change. Clay flipped the switch up to 200 watt seconds and Leif reapplied the paddles. This time, regular QRS complexes returned at a rate of about thirty per minute, but Ford was now unconscious and not breathing.

"Nurse," Leif called, "let's have a little help here." He pulled Ford around so that his head was leaning back over the edge of the bed and pried open his mouth. Then he unfolded a laryngoscope and inserted the blade into the mouth, pulling up on the tongue and jaw searching for the epiglottis and vocal cords. Secretions filled Ford's throat. Leif could not see the anatomy.

"Suction, please." Clay held out his hand for the polyethylene tubing. The nurse pushed the tubing into Ford's mouth and Clay drew out the foamy secretions.

Leif took the endotracheal tube and directed it along the blade through the cords into the trachea, then quickly blew into the tubing to see if the lungs expanded. He grabbed a Y tube and attached it to the oxygen supply and to the endotracheal tube. Leif pressed on the open end of the Y tube. Saw both sides of the chest expand. "Tape," he hollered. The nurse handed him a length of adhesive, which he wound around the endotracheal tube and plastered against Ford's cheeks to anchor the tube in the trachea. He listened to the air exchange with his stethoscope while pressing intermittently on the Y tube. "It's in the right place."

Now Clay's attention turned to the monitor. Ford was fibrillating again. "You breathe for him. I'm going to shock him. Stand clear." He applied the paddles once more, pressed the button, and the QRS complexes returned at a rate of about seventy.

Leif kept working the Y tube. "He's coming back." The rate was up to ninety. "We could use a little more help in here." But now the heart rate was beginning to slow again. There were long sinus pauses, then a straight line.

Clay applied the defibrillator paddles once more at 200 watt seconds. Ford again stiffened from the electrical charge, but his electrocardiogram remained flat. Another shock at 300 watt seconds. No heart beat. No spontaneous respirations. Brownish foam began to seep from Ford's mouth and nose as Leif began external cardiac massage.

Clay whispered, "What the hell are we doing to this poor guy, Leif? He's got a right to die."

Leif stopped cardiac massage. He looked at the flat lines on the monitor and said to the nurse: "He's dead. When Mrs. Ford gets here, please bring her to the chaplain's office and send for me."

The television set had remained on during the efforts to save Ford's life. Granny was now threatening to throw Mrs. Drysdale into the *see*-ment pond and Ellie May was clutching a chimpanzee in her arms as "The Beverly Hillbillies" faded into a commercial.

And before this disastrous day ended, Fred Berkowitz also died. His final opportunity to be in the newspapers was not all Fred would have hoped it to be. He would have to share the newspaper account with two fellow-patients.

Following their latest unsuccessful effort at resuscitation together—trying to save Berkowitz—Clay had started to walk with Leif towards his office. But it was as if Leif did not even realize that Clay was there. Clay stopped and watched him turn the corner. Alone. His usually straight shoulders stooped a little. Just a little. . . . Alone.

All five patients who would be subjects in Eric's book were now dead.

The headline in the *Houston Chronicle* read:
THREE HANSON
HEART TRANSPLANTS
DIE IN SINGLE DAY.

TWENTY-ONE

At Leif's request, the hospital administrator scheduled a memorial service for the three men the following morning. It quickly became apparent that the chapel could not hold the large number of people wishing to attend. Ardrey redirected the mourners to the auditorium, the place where so many press conferences on heart transplantation had taken place.

"We've got to sound a positive note. Somehow we've got to sound positive," Leif whispered to Clay as they walked down the hall. "Otherwise their lives will look like they've been wasted."

Even the auditorium could not provide seating for all who wished to pay their respects, the relatives and friends, the doctors and nurses, medical students, administrators, orderlies—and, of course, the media, including Eric.

Chaplain Ross opened the service, which he immediately shared with Rabbi Hirschfeld, who had ministered to Mike Goldman and Fred Berkowitz. Because the hospital was non-denominational, the clergymen restricted their contributions to providing certain biographical information in the context of reminiscences of their own encounters with the patients. The mourners learned that Martin Ford had been one of the most highly decorated

Canadian soldiers of World War 2. And Fred Berkowitz had played professional baseball, culminating in one season with the Brooklyn Dodgers.

Clay spoke next, sharing his experiences with, and fondest memories of, Martin Ford and Fred Berkowitz. But Clay could speak most intimately about Mike. "Dr. Goldman was given an extra year of life—and he filled that year with joy. He got to see his youngest child go off to her first day of school, holding tightly to her older brother's hand. He got to spend more time—precious time—with his beautiful family than most doctors ever have the opportunity to do. His family was his greatest source of happiness. And the Goldman family inherited the enormous fortune of an extra year together. He also wanted to learn to sail and to play the harmonica. I guess I don't know whether he got to sail or not, but he did learn to play the harmonica. He played it very well—like everything he did in his life, he did it well."

Now it was Leif's turn. He eulogized his patients in a manner that was both moving and heartfelt. But he went further: "These men were pioneers and heroes. They have helped advance medicine in ways that none of us dreamed of when we started this adventure together. We are deeply rewarded that we were able to add to their lives and permit them to enjoy time with loved ones that was being stolen from them. But this isn't the end—this is the beginning. What we have learned together with these pioneers is the path to new frontiers. The path to a victory that will add many years of life to potential victims of early death from heart disease."

Leif glanced over at Clay and caught the *what-the-hell-are-you-talking-about?* expression on his face. He turned back to the audience and continued: "I pledge to the memory of these heroes and to all others who have died too soon and to all assembled here—an early victory." He could see the newspaper people writing furiously—and yet he could not stop himself. These deaths had affected him more profoundly than he had realized. The Viking coat of armor that Leif Harald Hanson usually displayed to the world had not been worn today. He had left it in the longship.

"Outside, this is a cold, damp, winter day. Not uncommon for January in Houston. But I'm going to share with you that our goal is to have an important breakthrough by the time spring is here. We're committed to work to the limit of our endurance. And while we're striving for this major breakthrough, we pledge that every other new and promising advance will also be incorporated into our ongoing transplantation program." Leif looked again at Clay and saw him frowning.

But he would not submit to the deterrence of a Ducharme frown. "Although I attended a rival college, I visited Widener Library at Harvard on a couple of occasions. And I was deeply moved by a mural that may be seen as you climb the front stairs. It shows a mortally wounded World War 1 doughboy with his arms around two figures—one dark and one light. The inscription reads something like: 'Happy those who with a glowing faith in one embrace clasped Death and Victory.' . . . "I want to make certain that Mike and Martin and Fred clasp Victory."

Needless to say, the newspaper and television people crowded around Leif at the end of the service. What were these major breakthroughs? When in the spring? Leif said he was not at liberty to divulge the specifics. Something entirely new? Yes, perhaps something that could help many more people than the current transplants were helping. An artificial heart? No comment. Animal hearts? No comment.

"Have you flipped?" Clay asked Leif as they were leaving the auditorium.

Leif rubbed the flat of his hand across his chin and mumbled, "I guess I got carried away."

"Carried away?"

"All right, damn it, call it damage control."

"Damage control by raising false hopes? How cynical can you get?"

"No false hopes. I'm deadly serious. We're aiming for April 15. We're going to work our asses off, but we're going to go with an artificial heart or animal hearts sometime this spring. And to keep our program alive, we're going to do every heart transplant we can get our hands on until we're ready with the big breakthrough."

"Where do you get this *we*-stuff, paleface? You've really flipped."

True to his pledge to keep his program alive, Leif performed five more transplants during the next two months. He led DeBakey, but still lagged behind Cooley in the numbers game. Each of these last five transplants were vigorously opposed by Clay Ducharme, who said they were regressions to mindless activity and insisted that they now knew that the patients were doomed to early death.

Leif knew these facts as well as Clay.

But the difference between Leif and Clay in this matter was simply the urgency of their dreams.

TWENTY-TWO

Clay staggered into bed at 1:35 a.m., and in less than two hours the phone rang. He blindly pawed the bedside table for the intrusive noise—because he was unable to open his eyes.

"It's Mr. Holyoke," the nurse said. "He wonders if he could talk to you."

"Now?"

"Apparently there's a donor for him. And he'd like to talk to you."

"A donor? I didn't hear about that." Clay rubbed his eyes trying to force them open. "I'll be right over."

"This has got to stop," Betty Sue mumbled hoarsely after Clay had hung up the phone. "It's gone too far. There's a limit to everything and we've reached our limit," she now spoke more vigorously. "Andy was waiting all evening to tell you about his interview for Harvard—till he fell asleep. It's as if you don't care. But every time Leif Hanson decides to play God with another human life you come running."

"They're going to try to transplant Holyoke. He doesn't need a transplant any more than I do. I've got to stop those maniacs." Clay began pulling his pants on over his pajamas.

"And I've got to stop you. I'm getting tired of being

mother *and* father to this family. You work day and night, seven days a week. You have no time for the kids anymore. And no time for me. You've spent one weekend in an entire year with the family. And I think you're reaching a point where you don't know how to do anything but work. This has got to stop."

"I know," Clay said. He began buttoning his shirt.

"Honey, you don't know," Betty Sue said. "You don't even hear what I'm saying, do you?"

"I know," Clay said and limped from the bedroom, out of the house, into the February drizzle to his VW parked in the driveway. For the past month his feet and ankles had been painful early in the morning until they warmed up from activity.

He yanked open the unlocked door of his car and sat for a minute rubbing his ankles before fumbling with the ignition. The left ankle was actually a little swollen. This was definitely more than his old heel spurs from running. Arthritis. That was all he needed. He turned the key and the engine sputtered and coughed and died. For two minutes he cranked and pumped and finally elicited a sustained wheeze from the asthmatic VW. Perhaps, he thought, it would not be conspicuous consumption to trade this moribund vehicle for a new one. *Kind of stupid for a physician who needs his car for emergencies to drive a clunker. Even with the doors unlocked no one would ever steal it.* The windshield was already fogging. He turned on the defroster and half opened the door to crane his neck to see his way out of the driveway.

This early in the morning he should have been able to find a parking place only a few yards from the hospital entrance. But the night shift nurses and orderlies had filled up all the "physicians only" spaces. Circling the lot he searched for any available opening. Only one of the outdoor lights for the darkest section of the lot, where Clay had to park, was functioning. This created charcoal shadows, Rorschach figures of bats and projectiles, to fly noiselessly across the cars and land on the wet pavement. Clay scuffed his toe against a bat wing and felt pain shoot into his ankle.

He limped the remainder of the distance to the door of the hospital, limped up the stairs to his office, and after groping along the wall of the murky windowless room, he felt the light switch and snapped on the overhead fixture. He then traded his raincoat for a white coat and plopped heavily into a chair. Clay slouched forward to rub the painful ankle joint. Up to this morning the ankle and foot pain had disappeared within one or two minutes of rising. But not today. The joints had already been hurting for a half hour. *No time for this.* He had to see Holyoke. *See?* He could barely see. His eyes felt as if they had sand in them. More like gravel. *More like damned boulders!*

What the hell are Leif and Sellery up to? They're now stepping over the line. Definitely over the ethical line. But what could Clay do to stop them? Use reason? Logic? Try to wrestle with a truck? *Jesus, what can I do?* With hands on both thighs he climbed up himself to struggle out of the chair. As he locked his office door, he nodded to the night watchman making rounds down the corridor. And as a concession to his pain he rode the elevator to the transplant suite and took great care not to reveal his limp as he approached the nurses' station.

When Clay arrived at Holyoke's room, he saw a very thin, but otherwise vigorous looking, patient sitting up in bed. Holyoke wore Ben Franklin reading glasses and was holding a copy of *Life* in his lap.

"Good morning," he greeted Clay too cheerily, considering the hour.

"It's mighty early in the morning," Clay said. "You should still be asleep. And what's this about a transplant?"

"Dr. Sellery came in and told me Dr. Hanson has a donor for me. I thought you said I didn't need a transplant."

"You don't," Clay said, while trying to resist rubbing his burning eyes. "I'm going to make arrangements to discharge you from the hospital now."

"No, I couldn't do that," Holyoke said. "Dr. Hanson is getting everything ready for a transplant."

"Well, he can just get everything *un*ready."

"I don't want to disappoint him."

"It's your life we're talking about, Mr. Holyoke. Go ahead and disappoint him."

"He thinks I need a transplant. And the other cardiologists he sent in agree."

"My opinion is that you'd live longer and more comfortably without a transplant. Last year we thought differently. Last year we thought we might be offering you many years of life. Now we know we're only offering months of life, or a year or two, at best—until we come up with something new."

"I'm afraid."

"Of course you are. Let's discharge you."

"Let me think about it. You know my doctor sent me to Dr. Hanson for a transplant."

"I'll find Dr. Hanson," Clay said.

Sellery was at the nurses' station in the transplant suite when Clay came looking for Leif. He was jotting a progress note in Holyoke's chart. "We're planning on doing Holyoke," he announced before Clay could say anything.

"I just found out, no thanks to you."

"He's on the surgical service, you know," Sellery warned. "We were gonna let you sleep. I can medicate him."

"Where's Leif?"

"He's in his office."

"Let's go see him."

"No thanks, Ducharme. I'm busy right now." Sellery returned his gaze to the chart and rested his ballpoint pen on the paper.

"You won't come?"

"No. You can talk to Leif without me standing around with my finger up my nose."

"What is it with you, Sellery? Why are you egging Leif on?"

"Nobody eggs Leif Hanson on. He does exactly what he wants. He just selects the advice that goes best with his own opinion."

"This is sickness," Clay said and started down the hall.

"Heal yourself, physician," Sellery called after him.

Clay pushed into Leif's office without knocking. "Holyoke asked me to come in because he doesn't think he wants to be transplanted," he told Leif, while closing the office door behind him.

"He doesn't have to be transplanted," Leif said. He was sitting at his desk.

"What's more, he doesn't need to be transplanted." Clay remained standing by the door.

"Two distinguished and independent cardiologists say otherwise."

"What do they know?" Clay asked. "You turn on the Hanson pressure and they rubber stamp anything. And by the way, it's pretty damned strange that you've started getting outside cardiology consults. You trying to avoid knowledgeable peer review?"

"Holyoke is as sick as lots of people we've transplanted." Leif sidestepped Clay's last question.

"It's different this year than last year. We know we're only buying months not years."

"If we get the right combination we'll buy years *now*. I want to try heparinization on Holyoke. I understand that's what Kahn's been using. And he's been having great results." Leif stayed seated at his desk.

"We need more than gimmicks. We need an immunologic breakthrough." Clay continued to stand by the door, keeping his temper at a distance.

"I know that. But heparin could buy time until you turn loose your damned induction of tolerance. Or until I come up with it. Or till someone comes up with a new antirejection drug that really works. Or until the artificial heart is ready. I've pledged a breakthrough this spring—and I'm a man of my word."

"Don't operate on Holyoke. I mean it."

"I won't, for godsake. If he doesn't want it."

"Even if he does want it."

"That's another story."

"He's just worried that he'll disappoint you. Offend you. That's his main concern. That he'll disappoint or offend the great and famous Dr. Hanson, if he doesn't let you experiment on him."

"That's getting pretty strong, Clay."

"Just don't operate on him." Clay slammed the door behind him.

Clay could not believe it when he arrived at the hospital the next day. Not only had Leif and Sellery transplanted Holyoke, but they had not even completed tissue-matching before surgery, and had given inadequate preoperative medication. Then when Terasaki's report arrived two days later, Holyoke was found to be a D match with a positive lymphocyte cross-match.

Seven days after heart transplantation, Byron Holyoke died of acute rejection.

All Clay could think of was that this inoffensive pharmacist had not wished to offend the great and famous Dr. Hanson.

Following that definitive event, Clay Ducharme officially dissociated himself from the cardiac transplantation program at Southwest to return to his regular teaching duties, patient care, and the desperate pursuit of grant funds. He told Leif he would be happy to function occasionally as a consultant when his services would be needed and his recommendations were likely to be followed.

Quitting the heart transplant team made Clay feel physically ill for two days. The dean and hospital administration still refused to enforce a moratorium. So what could Clay do? The decisions were all in Leif's hands. No more checks and balances. But was Clay abandoning the patients? To an extent, yes. And yet he was being excluded from the process. The surgeons had taken the patients away from Clay. Reverse-abandonment.

What else could Clay do?

So why did he feel like hell?

TWENTY-THREE

Leif now had to confront the reality that he had no one left to provide the essential knowledge, intellectual stimulation, and quality interaction so vital to serious scientific inquiry. His setting the goal of having a major breakthrough in the spring had been deliberate and calculated—to force himself and the rest of the transplant team to push themselves to new and higher levels. *Why couldn't Clay understand and share the dream? Why couldn't he see that they were so close? Why the hell did he have to quit the team?*

So all that remained of the team were people like Frank Sellery, whose major contribution was making "ghoul rounds" to find heart donors. Of course, Sellery could help in the animal lab. Animal surgery was something he could do reasonably well. Yet when it came down to being able to help figure out why they could not induce tolerance the way Clay could, Sellery was a zero. Every transplant ended in acute rejection. Although some animals had lasted longer than others, none had survived more than three hours.

Then there was Haupt. Maybe the artificial heart was the way to go first. It was already late March. By the calendar and by the azaleas, spring had definitely arrived. Something had to happen soon. The team had not even had the possibility of a human donor in three weeks. What if they moved ahead and proposed the artificial heart simply as a temporary measure? At least it would be a first. Something to attract the media attention and stimulate further research. Something to let the world know that the team at Southwest was still in business, even though Cooley and DeBakey had been monopolizing the headlines lately.

"What do you think, Gerry?" Leif asked as soon as he reached the calf laboratory. "Will we be ready with the artificial heart by April 15?"

"Maybe yes. These three seem to be vorking fine. Now longer, I think, than any ever in calves before."

"They look as healthy as they did Christmas Eve." Leif inhaled the pungent smell of the domestic animal lab. He actually liked it. It smelled like his grandfather's barn.

"I think maybe the Hanson valve is the secret."

"I sure as hell hope so." Leif started to leave, but turned back. "Why do we need to wait until April 15? Could we start gearing up now? Start looking around for a suitable recipient. Maybe we could be ready in a week or so. And for the first trial, the strategy would be to put in the artificial heart, and as soon as it's in place, we put out a call for a human donor. We'll use the artificial heart as a bridge to a human donor."

"So hard to find human donors now."

"But with a patient waiting around with an artificial heart in his chest, the publicity, the urgency—we'll find a donor quickly. And that would start the donors coming back to Southwest again. And, bottom line, we'll be the first to actually use the artificial heart in the human."

"Then maybe for the next case, we leave the heart in longer—maybe a veek or a month?"

"Now you've got the picture." Leif smiled. "And before long, we'll start talking about the artificial heart as being permanent."

On the morning of April 4, two things happened.

First, the administrator of the Cohen Institute was finally able to establish an emergency one year grant for

Clay. The notification letter, of which Leif received a blind carbon, stated that the $600 thousand was from the Cohen Trust. At Leif's request, it was not revealed that the ultimate impetus for the funding was really Leif. Perhaps Clay would eventually be willing to work with the team again, but Leif was not going to allow the appearance that he was trying to buy Clay's help.

Second, an air compressor and other pieces of equipment were wheeled into location outside of operating room 1. The OR staff was setting the stage—and the title of this latest production should have been obvious to anyone who had been following the Houston heart transplant drama. For Leif there was a sense of opening night anticipation. Maybe the artificial heart could be a truly valuable contribution. At least it would be a Hanson first.

Leif was on the heart surgery ward reviewing the charts of his few remaining potential recipients when Sellery sought him out. Leif wanted to find the best possible candidate. "I think we should offer the artificial heart to Gabriel, what do you think?" he asked Sellery.

"I think we're a little too late," Sellery said.

"Has something changed with Gabriel?"

"No, something's changed with Cooley. Haven't you heard? It's on the radio and TV. Denton Cooley has just performed the world's first artificial heart operation in a human."

"Don't jerk me around," Leif said. "I've got too much of me invested in this to find that funny."

"I'm not joking. It's on TV and radio. Cooley has put in an artificial heart."

"Since when did Cooley get interested in the artificial heart?"

"Beats the hell out of me. But apparently Liotta, that guy from Argentina who used to work with DeBakey, is working with Cooley now."

"So he helped get Cooley into the artificial heart business?"

"I guess just like Haupt helped you."

"I suppose." Leif slammed Gabriel's chart back into

the rack.

"It's really tough having Cooley and DeBakey working in the same town with you, isn't it?"

"It's tough having them working on the same planet with me. Damn it! I was so god-damned close with the artificial heart." Leif allowed a tone of despair to color his words. "Only to have that damned Cooley beat me."

"But it's not nearly as good an idea as animal hearts. It's just that Cooley gets a first with it."

"A first is damned important."

"But the animal heart . . ."

"Yes, the god-damned animal hearts that we can't get to work for more than a few hours."

"Maybe we need to get Wendell doing a little more detective work in Clay's lab."

"Eck works in there all the time. He's shared everything he knows of."

"But something different must be going on."

"I don't know, Frank. I just need a little time to think, now. I guess talking about a breakthrough in the spring wasn't very bright of me."

"We still may make it. You never can tell. We've got two and a half months of spring left."

The next day, Denton Cooley and Mrs. Haskell Karp, the wife of his patient who had received the artificial heart, appeared on television together to explain that the reason for using the new device was that no human heart donor was available at the time of their urgent need. The artificial heart was a bridge to a donor heart. Thus, they were making a national appeal for a human donor. (And Leif could now vicariously follow what he might have experienced if he had beaten Denton Cooley to this particular breakthrough.)

Having been temporarily too immersed in the agenda of the artificial heart, Leif had allowed the animal heart work to slide. So now he had to return to these experiments with renewed dedication—if not desperation.

And for two months, what was left of the Hanson

team experienced failure after failure, acute rejection after acute rejection, until, at last, one pig heart, which was placed in the chest of a baboon did not go through rejection within minutes or hours. Rather it continued to function strongly for almost a full day. This small success occurred just before Leif was to leave for the Second World Symposium on Heart Transplantation in Montreal.

"All right, what did we do differently in this one?" Leif asked Sellery and Eck while they were walking down the basement corridor from the animal quarters to the hospital

"Beats me. Except maybe we were less careful than usual," was Sellery's answer. "Maybe got off our schedule a little."

"But it's the first good news we've had in a long time," Eck hastened to add.

"While we're away, can you review exactly what we did differently with this baboon—and how this might relate to the way Clay does things that are really succeeding?" Leif gave the assignment to Eck.

"I'll do my best."

"And maybe we can pick up a few pearls of wisdom while we're in Montreal."

TWENTY-FOUR

The stress in Clay's life had greatly dissipated since receiving the unexpected grant from the Cohen Trust. He now had a period of grace to resubmit the various components of the grant that Varney had sabotaged. And Clay had the commitment of the dean that he would prevent Varney from damaging future applications. The question that had been puzzling Clay was how he happened to receive a $600 thousand award that he had not applied for—the exact amount in the budget for the first year of the preventive cardiology grant. The most obvious explanation was that this was Leif's doing. After all, Leif was now the director of the Cohen Institute, and the Cohen Institute was also funded by the Cohen Trust. On the two occasions that Clay had tried to explore the origin of the grant with Leif, not only had Leif angrily denied involvement, but seemed to be positively resentful of Clay's having received the funds. Clay wondered if Leif could have been that good an actor. Of course Clay had been Seymour Cohen's cardiologist and had taken care of him before and after the transplant. Whether Cohen had directly stipulated that Clay receive the money or whether Leif was responsible remained a mystery to Clay.

Whatever the answer, the grant was saving Clay's cardiology program, his career, and probably his health and family. The two month period from April 2 to June 5, the day when Clay and Betty Sue left for the meeting in Montreal had been highly productive and rehabilitating, both professionally and personally. The warm weather brought relief from the arthritis that had often hobbled Clay during the winter. Of course the highlight of this time was Andy's graduation. Like his mother Andy was valedictorian. (Clay had been the salutatorian to Betty Sue in high school.) What was most rewarding was that Clay and Andy had never been closer. Tuesday nights were faithfully reserved for "Star Trek." And they were able to watch together the last filmed episode on June 3, while composing yet another letter to the network to urge continuing the series (as he and Andy had done two years before). Further, they spent hours talking about Harvard, now that Andy was accepted.

The Ducharmes were in a buoyant mood as they joined several other couples from Southwest and Baylor in boarding a Delta flight, the first leg of the trip to the Second International Symposium. Leif Hanson came on another flight without Elaine. Clay saw Leif in the Air France waiting area at O'Hare, but Leif and Denton Cooley went off with several reporters.

After their Air France flight had landed at Dorval, the participants traveled in taxis to the Chateau Champlain. Dr. Denis Tremblay was at the front desk in the lobby of the hotel when Clay and Betty Sue asked for their room. Denis was Clay's height and slender build with mouse-blond hair combed straight back. He was wearing a double-breasted blue suit with brass French designer buttons.

"*Bon jour*, Denis." Clay extended his hand. "*Comment ça va?*"

"*Ça va bien*, Clay. *Bienvenu au Canada.*" Denis shook Clay's hand vigorously. "And this charming lady must be Madame Ducharme."

"Betty Sue, I'd like you to meet Denis Tremblay, a fellow cardiologist at the Montreal Institute of Cardiology."

"Very pleased to meet you," Betty Sue and Denis said simultaneously.

"This is such a new and beautiful hotel."

"Nothing but the very best for the Second World Symposium."

"It looks like you have a good program," Clay said.

"I think it will be informative," Denis answered.

"By the way, how are your patients doing?"

Denis shook his head. "Discouraging. Most discouraging. They have all died. Every one."

"Last I heard, you had several alive."

"I know. But they are all dead now. And what about your patients, Clay?"

"We've lost eleven already. But we still have seven living."

"It started out so beautifully. It looked like we had the right answer."

"I'm afraid we're a long way from the right answer. In fact, I've dropped out of the clinical program. I'm devoting my time to research. What little time I have."

"Do Leif and Denton share your feelings?"

"No."

"I thought not. And Mike DeBakey? He's still doing a lot of transplants yet, isn't he?"

"He seems to be."

"We've stopped heart transplants entirely," Denis said. "But I hope we can come up with some new insights at this meeting."

"I hope so."

"It was a great honor to meet you, Betty Sue," Denis said, "and we'll be seeing each other many times over the next few days, Clay."

The bellman was leading the Ducharmes to the elevator when they saw Eric Kristensen. Eric had been working out of New York for the past few months.

"Eric," Betty Sue called. She had finally dropped the more formal, Mr. Kristensen.

"Betty Sue and Clay. It's been quite a long time."

"We *almost* miss your nosing around the hospital," Clay said. "How are things in New York?"

"Deteriorating," Eric said. "And how's the transplant scene?"

"Also deteriorating."

"That's what I've gathered," Eric said. "I'm looking forward to hearing you speak, Clay. I'd also like to have dinner with you, if you can fit it into your schedule."

"We'd like that too."

"Tomorrow night?"

"If there's no official function going on."

"See you then, if not sooner."

The Ducharmes continued on with their bellman to their room on the fourteenth floor looking out across Dorchester to Place Ville Marie and up to Mount Royal.

The first session of the symposium opened at an auditorium on *Ile Sainte-Hélène*—the Expo site. Christiaan Barnard, Leif Hanson, and Denton Cooley were among those who spoke at this plenary meeting. Norm Shumway and Mike DeBakey were not present. The rumor circulated that Shumway refused to appear on the same program with Barnard, and DeBakey refused to appear on the same program with Cooley. Shumway and DeBakey sent associates to present data from their groups. In contrast to the cheerless exchange of results between Clay Ducharme and Denis Tremblay in the hotel lobby, the presentations at the plenary session by the surgeons generated sanguine enthusiasm. The impression their talks produced was that heart transplantation, using present methodology (with variations), was now a valid and workable therapeutic approach to advanced cardiac disease.

During a break between presentations, Clay saw Lillihei at the phones calling his hospital to tell his associates to start the latest therapeutic variation he had just learned from the previous talk.

When Clay returned to his room at the close of the first day's meeting, he called Eric rather than waiting for Eric to call him. "Did you attend the presentations?"

"I did."

"What did you think?"

"I think the surgeons have lost touch with reality."

"You ready for supper?"

"Ready and starving."

"How about meeting Betty Sue and me in the lobby in five minutes?"

They walked the short distance to Place Ville-Marie, and took the elevator to the top, Altitude 737. The vista of Montreal spread out like an aerial photograph for miles around them. After cocktails, they filled their plates at the buffet and returned to their table by the window looking up towards McGill and Mount Royal.

"I'm going to turn the tables on you," Clay began. "You're always asking us questions. Now I'm going to ask you questions." The spicy aroma of the beef bourguignon was more than Clay could resist. He started on it even before the smoked Nova Scotia salmon. The burgundy-rich gravy was thick in his mouth and the chunks of beef marvelously tender. "We don't usually eat red meat, but the French really know how to make a stew," he said.

"I'll have to agree." Eric selected the salmon first.

Clay continued: "You spent several weeks on a number of different occasions with the patients and the transplanters. You must have learned quite a bit. And you've concluded, after hearing the surgeons today, that they've lost touch with reality." Clay paused to taste the salmon. "Why?"

"What they're saying doesn't bear any relationship to what I've seen," Eric said. "You remember, I was gung-ho for transplants—two articles in *Life*. But when I left Houston the last time, my impression was that it was back to the drawing board." Eric tried the beef now.

"Clay's been at the drawing board and might be close to a new immunologic approach," Betty Sue said. "We just need some time and patience." She smiled at Eric and added: "That's off the record."

"Can you keep doing transplants while looking for a new approach? Maybe there's a relatively simple new drug just around the corner," Eric suggested. "That's something Leif believes."

"I don't think so," Clay dismissed the proposition almost condescendingly. "But as Betty Sue said, I've been back to the drawing board. We were talking about the problem on the plane coming up here. Then . . . I was just sitting in the audience, barely listening to some surgeon trying to convince us that heart transplantation works fine the way it is and, like the proverbial bolt out of the blue, I think I got a hell of an insight." He stopped abruptly. "And—I'd better keep my big mouth shut."

"Do you think this conference will be in *Life*?" Betty Sue assisted in changing the subject.

"I'm not sure." Eric looked inquiringly at Clay. "But if it is, I'll try to make it a realistic report."

"I'm glad to hear it," Clay said. A reporter was not a person with whom he should share a scientific insight.

"You're scheduled to give three presentations, Clay. Why don't you come out and say that heart transplantation isn't working the way it is? Say it in such a way that the media will want to report it?"

"Two are strictly ten-minute, hard-data talks."

"But your last talk?"

"I might be able to work it in," Clay said. "But it won't carry the impact that it would if Hanson or Cooley or Barnard said the same thing."

"Is there any chance that these guys can be convinced to tell it like it really is?" Eric asked.

"Not much. Because they don't see it like we see it. I think they really believe what they're saying."

"Why don't we try to talk to Leif, anyway?" Eric asked. "Now if we're through discussing surgeons, what's this new insight of yours? Drop the other shoe. And this is off the record."

Clay repeated the restraining words: "This is absolutely off the record. Right now I can just say that my insight is on induction of tolerance. I think it may all be in the timing. . . . It's made me so anxious to get back home to review my data that I can hardly stand staying here in Montreal. I'm going to tell the meeting that we're probably two or more years away from animal to human transplants. But if my data show what I think, we may be a hell of a lot closer. I've just got to get back to Houston and check it out."

They strolled back to the Chateau Champlain. The

temperature had dropped precipitously. Clay put his arm around Betty Sue to keep her warm. As they crossed the street to the hotel, a taxi stopped at the entrance. Leif Hanson got out with none other than Roxanne Molnar.

"Why? Why does he have to do that?" Betty Sue asked.

"Apparently Roxanne Molnar's making a movie right here in Montreal," Clay said. "And in fairness to Leif, Elaine wouldn't come with him."

"I don't think we'll get to talk with Leif tonight," Betty Sue said, as she and Clay and Eric waited in the background where they would not be seen.

"Do you still want to go to the cabaret?" Clay asked.

"I'm afraid that's where Leif and his date are going."

"That's all right. There'll be dozens of other people from the symposium there."

"I'd just rather not." Betty Sue shook her head slowly from side to side.

"It's our chance to hear a good French *chanteuse*."

"Maybe another night."

There it was the next day on the front pages of both the *Montreal Star* and *Le Devoir*, Leif with Roxanne at *Caf' Conç'*. The caption in the *Montreal Star* read: "Hollywood star toasts famed heart transplant surgeon." The wire services widely distributed the picture and story, and the *Post, Chronicle,* and *News* all carried the item in Houston.

The section meetings of the symposium took place on Saturday at the University of Montreal. As on the previous day, the impression from the presentations was that heart transplantation was a valid clinical procedure. Clay challenged this concept during the panel discussion on rejection and found support from among those immunologists who had the most extensive clinical experience. Returning to his hotel following the afternoon session, Clay rewrote part of his presentation for the Sunday plenary session. He would have to hurry. Tonight there would be a formal reception in the Biosphere at the Expo site. Betty Sue was already in her evening gown. Emerald green satin that complemented her chestnut hair.

Chartered buses carried the guests of the symposium to Expo. In the distance the geodesic bubble—formerly the US Pavilion, now the Biosphere—sparkled like an enormous inverted Waterford crystal bowl. The couples entered the Biosphere on a red carpet and the mayor of Montreal shook hands with each of them. Inside the glass bubble were several levels of Renaissance-style formal gardens, fountains, and aviaries of tropical birds. Orchestras, bars, and buffets were also present on each level—with each orchestra playing a different style of music, from slow to fast tempos.

"This is right out of a fairy tale," Betty Sue said. "Cinderella never attended anything so elegant."

"Shall we dance to this orchestra? Or go up one more level?" Clay asked.

"Let's dance on every level," Betty Sue said. "I've never felt so elegant in my entire life."

One of the Baylor transplanters and his wife joined them for a few minutes on the next level. He asked Clay if he had seen Leif Hanson or Chris Barnard yet. "The rumor around the Biosphere is that Hanson is bringing Roxanne Molnar to the gala, and that Barnard is bringing Gina Lollabrigida."

The Ducharmes went up to the next level. "That's an unfortunate rumor," Betty Sue said.

"I know. I just wish Elaine would come to meetings with Leif. She used to come."

On the next landing, they paused to chat with couples from Stanford and Paris before going to the escalator leading to the top of the Biosphere. About a third of the way up, the escalator stopped abruptly and no one seemed to be able to move forward by walking. The word came back that there was such a crowd at the top that people could not get off the escalator. Finally, the escalator started again only to stop once more, two-thirds of the way to the top. After another wait, the escalator began to move and the source of the obstruction became apparent to Clay. Chris Barnard was standing right at the exit of the escalator surrounded by admirers—and smiling indulgently. But no Lollabrigida.

"He could damned will move back so people could get through," Clay said loudly.

Betty Sue quieted Clay by calling his attention to the view of Montreal at night from the top of the Biosphere.

On the way down, they saw Denton Cooley and Leif Hanson also attracting crowds. Roxanne Molnar was, fortunately, not with Leif.

More conversation with doctors from McGill. Dancing. Some trips to the buffet for pastries. And more dancing until the Biosphere was almost empty. A final ride to the top. "Why didn't we bring a camera?" Betty Sue asked.

"Too touristy," Clay said. "We'll just have to print these pictures in our memories."

"You know what, darling? I think that this has been the most glamorous evening of my life. Thank you for bringing me." She leaned her head against Clay's shoulder as they walked out on the red carpet into the chilly, Canadian-spring night to the last waiting bus.

The final session convened back at the Expo site at *Auditorium Sainte-Hélène*. Clay's assignment was to present, "Transplantation of the Heart: Prospects and Perspective."

Pierre Grondin introduced Clay in French rather than in English as he had been doing for the other American speakers. Clay answered in French, but then switched to English, explaining that his text was written in English and that it would be in the interest of speed and accuracy for him to give his presentation in the language with which he was most experienced.

Clay concluded his ten minute talk with: "The first round of heart transplantation is now over. The feasibility of the surgical procedure has been established. However, in the immunologic area, the human heart has proved to be highly vulnerable to rejection. We have tried unsuccessfully to bludgeon nature into submission. The second round of heart transplantation will have to use new immunologic methods."

Clay looked out into the audience hoping that the message was coming through. "The last few months have been disastrous for heart transplantation throughout the world. I have heard said in defense of the transplanters that they have had the courage to fail. The courage to fail when dealing only with one's own life is, perhaps, acceptable. But when dealing with the lives and dignity of other men, this courage to fail is immoral. We need no more of this courage to fail! What we now need is the wisdom to succeed. The wisdom to discover how to work with nature. New methodology. This is the legitimate goal of the second round of heart transplantation."

There was warm applause from the cardiologists and immunologists, but only a polite and restrained reception from the surgeons.

But did it matter how the surgeons received the message? If Clay's insight on the induction of tolerance was correct, the second round of heart transplants was ready to begin. He just had to get home and check his data.

TWENTY-FIVE

Leif took the same flights from Montreal to Houston as the Ducharmes, but he booked in first class while Clay and Betty Sue traveled in tourist. It was just as well. Leif was too tired to do anything but sleep during most of the return trip. He had two scotches on the Air France flight to Chicago, and two more on the Chicago-to-Houston Delta flight. As the plane circled Houston, Leif looked down at the new Intercontinental Airport. He had flown out of the old airport, but during the three days he had been away at the meeting the new airport had opened. The plane's wheels touched just once, softly. As a pilot, Leif could admire the captain's skill in "greasing" the landing. He fumbled under the seat for his carry-on bag, wanting to get off the plane quickly to hurry home to see Karen and Mark—and Elaine.

As Leif entered the circular reception area, he heard his name being called. It was Kenneth Price, a lawyer and friend of the family.

"Well, Kenneth, what brings you out here today?" Leif reached out and shook Kenneth's hand.

Price, eight inches shorter than Leif, reached up and put his other hand on Leif's shoulder and said, "Not a very pleasant mission, Leif." He wore a three piece suit and a long cigar. The three piece suit permitted him, even in hot spring weather, the opportunity to display a Phi Beta Kappa key on a vest pocket chain.

"What's wrong?"

"Can we get over here out of the traffic?" Price waved his cigar as if directing traffic with a police baton.

"Sure. But what's wrong?" Leif found an empty place in a row of newly installed black vinyl seats and sank into it.

Price handed Leif a legal document. "It's all in here. And I'm really sorry, Leif. But Elaine wants a divorce."

Leif looked at Price in disbelief—and yet believing. "This isn't a joke . . . is it?" Clay and Betty Sue were waving to him as they walked past. He waved back.

"This isn't a joke." Price joined him in the adjacent chair.

"Why? Why does she say she wants a divorce? And why send you out to the airport to tell me?"

"She says there's been no marriage for a long time. And she can't stand it anymore." Price spoke with a stuffy nasal twang. "And the ridicule over things like this Roxanne Molnar business and the other women. Like your nurse. Everyone around the medical center knows about that."

"Roxanne Molnar? That's really reaching for an excuse. And it's all over with the nurse. We don't even see each other outside the OR anymore. In fact she's moving to Dallas."

"I'm telling you what Elaine has said. Anyway, the Roxanne Molnar business was only the last straw. She has many reasons and we have them well documented." Then he added: "And we know it's over with the nurse."

"Oh *we* have them well documented, have *we*? Well, why isn't *she* telling me? What are *you* doing here, good friend?"

"I'm representing Elaine. And the reason I'm meeting you out here is that she doesn't want to see you. She and the kids will be at my house until ten o'clock, so you can go home and pack some things. Then she's coming home and she wants you to be gone."

"The hell I'm going to be gone."

"That paper in your hand is a court order, Leif. An order to show cause."

"What's that supposed to mean?"

"It means that you'd better be gone by ten o'clock with whatever you need to last you until Elaine and the kids go to Grosse Pointe in a week or two. Then you can have time to move out completely."

"I can't believe this." Leif yanked his underseater luggage closer to him out of the crush of passenger traffic.

"I know. I'm sorry." The cigar in his mouth and the smoke curling into his eyes was not compatible with the feeling that should accompany Kenneth's statement of regret.

"You're supposed to be our friend. Can't you get us together tonight? To work out a reconciliation?" Leif stopped. The words sounded strange.

"Elaine doesn't want to talk."

"Well let's give it a try anyway."

"It won't work, Leif. She absolutely doesn't want to talk."

"What kind of a friend are you? And what kind of lawyer? You worried about your fee?"

"That's not fair, Leif. It's because I'm a friend that I came down here. I could have sent you a telegram or called you long distance in Montreal."

"The hell you say. You come down here to the airport with your god-damn piece of paper . . ." Leif's voice was getting louder.

"Simmer down, Leif. People are watching," Price said. "Let me drive you home."

"I'll take a taxi." Leif lurched from his chair, jerked his bag off the floor, and walked away from Price.

"I'll be glad to drive you."

"Go to hell."

At his home, Leif packed two suitcases, two garment bags, and about ten of his favorite books. He thought of a short story, "The Portable Phonograph," in which the protagonist could only take with him into a destroyed world four books and a dozen records to last the rest of his life. What were the books? Shakespeare, *The Divine Comedy*. What else? *Moby Dick*. And of course, the *Bible*—probably the King James Version. But this wasn't for the rest of his life. The selection would not need to be so painstaking.

So he brought these few rapidly assembled possessions to his office at University Hospital. He opened the closet door, hung up the garment bags, and began to stack the books on a shelf. Then Leif paused to hold in his hand *Growth of the Soil*, the English translation of *Markens Grode*, the book by Knut Hamsun that his grandfather had given to him. He opened it. Pasted inside the front cover was a cracked and yellowed photograph of his father and grandfather together. How many years since he had last read this book? He would read some of it tonight. He placed it on the coffee table and stacked the rest of the books in the closet. He could still see his grandfather's face. See the country kitchen . . . with the oak dining table where they used to read together. Hear Bjorn Hanson say: "You keep your head high." So long ago . . . a lifetime.

It was now after ten. He picked up the phone and dialed his home.

"Hello." It was Elaine's voice.

"Sweetheart, what's going on?" Leif began.

"Don't call, Leif. I will not speak to you. And that's final."

"Just a word . . ." Leif heard the phone click off. He dialed again. This time there was no answer. So he put on a white coat to make late evening hospital rounds and locked the door to his closet. He did not want anyone to see that he had moved into his office.

In the transplant suite, Leif found Eck and Sellery talking together. "What's everybody doing here tonight? Why don't you all go home and get some rest?"

"Just making social rounds," Eck said. "Did you hear about Henry Knoblauch?"

"Nothing recently," Leif said.

"Well, while you all were up in Canada, Henry was committed."

"Committed?"

"Yeah," Eck said. "In the looney bin."

"Come on," Leif said.

"Honest. Of course, he's been seeing a psychiatrist for years. But then he got into drugs." Eck was smiling as he shared this latest gossip. "The poor guy. Varney tried to help. Tried to get him rehabilitated. It just didn't work out." Eck continued to smile.

"I'm very sorry to hear that," Leif said.

Sellery changed the subject abruptly. "I heard a lot of comments about Clay's talk this morning in Montreal. Some people were saying it was the best presentation of the entire meeting."

"It was good," Leif said.

"So when are we going to start the second round of transplants?"

"You mean using transplantation antigen and animal hearts?"

Sellery nodded affirmatively. "Or something."

"We still don't have the techniques. There's something missing," Leif said, too weary to get involved in this sort of discussion.

Wendell Eck could now spring his news. "I've found out what Clay does differently to make things work. It's really quite simple."

"That's the glory road," Sellery cut in, looking at Eck, encouraging him to continue. "We could be the first to do a xenograft with transplantation antigen, using a pig or baboon heart and a method that could make it the model for all future transplants."

Leif suddenly felt exhausted, although he had slept on the plane. There was also a heavy feeling in his chest, which he unconsciously rubbed for a moment. He said, "Let's think about it," and turned away.

He walked slowly down the half-lit corridor to his office and locked the door behind him. Then he removed his white coat, his tie, his shirt, and shoes. No damned blanket in the office. He lay on the slippery leather couch and pulled the white coat over him. The stethoscope in the pocket jabbed him. He yanked it out and put it on the coffee table, trying not to think of what was happening at home. Wondering if he would be able to sleep. He reached for *Growth of the Soil* and decided it would be easier to read at the oak dining table, so he jolted himself off the couch. Leif had finished almost half the book when he finally staggered back to the couch and fell asleep at about two in the morning.

After completing an abbreviated surgical schedule by early Monday afternoon, Leif saw Wendell Eck rounding in the recovery room. "Wendell, could we have a little talk in my office?" he said.

Eck followed Leif and paused to look admiringly at the office furnishings. "How was the Montreal meeting?"

"Very good," Leif said. "We really should have made some arrangements for you to go, too. You're as much involved in this as any of us."

"Someone had to mind the store."

"I guess. But I want you to know how we appreciate your work. We look on you as a coinvestigator." Leif sat at the oak conference table, signalling the serious regard he had for this meeting.

"It's an honor." Eck could strike the precise note of humility needed in these situations.

Leif rubbed the flat of his hand across his chin. "You mentioned last night that you'd figured out what Clay was doing right and we were still doing wrong."

"I sure did. I reviewed all the survival data." Eck took his place across the table from Leif, sitting tall, leaning his right elbow on the table, and pressing his left hand against his hip. "The ones who are really doing best are neither the high-zone nor the low-zone. But in between. It seems to be all in the timing of the antigen loads. And that's probably why we had that one baboon turn out better than the others. We got off on our usual timing."

"That sounds too simple." Leif adopted an adversary position.

"I know. But we've got the data."

"All in the timing?"

"Yes."

"Do you think we could take it to large animals, right now? Make some antigen from liver and spleen?"

"I'm sure we could."

Leif pushed his chair away from the table, gazed down at the floor, glanced over at the window—but did not look directly at Wendell Eck. He began slowly: "As a member of the faculty you are free to work with any other investigator. And I'd like you to be my coinvestigator in this and some other projects if you have the time and *if* it doesn't interfere with your work commitments with Clay."

"That's very nice of you."

"No question of nice." Now Leif was leaning forward looking closely at Eck. "I think we can work together to our mutual benefit. There's a lot to do and not much time to do it."

Eck nodded agreement and looked away. "I can make antigen in Clay's lab. He won't notice. We're always making some."

"No. That wouldn't be right. We'll have to use my lab."

"Whatever you say." Eck waited to see if there were any further instructions before slowly rising to his feet.

"By the way, Wendell," Leif said, "since you're on call tonight, are you going to have supper in the hospital?"

"Yes, but my friend's bringing me something from home at five."

"Right," Leif mumbled. "Right. I guess I'll be eating late anyway. You make the antigen and we'll start premedicating tonight." For a moment, Leif reflected on the fact that Eck had said friend—gender not specified, rather than wife—bringing something from *home*.

When Leif finally returned to his office, after injecting the baboons, it was almost nine. He called home. The phone was answered after several rings. It was Karen's voice. She said: "Hanson residence."

"Hi, honey," Leif said.

"Oh, Daddy. It's good to hear you," Karen said. "What's happening to you and Mom?"

"I don't know, honey."

"When are you coming home?"

"I don't know that either. Your mother doesn't want me to come home right now. But I'll be seeing you and Mark soon. I just have to work out the details."

"Hurry home."

"I'll do my best," Leif said. "Is your mother there?"

"She's upstairs."

"Would you ask her if she could talk to me?" Leif waited for what seemed to be five minutes before he heard Karen's voice again.

She was crying. "Mom doesn't want to talk, Daddy. She says you can come see us Saturday, but not to call before then."

"I'll pick you up at two o'clock."

"I've got to hurry and hang up, Daddy."

"I know. . ." Leif said. "I love you." But the phone clicked off before he finished the words.

Leif and his staff had already made rounds on the patients scheduled for surgery the next day. He would still have to make a last tour of the recovery room and transplant ward. Although he had not yet had supper, he was not hungry. Anyway, he was still slightly overweight—even though he had lost a few pounds since the transplantation program had begun. But somehow he would have to figure out how to get some meals at the hospital. Discreetly. He did not want people to know about his marriage. And he did not have time to go out to a restaurant.

Just before midnight Leif returned to his office. Again he locked the door so that no one from the housekeeping department would walk in on him. But he still had no blanket. He lay down on the cold leather couch, trying to cover part of his six-foot, six-inch, 250 pound mass with a size 48 long hospital coat. Somehow he'd have to find a better place to live than this damned office.

He twisted and turned trying to get comfortable. How could he sleep? The thoughts about his family kept intruding into his consciousness. All right, so he and Elaine had not had much of a marriage for several years. But it was a reasonable arrangement. They lived around each other and provided some basis of stability for the children and themselves. What a lousy thing for Elaine to do to him. And to the kids. At just this time when his work demanded so much. But she knew that. Sure. That was why she was doing it. This was the best time to get at him. To get at him for . . .

Leif got up and paced around the office. Now he was beginning to feel hungry. *What the hell kind of a way was this to live? A man who makes $2 million a year. And doesn't even have food or a decent place to sleep at night. Jesus. Like when I was a kid.* The times he and his mother were homeless. Sleeping in the park and in bus stations. *Jesus. The temporary Leif Hanson has come a full circle.* He sat down again. Musing: *how can you possibly feel sympathy for someone who makes the kind of money I make? But Elaine, for pure god-damned vengeance, would like to hit me for everything I've got. Except she's in no position to do it. Her drinking. Her affairs. I've got facts. If she wants a fight, she'll get it.* He stretched out on the cold couch again. After an hour he fell asleep.

The next day, Leif behaved most uncharacteristically in the OR. He chewed out two residents, a nurse, and even a medical student before the day's eight cases were completed. For the first time in his life he threw a surgical instrument. Threw it across the room. It was very much unlike Leif Hanson. Everything was just piling up after a year and a half of the tension and inhuman demands that the heart transplantation program had added to an already self-consuming schedule. And now the loss of his family. Leif was trying unsuccessfully not to allow himself to think about it. At the end of the day, he apologized for his behavior to the entire operating room staff.

Sellery came back to Leif's office after he had left the operating room. "Is it safe to come in?" he asked and remained standing by the door.

"Come on in," Leif said. "What have you heard?

That I was on a rampage today?"

"I've heard that the crews in rooms 1 and 2 did a lotta bleeding."

"I behaved like a horse's ass," Leif grumbled. "Sit down and take a load off."

"It shows you're human." Sellery sat across the room at the conference table.

"Too damned human." Leif remained behind his desk.

"What I came by to find out was: who're we giving the new pig transplant antigen to?"

"You mean *what* are we giving it to?"

"Maybe," Sellery said.

"*What* I'd like to give it to would be chimps."

"Do we have chimps?"

"No. They're damned hard to get. But we still have access to baboons. So we started premedicating a couple last night."

"Great," Sellery said. Then: "I've got an idea. Why don't we try it on Luce?"

"Luce?" Leif was puzzled for a moment.

"The guy from Atlanta that the GP sent to you." Sellery stepped away from the conference table and slid into a leather armchair closer to Leif's desk.

"That's the one that Clay says doesn't need a transplant."

"He's had three coronary occlusions already. And he's only forty-five. He insists he isn't leaving Houston till he gets a transplant."

"I remember him now. That guy's a nut like Schneider. He doesn't know whether he's here as a donor or a recipient."

Sellery laughed moistly. "He just doesn't know the right words."

"I'm not kidding. When I first saw him he told me he was here to donate his heart."

"Well, now he insists he won't leave till he gets a new heart," Sellery said. "Why does Ducharme say a forty-five year old who's had three coronary occlusions doesn't need a transplant?"

"Clay says he's got good myocardial function. He thinks he needs a coronary bypass graft. Clay is all hot on bypass grafts. He thinks that we should be emphasizing them more than transplants—the way DeBakey's group is."

"All I can say is this guy is anxious to volunteer himself to science."

"Come on, Frank, this guy isn't mentally competent to volunteer for anything."

"He came here referred by his doctor for a heart transplant. He was working a regular job until his last coronary. He owns a Chevrolet dealership in Atlanta. He's not a mental patient."

"He should be. He reminds me of the letter I got from that woman in Nicaragua. She wanted to donate her heart too. She sent her picture in a bathing suit. Very sexy. She said that her only question was: would all these pins she'd stuck under her skin interfere with the surgery?"

Sellery let out a small dry laugh, but would not allow himself to be sidetracked. "Look, what if we ask him if he'd like to be premedicated with transplant antigen?" He leaned forward, conspiratorially, in his chair, talking softly. "Explain it thoroughly. Have a chaplain there and an independent cardiologist. The idea being if the bypass graft isn't feasible—or if it fails—we'll have a transplant ready as a back-up procedure. Spell it out clearly in a written permit with plenty of witnesses."

"That's pretty far-out." Leif said slowly.

"You've gone in before to do a bypass and found it wasn't possible."

"Not on patients Clay has done the heart catheterization and coronary arteriography on."

"Clay Ducharme can be wrong once in a while."

"You're really pushing it, aren't you, Frank?"

"It's the glory road. And you promised a breakthrough for this spring."

"I know."

"Spring's almost over."

"For godsake, we've got to see if it works in animals

first."

"OK. OK." Sellery shifted himself to the back of the chair "Let's do some more animals. But I think the bad results we've been getting in animals are things we might not get in humans. Humans may be really different. And this new technique may be just the ticket."

"We'll see."

The seven living patients needed more and more reassurance from Leif and the remaining members of his team. Eleven of their number had already died. In the transplant suite there was no longer the feeling of exuberance of men beginning an exciting adventure. Rather, there was an atmosphere of stunned acquiescence mixed with intolerable anxiety, the ambient feeling of death row.

This evening Leif converged at the nurses' station with Webb, the psychologist who was still involved with heart transplant patients. Webb's "natural" hairstyle had become even more flamboyant. And he had now taken to wearing sunglasses indoors and a dashiki instead of a tie and jacket.

Webb started the conversation with: "Kind of shoots the program, doesn't it? I mean the way your prize guinea pigs are dying." Webb removed his sunglasses and held them in front of him.

"Some of our patients are dying," Leif said, trying to figure out what was on Webb's mind.

"Twenty-five to thirty thousand a month per patient, I hear. All down the drain."

"Nothing is down the drain. We've given life—and hope—to dying men. And we've learned a lot that will make future operations more successful."

"Ma-a-a-n, you don't think that all this has been a big-time failure and waste?" Webb asked.

"I gather that you feel that way," Leif said. "You thought that perhaps success would come with the first patient?"

"No. I'm not quite that immature," was Webb's answer. "But think what you could have done with all that money. Do you know that there are seventy thousand substandard dwellings in Houston? Do you know how many kids in this Texas-rich city don't get enough to eat? Do you know that kids are being bitten by rats in this damned city while you're wasting money and energy on this stupid game of playing mad scientists?"

"The money spent on heart transplants," Leif began slowly and deliberately, "is a drop in the bucket compared to the money being wasted on drugs, booze, cigarettes, cosmetics, and, worst of all, Vietnam. That's the kind of money that could do something about seventy thousand substandard dwellings—not the little piddling amount we spend on transplants. What do you want me to do? Go down to the Fifth Ward and set rat traps and spread rat poison? Anyone can do that—especially the people who live there. They don't need a cardiovascular surgeon to do it. But I can take a kid from the Fifth Ward, as I did today, and repair his heart."

"You think you can just live in your ivory tower? Do your own thing and not accept responsibility for anything else? Or anybody else?"

"I'm not saying that. What I'm saying is that there are some people in the world who are working to their absolute capacity—and making a real contribution. When they stay in their field of competence, they're professional. They contribute. When they get out of that field, they're bumbling amateurs."

"That's what you believe?"

"Yes."

"M-a-a-an, you don't know that the woods are on fire. You go home to your mansion in River Oaks every night. What do you know about rats?"

Leif unconsciously ran a finger across the scars above his right eye. What was the point in telling Webb that he did know about rats?

TWENTY-SIX

The following morning as Leif was finishing his coffee, alone at an isolated corner table of the hospital cafeteria, he saw Wendell Eck coming through the serving line picking up a sweet roll and a glass of milk.

Eck went out of his way to locate Leif's table. "Mind if I join you? I left home too early for breakfast. This is our early morning conference day."

"Please sit down," Leif said.

Eck unloaded his tray and sat across from Leif. "Both batches of transplant antigen we made from the donor pigs have plenty of activity." He glanced around as he spoke. "I've tested them and they're as good as any we've ever made."

"That's just what I like to hear." Leif smiled broadly. "Outstanding." He paused only a moment to reflect on what he was undertaking. This was Clay's work he was appropriating. *No. No damn it. It's fair game.* Clay had presented this information at conferences and had personally shown him the techniques. *No ethical problem here. None at all.* "What do you say we transplant the baboons tonight?"

"You name the time."

"Seven o'clock. The primate lab."

*

Before beginning his operating schedule, Leif made rounds on the floor where the potential heart recipients were. He saw Luce—who was large-bellied and balding and looked as if he should be wearing a county sheriff's uniform with a confederate patch on the sleeve—standing at the nurses' station in a crimson monogrammed bathrobe.

Luce waved and called out: "Dr. Hanson, could I see you?"

"I'll be right with you, Mr. Luce." Leif started looking through the charts in the rack. "I'll see you in your room." There were charts of only two potential recipients presently in the hospital. Several who had been candidates had returned home or gone elsewhere—including Gabriel, the man Leif had hoped would receive the artificial heart. Only two left—and Luce was one of them. Leif walked slowly to Luce's room, reading the progress notes and nurses' notes as he walked. Luce had been complaining constantly of chest pain, unrelieved by the usual medications, such as nitroglycerin. Lately he had been demanding narcotics frequently. Too frequently. The question now was whether or not he was becoming addicted.

"Doc," Luce began, as Leif walked into the room, "you've gotta do something. I cain't stan' it any longer." He rubbed his chest. "This waitin' for a heart . . . I've gotta hava heart. The pain, I cain't take the pain anymore."

"Mr. Luce, it's not that easy to find a heart donor."

"What am I gonna have to do? Go out and knock someone in the head to getta heart?"

"I'm afraid that's not the solution."

"Well, what *is* the solution?"

"First, Dr. Ducharme isn't sure you need a transplant."

"But you're my doctor here. My doctor at home sent me to you. He thought I needed a transplant. You think I need a transplant. So what do we care what Dr. Ducharme says?"

"Dr. Ducharme may be right," Leif said. "It may be that we only need to repair your coronary arteries. That's a new type of surgery that we've been doing the past year for cases that aren't bad enough to need transplants."

"And what if you cain't repair my coronary arteries?"

"There are some alternative possibilities."

In the evening, down in the pungent-smelling animal surgery lab, Leif and Sellery, with Eck assisting, bent over the side-by-side operating tables and performed the latest pig-to-baboon transplant. And they finally collected the reward they had been seeking. They watched the pig's heart beat vigorously and continue to beat . . . and beat in the baboon's chest. The new transplant antigen seemed to make all the difference.

For over an hour the men watched until Leif said, "By God, this one may be a winner—at last. It's not going to stop. Let's close the chest."

"We'd better set up a schedule of shifts to take care of this beast," Sellery said. "He may be our prize."

"I'll be happy to take a shift," Eck said.

"He's already waking up." Leif pointed to the spontaneous movements of the baboon's extremities as he snapped the last skin clips into the blue shaved skin over the breast bone. "He may not need much watching."

"I think we've really gotta winner, chief." Sellery pulled off his gloves and mask. "We've got the schedule that Clay uses to keep the mouse hearts going forever. That's a hell of a lot of background research. So when do we start on Luce?" He hastened into a supporting argument before Leif could answer. "We waited a day too long on Gabriel—and Cooley beat us with the artificial heart."

"Luce?" Eck looked surprised. "I thought he'd been discharged."

"No. We've talked to him about a bypass graft," Leif explained.

"But we should also get permission, if the bypass isn't satisfactory, to do a transplant. He's still on the surgery service," Sellery said.

"But there's such a shortage of donors," Eck mentioned the obvious.

"So if there's no human donor around, we could also get permission to use an animal heart," Sellery added. "Or even an artificial heart, as a bridge till we getta donor."

"That's heavy." Eck let out a soft whistle.

"That's also premature," Leif said.

"There's precedent for it," Sellery argued. "You know as well as I do that the first heart transplant to a man was done by Hardy using a chimpanzee heart. Back in 1964."

"It wasn't ready then and it's not ready now." Leif was enjoying playing devil's advocate. *Let's see how convincing an argument old Sellery can develop.*

"Others have tried animal hearts in men," Sellery continued. "Cooley used a sheep. Some guy in Poland, a calf. But if we did use a xenograft, we'd have the patient loaded with transplant antigen. A first."

Eck said, "Why are we thinking of putting a pig heart into a human instead of a chimpanzee or a baboon heart?"

Sellery, who tried to display his knowledge whenever possible, did not have a ready answer to this.

So Leif helped. "There are very, very few chimps in the world," he explained. "And while there are more baboons available, that supply is also extremely limited."

"But baboons are closer to man."

"And chimps are even closer. It was all right to use a chimp heart in 1964. You'd expect a chimp or baboon heart to be accepted better than a pig heart. But to stick a baboon heart into someone now is no advance."

"I guess not," Eck mumbled.

"What we need today is a supply of hearts to meet the demand. Hearts from the few baboons that are around won't even begin to do it. But pig hearts will. And pig hearts are anatomically quite similar to human hearts."

"Why don't we start giving the antigen to Luce now?" Sellery interrupted the lecture.

"Let's just cool it, Frank. What I'd appreciate is if you'd transplant the heart from pig B tomorrow night." Leif shrugged out of his surgical gown.

Sellery continued to press, "In the meantime we can

have Luce ready for whatever might happen."
"This is a hell of a big decision," Eck said.
"And it'll be a hell of a big accomplishment," Sellery added.

Sellery had the bit between his teeth now. The next morning he reported to Leif, "Wendell and I did the second baboon after you went home. Come on and look at them."

Leif went to the animal quarters and found both baboons awake and vigorous, screeching and poking their fingers through their wire cages. "My God," he said, "the second baboon looks even better than the first. And so does his ECG."

"We've got the answer," Sellery exulted.

Leif continued to look at the baboons. "Incredible. Clay says two or more years. But it looks like we may have done it in a week. I'd sure as hell like to show these results to Clay right now."

"Wouldn't it be better," Sellery countered, watching Leif's face for reaction, "to wait until *after* we do Luce?"

"You're still pushing for Luce?" Leif said the words flatly, not providing a clue to his position.

"What we've done here is worth a lead article in a basic science journal," Sellery said. "What we do with Luce is gonna go down in medical history."

Leif slowly rubbed his hand across his chin, keeping Sellery guessing. "I've already talked to Luce a little," he finally said. "I suppose it wouldn't hurt to talk to him a little more."

"All right! That's the way to go!"

"I can't get over it." Leif kept watching the baboons. "It finally seems so easy. And things usually aren't that easy in science."

"We just eventually put it all together," Sellery said. "And like I say, Ducharme has done years of background work on this. It hasn't been all that easy. There's solid research behind what we're planning."

From the animal quarters, Leif went directly to

Arthur Luce's room. "Mr. Luce," he said, "if you'd like, we could start thirty-six hours of a special treatment today and plan to try to repair your coronary arteries as soon as the treatment is over."

"Sounds great, Doc," Luce said. "Cain't wait."

"I want you to understand this too, Mrs. Luce. And I'm going to have other people talk to you so that it's clear in everyone's mind what we're doing. We think that there's a possibility that we can repair your coronary arteries, Mr. Luce. But we're not sure. So we can go ahead and try as we usually do. And if we get into trouble we can take our chances. Or we can have an ace in the hole."

"Tell me about the ace." Luce was sitting up in bed with his hands clasped over his bulging belly, as if he were actually looking at his hole cards.

"A transplant."

"That's what I'm here for."

"But as you know better than anybody, human donors are hard to find. So we'd plan on either a human transplant. If one is available. Or a pig heart, if there is no human heart available, and if we've prepared you with this special medicine."

Mrs. Luce let out a little gasp.

"And finally we have an artificial heart. I've brought one along." Leif held out the plastic chambers for Luce to inspect. "We can sustain you with the artificial heart until a human donor becomes available. Artificial hearts may be the wave of the future. This is an early model that has to be hooked up to an outside power source. But in a few years we should be able to have small, self-contained units."

"I'd rather have that," Mrs. Luce said, pointing to the yellow plastic heart. "The idea of a pig heart gives me the creeps." She was a thin, henna-rinsed, antebellum type, who looked as if she got the creeps or the vapors easily. There was a paper rose substance about her.

"The last artificial heart didn't work too well," Luce said. "I'd rather not have an artificial heart, if we can do something else. I heard that there's a big tube that sticks outta your chest. I mean, how can you even roll over in bed?

I came here for a heart transplant, anyway."

"But not a pig heart," Mrs. Luce said.

"I can only tell you we've done this in animal experiments. We now have pigs' hearts beating in baboons' chests as if they belonged there." Leif paused a moment to analyze what he had just said. The words gave the impression that more than two hearts and more than one day of observation were involved. Deceit was not his usual style. He was about to clarify what he had said. Then, of course, anyone with intelligence above that of the village idiot would decline the transplant. *But this wasn't really deceit. In the strictest sense it was true. Just a matter of interpretation. Someone had to take the step. Everything was on the line now.* "You see Mr. Luce, we could only have a successful transplant with a pig's heart if you get this special medicine for thirty-six hours. And I will assure you that the operation we plan to do is a coronary artery repair. No transplant of any kind. We'd only resort to a transplant if all else failed."

"As I told you, Doc, I'm here for a heart transplant or whatever you think is best," Luce said.

"Do you understand all of this, Mrs. Luce?"

"Yes. But I hope you don't have to use a pig's heart." Mrs. Luce now appeared to be one hyperventilated breath away from the vapors.

"I hope so, too," Leif said. "And the decision is up to you. We don't have to use this special medicine. We can go ahead and take our chances without it. Or we can use it as an ace in the hole."

"I'm a poker player, Doc," Luce said. "I like havin' an ace in the hole."

Luce opted for the pig heart antigen and also agreed to the artificial heart if it appeared to be the best alternative at the time of the operation. Premedication injections began immediately.

This crescendo of activity and preparation forced Leif to reduce his Saturday visitation with his children to only an hour drive around the park and the purchase of ice cream cones. He promised, however, that next Saturday they would go to Astroworld.

The meeting in Montreal had rekindled Eric's smoldering interest in heart transplantation, and in his proposed book on the subject. After he had checked into the Shamrock, he came over to the hospital on the chance that he could find Leif or Clay.

Leif was still in his office.

"Had supper yet?" Eric asked as he stuck his head through the half open door.

"Red, I was actually going to call you in New York, tonight." Leif got up and pumped his cousin's hand. "What brings you here?"

"I need a little more information for my book," Eric said. "But what about supper?"

"You bet, let's grab a bite."

"Shamrock?"

"How about Pier 21? I've got a craving for seafood." Leif threw his white coat on the chair and pulled on a summer-weight blue blazer.

"What were you going to call me about?" Eric asked.

"I was going to see if you could come down for a case tomorrow."

Eric didn't say anything.

"Something pretty exciting may happen."

Eric continued to wait for Leif to talk.

"Come on, let's get to my car."

"What's going to happen?" Eric finally asked, as they walked to the parking lot.

"I can't tell you. Just come to the OR tomorrow for my last case of the day."

"Have you got some new miracle of modern science to spring on us?"

"It's a possibility."

During supper they talked about several things. But not about the "happening" scheduled for the next day. And not about Leif's marital situation.

On returning from Pier 21, Leif called Clay's office.

Clay was also still at work. "I've got a couple of things I've got to show you. Can I come by and get you?"

They went first to the laboratory where the calves were walking "contentedly" on their treadmills with their artificial hearts in place.

"They look fine," Clay allowed.

"Gerhardt has seen them all. DeBakey's, the ones in Salt Lake, Minnesota, Chicago—he says these are doing the best."

"I'm glad to hear it."

"I think there's a place for the artificial heart in clinical medicine right now."

"Not for humans there isn't."

"I think there is."

"I wouldn't let my dog be chained in the yard. Much less have him exist chained by a tube sticking out of his chest and hooked up to an air compressor like these poor critters. And you know what happened with Cooley's artificial heart."

"Just want you to know that we've been ready to go with the artificial heart for months. We were as ready as Cooley was in April."

"You've been working hard. I'll grant you that."

"But I've got something else that relates directly to you, Clay. It's just down the hall from here."

"And what's that?"

"Come on I have to show this to you."

Clay followed Leif to the primate lab.

"Induction of tolerance with transplant antigen." Leif pointed to the two caged baboons. "They've got pig hearts in them."

"You've got to be kidding."

"I'm not. And just look at their ECGs."

Clay began unrolling the tracings and studying them. "This could be the beginning of the next step of our research. We may now be only a few months away from animal-to-human transplants."

"And it's mainly your methods I've used. So you share fully in this."

"How long since the transplants?" Clay didn't respond to the "sharing fully" offer.

"Three days."

"Three days? For crying-out-loud, you haven't had time for a first-set rejection yet."

"But look at them, Clay. Look at them."

Clay looked. "I admit they appear to be great. And I'm really impressed. You've achieved a hell of a lot. But we've still got a way to go." He turned back to Leif. "I know you're bright—too bright for a surgeon—but I don't understand how you learned my methods so well."

"You showed them to me, yourself."

"I know that." Clay started to roll up an ECG.

"But it took me years. And you seem to be doing at least as well, if not better. . . . Unless . . . did Eck help you?"

How could Leif answer? "A little. But with the full understanding that this is basically your baby. You'd certainly be first author of a pig-baboon article."

Clay replaced the ECGs on the table in front of the baboon cages and began slowly, "Since I've returned from Montreal, I've gone over my data. . . . The secret is in the timing. . . . We may not be years away from animal transplants. Maybe only months. So don't screw things up when we're so close."

"I know it's in the timing. That's why it's working in these baboons. We figured it out, too."

"*We* did, did we? My methods? My years of work?"

Now, how could Leif lead into the preparation of Luce for a possible pig heart transplant? "There's something else you need to know."

"I don't think I'm up to hearing anything more."

"I'm afraid you've got to."

"OK. Go ahead."

"Bottom line: I've already induced tolerance in a potential heart transplant patient."

"You've wha-a-at?"

"You heard. We're ready to go with this."

"The hell you are. Not with my methods you aren't.

You're not going to screw up years of my work by bringing this out before it's ready—and crapping out. And you're not going to experiment on a human being with something that's not ready yet for anything more than mice and baboons. This is crazy."

Apparently in response to Clay's yelling, one of the baboons began to screech and pound the screen of the cage.

"I think that both the artificial heart and animal hearts are ready right now. And, my God, Clay, Eck tells me your mouse and rat hearts are not being rejected anymore."

"I think this would be a page right out of Dachau if you tried it in a human before it's ready."

"Obviously, I completely disagree. Do you realize that these baboons are not getting Imuran or steroids? They're now functioning on induction of tolerance alone? Just like your mice and rats."

"I agree it's a beautiful result. But just stay with baboons. I'm not asking you. I'm telling you. Don't you dare use my methods on a human yet. We're too close for you to screw it up now."

Luce's name appeared on the schedule as the twelfth and last surgical case for Leif Hanson on the following day. The procedure designated for Luce was a coronary bypass graft. Eric waited in the doctors' on-call room.

Although Leif often completed comparably large surgical schedules by six o'clock, this day's case load seemed interminable—as if the delays were deliberate. Finally, at 10:15 p.m., Monday, June 15, Luce entered operating room 1, asleep on a gurney. Two people from the medical photography department were waiting in the corridor, and the platform that is used to suspend a movie photographer over the operating table stood at stainless steel attention just outside the door. Eric followed the camera crew into the OR.

The green-gowned surgical team surrounded the green-draped patient. Leif Hanson accepted the scalpel, then the electrical saw, which hummed its way through the sternum. Luce's chest gaped open, stretched by retractors.

Next, the slitting of the pericardium. At this point Sellery abruptly announced: "That's what we were worried about. Look at the ventricular aneurysm. And that's triple artery disease." As his fingers felt along the coronary arteries his hand covered the area where he had indicated the aneurysm existed. "How can you possibly revascularize that?"

Leif looked at Sellery's eyes peering over his mask. They were saying: *Up to you now. The opportunity. Up to you.*

But Leif said, "Let's do the best we can. We'll put him on the pump and remove the ventricular aneurysm first."

After all the tubes were in place and the heart-lung machine had taken over Luce's circulation, Leif began to cut out a piece of scarred left ventricle. Roughly. Not with his usual exquisitely precise strokes. The two surgical residents and the anesthesiologist kept trying to see what was happening, but Sellery's hands always seemed to be in the way. Leif handed the excised tissue to Sellery, who wrapped it in gauze, and dropped into a basin. Finally, Leif sutured the ragged hole that remained in the left ventricle and discontinued the heart-lung machine.

"The heart isn't beating," Sellery said. "We'd better go back on the pump."

Leif signaled for the team to restart the heart-lung machine. He stood quietly watching the motionless heart. *How would it respond to a little stimulation? . . .* And: *If I remove the heart, what should I use to replace it?*

The circulating nurse patted the sweat from Leif's forehead with a four-by-four gauze pad.

So much at stake. . . . Can't wait any longer. . . . Have to go through with it. Otherwise, everything that's gone before is meaningless. . . . All the losses. "There's not much point in going on with coronary surgery," he said. "This heart isn't going to function. Why don't you break scrub, Dr. Sellery, and see if there's any possibility of a human donor."

Sellery snapped off his gloves. "And if not, we'd better bring up the xenograft?"

"Or the artificial heart," Leif answered tentatively.

297

"Which?" Sellery came up behind Leif and whispered, "Just be the second to use the artificial heart?"

Leif turned his head towards Sellery and also whispered, "Clay doesn't want his methods used right now. He thinks they may be ready in only a few months...."

"To hell with Clay. These are our methods now." Still whispering.

Leif watched the telltale heart in Luce's chest for evidence of even a twitch. *The worst has already been done. Get on with it.* "If there's no human heart available—send for the xenograft," he said forcefully.

Sellery waved to the movie photographer in the corner of the operating room. Two orderlies wheeled the platform into place with the photographer poised over the operating table. Then Sellery told the photographer, "Now." The movie camera began to document that the heart would not beat after the aneurysm had been excised.

Sellery pulled off his gloves and gown and left the operating room. Within five minutes he called back the report that there was no possibility of a human donor and that the xenograft was ready. An intern had remained with the pig, which was anesthetized on a stretcher, in the animal surgery laboratory. Ten more minutes passed before Sellery and members of the surgical team pushed a stretcher transporting the pig, covered with a green surgical sheet. They wheeled the donor into operating room 2. An anesthesiologist and nurse were waiting. In twelve minutes the message came over the intercom that Sellery was now excising the donor heart. Leif turned to his patient and began to remove the heart.

Sellery transported the pig heart cross the hall in the traditional stainless steel basin as if carrying a crown on the traditional cushion. The trimming of the heart to conform to the residual atrial wall and great arteries and veins in Luce's chest took only two minutes. The excess pieces that Leif removed from the donor heart, went to Wendell Eck to make heart-specific transplant antigen as quickly as possible.

Eck left the OR immediately and walked and ran to Leif's laboratory. It was almost midnight.

Sewing the pig heart into Luce's chest required only fifteen minutes. Leif delayed another fifteen minutes before discontinuing the heart-lung machine, to provide as short a period of circulation as possible before the heart-specific antigen would arrive. But they had to maintain viability of this heart. He said, "Let's perfuse it." For a moment the heart contracted tightly in apparent hyperacute rejection, but then it relaxed and ventricular fibrillation appeared. The defibrillator paddles. Electrical shock. And the heart began to beat in sinus rhythm.

It was like the first heart transplant all over again. The murmur of excitement that sparked through the operating room discharged a current of *feeling* into Leif Hanson—up the damaged nerves that had been too scarred to feel anything since he had returned from Montreal.

"We've done it, chief," Sellery said. "Everything that everyone has done in heart transplantation before has just been a rehearsal for this. We've done it. A successful animal heart to a human."

"Let's watch the pressure," Leif said to the anesthesiologist. "It's dropping. How about a little calcium or Isuprel?"

The anesthesiologist gave calcium and the blood pressure responded promptly. "Behaving just like a human donor-heart," he said.

Staring down into the blood-splotched pulsating cavity, Leif waited for another thirty minutes before beginning to close the chest. The heart continued to function vigorously. By the time he had started to place the skin sutures, Wendell Eck arrived with the freshly made, heart-specific antigen.

At 7:00 a.m. Luce was nodding in response to questions and pointing to the tube in his throat, indicating that he wanted it removed so he could talk. He looked as good as the best heart transplant Leif had ever performed. A cautious press release was indicated. And could Leif now acknowledge—to himself—that this could possibly lead to a Nobel Prize?

Leif walked back to his office and, without recognizing what he was doing, he followed a well-worn habit path and dialed Elaine.

"Hello," Elaine answered.

"I'm sorry," Leif began. "I guess I forgot myself."

"Leif?"

"Yes."

"I've asked you not to call."

"I know. I just forgot myself. I guess I just wanted to share something with you."

There was no response from Elaine.

But Leif continued. "I think we've succeeded with a xenograft. You remember I told you about our experiments. Well, last night we transplanted a pig heart into a man. And it's working. A practically limitless supply of donor hearts. Do you know what kind of a breakthrough this is? This is a first. A major contribution. It makes all the sacrifices worthwhile."

A long silence. Then: "Leif, listen carefully. You don't seem to understand. What you do is no longer of any concern to me. You can transplant pig hearts into men or go to the moon. I don't care anymore. Don't you get it? You're a Phi Beta Kappa. Try to understand. I don't care anymore. It took me years to reach this point. But I'm here. And I'm not coming back from here. I simply don't care. And I don't want you to call me. Any further communication will have to come through my attorney."

"Well, could I speak to Karen?"

"No. You may see her on Saturday. I hope you spend a little more time with the kids this week than you did last. Then we're flying to Grosse Pointe on Sunday. And we'll be staying with my folks for a couple of weeks while our attorneys iron things out."

"Kenneth was my attorney. So I guess I don't have one now."

"Then you'd sure as hell better get one—if you want to come out of this with two dimes to rub together."

"Elaine, please . . ."

"Good-bye."

Leif replaced the phone in its cradle, changed into a fresh scrub suit, and walked to the surgical suite to begin another day's schedule of nine operations. Half-way down the hall he stopped. A feeling of heaviness in his chest. He rubbed his chest and took a few deep breaths. The heaviness disappeared.

The story of the xenograft appeared on the noon news broadcasts and in an early edition of the *Houston Chronicle*. The *Chronicle* headline read:

HANSON TEAM TRIUMPHS
First Successful
Animal to Man
Heart Transplant

Dr. Vincent Varney was outraged when he heard the news. And as the self-appointed spokesman for the critics of heart transplantation, he called the member of his department who was ostensibly most involved on the transplant team, Clay Ducharme. To his surprise, he found that Clay was not only not involved, but was equally outraged.

Clay went to the lobby of the hospital and bought a copy of the *Houston Chronicle* and carefully read the newspaper account before bursting into Leif's office.

Leif had just finished his fifth operation and was eating lunch at his conference table—fried chicken, which his secretary had brought on a tray from the hospital cafeteria.

"Leif, what the hell have you done?" Clay shouted.

"I've been trying to reach you. But I figured you'd get in touch, if I didn't."

"What the hell have you done?" Clay repeated.

"We've made a major breakthrough," Leif said. "And you'll share in it." He motioned to Clay to join him at the table. "Would you like some coffee?"

"Hell no." Clay didn't move to sit at the table. "You've used my method. Without my consent. Stole it. And described it in detail to the newspapers." His voice was growing louder. "You've used it long before it was ready to be used. And you've used a human being as an experimental animal."

"Watch what you're saying." Leif's jaw tightened and then relaxed. "No one is stealing your ideas. You're getting full credit for them. If this is a success, you share fully in the success. If it's a failure, I take all the blame. You can't lose."

"I can't lose?" Now Clay was shouting. "You steal my idea and misuse it before it has a chance to be developed. And I can't lose? All we needed was a few months to do it right. Safely."

"It could have dragged out to a few years. Someone had to have the courage to take a chance now. Sure there's a big risk. But I'm willing to take it. I've laid it all on the line. And it looks like we've won." Leif swallowed some coffee. "We've performed the first successful xenograft and established a model for all future heart transplants. No human donors needed. No plastic hearts that cause strokes. But the chance to raise new hearts just like we raise our food supply. We're first."

Clay stamped over to the couch and dropped heavily onto it, trying to capture his escaping rage. "What's this risk you're talking about?"

"I've put my reputation on the line."

"What you've done is you've put Luce's life on the line. You've taken a man who did not need a heart transplant—and stuck a pig's heart in his chest—and say you've taken a risk?" Clay jumped back to his feet. "Don't you understand?" he shouted. "It's Luce who's taken the risk. It's his life. And his big mistake was in ever trusting you. Listen to me, god-damn it! If Luce dies, you've actually committed a murder."

"I'm not going to take that."

"Go ahead and do something about it, you god-damned butcher."

Leif's secretary knocked on the door. "Did you call?"

"No. I didn't call," Leif said. "And we'll try to hold the noise down."

As the secretary closed the door, Clay began again:

"You've got this screwed-up, distorted, damned idea that being the first to do something is the same thing as being creative." He spoke less loudly, spitting the words from deep in his throat. "Be first. No matter what stupid thing it is that you do. Just so you're first to do it. No matter if some poor bastard trusted you and put his life in your hands. The thing to do is to use him. You're accustomed to using people. And this is the ultimate. Lord, this is the ultimate in using a human being. To puff up your enormous ego, you're taking a man's life. Using him. Damn it, murdering him!"

"Get out of here," Leif said through clenched teeth. "You're wrong about all of this. This is too big for you. One life for something to save thousands or millions. I'd put my life on the line just as quickly as Luce's. Because it's so important. But this is too big for you. Now get the hell out of here."

"I can't leave fast enough." Clay slammed the door.

On the plane to New York Eric made a few corrections in his latest manuscript. He played up the breakthrough angle. This indeed seemed to be *the major* accomplishment in the history of transplantation. It looked like Leif had really done it. Barnard, Shumway, Cooley, and DeBakey were no longer in the same league with Leif. Had the redwood at last sunk deep roots?

TWENTY-SEVEN

A benefit of the new regimen for combating rejection was that the very strict isolation procedures used in previous patients were unnecessary. So on Arthur Luce's second postoperative day medical photographers, wearing masks, but not gloves and gowns, recorded his first steps out of bed.

Then, just two hours later, unmistakable electrocardiographic signs of rejection appeared. The team gathered in Luce's flower-filled room, trying to exude confidence to match the roses, while Luce complained of difficulty in getting his breath and Mrs. Luce was hyperventilating even with a surgical mask covering her nose and mouth. She kept fanning herself with a magazine and moaning softly.

Leif motioned to Sellery and Eck to meet outside the room after Luce had stabilized. A nurse stood in the open door ready to signal the doctors to return.

"What the hell's happening?" Leif asked Wendell Eck. "Our prize case. What the hell's happening?"

"Jesus, I don't know," Eck said. "He'll have to stay on the Isuprel. We've had a couple of patients who did this before."

"This bad, this early?" Leif was looking back and forth between the Eck and the nurse—ready to rush back into Luce's room.

"Maybe not," Eck said. "I've got another piece of bad news, too. The heart-specific antigen I made from Luce's donor heart—it doesn't have any activity. I've tested it with tanned red cells and bentonite. And it just doesn't have any activity."

"Then what in hell went wrong?" Sellery demanded.

"I just don't know. I sonicated it and centrifuged it and millipored it the way I always do. Somehow the antigen mustn't have been in the supernatant—and I threw the baby away with the bath water."

"That's pretty damned casual," Sellery said.

"This is hardly a routine clinical procedure," Eck shot back. "And another piece of bad news: one of the baboons is dying. I just checked him. His electrocardiogram is almost a flat line. And he's lying in his cage gasping. I gave him intracardiac steroids and Cytoxan. But he's dying."

Sellery made a whistling sound. "The roof is caving in," he said.

Drones, the hospital public relations man, came down the hall, smiling. "Just wanted to let you know that the picture of Luce walking has been picked up by the wire services."

"Oh Jesus," Leif said, "is there any way to get it back?"

"It's already gone."

"That's all we needed," Sellery muttered, as the PR man turned away.

"We've got to keep Luce alive," Leif said. "I'll get in touch with Clay Ducharme. He'll have to help."

Eck frowned. "I don't think Dr. Ducharme knows I'm involved in this case."

"It's OK," Leif said, glancing at the nurse in the door to Luce's room.

"I think he's pissed at me."

"He'll get over it." Leif picked up the phone and dialed Clay's office. "Clay, you've got to help us," he said. "Luce is rejecting."

Clay put his personal anger aside and did everything he could to help save Luce. Massive doses of steroids and Isuprel temporarily restored Luce's blood pressure to a reasonable level. But Arthur Luce survived only until the next morning.

He had lived fifty-eight hours hours with a pig's heart beating in his chest.

After Luce's death, Leif and Clay went to the animal quarters. The first baboon had died, but the second was as vigorous as ever, yanking aggressively at the wire cage and showing its teeth.

"What medications has the living one had since surgery?" Clay asked.

"Nothing. The one that's alive is the one that Sellery and Eck did. Before I knew it, Eck blasted the other one with steroids and Cytoxan. But I told him to leave this one alone. We've got to see what the antigen can do by itself."

"I agree," Clay said. "And by the looks of it, the antigen is doing damned well."

"So why didn't it work in the other baboon? And in Luce?"

"Well, you said Eck didn't get the heart specific antigen prepared correctly for Luce. A human error."

The baboon was screeching and shaking the cage.

"But he said the antigen was great for both baboons—the one that died and the one that lived."

"There are probably other variables we don't understand yet," Clay said. "That's the whole point. Why couldn't you have waited? My rats and mice are much closer genetically than pigs are to men, for godsake. And there's a hell of a big difference between sticking a newborn rat heart into a mouse ear and not hooking up any blood vessels—and hooking up a pig's heart in a man and expecting it to keep him alive. We could and *should* have gone into this so well prepared that success would have been assured."

"Bad judgment," Leif said.

The baboon's screeching was making the conversation difficult to hear.

"And worrying about being first?"

"Bad judgment," Leif repeated.

"I imagine Sellery pushed pretty hard for this."

"My responsibility," Leif said.

"Unfortunately, it is." As he was leaving, Clay looked back once more at the healthy operated baboon. "I've got to admit you have one amazing success in that critter."

Leif wanted to say more. He mumbled, "Thanks for your help, Clay."

"It's OK," Clay said. "It was for the patient."

"I should have used the artificial heart. It was ready."

"No. Damn it! The artificial heart has already been tried in one patient. Neither option is ready yet. But maybe this one was slightly more humane."

Mrs. Luce was angry and distraught. The *Houston News* printed her allegations in an exclusive interview. She insisted that her husband had understood that he was to have a bypass vein graft and that the chances for a transplant (especially an animal heart) were highly remote. She described the sense of horror and revulsion that she and her husband had felt when they learned that a pig heart had been transplanted into him. She said that Luce could not believe it. That he had gone to sleep expecting to have his coronary arteries repaired and he had awakened to find the heart of a pig beating inside of him. A pig!

Several of Leif's surgical colleagues in medical centers throughout the world, as well as some self-appointed observers of the transplantation scene, were willing to be quoted in the media. The opinions ranged from a cautious questioning of Leif's judgment in performing the pig heart transplant to full-blown attacks and condemnation.

Within the University of the Southwest and University Hospital, there had always been opposition to heart transplantation—with the most vocal opponent, of course, being Dr. Vincent Varney. Now Varney possessed information from the pathology department that Luce's excised heart had reasonably good coronary arteries. And more damaging was the rumor that the piece of aneurysm, allegedly cut out of Luce's left ventricle, had never reached the surgical pathology laboratory. If the piece were lost, there would be no way to verify that Luce really had an aneurysm as Leif and Sellery contended. The heart catheterization and angiocardiogram that Clay had performed certainly did not suggest the presence of this aneurysm.

The governing boards of the hospital and the university were intensely concerned. The newspaper interview with Mrs. Luce, and the further news that she was presenting her story to the district attorney, called for immediate action—which Vincent Varney provided by submitting formal charges against Leif Hanson for unprofessional and unethical behavior. The Harris County Medical Society and the Texas State Board of Medical Examiners also expressed jurisdictional interest.

To parry the thrust of public and private outcry, the dean scheduled an immediate hearing of the charges against Leif in the board room of the University of the Southwest Medical School before the executive committee of the medical school (consisting of the chairmen of the major academic departments) and representatives of the boards of the University and the Hospital.

Leif awoke at six in the morning after hardly sleeping. He might as well be up. The housekeeping people would soon be trying to get into his office to clean it. He still had not found a place to live or contacted a lawyer. For a week and a half he had been living in his office—too numb from personal problems and too deeply involved in his work to worry about his living conditions. His major concern now was the hearing. And of no small concern was his visit with his children at two in the afternoon. Certainly the hearing would not extend beyond two. There would have to be a break for lunch. He had let the kids down so many times in the past. Today, no matter what, he would be there to take them out. They would go to Astroworld and battle the weekend crowds. Mark loved to ride the Black Dragon.

Leif shaved, dressed in a blue business suit—and found he was using his last clean shirt. After scanning the office to see that he had removed all evidence of his sleeping there, he unlocked the door and went down to the hospital cafeteria, picking up a morning newspaper on the way.

As he walked through the cafeteria serving line he sensed (or imagined) a difference in feeling towards him. The medical intern in front of him. The women behind the counter. A difference in attitude. Leif tried to be more outgoing than usual and joked as he walked down the line—pointedly ordering grits and drawling a little. He took a table in a far corner of the cafeteria and opened the newspaper. The banner headline proclaimed:

SOUTHWEST BEGINS HANSON HEARING

The information in today's report was a little more objective than the story of the previous day. Another story concerned Mrs. Luce and her visit to the district attorney. And a third front page report revealed that he and Elaine were separated.

Leif made his usual Saturday morning rounds with his staff. Again he perceived a change in attitude, which he once more tried to override with forced joviality. His patients were aware of what was happening and buoyed his morale with: "We're with you, Dr. Hanson." And: "Giv'm hell, Doc."

Promptly at 10:00 a.m., Dean Ernest Andrews stood up at the head of the table in the board room. Approximately twenty people were seated around the long, walnut table; and several others sat in chairs against the paneled walls, which displayed life-sized color portraits of the previous deans. Fifteen of the major department chairmen, minus the two who were on vacation, were there. Leif chose to sit against a wall.

Dean Andrews said, "I think we have enough people here to begin." Andrews was in his early fifties, but looked older—the price for being an administrator of a vigorous and tumultuous medical center. White hair, glasses, paunchy. He looked very tired as he spoke. "I also think we are quite familiar with the events which have led to this rather hastily assembled meeting. I have had a private discussion with Dr.

Hanson, as well as discussions with Dr. Varney and with attorneys from the law firms representing Southwest and University Hospital. It was on the advice of counsel that this meeting was called so abruptly to stanch a flow, which threatens to become a torrent of damaging criticism to the university and its teaching hospital. I don't believe that anyone who has read the newspapers for the past couple of days could disagree with the need for prompt action."

Varney was shuffling papers, obviously preparing for his presentation.

Andrews looked towards Varney, cleared his throat and continued: "Dr. Vincent Varney, professor and chairman of the Department of Medicine, has submitted charges against Dr. Leif Harald Hanson, professor and chairman of the Department of Surgery, relevant to the much publicized cardiac xenograft performed at University Hospital on the night of June 16, involving one Arthur Luce." He paused and looked over at the attorneys. "I will hasten to add that although we have two lawyers present, this is not a court of law, but a hearing to investigate certain charges and to take appropriate action specified by the constitution and by-laws of the University of the Southwest Medical School and University Hospital. The hearing will be as brief as possible and yet must provide the pertinent facts on which a decision can be based. I will now allow Dr. Varney to present his charges."

Varney began, "First, I am speaking as chairman of the research committee of University Hospital and a member of the research committee of the medical school when I present my first charge that Dr. Leif Hanson did not submit and receive approval of a research protocol permitting the investigation of a cardiac xenograft in the human subject." He glanced down at a three by five card. "This is in direct violation of the guidelines involving human experimentation established by the National Institutes of Health. Dr. Hanson, as a recipient of NIH grant funds awarded to this institution, has signed a pledge to abide by the rules established for investigations involving the human subject. He has flagrantly and irresponsibly broken his pledge."

"Second, as a member of the board of the Harris County Medical Society, I charge that Dr. Hanson has consistently and outrageously violated the rules of conduct regarding publicity."

"This is not a Harris County Medical Society hearing," Dean Andrews interrupted.

"Then as a *faculty member* of Southwest, I charge that Dr. Hanson's publicity-seeking conduct has been unprofessional, and has discredited the university as well as himself. Third, I raise the possibility of a criminal act . . ."

"I would ask you to modify that," Dean Andrews interrupted again.

"I call your attention next," Varney said, "to an occurrence that supports Mrs. Luce's discussion of criminal charges with the district attorney . . ."

"You will please not use the word *criminal*. This is not a court of law and you are not a lawyer," Andrews said. "Just describe the occurrence."

"The so-called left ventricular aneurysm that Hanson says he excised from Mr. Luce's heart never appeared in pathology. This raises the important question as to whether or not an aneurysm ever existed. And whether or not Dr. Hanson perpetrated a fraud to permit him to proceed with a clinically unjustified operation—to use one Arthur Luce as an experimental animal. In effect . . . to murder him."

"Dr. Varney, I'm going to have to ask you to be seated," Dean Andrews said. "And I'll give the substance of the last charge. I think that your presentation continues to be inappropriately emotional and prejudicial."

"But Dean Andrews . . ."

"I know what you think, Dr. Varney. And you're entitled to think what you wish and to discuss this in private with your colleagues. But we cannot support an emotional attack at this hearing."

Varney sat down.

"The substance of the last charge," Dean Andrews said, "is that Arthur Luce was deceived as to the operative procedure he was going to undergo. Now I have already studied all of these charges and have acquainted Dr. Hanson with them. And I've given him the opportunity to invite witnesses on his behalf. I have also invited other individuals who should be able to provide certain factual information which this hearing will require. I would now like to ask Dr. Hanson if he has any general statement he would like to make before we study each charge separately."

"No statement," Leif said. He sat stiffly in the straight-backed chair against the wall—his back to the wall—under the piercing gaze coming from the oil painting of Dean Archibald Stinson, 1934-1942.

"Then I'd like to take the charges in reverse order," Andrews said. "I've invited some witnesses here who will not have to stay for the entire meeting if they can give their testimony now. So let's address ourselves to the question of informed consent. Charge four. Did Mr. Luce agree to the possibility of a xenograft? Was he deceived? First, could we hear from Chaplain Ross, who witnessed Mr. Luce's signature on the operative permit to use a xenograft?"

Chaplain Ross remained seated at the conference table, but nodded towards Dean Andrews. He was a youthful, crew-cut, Presbyterian minister involved in full-time hospital work as chief of the chaplain training program at University Hospital. He wore a light gray suit over a pink clerical shirt and clerical collar. Chaplain Ross said, "Dr. Hanson asked me to witness the operative consent form and to go over it in private with Mr. and Mrs. Luce in lay terms, to be sure that they understood what was involved. It was my impression that both Mr. and Mrs. Luce understood that there was a distinct likelihood of a transplant using an animal heart, a human heart, or an artificial heart. And that in fact, Mr. Luce, just before leaving for surgery, indicated to me that he did not want the artificial heart, but he hoped he would have a transplant."

"He *hoped* he would have a transplant?" Dean Andrews asked.

"Yes, sir," Ross said. "I also considered the statement a little bizarre. But I've worked with many of these transplant patients. And I think they're a different breed. Mr. Luce said it was his turn to get his picture in the paper. And he's not the first transplant patient to emphasize just that aspect."

"So you would say that Mr. Luce knew what he was signing and actually hoped to have a xenograft?"

"I would say that, yes. A transplant of some sort."

"Now is the time to ask if members of the executive committee have any questions of Chaplain Ross."

"Did Mrs. Luce share Mr. Luce's enthusiasm for a transplant?" the chairman of biochemistry asked. He looked too young to be a chairman and was wearing an open-collared sport shirt under a white laboratory coat.

"I formed no judgment on that," Ross said. "I can only say that she understood that a transplant was a real possibility."

"How do you know she understood?" Varney asked.

"It would be pretty hard for her not to understand. I was in the room several times with her when Mr. Luce received the transplantation medicine—the antigen. And it was explained each time what the medication was and why it was being given. For an animal heart transplant."

"I'd like to ask Dr. Hanson a question about this." Varney motioned to the dean.

"In due course. Are there any further questions for the chaplain ?"

No questions.

"If you have other duties, Chaplain, we won't detain you," Dean Andrews said. "And we want to thank you for coming this morning."

Ross nodded and left the room.

"Mrs. Metzler, who is a social worker with the cardiovascular unit, also signed the operative permit as a witness," the dean said. "Mrs. Metzler, would you tell us your impression of the understanding which the Luces had regarding the contemplated surgery?"

"My impressions were very similar to those of Chaplain Ross," Mrs. Metzler answered. Her thin face and voice didn't quite fit her ample figure. "And I did what I very often do after a doctor has explained something to a patient. I went back alone to ask them if they really understood. So often a patient will seem to understand what a doctor has told them. Seem to agree. But when I go back and ask: 'What did the doctor say?' they can't tell me. Or they tell me something very unlike what the doctor was trying to convey. However, when I went back to talk to the Luces they seemed to understand quite clearly that an animal heart transplant was a likely possibility."

"Thank you for coming, Mrs. Metzler," the dean said. "And now Mr. Wells, who is an attorney for University Hospital, what is your opinion on the legality of the consent form for the xenograft?"

"Most hospital operative consent forms aren't worth the paper they're printed on," the pin-striped Mr. Wells said. "However, this form, used in this situation, and the witnessing of it are unequivocal and should be able to stand up in court. In my opinion."

"Thank you, Mr. Wells," Andrews said. "Now are there any more questions or statements regarding this charge? Dr. Hanson, would you like to make a statement?"

"No," Leif said softly.

"I'd like to ask Dr. Hanson a question," Varney said. "What was he thinking of when he brought Mr. Luce to the operating room? Was he going to give him a chance to have an operation other than a xenograft? Obviously he had Luce well prepared for a xenograft. And for an artificial heart, too. The air compressor was sitting right outside room 1. What chance was he giving him for the operation which the operating room schedule called for?" Varney waved a copy of the OR document. "A bypass graft."

"I believe that question to be out of order," Andrews said.

"I'll answer it," Leif said. "Until the last moment, when the patient could not come off the pump, I intended to do a bypass vein graft."

"Then why was Luce so well prepared with this transplant antigen?" Varney asked. "And why was the hospital's entire photography department so conveniently on hand?"

"Mr. Luce was well prepared—as will dozens of

patients in the future who might be candidates for a heart transplantation, if there is doubt about a lesser procedure succeeding. I think that the xenograft and the artificial heart are ways to go for a patient who dies on the table, who won't come off the pump. Instead of sending a corpse to pathology, we sent a living patient to the recovery room."

"You sent a corpse to pathology in a couple of days, anyway," Varney said. "But what about the cameras?"

"The cameras were there because there was a possibility that this would be the first of a kind. That's obvious. We weren't trying to hide anything. We wanted precise documentation of everything that happened."

"You wanted publicity," Varney said, "and had no intention of simply doing coronary surgery."

"We wanted to show a new approach to the high risk cases—double and triple valve disease, A-V canals, three and four vessel disease, hopeless myocardial damage . . ."

"But Dr. Hanson," the chairman of pathology stroked his closely cropped Freud-style beard and gazed over the top of his reading glasses, "was this a high risk case?" He was wearing a hearing aid.

"I considered it to be or I wouldn't have followed the course I did," Leif said.

"I believe we're getting into the province of the next charge," Andrews said. "And if everyone is through with the question of informed consent, we can carry on with this line."

"That suits me," Varney said.

Andrews nodded towards the chairman of pathology.

"Dr. Almeda was the pathologist on call who received Luce's heart from surgery," the pathology chairman said. "Dr. Almeda wrote up the report which is in Luce's hospital records. I have had the opportunity to study the specimen as have other members of my department. All we can say, Dr. Hanson, is that we all agree that the patient had a surprisingly good heart, good myocardium, and good coronary arteries, except for an occlusion of the anterior descending branch. There was, of course, also evidence of a recent excision of a piece of the left ventricular myocardium.

And that piece of excised myocardium never reached Dr. Almeda with the rest of the specimen."

"There is also ample evidence," Varney interrupted, "by heart catheterization data, X-ray, electrocardiogram, and left ventricular angiocardiogram that there was indeed no ventricular aneurysm. We also have a note on the chart by a highly experienced cardiologist, Dr. Clay Ducharme, that there was no evidence of ventricular aneurysm."

"Let's, at this time, confine ourselves to the pathologist's report, Dr. Varney," Dean Andrews said. "Dr. Almeda, how common is it for you not to receive all of the excised material from cardiovascular cases?"

"Extremely uncommon," Almeda jiggled his black horn-rim glasses into place and looked directly at Leif as he gave his answer. "It is almost unheard of for a specimen to disappear from which a diagnostic conclusion is needed."

"Has this ever happened before at University Hospital?" Varney asked.

"I'm not sure," Almeda said. "Maybe once since I've been here. And that's eight years. And I've been trying, since this happened, to recall a specific case. But since we never received a specimen, we wouldn't have a file on it."

"I'd like to say that we have many thousands of surgical specimens each year," the chairman of pathology added, "so even if this has happened once before in eight years, it is a very unusual event indeed."

"Dr. Hanson, could you shed any light on this?" Dean Andrews asked.

"Nothing at all," Leif said. "The specimen was handled in the usual manner."

"Dr. Sellery, you were with Dr. Hanson on this operation. Could you help us?"

"Only to support what Dr. Hanson stated," Sellery said. "I personally handed the specimen to the scrub nurse. It may have gotten covered by a sponge and thrown out with the sponges. You've gotta understand that there was an unusual amount of activity and excitement in this case. It wasn't like an ordinary case. And the focus of attention wasn't on the remains of the old heart as much as on the new heart."

"What about the ventricular aneurysm?" Dean Andrews asked Sellery. "Can you describe it?"

"It was not a large aneurysm, but it was thin, very thin. And it looked like it was in the site of a fairly fresh infarct." Sellery spoke with his customary self assurance. "So we elected to excise the aneurysm first. And then put the vein graft in where there'd be some good muscle."

"Dr. Hanson, does that about cover the appearance of Mr. Luce's heart?"

"Fairly well," Leif leaned forward in his chair. "Except I can tell you flatly that the coronary arteries appeared more diseased at operation than the autopsy specimen indicates. While the pathologists can make a judgment that this wasn't critical disease, I couldn't be that certain on the firing line. I was dealing with an emergency that had to be decided within minutes in a living patient, not an autopsy specimen I could study and argue about for weeks or months."

"That's a cop-out and you know it." Varney rapped the flat of his hand on the table and shifted his attention to Clay. "I'd like to ask Dr. Ducharme for an opinion."

Dean Andrews looked at Varney and then back at Clay before saying: "All right, Dr. Varney, ask Dr. Ducharme what you wish."

"Dr. Ducharme," Varney began, "you have written a cardiology consultation on Mr. Luce's chart in which you state that you felt that Luce did not need the heart transplantation for which he had been referred to Dr. Hanson. Is that correct?"

"That's right."

"You also performed the hemodynamic and angiocardiographic studies from which you concluded that a bypass graft would be the treatment of choice."

"That's correct. This would restore circulation to the heart muscle. I'd like to add that the circumflex and right coronary arteries also had compromised lumens which I considered to be major disease."

"Now what about the ventricular aneurysm?" Varney

asked. "You specifically stated that there was no evidence of this lesion."

"When I performed the cardiac catheterization, I could find no evidence of an aneurysm," Clay said. "But we were concerned about one, because he had persistent S-T segment elevation on his ECG. So we injected a small amount of dye under very low pressure into his left ventricle. By this very cautious examination, we found no aneurysm."

"That's what I wanted to hear." Varney, who had been standing, sat down smiling.

"There's something else you may not want to hear, though," Clay said. "Luce remained in the hospital for six more weeks. He had weekly ECGs after we did his heart catheterization, including one the day before his transplant. On all of these electrocardiograms, there was still persistence of the S-T segment changes consistent with a ventricular aneurysm. I can't dispute the observations of the surgeons if they found a small thin-walled defect that they considered to be an aneurysm. It could have developed during the interim."

Varney turned away and muttered, "Whitewash. God-damned whitewash."

Dean Andrews said: "If we may now proceed to the charge of unethical publicity, I will not ask for any witnesses. The Harris County Medical Society may hold its own hearing and reach its own conclusions. I will only offer my personal observation from the point of view of the medical center. I'm familiar with the original intent of this heart transplantation team to communicate only to scientific media. All of us in the medical profession deplore the sensationalism that has surrounded heart transplantation all over the world. I'm personally satisfied that Dr. Hanson's conduct with regard to the news media is not significantly different from that of the other heart transplanters."

"Apparently Dr. Hanson can do no wrong," Varney said, turning in his chair away from the table.

Andrews said, "Dr. Varney, a great deal is at stake here. The reputation of a medical school and a hospital is at stake—as well as the career of a man who has contributed enormously to these institutions. An honest decision must be reached, and reached quickly, on the basis of facts which are available to all. You will have an opportunity to vote on the publicity charge, as well as all the others."

"That's fine, Dean Andrews," Varney said. "Let's go on with the whitewash."

"That's unjustified," Andrews said. He closed his eyes for a moment and sighed.

"Then I apologize," Varney said. "But let's see how Hanson can answer the next charge."

"The final charge is that no research protocol was submitted for cardiac xenografts," Andrews said. "And the implication is that such an experimental procedure is unwarranted at our present stage of knowledge. I have read in our local papers statements made by Dr. Ducharme at the Montreal meeting that transplantation antigen induction of tolerance would not be ready for human trials for two or more years. Am I correct, Dr. Ducharme?"

"That's what I said when I was in Montreal." Clay remained seated.

"Do you feel otherwise now?"

"Well, since I've returned and reviewed all of our data—and since Dr. Hanson went ahead with xenografts in two baboons and the transplant antigen trial in Mr. Luce, I've concluded that we're closer to a breakthrough than I was able to acknowledge in Montreal. Specifically in transplants across species barriers."

"You mean you now think we are closer than two years to successful animal to human transplants?"

"Quite possibly," Clay said.

"How close are we?" Dean Andrews asked.

"I can't be sure. Perhaps we *were* only a few months away. But Luce's death is a great setback. It's damaged the credibility of the very research that put us so close to our goal. I suspect that because of failures here and at many other places, there will soon be a long-term moratorium on cardiac transplantation in all but one or two centers. It may take us ten or more years to recover."

"That's a rather gloomy forecast."

"It's been arrived at after considerable thought," Clay said.

"But let's return to the question at hand," Andrews said. "Do you think Dr. Hanson was irresponsibly premature in the clinical trial with Mr. Luce?"

"Probably no more premature than the majority of the heart transplanters throughout the world have been with their 'clinical trials' of allografts. And there was certainly precedent for the transplantation of an animal heart to a man. Hardy performed a chimpanzee-to-man transplant at the University of Mississippi almost four years before Barnard did man-to-man." Clay looked towards Leif and back to Andrews. "I would say that Dr. Hanson was not premature in this context of widespread prematurity."

"I suppose you also think that it was appropriate," Varney cut in, "for Hanson to do a xenograft without approval of the research committee."

"No. I wouldn't think so," Clay said. "However, I'm afraid that you didn't do your homework, Dr. Varney. The protocol for heart transplantation, approved by both the hospital and medical school research committees, specifically mentioned the possibility of a xenograft—or heterograft, which was the term I used, in 1968, when I wrote the proposal for the team."

"I can't believe that." Varney started riffling the pages of the protocol.

"You'll find it on page five," Clay said. "It goes something like: 'The initial clinical evaluation will be confined to human cardiac homografts and, depending on the development of new immunosuppressive techniques, cardiac heterografts may be undertaken in subsequent trials.'"

"I see it," Varney said.

"Allograft is the new terminology for homograft and means a transplant within the same species. And xenograft is the new term for heterograft. For transplants between different species."

"I know the terminology," Varney said.

"You seem to have missed it before," Clay jabbed the words at Varney.

"This one sentence is not a substitute for a complete protocol." Varney tried to speak calmly. "There is nothing here about transplant antigens. And nothing about how a xenograft would be approached differently than an allograft."

"And there's nothing about intravenous Cytoxan, either," Clay added softly. "But we began using it within weeks of starting our series of patients. We have a statement in the protocol following the list of anticipated medications, that agents other than those specified might be employed as the clinical situation warranted."

"There has to be a certain amount of latitude," Andrews said, "in a research undertaking of this type."

"All right," Varney said. "We've covered the charges. Now do we all rise and give Dr. Hanson a standing ovation?"

"No," Dean Andrews said wearily, "the executive committee will now adjourn to the next room to vote on these charges. It's getting on towards lunchtime, so we'll try to be expeditious."

TWENTY-EIGHT

The distress Clay felt as he remained alone in the board room with Leif could not have been greater had the charges been directed against him. He tried to think of something to say as he wandered around the room studying the portraits of the previous deans before returning to his chair to sit in uncomfortable silence. He looked across the room at the gilt-framed painting of Dean John J. Travis, 1942-1950. Supposed to have been a relative of the Travis at the Alamo. Dean Travis had a penetrating, disapproving look—the sort of look that Clay's father would shoot at him for the smallest behavioral infraction. The sort of look that Leif had probably never experienced in the absence of a father. But the disapproving look was all around them. And Clay felt the eyes of the deans burning into him as well as Leif.

What could he say at this time under these conditions? Apologize for the way he had verbally attacked Leif after the Luce transplant? He had called Leif a murderer.

But wasn't that exactly what Leif was? A prosecuting attorney could certainly make a good case for it, if he knew the inside story. Or was Leif was just trying to do something good for "mankind"... whatever he thinks that is. And something good for Leif Hanson. Maybe even something good for Luce. He just ended up committing a crime against against Luce, against the medical profession and science— and against himself. A man like Leif Hanson, committing such a crime. Oh God, how did we ever get into this mess?

After deliberating in the adjoining room for over an hour, the executive committee finally returned to their places, and Andrews announced: "The executive committee has voted on each of the four charges and has reached a decision." He looked directly at Leif. "As to the charge that informed consent was not obtained from Mr. Luce, the vote was 13 to 2 that the charge should be dismissed. The vote was 11 to 4 that the charge of unjustified surgery be dismissed, and 14 to 1 that the charge of inappropriate publicity be dismissed.

"However, with regard to the charge that Dr. Hanson violated research guidelines by not submitting a protocol, the executive committee has voted 9 to 6 that this charge be upheld. It is the further recommendation of the committee that Dr. Hanson be relieved of his chairmanship of the Department of Surgery at University of the Southwest as of Monday, and that Dr. Edward Noonan be appointed acting chairman. Dr. Hanson's position as a professor of surgery is not affected. It will be recommended to the board of University Hospital that the title of acting chief of surgery at that institution be conferred on Dr. Noonan. And finally, it is required that any future attempts at xenografts or artificial hearts must have an approved research protocol."

Dean Andrews looked from Leif Hanson to Clay Ducharme, who was slowly rising to his feet. "I know that there could be much more discussion," Andrews continued. "But there is a limit to the time that can be spent at this sitting. So I ask that any comments be brief, Dr. Ducharme."

"I don't want to interrupt, Dean Andrews," Clay said. "Is this it?"

"It is."

"I appreciate that you're striving for moderation, but this decision doesn't make sense. I was the one who wrote the overall protocol for the heart transplantation program, and I included a statement about xenografts. There was an approved protocol for xenografts consistent with our level of knowledge eighteen months ago." Clay paused. "It's the wrong charge against the wrong person and the punishment is excessive for that particular charge, even if the charge were correct. And I'm going to bring this up before the academic council of tenured professors. I don't believe that this decision of the executive committee will be upheld before the academic council."

"This doesn't go before the academic council," Varney interjected.

"I can speak for myself on these administrative matters," Dean Andrews said. "Dr. Hanson's tenure is not being violated. If his appointment as professor were being challenged, then you would be right, Dr. Ducharme, that this would have to be voted on by the academic council. However, it is the appointment as chairman of surgery that is under discussion."

"Dean Andrews, I appreciate that some positive action has to come out of this meeting," Clay said. "But this is wrong. I sent a memo to each of you urging that you support a moratorium on heart transplantation at Southwest. I enclosed our histocompatibility and rejection data. And I urged that further human experimentation be discontinued until new immunologic techniques could be developed. That was the time to review our research protocol and withdraw approval for xenografts *and* allografts."

"There are those of us who have *consistently* opposed heart transplantation," Varney postured.

"And I'll have to hand it to you, Dr. Varney, you've been consistent, all right." Clay almost added something about hobgoblins, but rejected the temptation. "But you had a chance to respond to the memo and support the moratorium I suggested. Why didn't you?"

"Everyone knew my position."

"I say your position in this is the same as it is in everything. To cover yourself while you're manipulating to gain your own destructive ends."

This caused a murmur around the table and a

momentary flash of anger to cross Varney's face. But he promptly slipped behind the mask of inscrutability that he presented to viewers. "My position was clear." The words came out through lips pressed tightly against the teeth.

"And among the Monday-morning quarterbacks, you alone can say I told you so on Friday. So you come off once more looking like you're in the right. But for the wrong reasons."

"You're in no position to make such a statement." Varney's lips were still tight against his teeth.

"Believe me, Dr. Varney, I know plenty about doing the right things for the wrong reasons. Unfortunately. But damn it, I'm talking responsibility and accountability. Not how to win power plays. The responsible thing for you and the dean and every other chairman who got my memo and had the good of the medical center and the good of the patients as highest priority was to support a moratorium before this happened. And I'm not talking meddling and jealous backbiting. I'm talking concerned responsibility. You can't just sit on the sidelines and watch disaster in the making—then take delight in saying, I told you so."

"I gave serious consideration to your memo, Dr. Ducharme," Andrews interrupted before Varney could respond. "But I considered your data insufficient evidence for taking the step you suggested."

"The data in that memo were better than the evidence presented here."

"That's your opinion," Varney said.

"My opinion is that we should reach a statesman-like decision. We should publicly renounce heart transplantation. Maybe this would be the first time in the history of science that people deliberately refrained from doing what they had the power to do."

"Spare us your sermonizing," Varney said.

"Varney, you're not . . ." Clay swallowed the next words. "Let me address my remarks to Dr. Hanson." Clay looked away from Varney. "Leif, maybe we can possibly solve the problems of heart transplants. But that's not important now. Look what we've done to ourselves and to other human beings. And for what? For our egos? More for ourselves than for the well-being of our patients? Among other things, we've confused quantity of life with quality of life. We've ended up doing great harm."

Leif was about to answer.

But Clay continued. "And maybe we can't solve the problems. This could also be the first time in our uncritical romance with science that we've discovered that there are limits. Maybe the honeymoon is over. Maybe we can't do everything we decide we want to do. Perhaps, we've recognized at last that there are some limits."

Leif stood up. "You're wrong, Clay. In this you're wrong. I got in on the ground floor of open heart surgery. And, really, what we've been doing in heart transplantation is no more radical now than open heart surgery was fifteen years ago. That's why so many heart surgeons got into transplantation. It was another frontier like the one they'd just explored and conquered. And we're close. We're too close to back off. If something new comes along, maybe only a new, but really effective drug, and we're shut down, we won't be able to take advantage of it. A new drug could change everything."

"A few extra months of life?"

"I'm not talking about keeping a sixty-year old alive for an extra few months. I'm talking about giving sixty years of life to a child with an inoperable congenital heart lesion. And giving decades of life to the thirty year old breadwinner who's about to die and leave his young children fatherless. Don't you see? Death is our opponent. Not the dignified death of a man or woman who has lived a full life. But the obscene death of a child who has never had the opportunity to experience his potential. Or the death of a young adult. As physicians and surgeons we're saying *No* to death every day of our lives. And, with the success of heart transplantation, I believe that the *No* we say to death will be as loud a *No* as death has ever heard."

"You're wrong! Heart transplantation is an obscene waste of resources. And because of irresponsible behavior, heart transplantation has now become a biological and ethical disaster," Clay argued. "A crime against life itself. Let's take the emphasis away from saying *No* to death and start saying *Yes* to life. Invest our resources in prevention . . ."

Varney got to his feet. "I'm sure we're all fascinated by this dialogue between Hanson and Ducharme. But I don't think we need to be their captive audience. I think that the meeting should be adjourned, and this private discussion can continue without us."

"I believe that I'm chairing this meeting, Dr. Varney," Andrews said. "Please sit down."

"Let me make this point," Leif said. "If we don't keep our momentum, we're going to decline. The future is in pushing science to the limits, not in backing away from it. It's not possible to coast in this world. It's either up or down. Britain has gone down as a nation because it deliberately decided to stop striving for dominance."

"Jesus," Varney interrupted, "Hanson's bringing in geopolitics."

Andrews said, "I do think you're getting away from the issue, Dr. Hanson."

"All right, look," Leif said, "in a month, NASA is going to have men walking on the moon. The space program didn't stop because of the deaths in Apollo 1. NASA redoubled its effort and we're soon going to see a scientific triumph . . ."

"Now we're into the space program," Varney interrupted again.

"Never mind," Leif said, "let me just ask a final question or two."

"Please do," Andrews said.

"Should I choose to remain on the faculty of Southwest and on the staff of University Hospital, what would happen if I were to submit specific protocols to do xenografts or to use an artificial heart? Would they be accepted?"

"I seriously doubt it," Andrews said. "In all honesty, I doubt it."

"Let me add," Varney said, "that I would fight them every step of the way. You can bet you won't have the freedom you've had in the past, big man. This is the end of the line, *big man*." The sweat was running down Varney's neck, soaking his collar. He looked furtively at the dean and at his fellow chairmen for a reaction to this intemperate outburst.

"I get the picture," Leif said to the dean. "And, of course, you want me to resign."

"No," Andrews said emphatically.

"Well, whatever you want," Leif said, "I resign."

"I cannot accept a verbal resignation at this meeting under these emotional circumstances."

"Then you'll receive written confirmation," Leif said. "As of Monday, when I cease to be chairman of the Department of Surgery, I terminate all affiliation with Southwest and University Hospital." He glanced at his adversary. "Look at how pleased Varney is."

"That's not true," Varney said.

"This is too hasty, Dr. Hanson," Andrews said. "You've got to reconsider."

"For godsake, what do you expect me to do? I don't have to reconsider," Leif said. "But I agree with you that this whole thing has been too hasty." Leif stood up. "I have nothing more to say. Varney is anxious that we adjourn, so please don't stay on my account."

Andrews looked at Leif. "I want you to reconsider, Dr. Hanson." Then he looked back at Varney. "I will now entertain a motion for adjournment."

"So moved," Varney said.

"Seconded," said the chairman of anatomy.

Leif Hanson looked at his watch. It was after one-thirty. He went over and extended his hand to Clay. "Thanks," was all he could manage to say.

"No need for thanks," Clay answered. "They were just pressing an incorrect charge. And you're still wrong as hell."

"I'm not wrong."

"It's pride, isn't it? And worse. Dishonesty."

"Pride, maybe. It's what I am. The devils and the angels, as Rilke said. But not dishonesty."

"Jesus, Leif, you don't even see it yet. Dishonesty. Cynical dishonesty. And lack of morality, where morality is essential—and absolutely expected."

"I'm going to have my victory."

"Your friends are trying to tell you you're wrong," Clay was shouting. "We were so close. Maybe only a few months away from doing it right. But you and some of your surgical cronies had to go and screw up heart transplantation for everybody. It'll take us years to recover from this madness. So you keep it up," he lowered his voice, "just keep it up and you'll be destroyed completely."

"Don't you believe it," Leif said.

"Let's go talk about this someplace."

"I can't today," Leif said. "I have an important engagement at two. I'm taking my kids to Astroworld."

Several reporters and photographers were standing outside the board room. As Leif came out, flashbulbs popped. "How about a statement, Dr. Hanson?" A *Houston Post* reporter blocked Leif's path.

"Dean Andrews will issue an official statement." Leif tried to pass, but found he was still being blocked. "Please let me by. I have an appointment at two."

"What was decided in there?" the reporter persisted.

"Dean Andrews may give you a full report." Leif sidestepped the reporter and moved quickly to his Mercedes.

Clay watched Leif drive away and turned to find Varney bristling at his side, sweat continuing to trickle into his collar in the heat of the day.

Varney began, "I wasn't really pleased with your performance in there. In fact I found it offensive." He wiped his neck and forehead with a folded handkerchief, but neglected the droplets decorating his upper lip.

"It wasn't intended to be," Clay said.

"You know it's very difficult for a chairman to have a division chief who doesn't support him. And someone he can't support in return. I need loyalty in my department."

"I'm sorry you feel that way."

"I really need someone like Eck in your slot. Someone I can relate to." Varney smiled abrasively. "You understand?"

"Spell it out." Clay felt a rage building inside.

"I've got letters on my desk for good jobs. Chief of medicine at Harlem Hospital—that's part of Columbia, you know. And in Detroit they're looking for a chairman of medicine."

"You'd like me to take one of those jobs?" Clay asked innocently as he watched Dean Andrews approaching from behind Varney.

"Yes, I would," Varney said. "You must regard it as an advancement."

"I love Houston. You're asking me to leave Houston?" Clay asked the question loudly enough for Andrews to hear.

"Yes," Varney said—also loudly enough for the dean to hear.

"It's very unlike you to behave so impulsively. Asking me to leave because you didn't like my performance at this hearing," Clay said.

Varney now twisted around and saw Andrews standing behind him.

Clay addressed his next remarks to the dean. "Dr. Varney has fired me as chief of cardiology because of my testimony in there. And he'd like me to leave Houston and take a job at Harlem Hospital. I don't want to leave. I don't accept his firing and replacing me with Eck. He's destroying the department and destroying the school. And he's destroyed lives along the way."

"That's slander," Varney said.

"Listen to who's talking about god-damned slander," Clay said.

"Gentlemen," Andrews said, "haven't we had enough for one day?"

"Apparently not for Varney. So I'm putting him on notice and the administration of the school on notice that I refuse to be fired. If that were to happen, tenure would be clearly shown to be a fraud at this medical school," Clay shouted.

"Please," Andrews said.

"I'm considering this move of Varney's as a violation of tenure. These actions against me and others aren't simple administrative adjustments. They're deliberate efforts to drive out tenured people. Varney doesn't just want me working in a different capacity. He wants me to leave the school and the city. And that is a clear violation of tenure. I will promptly notify the American Association of University Professors. I will also retain counsel and bring suit against the university, the hospital—and you, Varney—I'm going to sue your ass for everything you've got. On behalf of myself, Arthur Johnson, Henry Knoblauch, Leif Hanson, and everyone else you've screwed. But you made a mistake with me. I'm a hell of a lot meaner than you ever dreamed of. I'm going to kick your fat ass from one end of Texas to the other. I'm going to get you, you sonovabitch."

"Do you hear what he's saying to me?" Varney sputtered in the direction of the dean.

"You just better be sure you hear it," Clay said to Varney. "It's down to you and me now." The last words rolled out slowly. And for the briefest moment Clay could see New Orleans. He could see City Park. The Duelling Oaks. And under what remained of a thin civilized veneer, there was within him a thick rough-hewn longing for shotguns. "You and me, Varney," he repeated with bitter conviction. "You dirty bastard."

TWENTY-NINE

Leif returned to his office in University Hospital after leaving his children in the driveway of their house. He had savored the afternoon and evening at Astroworld like drops of brandy on his tongue. The children had been happy and Leif had been happy—when he could block out competing thoughts. And for a few hours there had been laughter.

But after he had locked his office door, he began to feel the walls hovering insolently close. He experienced a sense of oppression. And there was something wrong with the air conditioning. The humidity and heat were not under control. Rather than leave the door open, he removed his shirt and pants, put on a scrub suit, and went to his desk to begin writing his letters of resignation to the University of the Southwest and to University Hospital. He re-read each letter twice before sealing them in envelopes. It was done. He rubbed his chest. The sensation of heaviness had returned. Several times during the last few weeks he had had this chest pain. But why not? He was entitled to some crocky, somatic manifestations of tension. Forty-eight years old. Out of condition. Out of a family. And now out of a job.

Why should he not have chest pain or stomach pain?

Or something? Leif continued to rub his chest and take deep breaths. The pain began to ease. He stood up and walked to the closet to find a white coat. He would have to make rounds on his patients soon. But before that, call Elaine. He dialed. Elaine answered. "This is Leif. Please don't hang up. I have to tell you a few things before you leave for Detroit."

"Go ahead, Leif," Elaine said.

"I just want to tell you I'm sorry."

"It's a little too late for that."

"I guess so," Leif said. "These nights I've been trying *not* to think of what's been happening. And yet *trying* to think. I guess what happened to us happened a long time ago."

"You're becoming perceptive at this late stage."

"We shut each other out of each other's lives."

"We?"

"Yes, *we*. But I think I did more of the shutting. . . . It was after Davey died. We didn't know what to do—how to handle the loss. So we retreated. We crawled into foxholes of pain, where there was room for only one. . . ."

There was a pause before Elaine said: "Is there anything else you want to say? I'm in the midst of packing."

"Do you want to know what happened at the hearing today?"

"I was looking in the paper for it."

"It probably won't be out until Sunday. But what happened was that I've been relieved of my department chairmanship."

"I'm sorry to hear that," Elaine said. "I really am."

"I'm planning on resigning completely from Southwest and University Hospital."

"That's a drastic step."

"I have to do it," Leif said. "But what about us? Do you think we could try to start over again?"

"I don't think so."

"Please think about it."

"I have been. And if it's any consolation to you, my father is on your side. He's here now. We're going back to Detroit together. He's been talking with Kenneth Price. But

Kenneth tells him it's too early to be talking reconciliation."

"I don't know what that's supposed to mean."

"I don't either, but Kenneth is the expert in these matters. However, when I do think about it, I come to the conclusion that the present course is best."

"Please keep thinking."

"I've got to go now," Elaine said.

After he had finished his night rounds on his patients, Leif stopped at the drug closet in the recovery room and found tablets of nitroglycerin, which, when placed under the tongue, will relieve the anginal chest pain of coronary heart disease. Not that he felt that his chest pain had anything to do with his heart. Returning to his office, he once more locked the door behind him and stretched out on the couch.

For three hours he tried to sleep, rolling from side to side on the narrow leather couch, sitting up, lying down again, feeling progressively more uneasy.

It was all over.

Everything that he had worked for.

Everything that had been important. All over.

He abruptly pushed himself to a sitting position.

This ill-defined anxiety was becoming more and more intolerable. He tried pacing around the room, but the anxiety continued to build. Sweat began to trickle down his face and neck, and his shirt stuck wetly to his back. The anxiety expanded, filling the room. Pressing, squeezing, suffocating anxiety. *What the hell's happening?*

Leif turned on the overhead light, pulled on a dry scrub suit and a white coat, and walked out into the hospital—where there were people.

As he roamed the darkened halls, the anxiety began to dissipate slowly. He walked faster—into a dimly lit stairwell and up the stairs two at a time. Now he was beginning to feel better. Soon he would be able to sleep. He panted to catch his breath as he reached the eighth floor. Then his chest began to hurt again. But this was a pain to be preferred. Not like the uneasiness he had been experiencing in his office. Leif took some deep breaths, rubbed his chest and waited for the pain to disappear. He stood quietly in the eighth floor stairwell, expecting the pain to diminish. But it did not.

He finally reached into his white coat pocket, shook out a tablet of nitroglycerin, and put it under his tongue. He felt his pulse pound in his neck and his head throb. The chest pain promptly vanished.

Now he walked slowly down six flights of stairs and into the recovery room. Three of the nurses were off in a corner looking at a copy of *Cosmopolitan* when Leif entered. They separated quickly and two of them began to check patients as the third asked, "Is there anything I can help you with, Dr. Hanson?"

"I'd like to borrow an electrocardiograph for a few minutes."

"I'll call the night ECG technician for you," the nurse said.

"That won't be necessary," Leif said. "I'll bring it right back."

He wheeled the machine into his office. Next to his couch was an electrical outlet, into which Leif plugged the electrocardiograph. Then he smeared small patches of electrode paste on his forearms and over his shins and proceeded to record his tracing. Taking the six limb leads only required turning the dial. But to take the chest leads, it was necessary to apply another electrode to various places on the chest.

After recording his electrocardiogram, Leif unhooked the electrodes, wiped the sticky paste off his chest and arms and legs, and returned the machine to the recovery room.

Reading electrocardiograms with precision is not necessarily within the field of competence of the cardiovascular surgeon. But Leif Hanson had skill in this discipline. He glanced through the long paper streamer. The limb leads seemed to be normal except for some flattening of the T waves in leads I and AVL. But the chest leads appeared to be distinctly abnormal. T wave inversion was present across the left precordium. He remembered what

Clay had said about ex-athletes giving up exercise—as Leif had. And getting overweight. It was inviting heart disease. Leif thought his electrocardiogram reflected ischemic change. He would try to get Clay Ducharme to take a look at it.

Early Sunday morning, Leif dressed in a light cord suit and his cleanest shirt. (He still had not had time to buy new shirts or go to a laundry.) But today was the day he could return to the house to pack up his personal belongings. He drove to River Oaks and parked near his former residence. Shielded by a clump of oleander, he remained... on the outside looking in. A taxi drove up the driveway. He watched Elaine's father, then Elaine, and then the children leave the house. Mark and Karen were sunburned from the previous day's outing at Astroworld. They did not see their father. As Leif continued to watch, the taxi accelerated away. But he could not go into the house yet. Not just yet. So he started his Porsche and drove leisurely to Memorial Park, past the tennis courts. He would have to begin an exercise program. Elaine loved to play tennis. He drove back to the hospital.

Clay Ducharme's VW was in the parking lot. Leif retrieved the electrocardiogram he had taken in the middle of the night. He still needed to get Clay's opinion. But on the way he stopped at the animal quarters to take a look at the surviving baboon. Baboons are usually a surly and hostile species—and this baboon was true to form. Screeching aggressively. An unpleasant, threatening, and very active beast. Certainly not dying of rejection.

Leif walked slowly from the animal quarters into the hospital. No chest pain. He knocked at Clay's office door.

"It's open," was the response.

"No church this morning?"

"Just finishing up some data of Arthur's." Clay did not look up. "It'll make a strong paper to remember him by. His last paper."

"Nice gesture," Leif said as he handed the rolled-up

electrocardiogram to Clay and sat in the tweed chair at the side of the desk. "Wonder if you can look at this tracing for me?"

As Clay began to unroll the electrocardiogram he asked, "Who took this tracing? It's a terrible job."

"I did," Leif said. "I didn't want to call the night tech out of the sack."

"What's wrong with the patient?" Clay asked.

"Chest pain. Someone who recently had . . . a simple peripheral vascular procedure. So I thought I'd better check it," Leif said. "It looked like a little ischemia to me."

"Quite a bit of ischemia I'd say. And subendocardial injury," Clay added. "He's not on digitalis, is he?"

"No."

"Why don't you order a professional-type ECG and let us consult on him?" Clay said. "What did you do for his chest pain?"

"Gave him a little nitroglycerin and it cleared right up."

"That's pretty good evidence for the cause of the pain. Has he had much history of chest pain?"

"Just the past couple of weeks."

"How old is he?"

"In his forties."

"Well, I'd be worried that he's trying to have a coronary, so I sure would watch him." Clay took a notebook from his shirt pocket. "What's the name and room number?"

Leif did not answer for a moment. "I've got a block on his name, right now. He's on the second floor. I'll give you his name as soon as I think of it."

Clay frowned and tried to make eye contact with Leif. He asked very slowly, "This isn't your electrocardiogram, is it? The chairman of surgery does not usually take ECGs."

"It's not mine, for chrissake! And a soon-to-be ex-chairman can let a tech sleep, now and then."

"Be honest with me."

"I am."

"That's fine," Clay said. He looked at Leif,

337

searching. "It was kind of a miserable day yesterday, wasn't it?"

"I'm a big boy. I can take it."

"Did you get any sleep last night? Or do you always roam the wards taking electrocardiograms—just for the hell of it?"

"I got plenty of sleep."

"Well I didn't. I was worrying about you. And worrying about me. And . . . remembering my own screw-ups."

"I appreciate your worrying about me," Leif said and changed the subject. "I dropped by the animal quarters this morning."

"Oh? . . . So is the other baboon still alive?"

"Not only alive. But meaner than hell. It's as if he didn't even have a transplant."

Clay stopped what he was doing. He did not speak immediately. Then he asked cautiously, "Were you around—anywhere around when Sellery and Eck transplanted the second baboon?"

"They did it after I left. . . . Oh Jesus," Leif said. "You don't think? . . ."

"I wouldn't put anything past those two."

"Oh damn! Damn them if they did it! And damn me for being so stupid!"

"Let's get in touch with a pathologist and autopsy the beast."

"Sacrifice him when he's doing so well?"

"If the method's good it'll work again," Clay said.

Leif felt a heaviness return to his chest. He leaned back in the chair as unobtrusively as possible, waiting for the pain to disappear.

"Are you all right?" Clay asked.

"Just trying to figure things out."

"Let me take care of the arrangements." Clay made some phone calls. To the veterinarian in charge of the experimental animals. To the technician who had been caring for this specific baboon since surgery. And to the chairman of pathology. Then they waited.

A half hour later, the door to Clay's office opened

and the chairman of pathology entered with: "I hope this is something good, Clay. This is Sunday. And I'm not on call." He was wearing Bermuda shorts.

Clay said, "I suspect it's something bad rather than good. But it demands your attention."

They went back down to the animal quarters where the veterinarian and technician had the baboon in question already sacrificed and in position on the autopsy table. The chairman of pathology made the initial incision as Clay gave him the details of the Sellery-Eck presumed transplant.

"All I can say is there'd better be a pig heart in that baboon." Leif watched the pathologist at work. "But I should have suspected something when the electrocardiogram on this beast looked so damned good."

The pathologist held up the excised heart and lungs. Turned them over in his hands. Allowed everybody to look. "There's no pig heart here," he said. "They only had the cunning to put a few stitches in the back of the heart to make it look good."

"Sellery and Eck just opened and closed the chest," Clay said. "You can believe that the dean will hear of this."

Leif started to walk away. *Stupid*, he thought. *Stupid!*

Clay called after him: "Leif. Leif, I can't tell you . . . I mean, we're damned sorry. Damned sorry."

Leif kept walking. How could he have been so stupid?

The remainder of Sunday afternoon, Leif should have spent packing his belongings at Gray Rocks. That certainly had been his intention. But while he was walking briskly down the hall to his hospital office, the chest pain returned. This time he did not wait to take a nitroglycerin. He placed a tablet under his tongue and lay down on his couch as soon as he reached the room. Within two minutes the pain was gone. The question was what should be done. If just walking down the hall set it off, packing and lugging boxes of books would guarantee an episode. He had thousands of books for him or movers to pack. Should he alert Clay? Clay would be the cardiologist he would want to take care of him. But what if he needed surgery? Sellery had not even done a coronary bypass graft by himself yet. Besides, by now it was clear that Sellery was too crooked to be trusted with clinical responsibility of any kind. Cooley was doing bypasses. And Leif knew that DeBakey's group was strongly pushing bypass surgery.

Damn it. With all the things happening, he could not afford to be sick right now. There was the divorce. A possible suit from Mrs. Luce. And there would be the fight over the Cohen Heart Institute. Although the building was a year from being completed, the battle would begin immediately. The affiliation with Southwest would be the nidus of this political boil. The assumption under the agreement was that Leif would continue to be chairman of surgery at Southwest.

The jarring ring of the phone. It was Eric.

"You're calling to get my opinion about this guy Barnard and his new operation?" Leif asked with as much irony as he could muster.

"Not this time," Eric said. "I just wanted to call to tell you I've heard about the problem. And to tell you how sorry I am."

"Thanks, Red." Leif tried to sound casual about the crisis.

"I'll be in Houston to cover the moon landing next month. Just wanted to visit, if I could. I've almost finished my book."

"That must be very satisfying," Leif said. "What're you calling it?"

"Well, my book covers both the transplanters and the astronauts. So I've obviously got to include the moon landing."

"And . . ."

"Well, I took a cue from that *Life* cover story. Houston is a place for explorers."

"Another *New Vikings*?"

"Not exactly. . . . I'm calling it *The Last Vikings*."

"I'm not sure how to take that," Leif said.

Eric didn't respond to the remark.

After the phone call, Leif decided to stay in the hospital and pack things in his office rather than try to do anything at home. Not that he thought he was really going to have a coronary—but what safer place for the unlikely event to happen?

On the floor next to his desk was a box of transplant data on which he had written Clay's name. He opened the lower right hand drawer of his desk and pulled out a manuscript—the poems he had hoped to publish and dedicate to Davey. He would have to speak to Eric about this in July. Maybe they were actually publishable. After all, one had already appeared in *Life*. The next drawer contained a stack of reprint request cards that he had neglected to give to his secretary. And letterhead paper with his title that would no longer be valid tomorrow. He would just leave that stuff.

Then Leif opened the middle drawer where he kept other personal items. Some medals and certificates from foreign governments. An unfinished letter to Yale to inquire about the procedure for endowing a scholarship in the name of David Bjorn Hanson. A brochure from the Save-the-Redwoods League detailing how to dedicate a memorial grove.

He placed these latter two items in a stack on top of the manuscript of poems, wondering how this funding could be accomplished now that his assets would be tied up in the divorce action. Elaine would at least be in favor of the scholarship and the redwoods—if he brought them to her attention in just the right way. If the divorce went through, this could be part of the settlement.

Finally he withdrew a small framed color snapshot of Davey, which the light had faded so badly that it had to stay in the drawer to protect it.

Leif studied the picture of this fair-haired child with an enormous and mischievous grin. He smiled back at the photo and placed it on top of the brochure from the Save-the-Redwoods League. Davey had never seen the redwoods ... but how he would have loved them.

The chest pain was returning.

Occurring at rest. Unstable angina. An impending heart attack. The emergency room was just down the hall.

The pain. Crushing pain. The elephant on the chest. The shoulders. Down the arms. Into the jaw. He took a nitroglycerin and rose to his feet.

Unsteady. Sweating. Nausea. He wiped the sweat from his face with the back of his hand.

More fastidiously, Dr. Leif Harald Hanson put on his long white coat and carefully adjusted his tie. He touched his right hand to his hip, checking that his stethoscope was securely holstered in his coat pocket. Now he straightened himself to his full imposing height. His head high. Always high in battle.

As he stood there, he could almost feel a small hand slip into his, and hear the laughter as they began to walk together—then run. Running through a grove of redwoods.

Then perhaps Davey would stop and say, as he often did: "Lift me up, Daddy, so I can touch the ceiling."

"But we're outside, son. There is no ceiling."

"Then help me touch the sky."

MAIN

Nora, James J.
The upstart spring

This book has been
withdrawn from the
St. Joseph County Public Library
due to:

— deteriorated/defective condition
— obsolete information
— superceded by newer holdings
✓ excess copies/reduced demand
— other _____

7/94 Date _____ Staff